EDGEWOOD ACADEMY ELITE BOOK 2

RUTHLESS
Rejection

P.H. NIX

For all the tissues, cold showers, and cursing.

CONTENT WARNING

Content Warning: Ruthless Rejection is an 18+ novel that has triggers. If you have any triggers, this series may not be for you. Please also remember self-care when reading.

Some potential triggers include bullying, anxiety disorder, torture scenes, and kidnapping. Please visit https://linktr.ee/authorphnix for a more detailed list of triggers.

BLURB

Edgewood threatens to chew me up and spit me out.
Since moving to town, my life has been turned on its axis. Everything
I thought I knew is a lie, and even as secrets are revealed, more
questions arise.

I've been forced into a ruthless game—one with deadly
consequences in order to take care of my siblings in my parents'
absence. A game that has the Queen Bee of the school out for my
blood because the heirs of the school are fighting to win me over.
The question is, are their motives pure, or will I be on the receiving
end of a Ruthless Rejection?

Ruthless Rejection is book two in the Edgewood Academy Elite
Series. It is a slow burn, why choose, dark high school bully romance.
Meaning the main character will end up with more than one love
interest. As the series progresses, so will the level of darkness.
It is an 18+ series with profanity, a feisty heroine, bullying, and
obsessive and possessive themes.

GLOSSARY

To help with some of the Jamaican Patios in this series, I've provided a glossary of terms.

Dem: them
    Dem don't righted: they're not okay
    Fi: to
    Gal: Girl
    Haffi: Have to
    Irie: cool/good
    Mi den yah: I'm okay
    Not ah bumbo: Not a fucking chance
    No suh: no sir
    Pum pum: pussy
    Quint it: clench around it
    Siddown pon di buddy: ride the dick
    Suh: So
    Unnuh: one or more people
    Wah gwan: Hello/What's up
    Wha di ras: what the hell/fuck

PLAYLIST

Listen on Spotify: Ruthless Rejection (Edgewood Academy Elite Series)

Blood//Water- Grandson

Bodies- Drowning Pool

Dangerous- DeathbyRomy f. Blackbear

The Hell I Overcame- Bad Omen

I Feel Like I'm Drowning- Two Feet

PillowTalk- ZAYN

Go Down Deh- Spice f. Shaggy & Sean Paul

Calm Down- Rema f. Selena Gomez

Heart-Shaped Box- Nirvana

Take Me To Church- Hozier

Secrets Kill- Ely Eira

Motivation- Kelly Rowland f. Lil Wayne

Earned It- The Weekend

Meet Your Master- Nine Inch Nails

The Death Of Peace Of Mind- Bad Omens

Sure Thing- Miguel

Bad Guy- Billie Eilish

Heaven- Julia Michaels
I Run To You- MISSIO
In The Blood- Red Rosamond
Coming Undone- Korn
I See You- MISSIO
Dark Red- Steve Lacy
Elastic Heart- Sia
Cinderella's Dead- EMELINE
Someone You Loved- Lewis Capaldi

PROLOGUE

I watch as they scramble. *Stupid fucking idiots.*
You'd think by now they would've figured out I'm the puppet master— all of their movements are controlled by me.

Ariah didn't understand, and neither did they— forcing my hand. There's a plan, and I won't allow any of them to deter what's coming.

The power that will come with the union between the girl chosen and the heirs of Edgewood is too great to let some stupid decree created by dead men centuries ago dictate what was never the Fraternitas' in the first place.

Men have ruled this world for far too long— foolishly. Wars, famines, and gluttony have destroyed us while they were at the ship's helm, bringing us to calamitous existence.

It's time for a woman to wield power— for us to finally get the job done– and in order for that to happen, the Fraternitas must fall.

"Are you ready?" I ask

"You know I'll do anything for you," Senator Baker says.

The fucking gullible fool.

Smiling, I say, "Soon, you'll have it all. Just remember the plan."

He walks closer, and I know what he wants— a small sacrifice for what I'll gain.

I begin to strip off my clothes as he makes his final approach, his mouth finding my neck, causing me to groan.

He lifts his mouth from my skin. "Soon, my father will bow at my feet."

Not wanting him to see me roll my eyes at his ridiculous notion that anyone would bow to him, I put his mouth to better use, pushing him down to his knees and opening my legs.

That's the only place men belong.

As I grind his face into my pussy, I recite the only edict that matters.

Largitor vitae tuam divinam amplectitur foeminam pro eo quod gentes peperit.

I want this event to hurry up and end so I can test just how well Ariah can keep up with me. She told me to bring it, and I fully intend to do just that.

I make my way around the room for the bar when I see Lydia rounding the table and heading for the exit. *Lucky*. At least she gets to leave this stuffy-ass party.

"What can I get you?" the man behind the bar asks.

"Just give me two bottles of water, please."

It doesn't make sense to drink anything else if I'm trying to exit stage left at the earliest possible moment.

"Here you go, sir." He hands me the waters, and I make my way back into the crowd, hoping to find Riri and get out of this damn tie.

Whose idea was it to invent the damn bowtie?

Reaching up with my free hand, I loosen the band I feel is trying to choke the life out of me, and head for the door I saw Riri leave through earlier— she's been gone too long.

I'm at the door when Lev nearly tackles me. He's moving so fast.

"Slow the hell down," I grunt, grabbing his shoulder to slow his forward momentum. "Where the hell are you coming from?" I growl, staring behind him to the path that leads to where my Riri went.

I wanted to track her down immediately but recognized the look of exasperation coating her face. The tensed set of her jaw and clenched hands— a telltale sign she wanted air and time to herself.

"I went to give some friendly advice to your *Selected*." His lips curl like the thought of her being our potential wife leaves a bad taste in his mouth.

Gritting my teeth, I try to remember he's just too focused on what's going on with the Fraternitas to see Ariah's greatness.

"What do you mean you gave her some advice?" My grip on his shoulder intensifies, squeezing until he visibly winces. "What did you say?" I growl.

"I simply suggested she leave town," he states, stepping back until my hold loosens.

I feel the shift in my mood, my eyes narrowing as my annoyance grows. *Why does he have to be this obstinate?* There's apprehension, and then there's Lev and Wes. *Fucking idiots.*

Rolling my eyes, I say, "You're a tool. You know that? You and Wes are going to die on this hill of denial, and I can't wait to make you both eat crow when you have to grovel for forgiveness."

"No, I'm just the last of the remaining rational thinkers," he mumbles, the last part so low I almost miss it. *Does this mean Wes is coming around?*

"What do you mean the last? I thought Wes was the conductor of the 'Ariah is trash' express?"

Lev pulls his hair from the styled bun, letting it fall down the sides of his shaved head to his shoulders before responding. "I don't think she's trash. So I was never on that damn track. She's an un-fucking-known that showed up at a far too convenient-."

Whatever bullshit he was about to finish spewing is cut off when I see Ariah's guards fly past us, nearly bowling us over.

I don't stop to see if Lev is following. I take off— flying out the estate's wooden doors, trying to catch up toward the gazebo.

When I reach the opening, all I see is the spot where Ariah's shoes are strewn on the ground next to her watch. The watch that's always supposed to be attached to her wrist. The only evidence she was here. I spin, peering into the darkness— hoping she'll appear out of the abyss.

My pulse pounds, drowning out all the noise of the scene around me. I see the scrambling of her guards. I see their mouths move, and I'm sure someone is calling Thomas, but none of the sounds permeate the roaring sound of my blood throbbing in my ears.

A hand waves in my face. I recognize Lev. He must have followed me here. He's trying to speak to me, but my mind locks on to his earlier words, *'I simply suggested she leave town.'*

My hand shoots forward before the sly fucker can move— wrapping around his throat and squeezing.

"What the fuck did you do?" I snarl, shocking him as I apply pressure against his trachea. *The stupid fuck. He'll die if he did something to her.*

"Wy. Wy, let him go. It wasn't him." Sebastian's hand grips my wrist, squeezing to garner my attention.

Turning, I face him but don't loosen my grip. I growl, "What do you mean he has nothing to do with it? He said it himself. He suggested she leave, and then she goes missing?"

I return my focus back to the last fucker to see her. "Where the fuck is she? If you weren't so goddamn stuck up Wes's ass-."

Sebastian's hand shoots out, gripping my wrist. "If you would let him go, we can go get the damn update. Now let him go. We don't have time for this shit," he snarls, moving to stand in front of me.

As his words register, I release my hold and choked gasps shift my attention back to Lev in time to see the color returning to his face and hurt fill his electric-blue eyes.

"How could you ever think I would do something like that? After everything that happened?" he rasps.

"He's not thinking straight, Lev. He knows you would never do something so vile," Owen says, coming to my defense.

I'm not sure when they all arrived. But Owen's right. I know deep down Lev would never, not after what happened to him and Owen.

"I'm sorry, man. I jus...No, I'm sorry. There's no just. I was out of line, and I'm sorry," I state.

He pauses before nodding, "Let's go find out what happened to your girl."

"*Our girl*. She's *ours*," I snarl, stalking toward the area the guards are still combing over.

"What the fuck happened here?" Wes shouts, storming in until he's face to face with a guard.

"Sir, we're not sure," a beast of a man answers. I think his name is Antonio. He's easily the size of Thomas, but his muscles' muscles have muscles. I'd typically have some slick shit to say about staying away from creatine, but I'm too fucking livid to joke.

"You don't get paid not to know. I want to know what happened here and fast," I bark. The composure on my control is hanging by the thinnest of hairs.

Giggles sound. "Oh look, your pet reject has finally recognized her betters and left before she lost. Here I thought she was stupid," Samantha's smarmy voice announces her arrival. *Not today, Satan.*

My shoulders stiffen at her words. I know if I look in her direction, I'll tear her vocal cords out. Instead, I turn to the only reason she'd be down here at all.

"Wes, if you don't get your cum catcher out of here, I won't be responsible for her joining the ranks of the other dearly departed Selected girls."

His face flushes with anger. Whether it's at her words or mine, I'm not sure. Nor do I care as long as he gets rid of her.

Before he can react, our fathers are walking into the clearing, shouting orders and clearing everyone but the bodyguards and us from the area.

"Who would like to tell me how the fuck a girl was taken from under our noses?" Mr. Edgewood's tone is lethal as he walks up to where Tony is standing next to Erik.

"Sir... Mr. Edgewood, the camera feeds and security were compromised. We're still doing a detailed analysis, but from what we can see, someone looped the feed showing Miss Bishop still out by the gazebo. Whoever took her was let in. There have been no unauthorized entrances detected," Erik reports.

"Well, Erik, that's obvious bullshit, or Miss Bishop would still be on the premises. Wouldn't she?" My father snaps.

"Yes Sir. We're currently looking into it," Erik continues, but I stop listening. He's not telling me anything I want to hear right now. His mouth isn't stating, 'We have her location and are currently en route to kill any fucker that has her.' Those are the only damn words I want to hear out of his mouth.

Turning to Lev, whose color has finally returned to normal, I command, "Locate her chip."

Nodding, our earlier dispute not solved but not as crucial as locating Ariah, he pulls out his phone, and his fingers fly away on the screen.

"You chipped her?" Sebastian asks, a sly smile of approval appearing on his face.

"Of course we chipped her. You don't think Wy and I would let our little angel only have one line of defense, do you?" Owen responds.

"I chipped her. You just co-signed the idea," I remind him. I momentarily think back and enjoy the night I made her come on my fingers in her sleep. She was so high off her climax that she didn't recognize the pinch to her skin when I was embedding the tracker. *Thank fuck for that.* She'll have my balls for it when she finds out, and I can't wait for that fight. First, we have to get her home.

"Find out what happened here and find Ariah Bishop or else," I hear Wes's dad bark before walking in our direction.

"Wesley, I want this handled and I want her found immediately. Drop everything else. This is priority number one. Do I make myself clear, boys?" Mr. Edgewood commands, staring as his brown eyes appear almost black.

We all grunt our agreement, but he didn't need to make that statement at all. I'll burn this whole fucking planet down to get my Riri back. There isn't a hole deep enough or a security measure secure enough to keep me out.

"Have you found anything, Lev? Where's the signal say she is?" Owen asks. Lola flips between his fingers— he's itching to cut his way to answers.

"The signal can't be located. The last ping was right outside the town line, and then it disappeared," Lev grits through clenched teeth, his hands still moving a mile a second.

The last shred of control I have evaporates. "What the fuck do you mean 'disappeared'? How is that possible?" I start pacing. My fear is palpable with the thought that someone has taken my girl and they're untraceable. I need to hit something— more preferably, someone. *Where the fuck is she?*

I run my hands through my now unruly hair, trying to find something, anything, to keep me from snapping the closest person in half. If Lev doesn't answer me, I might ignore my earlier decision to not cut Samantha's lifeline short. *Stupid bitch.*

Lev answers, cutting off my spiraling thoughts. "It means they either found the chip or they've gone somewhere out of signal range. I won't know until I run my diagnostics."

His comments set my teeth on edge. My gums begin to throb, pulsing to the same tempo as my anger.

"There's no fucking way they found that chip. It's fucking untraceable. Those were your words to me-." My sentence is cut short by the commotion to our left.

"We've got something," Erik shouts, and I'm over to the car before he can utter his next words.

Stopping once I'm at Erik's side, I take in the iPad in his hand. What I see makes my vision blink out, then blur before righting itself. It can't be. The rage that fills my blood vows retribution.

With nothing around to punch, I shout, "What the fuck?"

L ydia. *Lydia fucking Givens.*

The stupid cunt had something to do with this. She was at the party rubbing elbows and smiling in everyone's faces. I can't believe Wyatt's dad's assistant would betray us, but she's caught on camera punching a code in, letting an unmarked black van with blacked-out windows into the delivery area.

At least we know Lydia wasn't working with anyone on the Council.

We've spent the last five hours combing through countless videos from the party. The main cameras were hacked, but whoever was responsible didn't know about the cameras on the separate server for deliveries, allowing us a clear view of Lydia's face. We know she's working with someone, but because she isn't part of the inner circle, she wasn't privy to the upgraded security measures put in place after the two other girls were murdered. It's too bad she left the party early. She's just delaying the inevitable.

I look around the car at the varying expressions of my friends. Sebastian looks perplexed. A combination of puzzlement and anger mars his face, making me confused.

Leaning over, I whisper, "Why are you so concerned about her? You have barely spent any time with Ariah."

"I don't have to know her to be worried, Wesley," he retorts, his tone chastising, like the idea of my question was ridiculous. "I could ask you the same question. Why are you so upset? Have you finally decided to stop being a dick?" He rapidly fires question after question driving his point home.

"Point taken, and no, I still don't think she's the right choice." My answer feels like a lie coming across my tongue. One I'm not ready to admit to myself, much less out loud to anyone else.

Ariah is a conundrum that I'm not even trying to figure out. She is trying, stubborn, and not Elite wife material. I stand by that point, but she's not a plant. *Fuck.*

I rub my hands down my face, trying to work through all the shit that's happened since her arrival. Now's not the time for this shit. Right now, we just need to get her back safely. I can deal with my confused feelings another time.

Looking up, I see we've passed the diner. We're on our way to The Tombs. Lev has a better setup there. That prompts me to turn my gaze to him. He has pictures of the van up on his laptop. It has no plates or identifiable markers that could be immediately used to track it. Lev's already at work tracing its route through CCTV. We should at least have an idea of where Ariah's GPS signal went out.

I never thought I'd be happier about the level of stalker Wyatt is, but his overzealous need to protect Ariah might save her life.

"Do we have a lock on that traitorous skank yet?" Owen snarls from the back of the car. He hasn't stopped playing with his knife. I'm almost afraid he will use it on just about anyone to calm his twitchy fingers.

The blaring of my phone draws my attention to the inner breast pocket of my tux. Thinking it could be my Dad with updates, I reach in and answer without looking at the caller ID. That was my first mistake.

"Wes, where are you? My pussy is wet and waiting."

Cringing, I pull the phone from my ear and peer down to confirm the whiney voice on the end of the line is Samantha. *She's going to be a nightmare through this fucking process.*

Refusing to deal with her selfish shit right now, I hang up and block her number for the time being. Dick move I'm sure, but I don't a give fuck.

Ariah may not be my choice, but someone's well past their place snatching her after she was officially pinned.

We pull up outside the Fraternitas, and a large frame is waiting — Thomas. Of course he'd forego recovery to ensure the search for his charge is handled correctly.

Doors snap open, and the five of us exit from the blacked-out Chevy Suburban.

"I've already been briefed on the situation. I'll have everyone's balls who was on duty tonight for this clusterfuck of fuck ups," Thomas states. He appears composed, but the rigid set of his jaw and the focus in his eyes bring his anger at the situation into complete focus. He's pissed— livid. If he wasn't a consummate professional, he'd probably be flipping shit. This has to remind him too much of her— *Tegan.*

"Not if I have them first," Wyatt mumbles as we head for the door.

The sound of a throat clearing shifts our attention to Sebastian. He loosens his bowtie and interjects, "Let's just get the spitfire home, and we can Bobbit everyone who deserves it after she's safe."

"No, there will be carnage long before Ariah's return. Lydia will be the first to taste my blade, and I'm certain she won't be the last to lose their entrails before my angel's home," Owen huffs, picking something invisible from his teeth with Lola.

None of us bother correcting him as we walk through the halls because he's right. The streets will be lined with bodies before this is all over.

"Damn fucking right there will be," Wyatt agrees, pacing the floor, unsure what to do with all his restless energy.

Running his hands through his wheat-colored waves, Sebastian states, "Wy, sit down so we can plan."

Ignoring Sebastian, Wyatt strides toward the bar instead, banging and slamming things in his effort to make a drink. Amber liquid sloshes the sides of the glass as he throws it back.

"You don't fuck with the queen on the board unless you know you have checkmate," he grunts, finally relenting and takes a seat around the table.

Someone made a significant tactical error in taking Ariah. As incorrect of choice I know she'd be as our wife, she's still a Selected, which awards her certain protections.

Lev pushes some buttons on his phone, and a panoramic screen comes down from the ceiling, lighting up once it reaches its final spot.

"Here's what we know. Lydia was contacted shortly before Ariah's arrival," Lev begins, and Owen immediately cuts him off.

"Are you trying to tell me Ariah's arrival was known, and her kidnapping was planned long before she even moved here?"

Pulling up an email exchange between Lydia and someone, Lev explains, "We had some idea Ariah was connected to what's happening because of the packages she's been receiving and the attempted kidnapping from school."

He shows the timeline of messages between Lydia and someone she addressed as A.

"The problem we are working on is linking the timing. Did her arrival start this, or was this always in the works? It seems, at least at this moment, it was planned," he finishes, turning his gaze from the screen to us at the table.

I knew something about her appearance here didn't sit right. Lev and I have been saying this all along. The timing was just too coincidental. I want to feel vindicated in this, but she doesn't appear to be the enemy— more like someone caught in a war not of her making.

"The real question is, did Lydia tell them of her arrival, or did Lydia take this position because she moved here?" Sebastian asks.

"Something I'm looking forward to finding the answer to. Where is the bitch?" Owen shouts, not as interested in the backstory. He wants to peel the answers from her flesh.

"We're still not sure. We know she didn't leave with the van because she was seen entering the estate after letting the van out. But with the camera feed on a loop, there's no telling where and when she actually left," Lev says.

Clearing his throat, Thomas draws our attention in his direction. "Her house was empty by the time my team arrived. Either *Miss Givens* moved her belongings ahead of tonight's plan, or she never had anything there. Lev, please pull up the file I just airdropped to you."

My eyes bulge at what comes on the screen. "What the fuck?" I snap, my head looking back and forth between what I see and Thomas. "I thought you said you didn't find Lydia?"

Standing, Thomas walks to the screen, "Well, we did and we didn't," he says, pointing to the body, or what's left of it, on the metal slab.

"This is Lydia Givens. The real Lydia Givens. She's been dead for weeks."

There on the screen is an identical-looking Lydia, or what's left of her. Her graying skin shows the level of decay setting in. Her throat slashed.

"Are you telling me Lydia isn't actually Lydia?"

"It would appear Lydia Givens was murdered weeks ago, and Madeline Rutherford took her place, pretending to be Miss Givens since Ariah's arrival. We don't have all the details, but it explains why we had initial issues locating Miss Givens."

Our fathers will flip their shit when they find out we had a mole.

As if my thoughts summoned them, in walks Mr. Grant, Mr. Washington, Mr. Jefferson, and my father.

My dad steps forward, eyes filled with fury, but his mask is fully set in place. Whatever he's about to say, he doesn't want to. With Ariah being taken and the news of the mole, his hand is being forced.

"Boys, with the information we've just been given, it's time we fill you in on a few things."

3
ARIAH

A throbbing in my skull slowly wakes me. Damn. What the hell was in that champagne? *I thought expensive shit was supposed to hit differently?* My eyelids feel like they're sewn shut.

"Uh-," I try to croak, but my mouth feels like it's stuffed full of cotton.

The pulsing in my skull magnifies at my sudden attempt to speak. *I'm never trusting rich people alcohol again.*

I move to lift my hand, and I'm met with resistance. I tug, and still nothing. The distinct feeling of metal rubs against my skin. *What the fuck?*

"Oh, I wouldn't do that if I were you. You wouldn't want to hurt yourself. You're strapped in pretty tight," a voice singsongs.

My neck whips in the direction of the voice as I will my eyes open, but they remain unresponsive.

"Don't worry, you'll have bodily autonomy soon enough. Well, you'll be able to open your eyes at least," the fucking voice says.

I can't determine who it is, but I think it's a woman. The pitch of her voice is somewhere between alto and soprano and nasally.

Where the hell am I, and what the fuck happened? I work my memory, trying to figure out what's going on. I remember being outside by the gazebo and then jackass Lev suggesting I tuck tail and run, but everything is blank after that. Every time I reach for what happened, I'm met with fog, and my brain beats against my head. *Fucking hell.*

"Wh-," I try to force the words out, but the burn to the back of my throat screams for water.

"Thirsty, are we? Well, that's too bad for you, isn't it?" I hear her say and then hear the distinct sound of liquid being poured and the sound of someone gulping said liquid. "Wouldn't it be great if someone had something for you to drink? Help quench your parched mouth?"

Ugh. I don't know who this fucker is, but I swear she'd get a cunt kick if I wasn't in my current state.

"It's too bad-." Whatever she was about to say is cut off at the sound of a door opening.

"What are you doing in here? You're not supposed to be here at all! What if she opens her eyes? Are you trying to fuck this up?" another voice says.

"I'm doing whatever the fuck I want, and the skank can't see shit yet," the tormenting bitch says.

"If I were you, I'd get out before they see you in here. You might have some power, but you're not so important you can't be replaced. Get the fuck out, or I'm making the call," I hear the newcomer say.

"Fucking fine. The stupid bitch was boring me anyway. She can't even talk yet."

I hear feet stomp and then a loud bang. I'm assuming it was the door hitting the wall or slamming shut.

"You must be thirsty, Ariah."

I'm still not alone.

I hear the sound of shoes once again moving across the floor and something being poured before the feet move again. The sound is coming closer to me. My body tenses as I feel the person's body heat against my exposed arm.

The feeling makes me check to see if I feel bare all over. I inwardly sigh with relief when I sense my dress against my skin. *At least these assholes haven't stripped me.*

"I'm going to pour a little water in your mouth at a time. I can't untie you, so I need to give you a little at a time, or you'll drown."

Thankful for something to drink, I slowly nod.

A trickle of water falls against my chapped lips, and I whimper in relief at the feeling, my tongue gleeful at the first cold drop.

I'm basking in the taste when suddenly the trickle becomes a stream and then a flood, pouring all over my face making it hard to suck in air without choking.

I hear the hyena cackle before the person I thought was helping speaks while attempting to drown me. "You stupid bitch. You thought I was here to help. Welcome to Hell."

Water continues to fall on my face, and I turn my face to the side, escaping the endless stream. Sputtering a cough, I clear my throat and suck in desperate air in time to realize the water has stopped.

"You'd be wise to do what you're told, or your stay here won't be a pleasant one."

With that statement, the clicking of shoes moves away from me, and I hear a door open, close, and then a lock engage.

I need to remember what the hell happened and get the fuck out of here.

4
LEV

When I saw Ariah a couple of nights ago at the party, I meant she should get out while she could. I didn't mean she should be taken.

"Go get help. Please, Lev. One of us has to get help."

Owen's last words from that day years ago play on repeat in my mind, refusing to let me focus.

"I'll be back. I promise."

But I wasn't back in time. Owen was taken and abused. Different from the fun loving friend I remember. He never talks about his time in captivity. His scarred body and haunted eyes told more of the story than his lips ever could.

I can't let that happen to Ariah. *I'm a fucking asshole for what I said to her.* Wyatt was right to choke the life out of me. I'd have done the same. *What if they're torturing her or worse— raping her?*

Shaking my head, I try to clear my thoughts. I can't let 'what-ifs' distract me from finding her. My fingers fly across the keyboard as I watch the monitor to my left before shifting to the monitor to my right. Many programs run simultaneously— facial recognition to locate Ly- Madeline, software scripts to remotely override whatever is blocking the signal to her chip, and a search for the van. I need something to give to Thomas and his team.

A yawn breaks my concentration on the monitors, reminding me I haven't slept since we arrived at the Tombs yesterday. I grab my energy drink and bring it to my chapped lips, gulping down my caffeine boost. *I'll sleep when she's safe.*

I didn't mean for any of this to happen. I just wanted her out of the way. She was distracting us from what needed to happen. If I had only stayed longer. Maybe if I got to know her better instead of trying to force her into leaving I'd have been there, or at least close enough to hear something happen. Instead, I let my pigheadedness rule— essentially kicking her out of town.

"Stop beating yourself up," Sebastian chimes, stepping fully into the room.

I'm out of it. I wasn't even aware that I wasn't alone any longer. *If you'd been aware of your surroundings or bothered to run your own surveillance, Ariah would be here now— annoying the shit out of me with her bullheaded presence.*

"Stop it, Lev. You didn't do this. The people who-."

"Don't finish that fucking cliché sentence. 'The people who took her are responsible'," I mock.

"It's bullshit and you know it. I should've been there. This is the second time I was present at a kidnapping and I was powerless to do something about it." Turning, I snap, "I should've been able to do something!"

Clapping fills the air. *This motherfucker is clapping.*

"Aww, poor Levi. You weren't there so that's why they made their move, " Sebastian starts. "Way to make this about you. It's a little on the pretentious side if you ask me. I expected this behavior from Wes, not you."

Affronted by the accusation, I shout, "You don't know what you're talking about. I don't think this is about me." *I don't.* "I just know I fucked up and left her there and she was fucking kidnapped. So, excuse me for feeling some remorse."

Not compelled by my statement, Sebastian steps in my direction. He's wearing gray sweats and an LWU t-shirt, foregoing his usual stuffy suit and tie. His long legs stride across the room until he's standing feet away. His dirty blond hair is tousled, but he still manages to look like a dapper gentleman. Meanwhile, I probably smell and look like I have the hangover from hell or something.

That thought prompts me to assess myself. I'm in a pair of blue joggers and a black hoodie— a mismatched pairing of things I've left here. I could've gone home or had someone grab me something, but it didn't seem important.

A smack to the back of my head has me glaring at him.

"What the hell, Seb?"

"You need to snap the fuck out of whatever this is and find Ariah. You're distracted, Lev," he growls. "And that distraction could get her killed. Focus and find her," he commands and then turns, exiting as fast as he entered.

Am I really distracted?

I don't think I am. I think I'm doing everything in my power to find Ariah.

As if synched to my thoughts, an alarm signals something's been found.

I refocus my attention on my screen.

"Fuck yes!" This is exactly what I needed.

Picking up my phone, I dial Thomas. He picks up before the phone even has a chance to ring. "What have you found?" he rushes out.

"I have a lead. Meet me here in five."

"I'm already here. I'll be down in two minutes," he replies and ends the call.

Hopefully, this is what we needed.

"**W**es! Where the hell have you been and why have you been ignoring my calls?"

For fuck's sake. Who let the banshee in here?

"What do you want, Samantha, and how the hell did you even get in here?" Wes quips. He's had little to no patience for anyone since everything went down at the Selection ceremony.

I don't think he realizes it yet, but he's got some feelings for the new girl. He's in denial, but I see it. He's always watching her when he thinks no one is looking, and the fact that the GPS was something he talked about with Wyatt... Though he tried to sell it as a way to keep tabs on her, ensuring she wasn't up to no good.

Wes is a softie. I'm the only one left who's really thinking straight— and I'm not sure my earlier inclinations are sensible anymore.

Walking her high-heeled feet across the room, she stops and begins speaking only once she has everyone's attention. "Wesley, you're all supposed to be courting the Selected. You know, the ones that are still here."

"If you haven't noticed, Silicone Sammy, one of the girls chosen was fucking kidnapped!" Wyatt shouts from his perch by the bar.

"You never cared before. Two other girls are dead, and you didn't lift a pinky finger to find either of them," she snarks, confident that her jibe has landed.

Owen's menacing laugh fills the room before a glint of silver catches the light. That's the only warning given before a whirring sound flits through the air. A shrill, screamed curse is heard before a thrown knife embeds itself in the wall.

"What the fuck, Owen?" Samantha snarls, pressing her lime green-tipped fingers to her ear, her hand coming away with red as small rivulets of blood trickle down her ear.

Readying another blade between his fingers, Owen glares at a shocked Samantha, taunting, "If you don't want Daddy to have to pay for nose job number five, I highly suggest you scamper off to whatever animal pen you escaped from."

Not deterred by his threat, she looks to Wes, like he'll save her. I've honestly never encountered someone so delusional in all of my life.

Before Wes can utter a word, Sebastian grabs her face and growls, "Your desperation is showing, and it doesn't smell very good on you." Then, he shoves her toward the door.

She attempts to protest, but I cut her off, "That was your cue to get the fuck out of here. You're not needed, and you're definitely not wanted."

Her hands ball into fists as the frozen set of her face tries to morph into anger, but the injected nerves refuse to cooperate. Indignation fills her glacial blue eyes as she growls in frustration, turning and storming through the same door she entered.

Now that the stench of bitch is fading from the room we can focus back on what's important.

"We have a lead on Madeline," I state as I open the video footage I was able to find.

"Fuck, Lev, why didn't you say something earlier?" Wyatt asks moving from the bar to the table, his usually playful demeanor far too serious.

"I would've, but clingy-in-heels stormed in. Remind me to check with security to see how she was even able to gain access," I say, also making a mental note for myself.

Hitting play on the video, I see a very comfortable Madeline walking into a grocery store. Her hair is now golden brown and styled in a pixie cut. Her once green eyes are now coffee-brown. The makeup she's wearing hides the prosthetic nose and jawbones she used to change the shape of her face. It wasn't enough to keep her hidden from my facial rec programming— *too bad for her.*

Twenty minutes later we see her walk out with a few bags but instead of heading to her car, she walks down the street four blocks and turns into a parking garage. *Why do they always meet in garages like they don't have cameras in there?*

"Where'd she go?" Sebastian asks.

I point to the entrance of the garage, replying, "Just keep watching."

As I state my last word, a black 2018 Nissan Rogue exits where my finger was pointing. Two people sit in the front seat, one of them being Madeline. But that's not the shocking part. It's who's in the driver's seat that has everyone gasping.

Wyatt kicks back his chair, causing it to topple over as he barks, "Senator fucking Baker!"

5

SEBASTIAN

I stare around my office, trying to take my mind off this clusterfuck of a situation. Ariah being taken has shaken the core of our group.

While I haven't spent as much time with her, I've seen the impact the spitfire's had on the guys. The most significant change is Lev. Wes is still apprehensive. You can see how much he wants to care, but his bullheadedness won't allow him to admit he was wrong.

Lev— he's going to be putty in Ariah's hands when we get her back. Oh, he'll have to grovel, and I'm looking forward to watching it all.

"Where the fuck is my friend, Sebastian?!"

I turn to see a very irate Shay blow through my once-closed door.

"And don't give me any shit. Wyatt and Owen already tried that, and it didn't go well for them. I want updates, and I want them now, or I'm storming the Fraternitas and knocking on Daddy Edgewood's door, and none of you want that stress," she continues to rattle on.

I attempt to speak, but she puts up her hand, essentially silencing me.

"I'm not finished. I've played by the fucked up rules of this town and kept quiet because I had to, but if you fuckheads did something to my girl, then not even the Council will keep you safe from me," she finally huffs, crossing her arms and nodding.

Quirking a brow, I fix my gaze on her. "Are you quite finished, Miss Warren?"

Shay rolls her eyes. She's never been one to take our bullshit— not even when I started working here. "I stopped speaking, didn't I? So that means I'm done unless you give me a reason to keep going. Now spill it. I haven't seen Ariah since the party."

I massage my temples, trying to alleviate the building headache.

"She's been kidnapped," I state, seeing no point in sugarcoating the situation— I go for the rip-the-band-aid-off approach.

"What the bumbo ras claat?" she shouts. Her fist clenches at her side, her face going three different shades of red, and her nostrils flare as Shay tries to reign in her temper. "What do you mean she's been kidnapped? How the fuck does that happen on *your* fucking property?"

Sighing, I run my hands through my loosely styled hair before sitting on my desk and resting them at my sides. "She was drugged and taken with the help of someone posing as Lydia," I inform her.

Shay doesn't know all the details of the Fraternitas' requirements for the town, but as her family has been here a few generations now, she knows enough.

I stand and begin packing my office again, walking over to the bookcase and grabbing a stack of books to place in the box on the table.

"So, what's the plan, and how can I help?"

I pause at her question, then resume my trek toward the bookshelf.

She's about to say something when we're interrupted.

"Have you been ignoring me, Bastian?" Vivian's voice sounds from my office door.

The throbbing in my head intensifies. *Fuck, she's annoying.*

I remember a time when that voice would harden my dick with its sultry tone. Now, it just grates my nerves.

Seeing that we won't be able to discuss anything further with Vivian here, Shay announces, "Thank you, Mr. Grant. I'll wait to hear from you." Then she strides for the door, brushing past Vivian, curling her lip in disgust.

Sighing, I stop boxing up my things, "How can I help you, *Miss Taylor?*"

I don't have time for her shit. I came to pack up my things while the guys look for leads on the Senator and Madeline.

After the video footage Lev showed yesterday, it's been all hands on deck, but I needed to clear out my office before all this damn courting begins.

Her body stiffens as if I struck her with my formal address. Recovering quickly, the wince she donned transforms into a smile. *I wonder if she knows she has burgundy lipstick on her teeth?*

"Don't be like that. Just because you've made your *Selection,* it doesn't mean anything has to change between us. How will they know?"

Rolling my eyes, I return to packing the things on my desk. "Miss Taylor, everything's changed. The primary change being I can finally stop fucking you." My voice is venomous when I make my next point. "Did you honestly think there was a future here?" I look and see the hurt in her eyes. "Oh, you did. Well, that's too bad for you. After you not only fucked my father, but then married my former best friend, I think that ship has sailed. Now please get the fuck out of here so I can finish this in peace."

"Sebastian!" She storms into the room shouting, "How can you speak to me like that? I've apologized." She grabs me, trying to make me face her. "I had to."

Turning my neck slightly, I peer down at where her hand grasps my arm, trailing my gaze slowly until our eyes connect. My stare is glacial, causing her to drop her hand immediately.

"Bash, baby. Please don't do this. None of those girls have what you need. They can't satisfy your hunger."

"Step back, Vivian, and stop fucking begging. You look ridiculous," I demand and return to packing.

"Sebastian, please?" she pleads, but I ignore her. Vivian Taylor had my heart once, and she crushed it. I'll never trust another woman with it again.

That thought makes me think of how Owen and Wyatt look at Ariah. That girl has them lost with no hope of return.

She intrigues me. All her fire and her refusal to accept anything Wes or Lev dish out? It makes me look twice, something I haven't done in years. But I can't allow myself to be that vulnerable again. I'll marry and procreate with anyone we choose, but loving them is not on the table.

"Sebastian! Did you hear me?" Vivian wails. I've had enough of her bullshit to last me five millennia.

A knock on my office door cuts off my pending words.

"I strongly suggest you accept your dismissal, use your fucking vibrator and imagination, and take your fucking leave, *Vivian*," Owen grits out, striding in her direction, stopping only once he's standing in front of her and whipping out his knife faster than she can react. He holds it to her pulse point at her throat. "Or you won't like the outcome."

To say Owen has been on edge is an understatement. Ariah's kidnapping has impacted him and Lev in similar but different ways. Lev buries himself in every database and computer programming software to try and activate Ariah's tracker even while out of range. Owen, well, he has no true outlet until we find people to carve up. His other outlet is off the table. *Sex.* He refuses to entertain anyone else.

A squeal interrupts my thoughts, and I turn in time to see Owen has Vivian scurrying to the door. She pauses at the threshold, turning, her eyes imploring me.

"Goodbye, Miss Taylor. I hope never to have to see you again," I state, and water wells in her eyes, pooling before escaping down her cheeks, and with one more glance she finally exits the room.

"Too bad she decided to leave. I always wanted to see if she truly has a heart," Owen quips.

Shaking my head– *crazy knife-obsessed fucker*– I return to packing the last of my belongings.

"I t's been three fucking days! What do you mean you still haven't found her? Why can't we find anything new?" Wyatt shouts as he punches the bag.

We've had to bring him in here at least twice a day before he kills someone. The punching bag swings from the momentum of his strikes— left and right hooks in rapid succession– causing his pale skin to bloom red, not so much from exertion, but from his constant state of rage. I don't know that I've ever seen Wyatt so angry.

Owen isn't faring much better. I'm unsure how many more people he can slice up to get answers.

"I mean, until the chip comes back online, we won't find her that way. I'm already running facial recognition on the driver of the van, and we're tracking Madeline down now," Lev states from his spot on the couch.

He looks haggard— his usually stubbled beard fuller from lack of shaving. The most the man has done in the last seventy-two-plus hours is shower and occasionally eat. He's still not Team Ariah, but he wants her out of the clutches of whoever took her.

Owen steps into the room, wiping the remnants of blood from his hands.

"What did he say?" Wes asks, moving to the side so Owen can get to the bathroom.

The faucet turns on before Owen replies, "He wouldn't say much else other than we'll never find her in time."

"This is getting out of hand. Why won't anyone talk?" Wyatt mumbles as he hammers his fist into the punching bag, making the ring holding it to the ceiling creak at the impact of his blows.

"Take it easy on the bag," Wes quips.

His jibe grabs Lev's attention, causing him to stop typing and train his gaze on Wes. "Why? Are you worried he's honing his skills for when he finds out about what happened in the hallway with Ariah?"

Oh, this is going to be great.

"What scene in the hallway?" Wyatt's face swivels mid-swing. "What. The fuck. Is he. Talking about, Wes?"

"What the hell, Lev?" Wes gripes, tossing his empty energy drink can at his back.

Shrugging, Lev tips his head to the side, and the can sails past. "What? You didn't tell them?" he asks, a full-toothed grin lining his face, knowing the chaos he just unleashed.

I should step in, but this is just the outlet Wyatt needs. I unbutton the top buttons of my shirt and loosen my tie. This should be good.

"So what? I touched her pussy. How is that any different than what you and Owen did?" Wes retorts.

I lift three fingers to rub the lines of my forehead. *I know Wes isn't always the wisest but talk about throwing gasoline on a fire.*

Sighing, I groan, "Are you trying to die in here tonight, Wes?"

Wyatt's growl is almost feral. His lip lifts above his teeth, canines pronounced as his shoulder and neck muscles ripple. If I believed in the paranormal, I'd think he was shifting into a fucking wolf. The man might actually Hulk out.

"No, you dick. You don't like her. So, you," he points, taking his first step in Wes's direction, "don't get to fucking touch her. Ever. Not until you respect her."

"She didn't seem to mind my dislike of her when I squeezed her throat and had her riding my fin-."

Wes doesn't get to finish his statement— his head snaps left. Wyatt's right hook connects with no hesitation.

"You don't ever get to disrespect her like that," he spits, aiming to take another swing, but Thomas grabs him from behind.

Where the big fucker came from, I'm not sure. I would've eventually stepped in after letting Wyatt get in a couple more swings. Wes deserves more for being a taunting dick.

"Both of you cut it the fuck out. We have a lead, so save your wrath for who deserves it and not each other," Thomas snaps. It's the first time I've seen him raise his voice at one of us.

His words stop Wyatt's flailing. "What did you find?" Wyatt asks, glaring in Wes's direction, a promise of retribution before composing himself.

"We were able to locate the owner of the van company they used. He's in a holding cell downstairs."

"Finally! Some good fucking news," Owen shouts, already striding for the door, stopping to throw his elbow into Wes's side, causing him to double over with a groan of pain.

"Next time you touch my angel without her expressed consent, I'll cut your fingers off and fuck you with them." Then he strolls out the door, whistling what sounds like Sir Mix-A-Lot, without looking back. *Crazy fucker.*

Ignoring the hypocritical command, I try to gather more information from Thomas.

"Has he said anything?" I ask.

Thomas shakes his head before responding, "Just 'our time will come' repeatedly— like the guys who tried to kidnap Ariah from the locker room at the school."

I remember the guys filling me in on their extensive interrogation tactics. The thoughts inspire an idea.

A smile slowly etches my face. It's been a long time since I was able to dabble in some fun. Jumping at the idea of getting to play a game, I shout, "I know how we should question our *friend.*"

forgot how much fun it is having Sebastian around. His ideas often line up very nicely with mine.

I look at the table lined with weapons of our varied tastes. Axes, knives, guns, throwing stars, and whips lay among the assortment of options— like a buffet.

Gleeful at the prospect of what's to come, I quirk a brow in Sebastian's direction, "What exactly do you have in mind?" Excitement is pooling in my groin at the idea of the pain I'll get to inflict on the piece of shit who played a role in taking Ariah out from under my nose.

"Let's vote on it, shall we? Pin the tail on the asshole, or a game of good old fashioned darts?" he asks, flipping the switch. The light at the front of the room turns on, and there's a man tied to a solid wood board in the shape of a circle— *the impalement art*s.

My smile grows. "Wheel of Death?"

"Of sorts," Sebastian replies, walking to the table of goodies. "I figured this would be an interesting way to see if we can't get him talking and burn off a little tension. You've all been wound incredibly tight," he smirks, "for obvious reasons, of course."

"I like where this is going," Wes says, smiling for the first time in the last few days.

"So. What will it be, boys?" Seb asks

"I say we play darts and make a true sport of it," I suggest.

Hums of agreement confirm our plan of action.

I walk to the man donned in only boxers strapped to the wheel. He can't hear or see my approach, but his body is tense, sensing the predator nearby. My pulse skitters before thrumming a steady beat — anticipation of what's to come driving my steps forward.

Reaching the front of the room, I step up the short ladder until I'm comfortably level with his ears. Carefully, I pull the noise-canceling headphones off. I shout, "Boo!" startling him before he quickly recovers, clamping his mouth shut. Not even that annoying ass chant passes his lips.

"Oh, you're no fun," I heckle. "No worries. You're about to be the star of the show." I double-swat his left cheek and climb back down the step ladder.

Once my boots hit the concrete floor, I twirl, lips quirked and arms spread wide like the Greatest Showman. "Step right up, gents. Place your bets. Our main attraction of the night is about to begin, and it's interactive. The rules are simple. Cause him to bleed, you score a point. Cause him to yell or shout, and you score five points. Make him cry or beg, score fifteen points. Hit the bullseye, score twenty-five. And if you can make him talk? You win the pot and the game."

Stepping up to the table, I continue, "Each round is a different weapon. We'll start with throwing stars and end with guns." I pause, turning, taking in the blindfolded man whose life will end here tonight. He already looks like his ride here was a bumpy one with no seatbelt. "If he lasts that long," I snicker.

I hear a mixture of their reactions. Wyatt's cackle and Lev's scoff at my stupidity. Not wanting this to be too mundane, I decide to up the ante.

"I forgot to mention, to keep things interesting, you can't bet on yourself." My hands instinctively gravitate to the throwing knives— itching to feel the cool metal against my fingertips. I grab the matte raven-colored stars, foregoing Lola for the moment. Bringing one point to my lip, I open my mouth and test the sharpness against the tip of my tongue— *perfection.* If only my angel was here to christen its point with the iron of her blood.

The reminder of her absence reinvigorates my hunger for the man on the wheel's end. The fucking audacity of this amoeba to help facilitate her being taken from us means he'll be skull fucked by Lola before this is over.

Sebastian's voice cuts off my thoughts, "Five thousand and the keys to my cabin in Aspen for a year. I think Wes will get him to talk first."

Clutching my chest in faux heartbreak, "You wound me. I thought for sure I'd be your pick."

Chuckling, Seb replies, "I don't doubt your skill," he pauses, pointing to the ax in Wes's hand, "but I think the hardware he's wielding will make our boy there sing. Either way, it'll make him talk."

Silly Seb. How quickly he forgets.

"It's not the size of the tool. It's how you use it." I begin, readying the blade. "Or in my case— it's both." I sail the blade through the air, eyes following its progression until it lands right between our guest's legs, under his ball sack.

A quick grunt and jerking of arms can be heard from the front of the room.

"Careful, buddy, or you'll be nutless," Lev jokes from his spot on the wall. His arms are crossed, studying the man— observing every tick, twitch, or hitch of breath. It'll be him or me that makes this man talk.

"That doesn't count," Wyatt shouts, pausing his examination of his throwing stars.

"Just a little test run. Making sure our friend here is awake," I reassure.

Wyatt is a joking bastard, but he's competitive as fuck sometimes. However, this time I think it's the combination of wanting answers and wanting retribution driving him to want to win.

"Okay, I got five and my bike for a weekend on Wy making the fucker crack," Wes shouts.

"You can't do this!" the idiot from the front of the room screams.

"Au contraire mon ami. We can do whatever the fuck we want." Lev's tone is arctic as he continues. "Did whomever you work for not tell you how this all works?" he mocks, his deft fingers grabbing the pliers from the table, and I already know what's about to happen when he prowls to the unseeing man.

I follow his stride with my eyes, watching his approach. He looks like a panther on the prowl. Each time his long legs step soundlessly closer, my smile grows. It's like watching the Discovery Channel or some shit.

The wail that engulfs the room is like an adrenaline shot to my dick— *fuck,* Lev's pulled a tooth from the man's mouth. I inhale his screams like it's a fresh brew after a late night.

"Hey, that doesn't count either. If he squeals before we start, I say we still play just for bragging rights," Wyatt voices, determined to make this a real competition.

I chuckle at his eagerness. We need to get this show on the road.

"Not the teeth, eager beaver. We need him to talk," Sebastian jeers.

"What? I left his tongue, didn't I? You don't need teeth to talk, and I only took one." He shrugs. *Lev is a sicker fuck than even I am. People just don't seem to notice.*

"Finish placing bets so we can announce me as the winner already," Wyatt demands.

"Fine. Five grand and keys to Rubi for a day on bloodthirsty Lev over there," I state.

"Finally, someone with some sense," he responds. It's an unusual display of confidence— one I hope he exudes more often.

"I've got five large and a tattoo on me that Sebastian's going to be the one to do it," Wyatt states. "He can't wear those uptight wedgie-inflicting suits for nothing," he tacks on— his coppery brows wiggling in jest.

Raucous laughter erupts in the room, causing the man to shriek in surprise.

With bets placed and the order chosen, we line up by the table.

Wes steps forward, five six-point ninja stars at the ready, "Do you want to make this easy and just answer who ordered the van and where it was going?" he probes, but the man remains silent.

It's better this way or at least more fulfilling.

Determining he won't get a response, Wes pinches a star between the knuckle of his index finger and thumb, lining it up with one of the points— great form.

The whirring of gears turning brings my focus away from Wes momentarily to see the wheel begin to spin.

My smile grows. "Oh, this is going to be much more fun than I originally thought," I mumble as a shocked cry bursts from the now spinning man's lips.

"I say the stars should just be a practice round, and then we can question the dumb fuck," Wes suggests, and then he whips his through the air.

A shriek sounds. "That's a motherfucking hit," Wes shouts before launching the four remaining stars in rapid succession. Each time a whimper or scream is heard, but no other indication our guest is primed to talk.

We each take our turn, eager to move on to something more lethal and finally get some answers.

After the first round, Sebastian has edged me out by five points. *The ass. He always loved to be the one edging someone.*

The wheel stops. Once the dude is upright, he opens his mouth and spews vomit everywhere. *Fucking gross.*

"Someone's made a mess of themselves," Lev taunts.

This is his wheelhouse. The weapons serve a purpose, but the mind games he's sowing are precisely why he's my choice to win.

Blood runs in rivulets down his body, his skin oozing from head to toe in twenty-five varying levels of cuts— some superficial, others more profound. A few stars are protruding from his torso.

Eager to continue, Wyatt picks up the throwing knives. "I'm up first this time," he asserts. He doesn't wait for consensus. Instead, he throws his blade, and it impales itself into the man's closed fists.

Screams and curses fly from the man's mouth, but Wyatt doesn't wait— there will be no reprieve for him. He sails the next one into the man's muscled thigh.

"Still want to keep your fucked up vow of secrecy, Stephen?" Wyatt asks. The anger lacing his question is enough to make me pause. Stephen should probably answer.

"Fuck you," Stephen chokes out, spittles of snot and blood spraying around him. He's not surprised we know his name. He's, at least, not a complete idiot.

Needing no further encouragement, Wyatt sends his remaining three knives into Stephen's various body parts— a shoulder, a foot, and his other thigh.

Watching the blood run from each wound causes a pull in my groin. I grab hard at my dick, adjusting it while I try to give it a 'now's not a good time' pep talk. Normally I'd be all over the high this brings, but without Ariah being the one screaming in pain and pleasure while her blood touches my lips, it feels less rewarding. Pain and blood seeping from blades will always make my balls draw tight and my cock rock hard, but now I want to be able to sink that dick in my angel. *Fuck! Now I'm harder.*

"Where the fuck did the van go?" Wyatt growls.

I must have been too focused on my growing erection that I missed both Wes and Sebastian's throws and the escalation of questions.

Annoyed by Stephen's sniffles and refusal to still answer, I pick up my blades and wheel them through the air, one immediately after the other, like I'm throwing frisbees. One makes slices through the tendon in his forearm into the wood— another in his side, and the other three line his femur.

"Answer the fucking question because the axes are next, and we're going to spin you again for that round," I snarl.

"I-I-I was con-contacted a mon- a mon-th ago and told to have a v-van ready and untrac-untraceable," he finally spits out.

"Now we're getting somewhere," Wyatt says, pushing the button to spin the wheel again.

Sebastian stands, arm bent to the elbow, ax ready.

"Wait," Wyatt shouts, halting Seb's movements. "I think we need to speed this up. I say Seb throws the ax, but each of us should do something different until he finally spills." He picks up the flare gun and adds, "The bet stands, though."

We all nod in agreement, and Sebastian takes aim at the spinning wheel, his forearm extending back before snapping forward and aiming downward.

The howl that comes from the now slowing man on the wheel makes me laugh. The blade of the ax has split his kneecap wide open.

"We probably shouldn't have made him spin. The ax could've easily split his skull open," Wes announces.

"Hindsight is twenty-twenty or whatever," I shrug.

Lev walks up to Stephen, his dark denim-washed jeans and black shirt hiding the blood from our sight, and yanks the ax from Stephen's leg with his left hand before quickly digging the finger of his right hand into the open wound as he demands, "Tell me the name of the person who hired you?"

A blood-curdling scream rips from the soul of a now writhing Stephen.

"Seline Bishop," he stutters.

Silence.

That's all that can be heard outside the snot-crying fool who just threw a nuke-sized bomb in the room.

"What the fuck did he say? Did I hear him correctly?" Sebastian shouts, but it barely registers over the pounding of the pulsating beat in my ears, buffering his words.

"You did," Wes croaks.

"Where the fuck did they take her?" I snarl. My patience is lost. *I need answers now.*

Lev squeezes his knee again, and Stephen wails, "I don't know. We had nothing to do with it outside getting the van. You'll need the driver to know where they went, but he's probably dead already."

"What do you mean, probably dead?" I ask.

"I mean, I was leaving town when you fucks kidnapped me. My house was blown up with my men inside. I was supposed to be there, but I went to get dinner."

Stephen is finally spewing his guts.

"You chose the wrong business," I state.

"And the wrong girl to help take," Sebastian adds, grabbing the gun from the table, firing three rounds into Stephen's already battered body.

We're finished with him, and I grab the water gun. An idea hits me— sparked by the flare gun Wy had earlier.

"Lev. Wy. Help me with something?" I ask, using my eyes to signal what I have planned.

Understanding dawning, Wes walks Lev over a pair of gloves, and without saying a word Lev covers his hands, steps up the ladder, and yanks open Stephen's mouth— *his time is motherfucking up.*

Holding up the gasoline-filled gun, I step in range and aim for his uvula like this is a carnival game, and I'm trying to win Ariah a giant stuffed frog or some shit.

Stephen chokes and gurgles, trying to snap his mouth closed, but Lev's muscles are locked in— his grip on Stephen's mouth firm.

Gasoline pours down his body, flowing like a stream out of his mouth.

Satisfied with my efforts, I turn to Wyatt and nod, ready to take my spot. Wyatt takes position, aims, and before he fires the flare, he roars, "Burn in fucking hell!"

Lev jumps out of the way before the flare can completely catch fire. His flame-resistant gloves keep his hands safe.

We all hold our positions around the room, watching as his skin melts away from his bones.

The smell of charred flesh permeates the air, roiling my stomach, but I still don't make a move. The euphoria of avenging my angel is enough to negate any sick feeling that's building. Shit, if I had them, I'd toast marshmallows on the fuck.

"We need to go tell our dads what we know," Wes says.

The door swings open interrupting Wes's next words, shifting all of our attention from the still twitching but dead Stephen.

Erik storms through the door, pausing at the sight of the burning corpse.

Remembering himself, he shakes his head clear, oscillating his focus to our varying spots around the room.

"Sam's been kidnapped," he grits through clenched teeth—effectively killing the high of the interrogation from moments before.

7
ARIAH

"Let me the fuck out of here, you diseased cunts," I shout to anyone who's listening.

I know they're watching. There's no way they trapped me in this fucked up room without having cameras on me. I'm not sure how long I've been stuck in this dank fucking space.

My vision finally returned to me, and at some point, I was untied from lying on the slab and chained by my ankle to a concrete wall. My gaze surveys the room for the hundred-and-fifth time. A large metal table is sealed to a wall, but no chair accompanies it. *Smart.* No weapons. There are two examination-like tables in the center of the room, a small bed mat with a flat sterile pillow, and a scratchy blanket. My accommodations have been less than stellar. *I'm totally leaving a negative star rating on Yelp.*

The only saving grace in this whole fucked situation is knowing my siblings are safe. I know security will have tripled since I was kidnapped. Thomas will have ensured it and Tabitha will make sure Jamie, Ky, and Kellan don't worry. *I need out.*

I study the room again, preparing to stand when the sound of a lock turning snaps my attention away from the barren room.

The door pushes open and two men walk in. One of them is holding something.

Shit. It's a girl.

Long black hair hangs, and a slender arm dangles as they bring her to the examination table on the left and toss her down. I still can't see her face, but when they walk around the table and begin to strap her in, my pulse starts to race.

They know I'm here. It's evident when the one with brunette hair swings his muddy-brown gaze in my direction. Smirking, he says, "You're next."

What the fuck? Next for what?

Both men are dressed in identical black pants and t-shirts. The one with the jet-black hair pulls something from his back pocket. I can't tell what it is until the glint of metal exposes the blade. I bite my tongue to prevent the scream building in my throat.

I watch in horror as the man begins to cut the clothes off of the girl. I hope they're just undressing her to redress her, but I know in my gut that's not the case long before the knife cuts the band of her bra, exposing her naked breasts.

I turn away, not wanting to be part of her violation. At least, I do until I hear a groaned question. "Wh-where am I?"

My head whips back at the sound of that voice. A voice I've grown to hate but would never wish to be here, in this situation, ever.

"Sam?" I croak.

My suspicion of her identity is confirmed when her tear streaked face turns, meeting my stunned gray eyes. Her shrill cries fill the room, and I want to cover my ears and close my eyes as I take in the men stripping out of their clothes.

My stomach is churning at the prospect of what's to come.

"Don't you fucking touch her," I shout, finding whatever courage I can in this fucked up circumstance.

The douche with the crooked nose and hairy ass turns, chuckling, "Do you want to take her place? Because that can be arranged, sweetheart." I'm sure many women might find his smarmy smile attractive, but the brown-eyed pencil dick can fall into a vat of acid after being tripped for all I care.

Satisfied with my silence, he turns back on a screaming Sam.

"Shut your mouth, you dumb bitch," the taller one with black hair shouts, slapping her across the cheek at full force, her face snapping in the opposite direction. "The only time I want that mouth open is when it's stuffed with cock," he snarls, yanking her head back. She's dazed, so much that she doesn't fight when he stands in front of her and jams his dick right in her throat.

I dry heave at the sound of grunting noises and whimpers. I hate the bitch but not this much. No one should ever be subjected to this.

"Nooo!" The shout makes me lift my gaze in time to see the bastard has pulled out of her mouth, but the other fucker has positioned himself over her.

Oh fuck! I can't watch this. But before I can get my brain and eyes to communicate, hairy ass slams home with such a brutal force, I'm sure he's broken something.

"Fuck, you stupid bitch," the man screams as he slams his hand across Samantha's face. "Bite me again and I'll knock out all of your teeth," he growls before his hips piston back in and out of her mouth.

My eyes travel to Sam's, and hers connect with mine again. I want to shout I'm sorry, but what the fuck will that help? I watch as streams of tears glisten, running down her already swelling face. I want to turn away, but her icy eyes look as if they're begging me not to leave her alone at this moment.

I mouth, "I'm here," not knowing if she can truly see my lips to read them, but I refuse to say anything out loud for fear of them taking it out on her.

The smacking of flesh hitting flesh as the vibrancy in her eyes slowly dulls makes my blood boil. How the fuck dare they?

"Hurry up. It's my turn," the other sick fuck says.

"Fuck you. Take her mouth again until I'm finished. It's been too long since I've had pussy this young and tight," the hairy-ass fuck snaps back.

Spurred by the guy's directive, the other man walks around the table, blocking my connection with Sam, and bends his head, then bites her nipple so hard she screams. She tries desperately to move, but she can't.

Her screams make me forget I'm chained to a wall. I jump up, charging toward them, only to be halted in my tracks when the chain snaps taut. No give in the links whatsoever.

"Open up, you stuck-up cunt, or I'll punch your pretty face this time. And if you even think to bite, I'll turn you over and take your ass instead. So it's your choice, face fucks or ass ones?" he barks.

I don't feel my body falling until I hit the floor as I watch Sam comply, choosing the lesser of two evils, parting her lips and unwillingly accepting as he thrusts in and out of her mouth.

The tears build in my eyes, cascading down my face at the helplessness I feel at the sound of pleasured moans and gagging sobs.

At the sound of a guttural moan, I know one of them has finished, but I refuse to turn and discover which one. I don't have to wait long to know, though.

"Done. Now let me see what her mouth can do," hairy ass says, sounding so pleased with his vileness.

They must swap places because the sound of flesh pounding against flesh starts again, and Sam's cries are louder. So loud that I turn to see the guy with black hair angling her body up. *Shit. Fuck.*

He wastes no time slamming into Samantha's ass. No prep. The only lube, whatever blood and juices from his friend's time inside her pussy. Her scream is cut off as the other guy grabs her throat and shoves himself in her mouth.

I can't take it anymore. I'll never be able to unsee what I've seen, so I can't begin to imagine what the fuck Sam is going to have to go through.

I close my eyes and cover my ears. I won't turn my back, so she's not completely alone, but I can't stomach another sound or chance another forced look at the horrific scene before me.

I'm not sure how long I sit waiting for it all to be over, but when I hear the door slam, I open my eyes and take in a broken Samantha Davenport covered in cum, handprints, and a swollen face.

She's staring in my direction, but she's not seeing me. She's seeing past me, staring blankly into nothingness.

I find my voice, "Listen to me. We'll get out of here, and we'll kill these gutless fucks when we do."

She says nothing in response, but I don't expect her to. I just need her to know that we'll survive this.

I don't know who the hell these people are, but they're far worse than I could've imagined.

I take one more look at Sam, determination building along with my festering rage. We need to get the fuck out of here.

8

WES

"This is a major fuck up. How the hell did the Davenport brat get taken?"

I eavesdrop on my dad, listening as he speaks with Wyatt, Owen, and Lev's fathers.

Sebastian's dad isn't as high up— he's on the Council, but Wyatt's dad is the heir of the original bloodline.

"That girl has more security watching her than we even had on the Br-Bishop girl," I hear Mr. Jefferson say.

Why did it sound like he was going to call Ariah by a different name?

"Do you think she did it on purpose? Have we found anything new?" Mr. Grant asks.

I really shouldn't be out here. If my father finds out I'm snooping, I'm fucked. But they aren't telling us things, and if there's anything I hate more than Sam's annoying ass, it's being in the dark.

We've trusted the Fraternitas and done everything ordered of us — including getting close to someone we all believe probably got herself kidnapped.

"There's still no evidence of treachery, but you know I haven't trusted that family since the day Owen and Lev were taken," Mr. Washington grits, voicing the sentiments of all of us.

Nothing could ever be proven, and they always said Sam was too young to be in on it, but they didn't see her smile after she came back inside without Owen and Lev. She was dead to us after that day. It stayed that way until I got my order last year: Get close to her— do whatever it takes to get her to trust you.

I snort and quickly cover my mouth, remembering where I am.

"Wesley," my father's voice booms through the door, "you might as well come in, instead of sneaking around like a petulant child. We've known you were out there since you arrived. Did you forget about the cameras, son?"

Shit!

In my eagerness to get information, I forgot about all the goddamn tech.

Sighing, I push open the door. "I did," I mumble, sheepishly, but don't apologize— because I'm not sorry, unless you count being sorry I was caught.

"Continue. The boy needs to hear this," my father instructs, and Owen's father speaks next.

"Bobby's coming up clean. Blair's background has some flags that are being checked out."

So maybe our suspicions weren't off base.

"How did she go unnoticed?" I blurt out, my shoulders tensing, hoping I wasn't just meant to be a spectator in this conversation.

When my father's smile grows, and he nods approvingly, I relax a bit.

"Blair Davenport was born in this town. Her family has been loyal to the Fraternitas for generations. However, that doesn't mean she's loyal. It could be nothing, but we'll investigate," Lev's father states.

I listen as they finish talking. The list of people who could be turncoats is growing exponentially.

They rise when they're done, preparing to leave. I stand to follow suit, but my father's hand grips my shoulder, halting my exit.

"I need to talk to you, son." He says his goodbyes while I return to my seat, waiting for him to do the same.

Donald Edgewood feels like a new person. The man who I remember growing up with as a kid seems to be more present than the monster I've known for the last five years— ever since the kidnapping.

My father closes his office door, then strides across the room. His long legs cut the distance in a fraction of the time. He takes his seat, his imposing form still as intimidating as when I was ten.

"Wesley, I know..." he pauses, clearing his throat. "I know I have much to explain about my behavior, and I have every intention of doing so as soon as we get Ariah back. She's important, and her safety is paramount."

I nod but keep quiet. This isn't anything I don't already know.

He continues, "When we get the Davenport trash back, you need to find a way to get her to talk. I know what we said in the meeting, and we'll look into her mother, but I'm not convinced it's not both of them. I think Samantha wormed her way into this Selection. We don't have any evidence of it. It's just all too convenient."

"What is it you want me to do? I won't sleep with that bitch again— not even for the Fraternitas. I'll take whatever bullshit punishment— even the branding," I exclaim.

There's not a chance in hell I'm dipping my dick back in there. I shouldn't have the last time, but I figured it would be a great send-off.

I chuckle at the image of her flailing and cursing over the gag as I walked away from her after coming with Ariah's name on my lips.

My father cuts off my train of thought. "No! Listen to me, Wesley. Under no circumstances are you to put your dick in her ever again. We can't risk any slip-ups. A baby would guarantee her the spot. Any girl but her would be better— especially the Bishop one."

Right, because she'd let me anywhere near that delectable pussy again. My dick gets hard remembering the way she responded to me, and then immediately deflates when I remember where I am.

"Why her? She's not even from here. Why did you let her become Wyatt's Selected?" I probe, hoping he'll let something slip and answer questions that have been plaguing me since Wy made his choice known.

Even with the small bit of information they've given us. None of it has been explained. Why *her*?

"That's not important. What's important is that you and the boys find her and fast. Life would be easier if Samantha dies, but in the event she's alive, make sure she comes back as well," he instructs, and I know that's my cue to leave.

Standing, I make my way to the door, grabbing the handle and turning before I pause and look back at my father, asking a question that's haunted me for almost a decade.

"Why did you change after Owen came back?"

He grinds his molars, closing his eyes before reopening and focusing his identical gaze on mine. "It was the only way to make sure they couldn't use you against me. If they thought you were nothing to me, then you'd be useless to be used against me."

My father stands, moving around his desk, and before I can blink, has me wrapped in an embrace I never knew I needed. The shock wears off long enough for me to return his affection with a hug of my own.

"I've always loved you, son. I'm sorry I could never let you know just how much," he mutters, planting a kiss on the top of my head.

As he pulls away and our arms fall to our sides, something in my chest shifts and the pressure on my shoulders lifts. It's strange to know how much the lack of a parent's love can weigh on you. Our relationship is not magically fixed, but at least now I understand.

He pats my back, "Go update the guys. Let's bring Ariah home."

9
ARIAH

L ifeless. That's how Sam's eyes looked.

After some woman came in and cleaned up a catatonic Sam, I knew she didn't want to speak. She doesn't eat, talk, or move, and I don't blame her.

I haven't attempted to talk to her since my promise two days ago. I know it's been at least two days because we've gotten six meals.

It's been six meals since Samantha's world was irrevocably changed. Six meals since I discovered whoever took us is merciless.

There's a different level of ruthlessness someone has to have to not only rape someone but also make someone watch the gruesome violation and meticulous destruction of one's core self.

I haven't been able to close my eyes for more than fifteen, maybe twenty, minutes tops. Watching what happened to her keeps playing on a loop in my mind, refusing to give me a moment's peace.

I peer down at the charcoal gray sweats. I've had them on for days, refusing to let anyone touch me for fear of what could happen if I allow myself to be vulnerable in any capacity. Especially not after what that disgusting man tried to do to me. *No, don't go there.*

I shake off my intrusive thoughts when I hear the door creak. Not wanting to be obvious that I'm watching, I lift my eyes, but not my head, at the sudden burst of light chasing away the dark of our prison.

It's not time to eat, so whoever walks through that door isn't here to feed us.

My body tenses, every nerve ending instantly turns on high alert, ready to spring into whatever limited action I can take.

Two large bodies appear, blocking the sliver of light to whatever lays outside the door.

It's two men, not the same ones from days ago, both burly, their clothes looking like they're fighting for their lives, stretched to the full ability of the fabric.

They both approach the table Sam is strapped to, unbuckling the straps at her feet and arms. The minute she's free, Sam's arms soar into the air, her nails raking down the face of the man closest to her hands.

"You sick twisted bastards," she screams, clawing at the man's neck before the other one moves to restrain her.

"For fuck's sake, Murray, you can't control one puny girl?" the other guy asks, squeezing Sam's throat with the crook of his elbow, putting her into a chokehold, and yanking her hair back with the other.

Jumping from my seated position on the floor, I shout, "Leave her alone. Haven't you assholes done enough?"

They don't even acknowledge my existence. Instead, the other guy, not Murray, flexes his tricep and bicep muscles until Sam's face falls forward from lack of oxygen.

Murray leans forward, scooping Sam's prone form over his shoulders, and both men exit the room without a backward glance.

I don't have enough time to wonder what will happen to her or what's coming next as I hear the distinct sound of heels clicking against concrete.

"Hello, Ariah," a voice so familiar I think I'm hallucinating says, because there's no way what I'm hearing can be true.

Closing my eyes, I try to bask in the last moment my life was normal. When my father wasn't missing, and our family was whole, but most importantly, when my fucking mother was soothing my worries and not the one part of my entrapment.

My eyelids pop open—my pupils dilate at least five times their size.

Standing five feet into my cage stands Seline Bishop, my mother.

Her heart-shaped face glows with a vitality far from the emaciated strung-out junkie in the video weeks ago. Her once gaunt cheekbones, now full, have a rosy hue.

"Aren't you going to greet me, *Daughter*?" The venomous way she says daughter feels like a punch in the tit. *What the fuck?*

I want to ask why she's here or if this is some mistake, but I don't want to waste a breath I might need at the end of my life on the likes of this mess in front of me.

My mother's spirit left the day my dad went missing, and I tried to hold out for her return, but she's dead inside.

"It would seem your time in isolation hasn't done much for your manners. Your father is to blame for that," she states, like the mention of him sours her taste buds.

I continue to bite my tongue, my silence my only weapon.

Not deterred by my insolence, she strolls deeper into the room. Her coral suit perfectly outlines her petite pear frame, which is lengthened by her sky-high stilettos. If I wasn't so annoyed at the cunt who birthed me, I'd tell her she looks immaculate, but she can break a heel and twist her kneecap on the way down.

"The time has come for you to fulfill your birthright. I've sacrificed far too much for you to fuck this up for us."

Us? Sighing, I roll my eyes at another group having some nefarious plan for my fucking life. At least the other group never chained me to a goddamn wall.

"Do you know how many generations have planned to get us to this very moment," she babbles on.

Generations? My damn curiosity can't take anymore.

"What are you talking about?" I ask, my voice a little scratchy from lack of use.

"She speaks." My mother turns, striding gracefully toward me and stopping so she's still five feet away from any attempted stealth attack I might have been planning to utilize. "I was truly beginning to think we were going to need to increase our tactics,"

Increase our tactics?

"What the fuck could be worse than someone getting raped?" My stomach churns at the thought of what happened here only days ago.

Her head jerks back as if I struck her, but she quickly smooths out her features.

Did she not know what happened in here?

My mother's slender hand reaches up to adjust the broach on her jacket, focusing my attention on the profile of a skull wearing a gold military-styled headpiece circa the Roman Empire.

What is it with these people and fucking skulls?

The broach is not something I'd expect to see paired with her outfit. Hell, I've never seen her with a broach in my life.

Squatting just out of my reach, she whispers, "Far worse things can happen in this place, Daughter. You've been sheltered far too long. It's time you recognize your power and the prominent position in which you've been placed."

"What the hell are you talking about?" I yell, exasperated at the continuous subliminal messages I've received since I stepped foot in Edgewood.

"Temper, temper, my dear," her tone condescending. "We'll have to work on that if you're to come fully into your true potential."

She stands, dusting off invisible dirt from her pants before continuing, "You must not remember my words before the prick to your neck."

Seeing the confusion in my scrunched face and arched eyebrows, she titters a laugh, only growing my frustration with this whole damn conversation.

Clapping her hands, gleeful at whatever this news is she's about to unload, her candy apple red-covered lips break into a wide smile, brilliant white teeth a stark contrast to her lipstick. "Let me have the distinct pleasure of reintroducing you to who you really are," she pauses for annoyingly too long. "Ariah Elaine Bradford," she singsongs.

At the mention of that name, the block on the night of the party is lifted. I see the moment my mom comes into the clearing by the gazebo. I turned, expecting to ream Lev out for not taking the hint, only to be greeted by a woman I thought was hurt or dead somewhere. But she wasn't. She was standing in front of me like a proud fucking peacock, preening, right before I felt the prick and her call me by someone else's last name.

"That's not my name," I grit through clenched teeth, holding out hope that this is part of this mindfuck, another way for whoever they are to mess with me more.

My denial makes her laugh fully. My life is being tilted on its axis, fodder for her amusement.

"Oh, you poor stupid girl. You truly believe you're a Bishop, don't you?"

"Why would I ever think otherwise? You and dad never gave any indication that I should doubt my surname." I retort.

Her mouth twists at the mention of dad, like the idea of him is repulsive to her.

Who the hell is this woman? I begin to question every interaction they ever had. She never looked at my dad, *her* husband, with anything but adoration. Her cries and look of devastation on the day she received the news of his disappearance are burned into my memory. How could she fake that?

"Let's not mention *that* man. My duty to him is over. His purpose was fulfilled."

My throat tightens at her words, and there is a foreboding feeling stirring in my gut. I hesitate but find my voice, "What do you mean fulfilled his purpose? He's your husband."

"He almost fucked this all up, but luckily-," she trails off like her last words were only meant to be heard by her. My heart begins to race, pounding like a stampeding herd of elephants. Sweat starts to build on my upper lip, a telltale sign of what's to come. I gulp in a lungful of air, trying to stave off this dreaded feeling, but the dots appear. Each blink brings on double the number than just seconds before.

My neck wheels left at the same time the crack of a hand connects with my cheek.

"Oh no you don't, you little shit. We don't have time for your bullshit panic attacks," she snarls.

The smack stuns me breathless momentarily.

"You always were an attention-seeking little brat. Your dad goes missing, and you develop these *attacks*. Well, that stops now. We have too much to do and no time for your selfishness."

Selfishness? Is she kidding me?

Rearing my arm back, I throw my fist, punching her in her hateful mouth. *I hope I fuck up her perfect smile.*

She shrieks, falling backward on her ass, one heel falling askew.

Two men rush into the room, and I instantly recognize who they are: the men that raped Sam.

I scurry back into the wall, fearful of what they'll do. My anger made me forget my predicament.

"You were always an impulsive bitch," she huffs, holding herself up, stopping the two goons from further entering the room.

Standing, she rights herself, putting her heel back on and brushing the butt of her pants. Now she has a reason to dust her suit. I smirk at that small win. Once she's situated her clothing, she lifts her thumb to her mouth, wiping at the trail of blood from her bottom lip.

"You're lucky we need you to accomplish this plan, or I would've killed you by now," she snaps.

Her words strike my heart with the precision of a sniper, directly through the center of the organ lying to the left of my chest, causing a stuttering beat before it stalls, killing the last of my love for the woman before me.

Closing my eyes, I try to reconcile that I might be an orphan– a missing father and a dead-to-me mother.

"Again, you heartless hag, what the fuck are you talking about?" I demand, meeting the green eyes that match my sister with the cold gray of my own.

At the thought of Jamie, my stomach sinks. What will I tell her and the boys? *Fuck!* How do I broach such a subject? *By first getting out of here! Focus!* I remind myself. I can't tell them shit if I never make it out of here. I cut off that thought process immediately. I'll be getting out of here and with Sam.

"Right, you don't know anything, do you? Well, let's fix that, shall we." She begins to pace the room, now far out of my reach. It's smart on her part. I might risk her wrath for an opportunity to deck her again.

"I'd give you the whole long drawn out history of the five original families of Edgewood and their arrival to this country and settling in the English colonies, but it's dreadfully boring. Let's skip to about a generation or two ago when your father's father, your grandfather if you will, started to get wind of our plan."

She walks toward the table embedded in the wall, presumably tired of pacing, and takes a seat, crossing her legs before she continues. "You see, my family, the Lockwoods quickly recognized that chaos ensues with men in charge. A plan was hatched generations ago, long before you or me, to seat a woman of both original bloodlines at the helm under the Filiae Bellonae." Her gaze connects with mine before she says everything I've dreaded since this horrible story began, "And you are that woman, my dear sweet *daughter.*"

I can't blend this version of the woman before me with my mother. She's worn so many faces. First, she was the nurturer, the one who was our constant when Dad would be out on missions. Then, she was unreliable, drugs and alcohol dictating her actions, forcing me to become what she once was. Now. Now, she's something unrecognizable, leading some fucked up version of a hostile takeover.

"I won't do it," I exclaim, returning her hard stare with one of my own.

She throws her head back, exposing her throat as she laughs hysterically before abruptly stopping, her face morphing, lips drawing tight as her eyes narrow and her brows arch. It's like watching someone possessed.

Ignoring my rebuff, she sighs and states, "Here's how this will work. You'll take your place as the rightful head of the Bradford line and win the spot as the heirs' wife, giving me what I sacrificed my life and body for. Do you understand me, you ungrateful b-?"

Her words cut off as the door she entered opens, smacking against the wall. A short, stout woman stumbles in, rushing in her direction.

"What is it, Paulette? Can't you see I'm busy catching up with my daughter?"

I roll my eyes at her use of that word. I have no mother, so she has no daughter.

Paulette reaches her, signaling for her to lean forward. She whispers something into Seline's ears, causing her to whip her gaze up to Paulette. Seline quickly turns in my direction as she jumps down from the table and yells, "For fuck's sake! Can no one do anything around here?"

She's stomping toward the door when I hear someone shout, "Seline, where are you, you traitorous bitch?"

And for the second time today, my body freezes at the sound of a voice so familiar I'd know it anywhere.

"Dad?"

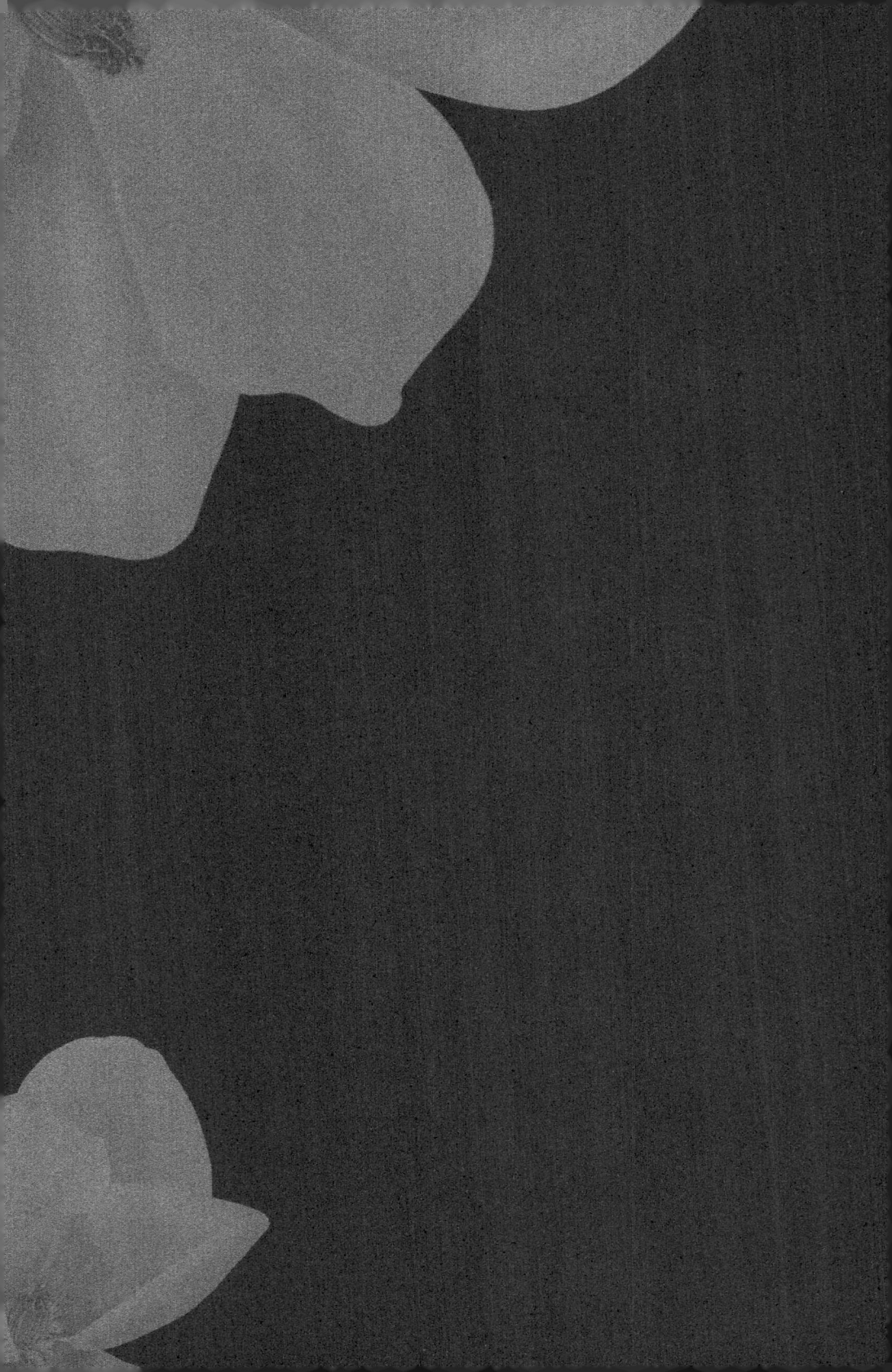

10

WYATT

Sam's finally done something for the greater good for once in her life. She went and got herself kidnapped.

The Filiae Bellonae are either incredibly cocky or stupid. I haven't made my final assessment on whether it's the former or the latter. Lev upped our technology after Ariah was taken, and her chip went offline. Once the girls were selected, they're required to wear pins at all times. We replaced those pins with new ones that contain GPS locator chips, so even if they were sunk to the bottom of the ocean, we'd still find their body's location.

It was too late for Ariah, but once she's home, I'm super gluing her to my side. She's lucky I can't find someone to make us one person.

When they took Sam, they led us right to them. It took a couple of days to work through some encryptions that initially blocked the GPS coordinates, bouncing them all over the world, making us think we were fucked again, but Lev called ten minutes ago saying he had confirmed the location with satellite and drone images.

"Are you ready?" Wes asks, suited up in tactical gear.

We could've let Thomas and his team go in alone, but a snowball has a better chance in hell than they would've in convincing any of us, especially me, to stay behind.

Turning to him, I nod. "I've never been more ready in my life. Let's play Catch or Kill. The person with the highest kill count gets to torture and kill Seline Bishop, and the person with the highest catches gets to have the Madeline skank."

It might as well be a game because there's no way this doesn't end with the streets of Lincolnville running crimson.

I grind my teeth at the knowledge of her location. She was so close. I should've felt her.

"Get your fucking head out of your ass, Grant, or you'll be left behind," Sebastian orders, and I immediately focus, clearing my thoughts of the guilt I feel for not being there to stop this or find her sooner from eating me alive. I'll never let her go again. Death himself would have to come for me, and I'd kill him too if he was in the way.

"Okay, there are over three dozen people on the property. We know Ariah is somewhere on or below the basement level, which is why we can't get the signal from her chip. Sam's chip is shown to be on level four, right above the basement in this corner left room," Thomas explains, pointing to the 3D image of the inconspicuous building.

The top ten floors make it look like a typical corporate office. The off-book blueprint we're looking at now tells the truth. Below the ten-story building are four floors, a basement, and a sub-basement.

Thomas stands, bending to strap his holster to his thigh. Once his gun and knife are positioned, he rights himself and continues, "By the time we arrive, we'll have all roads leading to and from Lock-Core Inc. under our control. The plan is to send in the Gamma and Sigma teams to secure the upper levels while the Beta and Delta teams secure the lower levels, clearing the way for Alpha team to breach the two levels on which Ariah may be held."

With the instructions provided and our plan laid out, we finish gearing up.

"Let's go bring our girl back," I state and head for the door, not waiting for the rebuff or concurring of any of the guys. She's ours. Some of us are just further along in our acceptance and devotion to the fact.

"I've never been so ready to unleash pain on someone as I am right now," Owen says as he steps up to the truck. He's decked out in more knives than I even knew he owned. Lola sits on his hip, but the long-bladed machete sitting past mid-thigh and push dagger are two new additions.

"Try to remember the objective is to bring both girls home. Even if one of them is a raging bitch, we can't leave her behind," Sebastian reminds us.

Lev rolls his eyes and mumbles, "I wouldn't be surprised if the bitch was part of this and planned it all from the beginning."

Laughing, I nod in agreement. "Samantha Davenport is exactly the type of crazy to stage her own kidnapping so that everyone will pay attention to her."

A derisive snort comes from the driver's seat. Erik doesn't seem to agree.

"You think she'd really kidnap herself for attention?" he asks.

"Have you met the girl?" Wes quips back.

At least we're in agreement that she's conniving enough to get herself kidnapped. I'm just not sure she's at the mastermind level to plan all of this, though. After the bullshit she pulled with Lev's attempted kidnapping and Owen's actually being taken. She was the reason they were outside in the first place.

"Focus! We can discuss the probability of Miss Davenport's involvement at a later time. Right now, our goal is to bring them both home," Thomas commands from the front of the armored truck.

The stubborn man refused to stay behind. He's not one hundred percent, but even at a diminished capacity, he's worth five of Erik, so he'll be more than fine.

"You make sure you don't go getting shot again. Ariah will kill us if anything happens to you on our watch," Owen half jokes.

"I'll be fine. Let's bring Miss Bishop home," Thomas replies but reaches to adjust his bulletproof vest to cover the area he was shot. Whether it's consciously or subconsciously being done, I'm not sure.

Needing a minute to refocus, I turn and peer out the window, watching as Edgewood blurs into Lincolnville. My mind replaying the information Mr. Edgewood shared after discovering Lydia's doppelgänger.

"Ariah was brought to Edgewood for a purpose. One I can't divulge. Just know she's important, and we must get her home before it's too late."

His words are more ominous than they are helpful, leaving me to have more questions than answers. I already know she's important, though I'm sure his reasons for wanting her back are vastly different from mine.

"We're here," Thomas's voice breaks me from my wandering mind. All distractions are cast aside until the beat of my heart resyncs with hers—Riri comes home now.

11
OWEN

The truck stops outside LockCore Inc., and I pull down my balaclava, the white skulled bones etched into its fabric.

The guys do the same, their guns rechecked, ready to wreak havoc. I pull out my latest toys— Thelma and Louise. Guns work, but the blade is so much more thrilling. The machete and dagger are the perfect combination for the level of hell I plan to unleash in this building.

"Did you even bring a gun, you idiot?" Wes asks, jumping from the back of the truck. His masked face matches my own.

"Of course I did," I turn my hip so he can see the FNX-45 Tactical. "You know how much I enjoy making it personal, and this is as personal as it gets."

Straightening, I put my blades away and double-check my gun— the magazine full and the safety off. With the built-in suppressor, we can light this building up like Christmas.

"Okay, two-person team entries, watch your partner's six. Gamma and Sigma have cleared the entryway and are making their way to the upper levels. Beta and Delta will enter the lower levels first, and Alpha will follow. Remember why we're here. Let's get these girls home," Thomas directs, and the teams file out.

Just as we walk toward the entrance, a man in a black suit runs out of the door, gun drawn, preparing to fire, but before he can lift the barrel of his weapon, there's a hole between his eyes. His body drops to the ground.

I peer over my shoulder, trying to find where the sniper is.

"You won't be able to see him from here. Eyes front— head on a swivel," Sebastian orders.

As soon as we enter the building gunfire is heard, but no one breaks formation. Thomas and Erik are in front, Wyatt and I in the rear.

We walk down the main floor hallway, heading for the stairs. Thomas aims his gun up then down, surveying the stairwell, "Clear."

Once we hit the bottom landing the door to the lower level entrance is already open, Beta and Delta having cleared the way initially. But once we step onto the floor, chaos ensues.

Our team is in combinations of shootouts or hand-to-hand combat.

Wes takes out two men before Thomas utters, "Stay safe and stay focused. Let's get to the rooms so we can start our search."

We pick off people but don't stop our forward progress. The teams have it under control.

I sense movement as we're about to enter the first room. Snatching my push dagger, I wheel around and upper-cut the man rushing from my left flank—nailing him under his chin. Surprise lights his eyes as blood pools in his mouth. Grabbing my machete, I slice through his carotid artery and rip my dagger from his chin, letting him drop to the floor before I stomp on his skull.

As his body hit the ground with a thump, I wonder if people think, 'This is it. This will be the one bad decision that causes my death.' Do they ponder the moment that caused the domino effect that brought about their end? If they don't, they should.

"You stupid fucks chose the wrong girl," I shout, stepping over the asshole's body.

"She's not in here," Lev shouts.

Fuck.

"Keep going," Sebastian snaps.

Moving through the hallway, we enter room after room and still nothing. Frustration mounts every time we turn up nothing— no Ariah, no Sam, and no people.

We're at the last room on this floor, and Lev kicks it open, breaking formation.

I see Thomas gritting his teeth as the giant tries to reign in his temper. He wants Ariah back just as much as we do, but he doesn't want any of us getting killed in the process. Our dads would have his head.

"Can you please follow orders? If not, I'll send you back to the truck," his tone placating but firm.

"She's not in here either," Lev grumbles, holding one hand up to indicate his apology for his error. "Sorry, T, it won't happen again."

Huffing, Thomas delivers his next command, "The next level is the basement, and since Beta and Delta are tied up here, it means we'll have to clear the floor before we search. Have your guns ready and your eyes and ears open."

We reach the basement with no initial resistance. It's looking like they didn't expect us to make it this far down. *Stupid on their part.* Our movements slow as we travel down the dark corridor, only the emergency lights guiding the way.

Thomas gives the signal for us to break out into smaller teams. Wyatt and I are in step, moving together to form a unit without a second thought. The minute we enter the first room, someone drops from the ceiling, landing on both of us, sending our guns scattering.

Wyatt rears his elbow back, smashing the man in the face. I'm about to grab Lola when I'm kicked in the side.

Grunting, I grab his foot before the next hit can land, knocking him off balance. As he falls to the ground, I jump on top of him, balling my fist, and take aim.

Punch after punch. His face whipping left then right with each blow. I don't stop until I hear the crack of bone.

"You picked the wrong day to show up to work," I snarl, grabbing his neck with my left hand, my thumb pushing down on his throat. I watch his light blue eyes blow wide as his mind struggles to figure out why it's not breathing freely anymore.

As he fights to breathe, I pull Lola from her sheath, releasing his throat long enough for him to gasp in one lung full of air before I plunge the blade through his Adam's apple.

Wasting no time, I don't bother to enjoy watching the light leave his pathetic eyes. I retrieve my blade, wiping his blood on his now dead face. *Can't leave it dirty. She has more blood to collect.*

Standing, I turn to see if Wyatt needs help only to discover he's currently stomping his attacker's face in, or what's left of it.

"Wy, I think you missed a spot," I joke, pointing to the part of the man's eye, which is the only distinguishable thing left on his face.

Wyatt turns his maskless blood spattered face to me but doesn't stop, moving from the dead man's head and slamming his boot on his nuts.

"He died too quickly. He's lucky my rage won out, or I would've saved him."

Wyatt's gaze looks crazed, his auburn curls wild as he speaks again, "He said he was going to take his turn with the fat blue-haired slut like he did with the mouthy bitch he had the other night."

My body locks as his words register in my brain. I'm going to burn this whole fucking place to the ground.

I don't allow myself to go back— blocking my mind from the memories that consistently linger right on the edge of my psyche. Instead, I channel my rage. Pulling my machete from my hip, I pick my gun up off the floor, and without looking back, I growl, "Let's fucking go."

Every room we enter and Ariah's not inside, the more my anger grows. I shoot and slice through bodies on autopilot. I don't speak. I just move. Every person we encounter, Wyatt and I move like we're one person. We move like we share a brain with a singular focus—*bring our girl home.* I hear voices when we reach the last room on our side of the floor.

Turning to Wyatt, I put my gloved pointer finger to my lips and then to my ear, signaling for him to be quiet because I heard something.

My knee-jerk reaction is to rush the door and exterminate anything that stands between me and my angel, but something in my gut tells me it's not her inside, and even if it was, rushing the door could get her killed.

I send a signal through our earpiece to get everyone to our area. I'm going to play it smart. Ariah's life could very well depend on it.

While we wait for the guys and Thomas to arrive, I keep listening to the muffled sounds through the door. It sounds like arguing, but I can't be sure.

Just as my patience is about to run out, I see Lev and Sebastian creep down the hall. Before they make it to us, Wes, Thomas, and Erik follow quietly behind.

Thomas takes point, signaling his instruction for breaching. Once we're all in position, he kicks the door open and jumps to the side as shots ring. Erik quickly returns fire, and someone inside curses before a crash is heard.

"You stupid fucks. You shot my brother," a gruff voice shouts from inside.

Filing in, we see a man standing and one lying on the floor, a gunshot wound to his shoulder.

"We're the stupid fucks, but your brother was shoot-." A shot rings out, cutting off Erik's rebuttal.

The man that was standing there is now dead, lying in a heap next to his brother, who is still clutching his shoulder.

Erik turns to see who fired the shot, only to see Sebastian fire three more rounds into both men.

"We don't have time for useless banter. If you want to talk it out, find a therapist. Let's move to the next floor," Sebastian orders as he exits the room, waiting for us to follow.

"Where the fuck is she? She has to be here," Lev snaps.

It's an outburst I'm not expecting from him, but one I should've seen coming. This has to feel like seven years ago all over again.

Moving to his side as we make our way out of the room, I lean over and whisper in his ear, "It's not your fault. We'll find her because of you."

His masked face is unable to hide the dejection in his eyes— he's wrecked, and if we don't get our girl home soon, I'm not sure what state he'll be in.

Knocking his shoulder with mine to snap him out of it, I say, "Let's go get her, Lev."

12

LEV

There is silence when we enter the bottom level. It's eerily quiet.

All of the teams have been met with resistance. Peering around, I look at the guys and see they've all had their share of close-quarter combat.

Wyatt's exposed face, splattered with blood, the sleeves of Sebastian's shirt torn, exposing some of his hidden ink, Owen's vest covered in blood— his kills are always the bloodiest– and Wes is missing gloves, his knuckles bruised and split from where he broke a man's jaw with one blow to the face.

We slowly make our way down the hall and are met with no resistance. I'd think this was a trap if it weren't for the trail of dead bodies lining the floor, blood splattered across the white walls like a Jackson Pollock.

I turn back to confirm the guys are seeing havoc before us. Body parts are everywhere. Whoever did this was like a rabid animal. Jagged pieces of flesh are strewn in the path before me. Someone has hacked these people to pieces. An arm hangs from a black rollout office chair, blood spurts from a vein that doesn't recognize its job is done. A head lies adjacent to it on the floor, vacated mahogany eyes stare in shock— frozen forever at the sight of their killer. *It's a fucking masterpiece.* The rage displayed in each kill, the skill someone would have to possess to chop a man's head clear off.

"What or who the fuck did this?" Sebastian murmurs. When I turn, I see the smirk I knew I heard in his question painted on his face. He's impressed. I am too.

"Whoever it is, better not have touched my angel, or I'll skin them alive with a hot fireplace poker before I rip off his dick and fuck him in his ear with it," Owen snaps, reminding us that this person could very well be a foe and not a friend.

With that thought put in the atmosphere, we ready our weapons, guns drawn, as we make our way through the halls.

A groan comes from my right. A man is pulling himself across the floor with his forearms. I contemplate for one moment— end his miserable life quickly or slow suffering? The choice is easy.

Walking until I'm standing over his slowly moving form, I raise my gun, firing a bullet in each arm. He cries out in pain, "Please."

"Why do you fucks always beg in the end?" I ask before I put a bullet through the back of his skull.

I was going for slow, but then he annoyed me with his begging.

"Enough playing. Let's go," Thomas instructs.

Nodding, I rejoin the group as we continue to step over limbs and walk around pools of blood. We're at a fork in the hallway when I hear something.

"Holy shit!" A scream comes from down the hall, and I instantly know it's her. I'd recognize the voice that's been playing on repeat since our last conversation. The one that I hope will forgive me for my follies.

I don't think. I just run in the direction of her voice. My legs can't move fast enough. Even the added weight of the tactical gear isn't slowing me down. I hear her again, my heart pounds with the spike of adrenaline shooting through my system.

"Fuck. Fuck. Dad, is that really you?" Ariah's voice is more pronounced with each pounding step I make. Remembering that I'm not sure what or who is down the hall, I slow my approach and breathing to ensure I can hear everything.

"It's me, Ry. It's me," an unfamiliar voice says. I assume it's her dad.

"Oh, isn't this just fucking touching? Reunited once again," a woman's voice snarks, sounding the very antithesis of warm and fuzzy.

I'm nearing a doorway when the woman continues, "Well, as exciting as this reunion has been, you've fucked me again, Aaron, and this time, it's for the last time."

The distinguishable pop of a gunshot sounds, and then Ariah's screams spring me into action. I'm sure the guys are almost here, so if anything happens to me they'll ensure her safety, but I won't fuck this up again.

I run into the room in time to see Ariah hovering over Aaron Bishop's body— blood leaking profusely onto the floor, but I don't have time to examine how deadly his wound is. My head snaps up in time to see the back of a blonde-haired woman in a navy suit attempting to slip through a door in the wall.

I aim my gun and fire three rounds. "For fuck's sake," she screams, grabbing her shoulder but not stopping just as the door in the wall closes behind her, preventing me from shooting again.

"Dad. Dad, no, Dad, please. Please, please, please," Ariah's gut-wrenching cries fill the room.

I turn, racing to her. The sounds she's making are cracking something inside of me. The pain in each of her screams assaults the barrier around my heart. No one should feel that level of hurt— her sobs catapult me back to the helplessness I felt for Owen.

"Let me take a look." I'm gentle with my approach, touching her shoulder lightly.

Her gaze whips in my direction, her face covered in spatters of blood and dirt.

"Lev, where the fuck are you?" I hear Wyatt growl in my earpiece.

"Go down the hall you saw me take off down and take a left when you get to the end. We're at the end of that hall. She's in here, Wy. She needs you," I state as I survey Aaron's body to see where he's been shot.

"I'm fine," Aaron coughs. "It's not that bad. I'll be okay," he says, but he has to know there's internal damage from the injuries he sustained. I know he's trying to alleviate her worry, but he shouldn't downplay it.

"You were shot," she shouts back.

"She has terrible aim," he jokes, attempting a laugh but the jolt to his shoulder makes his bearded face grimace.

Crunching boots and shouts sound as the guys enter the room.

"Riri," Wyatt gasps, rushing to her, but I stop him.

"Not yet, Wy. We need to make sure her dad's okay first."

Ariah's steel eyes soften, grateful for my help.

She should hate me. I left her. Instead, she's thanking me. I've done nothing but be an ass to her, and she's thanking me.

"I got it from here. Get her checked out by the table, and let me look at her dad." Thomas's hulking frame lowers to the ground taking control of the situation.

I don't know if she means for anyone to see it, but Ariah's body stiffens at the mention of the examination table. The hairs on the back of my neck stand. My eyes make a quick survey of the room. A woman lies dead on the floor, a knife sticking through her throat. I peer back at the man being treated on the floor, remembering the body parts littering the hallway. *Did one man do all of that?* Something to examine later. Right now, I need to know what has Ariah shaking at the thought of being on that table.

What happened to her in here?

I want to ask, but I already know something horrible happened, and she'll talk only when and if she's ready.

"Hey," I start, holding out my hand to help her up, "let's go outside. I'm sure someone can check you over out there."

She nods, beginning to take my hand, hesitating only long enough for her dad to nod for her to go.

"I'll be alright, Ry. I told you, your hag of mom was a terrible shot," he assures her.

Standing to her feet, her shoulders pull back, her posture straightens— steeling her spine, she gazes down at her father as she exclaims, "My mother's dead." Without another word, she turns and walks as if on autopilot for the door.

I take a moment to watch the goddess level of strength she exudes, walking from whatever hell she experienced with her head held high.

Ariah Bishop isn't a problem. She isn't a distraction or a weakness.

She's the fucking truth.

"Close your mouth, Levi. You're drooling," Sebastian mocks.

Clearing my throat, I deny his accurate assessment, "I don't know what you're talking about."

Sebastian snorts, clapping me on my shoulder, "Sure, man. Just go make sure she's okay." Then his face turns serious, "Until we know exactly what, she shouldn't be alone."

I shake my head, "Wy or O should be the ones to be with her."

"They will be, but there's no limit on who can support her. Go," he commands.

Sensing my hesitation, he pushes me in the direction Ariah just went, and my feet move before my brain can object.

I go over all of the instances I doubted her— all of the times I gave Wyatt and Owen shit for letting some girl mess with their minds, accusing them of not having their heads in the game.

Fuck. I got this one all wrong.

13
ARIAH

My mind keeps playing the last five days on a loop. That's how long I've been gone. *Almost a goddamn week.*

I sit in the open back of the SUV as some doctor checks my vitals. She's nice enough, but I'm less focused on her bedside manner. All I see is water being poured in my face, Sam being assaulted, and my dad being shot.

My dad.

I can't believe the man covered in blood was him. He looked disheveled like someone left out in the Alaskan wilderness to fend for themselves.

His usually cropped short hair was a tangled mess, his bearded face paler than his typically clean-shaven alabaster complexion, making his freckled cheeks more pronounced. He looked like he'd lost ten pounds and some muscle. *What did they do to him?*

I step down from the truck, hoping to find someone to update me on my father. My thoughts drift to the hate in my mother's eyes. The revulsion and contempt in every word spewed from her mouth, the power in the slap she planted on my cheek. I mindlessly raise my hand to the spot, wincing as my cold hands graze the still warm skin.

A hand slides up my arm, making me jump and attempt to tug away until I smell him. *Wyatt.*

I look up into the distraught amber eyes, my mouth parting to speak, but he envelops me. My face presses against the black bullet-proof vest as I inhale him. His scent mixes in with the metallic smell of blood, but it's his scent that reminds me I'm not in that room anymore.

His hands slide down my form, scooping me up by my butt into his chest. I squeal in surprise, wrapping my arms around his neck and my legs around his waist as I rest my head in the crook of his shoulder.

"Never letting you go. I'll kill anyone who tries to take you from me again," he growls in my ear.

The bass in his voice sends shivers down my spine, but it's his words that settle me.

"You came for me," I whisper, lifting my gaze until our eyes lock.

Wyatt angles his neck, lowering his mouth a hairbreadth from mine as he professes, "I will. Every single fucking time, Love. We all will," before claiming my lips with his in an all consuming kiss.

I'm caught in his spell, lost in a tangle of tongues, groaning at the feel of him hardening beneath.

"Hey, fucker. Stop hogging her." Owen yanks me backward into a bridal hold before planting me on my feet. "Angel," he chokes out as his calloused hands run along my skin, gliding across the spot where Seline smacked me.

Owen's eyes light with rage, his jaw clenches, but his touch is gentle as he tilts my face to the side to better examine the still forming bruise.

"Who did this?" he mutters through gritted teeth.

"Seline," is all I say, and I hear Wyatt curse.

Not wanting everyone to fuss over me, I redirect the conversation. "How's my dad, and have you guys found Sam?"

Lev answers, shocking me. "He's being treated, and then they'll take him to the hospital. Sam wasn't on any of the lower levels, but the building is still being searched."

I didn't hear him approach, and with the way he made his feelings about me clear the night of the Selection ceremony, I didn't anticipate him speaking to me at all.

"We need to find her." I pause, choking on the memory of her time here. "She can't be left behind."

Lev must see the fear in my eyes. He doesn't question my worry for someone who's made my first few months in Edgewood hell.

"We'll find her," he says, opening up his phone and pushing a few buttons. Lifting his gaze, he examines me with a level of scrutiny that resembles concern. I have to be imagining it. Lev doesn't tolerate me much less like me.

"They're bringing her down now," he smiles reassuringly, confusing me even more. It has to be the situation. *He feels bad, nothing more.*

My dad is wheeled out, and I take off. He sees my approach and pulls down the oxygen mask. "I told you she was a bad shot, Ry." His smile is pained.

"I'm riding with you," I state, leaving no room for argument.

"Whatever you want, Angel, but we're all riding together," Owen says.

"But sir," the medic tries to object, but whatever look Owen gives shuts him up.

As I step up into the back of the transport, I see someone carrying out Sam. Her head hangs on the guy's shoulder. It's not one of the guys, so it must be someone they came with.

I want to check on her, but I don't think she will want me anywhere near her. She lifts her gaze, seeing all of the guys crowding me, and the glare she sends me confirms my assessment.

She stares longingly at Wes, whose back is to her, and I feel bad for her. She's alone, and after everything that happened, she shouldn't be, but I'm not the one to comfort her.

"One of you should go check on her," I say to no one in particular.

They all follow my line of sight.

"Will has her. She'll be fine," Wes says dismissively.

They all climb into the back and I'm tempted to ask why Wes or Lev would even bother but think better of it. They did just risk their lives to come and save mine, leading to saving my dad's in the process.

"Our focus is you," Lev says, his gaze trained on me, and if he notices my shock, he doesn't acknowledge it. He's trying to convey something, but if he thinks this clears his slate, he forgot who the hell I am.

My dad's coughing pulls my attention from Lev's probing stare.

I peer down at his pale face, reaching for his hand as tears fill my eyes. "I still can't believe you're here," I choke out.

"Shh, shh, shhh. Don't cry. I'm here, Ry," he choppily soothes.

"Let's refrain from making him do anything too strenuous until we get him proper medical treatment," the female medic says.

A phone rings before we pull off.

"Yes, Dad, we got them both. We have a lot to update you on, but Seline got away," Wes reports. His dad says something else, making his lips draw tight into a grim line before he responds, "She's here, and so is her dad."

I hear Wes's dad's voice rising, but his words are inaudible.

"Right away. I'll let them know," Wes mumbles, ending the call as he turns his gaze to the medic. "Bring us to the Edgewood estate."

"What? My dad needs medical attention!" I shout.

He nods. "And he'll get the best attention in our medical wing. My dad has already called in an entire team. He doesn't want you or your dad out in the open until he has a complete update on the situation."

"He's right, Ry. It's the safest way to handle this," my dad interjects, cutting off my rising protest.

Puffing out my cheeks in resignation, I acquiesce. "Fine, but you better have the best doctors in the world because if anything happens to my dad, I'll feed you your balls for breakfast."

I sit back against the wall of the ambulance, taking it in. This isn't like any medical transport I've ever seen. It's about the size of an emptied out UPS truck, but it's filled with medical supplies and even a surgical table. The thing could be a hospital on wheels and it still has enough space for all of us to comfortably fit back here.

A hand lands on my thigh. "What's going on in that mind of yours, Angel?" Owen studies me like he's trying to see into my thoughts.

Definitely not a place I want him to be, not after everything that happened. I need time to process it myself.

"Don't hide from me." He sees me without even trying. "You don't have to tell me if you're not ready. Just don't hide from me," he whispers the last part as he lifts his hand, brushing his thumb over my chapped lips.

A pained grunt breaks the moment.

"I know I haven't been around, but, umm, Dad in the room," my father jokes, making us all laugh.

Owen doesn't remove his hand from my thigh, but removes the one from my lip. His eyes pin me, communicating the promise that this conversation isn't over.

"Right, so hands only in places you can't see. Got it," Wyatt quips. My cheeks bloom red and hang my head, trying to hide my embarrassment.

I hear a smack and look up to see Wyatt rubbing the back of his neck.

"What? I was just saying," he mumbles.

I snort, bringing my hand to my mouth and cough, trying to cover up my amusement.

It feels good to laugh after so many days of feeling despair.

"How did you guys find me?" I ask, hoping my question doesn't completely kill the lighthearted vibe.

Wes answers, "Samantha finally did something unselfish— not knowingly, but in this instance, we'll take it."

"What did she do?" I question, furrowing my brow in confusion.

As bad as I feel for Sam, I know her. She's not the selfless type, especially when it comes to me.

Sebastian clears his throat. "After you were taken, we made all the Selected girls wear pins with GPS locators in them. When Sam was kidnapped, she was still wearing hers. We just had to wait for her to be taken somewhere the signal wasn't jammed," he explains.

"They took her out of the room. I don't know where they brought her, but it must have come back online when they did that," I state.

Lev nods, confirming. "Yeah, she was found on the floor above where you were. Their fuck up was our gain."

I still have so many questions. I didn't see a pin anywhere on her, but I can analyze that another time. I'm just happy to no longer be stuck in the clutches of that bitch Seline and to have my dad back home. My gaze shifts to my dad. The medic has stopped the bleeding. He catches my eye, a small smile on his lips, and he mouths, 'I love you, Ry.'

It's not a magical happily ever after, but the nightmare is hopefully ending.

14

WES

She's *safe*. I keep repeating that as I watch Ariah with her dad from the door.

Last night could've gone so many ways, but thankfully we were able to get her back. It's good we got Samantha back too. I'm just not convinced she didn't have something to do with her own disappearance. It's why I pull myself away from the girl who's been monopolizing my thoughts since she arrived in Edgewood.

I make my way to my father's office, trying to mentally prepare myself for the grilling we're about to get. When I arrive, his door is open, and the guys and our dads are already inside, sitting around the table waiting for me. *Shit.* I curse myself for needing to see she was truly safe with my own eyes. *She's not my problem.* I taste the lie — ignoring its bitterness as I take my seat.

"I apologize for being late. I wanted to make another round before the meeting," I explain, looking at my father, hoping my explanation softens the blow.

To my shock, he smirks, "Perfectly understandable, Wesley," and the look is gone as quickly as it appeared. "Let's get down to business, shall we? Now that everyone injured is being taken care of in the medical wing, we have some things to discuss. There's a lot we need to update you all on in order to move forward accordingly."

A sharp jab in my side takes my attention away from his words, "Are you finally ready to eat crow, Edgewood?" Sebastian asks.

"I don't know what you're talking about. Nothing's changed," I mumble.

A throat clear. "If you two are finished, we need to get started," my dad says.

Did this man get a personality transplant? He's serious, but any other time my not providing my undivided attention would've landed me a swift reprimand— not a clearing of the throat.

"We've updated you on Aaron Bishop's capture and being one of the highest priorities to retrieve, second only to his daughter Ariah's safe return, but what we haven't told you is that Ariah Bishop is Ariah Bradford."

My head snaps up— eyes going wide in shock. A Bradford?

"What the fuck?" Lev shouts but quickly shuts his mouth at my father's stern glare— now that's the man I grew up with.

"How's that possible?" Sebastian voices, saving Lev.

Shifting his furrowed gaze from Lev, my father surveys the room, his jaw flexing as though he's trying to find the right words to explain the bullshit lies they've been telling us for all of our lives.

"We can't give you all of the details. Just know it was for her safety that she was hidden. And as you've observed, it was for a good reason."

He stands, moving to his desk to retrieve something before he continues, "The Filiae Bellonae has been a shadow organization we've known about for generations, but they've kept themselves hidden, only striking in recent years."

I look to my brothers. We all have a variation of the same look— confusion, frustration, and shock. How could they keep this from us? Why would they?

"How... why would you not tell us any of this?" Owen inquires as if hearing my inner thoughts.

Expecting our questions, a screen rises from the stand at the front of the table. An image on the monitor appears.

"Elise Lockwood, or Seline Bishop as she's been going by, was high on our radar, but we couldn't confirm our suspicions until Ariah's arrival to town."

"Lockwood? As in *the Lockwoods?*" I ask, remembering one of the families that left Edgewood when they felt snubbed for not being part of the founding families because they had no male heirs at the time. Women aren't allowed to be Fraternitas members. It's not allowed and will never be done.

"The very same. Seline Bishop was born under the alias of Seline Stephens, a name she was given at birth to hide her true identity. She was given up for adoption to a family to hide her true lineage but raised under the tutelage of the Filiae Bellonae."

We stare at the birth certificate of both names. This group has been planning for a long time.

"Do we know who the members of their leadership are?" Wyatt asks. His hands balled into fists, no doubt trying to reign in the rising anger— evident by the reddening tips of his ears nearly matching his ginger hair.

"Not enough. They're hiding in plain sight. We're slowly gaining some insight based on the members we've identified."

"Do we think Samantha Davenport is a member?" Lev voices.

"We're still unsure. After she was taken and assaulted, we believe she may not be a member, but suspicion remains. We're just lucky the idiots that took her didn't realize that the pin she was wearing had the GPS chip in it," my father replies.

When news of Sam's rape broke, I felt horrible for my initial suspicion of her, but then I remembered who she is. Would someone stage their own kidnapping and rape? That would be vile even for her usual antics.

My father continues, "We'll be keeping an eye on her, but for now, given all that's occurred, we will pull back on our surveillance to give her time to heal. She's bruised and has a broken cheekbone so she'll be home resting for the foreseeable future."

"How can they be so hidden? Why don't we know more?" Lev starts. He pulls his hair from its bun and redoes it, a sign of his mounting frustration with being so far out of the loop. But Lev knows we never get all of the information. He needs to tread lightly here.

"If we had known even a quarter of this information, Ariah might not have been taken. We could've done more," he growls.

Rubbing the back of my neck, I finally recognize where his frustration lies— his guilt. He's trying to make sense of a fucked up situation.

"You were all told what you needed to know," my father barks, his patience with Lev's outburst spent. "With the information you did have, you didn't discover enough to do what's required. See that you all rectify that moving forward. You're all dismissed."

We rise from the table, silent as we make our way to my side of the house, so we can discuss everything festering after the cluster fuck of information dump we just received.

"How the hell did we not know any of this? How were we supposed to keep her safe without knowing all of this?" Lev snarls, punching the wall as we enter my room.

This is more than just guilt. I snort, "Let me guess, you're team Ariah now?"

He works his jaw, glaring at me.

"Will you cut it the fuck out? We don't have time for your shit, Wes," Sebastian snaps. "We have a serious problem on our hands and too many variables up in the air. Lev's right. We need to know everything if we're going to keep her and any of the other girls safe. They didn't just take her. They took Sam and killed two other girls."

Sebastian's words illuminate the severity of the situation. I know Lev's right, and I know I'm being a dick, but it's hilarious to see the change in him. He was more anti-Ariah than I was.

"You three can bicker like housewives trying to decide who gets to throw the next garden party later. We need to discuss our next steps so I can go see my Riri," Wyatt demands.

"So *we* can go see *our* girl," Owen adds, giving Wyatt a pointed look, and I know Frick and Frack are going to find a way into her house tonight.

Agreeing that we need to do something to get a handle on everything so that we can keep Ariah and the rest of the girls safe, I state, "You're right. Let's plan."

15

ARIAH

I sit in the chair across from dad, whose reappearance I'm still trying to wrap my head around. He's here, in front of me.

"Where have you been?" I need to know what has happened in the last two years. No. My entire life. It seems to have been a complete lie.

He grunts as he raises the back of his hospital bed from a lying position. "There is a lot I can't say," he mumbles.

I narrow my eyes, clenching my jaw at his bullshit answer. "What do you mean there's a lot you can't tell me?" I whisper yell, aware that people are walking in and out.

"Ry, there is so much that's happened that I can't begin to apologize for, but I need you to know it was all done to keep you safe. As soon as I knew your mother–" he starts, but I cut him off.

"That woman is not my mother!"

"Right. Well, I discovered Seline wasn't who I thought I married after I was taken as I was leaving the Fraternitas to return home two years ago."

His words register, and my mind tries to make sense of what he just told me.

"Are you telling me that my moth– Seline knew where you were the entire time you were missing?"

"Yes, and she was responsible for my prolonged absence. After I was released from the Fraternitas, I was taken while on my way to the airport. That's where I discovered Seline Bishop was really born Elise Lockwood."

The sheer number of revelations I've received since I stepped foot in this town is baffling. Sel-Elise having an alias is high on the list of shit I wasn't expecting, but my mind kept repeating, 'after I was released from the Fraternitas.' *What the fuck?*

"What do you mean released from the Fraternitas? They took you too?"

"I was trying to keep you safe for a little longer," he starts, reaching his hand for mine. "I needed to let you be my baby girl a little longer, and they just wouldn't let it happen."

My brows knit together, even more confused. Who was he trying to keep me safe from? I want to ask him, but his eyes begin to droop, and I know his latest dose of medication has been distributed.

The door to his room opens, and a petite nurse with mahogany hair and pixie features steps inside.

"Hello, I'm Sarina. I'll be your father's nurse for the night. I'm just here to check his vitals before he goes to bed," she explains, walking to his side and examining the machine measuring his blood pressure and heart rate.

As she writes the information on her tablet, she speaks. "While it's okay for you to be here a bit longer, I recommend you don't spend the night and give your father some time to rest." Lifting her eyes from the device, she pauses, surveying my still unkempt state, "And you should go get yourself properly checked out."

"Yes, Ry. Please go get yourself looked at and then go home to your sister and brothers. Come back tomorrow, and we'll talk more then," he slurs, his head lulling to the side, half in and out of sleep.

Sighing, I stand from my seat. They're right. I need to check on the kids. I can't begin to process how I will tell them Dad's back or that their mom is a conniving bitch who tried to kill our dad.

I rub my fingers across my forehead, feeling the dried blood caked on my skin, the realization making me itchy.

"Okay, Dad. I'll be back tomorrow," I say as I bend, kissing the top of his head, "with the kids. They'll be so excited to see you."

I want to tell him how big they've grown and how hard it's been, but his light snores signal he's no longer awake. I peer down at him one more time, soaking in the fact that he's here before I turn to exit the room.

Walking down the hallway, I pass room after room, each filled with someone injured from tonight's rescue. A level of guilt hits me. They're here because they came to save me. That feeling quickly morphs into a simmering rage. Rage at so many people but specifically the incubator that birthed me.

I'm coming to the end of the hall when I catch a glimpse of a slender frame with black hair. *Sam.* Her body is facing away from the glass.

Do I go inside? I should go inside. Steeling myself, I push open the door. She doesn't even react. I don't want to spook her by getting too close.

Clearing my throat, my words soft, "Sam." She still jumps at the sounds of my voice. *Shit.*

"Sorry," I whisper, "I didn't mean to startle you. I just wanted to check on you before I go home."

Sam slowly turns, mottled bruises line her face, and a splint covers her nose. She looks awful, but that's not what shocks me. It's the glare she levels me with. Her ice-blue eyes pierce the dimly lit room. I'm sure her nose would be scrunched in disdain if it wasn't immobilized.

"What the fuck do you want, you gutter troll? Did you think we would magically be friends because we were taken together?" she snaps.

Rolling my eyes, I try to remind myself of what she's been through, but fuck that.

"Good to see your glowing personality is alive and well. I just wanted to make sure you're okay."

She huffs a laugh, "Okay? I was fucking raped, and no one came to look for me when the rescue happened. Instead, they were all too busy trying to find you."

My heart breaks a fraction at her words. She's angry. Her following words incinerate any sympathy I had for her.

"It should've been you having your face smashed as two men fucked you. You probably would've enjoyed it like the skank you are."

I gasp, my jaw dropping at her acerbic words.

"You might be hurting, but you don't get to be a fucking spineless bitch because of it," I yell. Fuck decorum. Who the hell says shit like that to someone? "Wes probably didn't look for you because you're dead inside. And yes, I know you meant *Wes* didn't look for you. He's who you care about, isn't he?" I ask, my head tilting to the side. She flinches at my pointed question.

"How does it feel to know that he came to find me, *the trash,* and not once sought you out? Has he even checked in on you?" I jibe, relentless in the evisceration of her. She never knows when to keep her fake ass lips shut.

"They all came for me, even Wes. I'm the reason they were there. You weren't even an afterthought," I grit through clenched teeth. "You might be a decent person if your mouth could be glued shut."

Turning, I yank the door open, ignoring whatever the ungrateful brat squawks. *Fuck that stupid hoe.*

"I can't believe you ignored the doctor's orders and came to get me. Thomas, are you crazy? What if you got hurt or, worse, killed?" I shout at the giant man driving.

"I assure you, Ariah, I was fine. I am fine."

Crossing my arms over my chest, I suck my teeth. *Big dummy.* Why don't men ever want to listen to doctors' orders?

"Right, your zero years of medical school allowed you to give yourself a clean bill of health," I mumble, and the big oaf bursts out laughing.

"No medical school, but I'd say my years in the military provided me with some experience."

"Okay, I'll give you that," I snark. He's more than proven his capabilities. I'm just worried. An image of him lying on the pavement as blood pools around him flickers across my mind. *That can't happen again.*

My voice cracks, "Look. I just don't want you to get hurt because of me. I'm beyond thankful you came for me, that all of you came for me."

The car pulls to a stop, causing me to look up and realize we're home. His throat clears, making me turn. His hand resting on the door handle but not pulling it open. His stare pins me to the spot. "I know you're worried about my well-being, and I greatly appreciate you for it, but you're like a daughter to me, so know if the choice is ever your life or mine, there is no choice. It will be yours."

The surety in his words freezes me to my spot. Since coming into my life, Thomas filled the role that my parents haven't been able to over the last two years.

Warmth envelops me at his willingness to care for my well being, "How about I don't put myself in situations to make that a viable option?"

He smiles, nodding as he opens the door, "That sounds like a smart plan."

Squeals shift my focus to the window in time to see Jamie,

Kellan, and Kylan torpedoing for the car. I don't wait for Thomas to come around. Pushing out the door, I jump out and open my arms as my three siblings tackle me.

"Ry," they all scream. I bask in the warmth of their hugs as tears stream down my face. *I thought I might not ever see them again.*

Squeezing them tighter, I say, "I missed you all so much."

"Let's get you all inside," Thomas states. I jump at his words. I didn't hear him approach. *I have to be more alert.* I can't let what happened to me at that party ever happen again.

Giggling, the kids let me up from the hug pile on the ground. As I stand, I feel Jamie's penetrating gaze taking me in, noting every scrape and bruise.

"Where were you? What happened? Why could no one find you? Why the heck do you have a handprint on your cheek?" she asks as we make our walk to the house. The boys have already run ahead, safely out of earshot from the rapid firing of her questions.

I'm not going to hide anything from her, but I damn sure will not give her all the finite details either. I need to talk with dad before I share too much. I still don't have all the answers, but I know there are things she can't know, and shouldn't know.

Putting my hand around her shoulder as we walk through the door, I explain, "There's a lot you need to be filled in on, but I'm exhausted. Let me shower, and then we can all dogpile on my bed. In the morning, we can talk more."

Her emerald eyes narrow before she nods in agreement, showing again she's far more mature than she should have to be. In this instance, I'm okay with it. I'm just too tired to combat any onslaught of her questions.

I make it ten steps into the house before Tabitha wraps me in her arms and whispers in my ear, "Don't ever scare an old woman like that again, child."

"I won't. I promise," I say, pulling back from her embrace and smiling.

"You must be so tired. Go get cleaned up, and I'll bring you something hot to drink and light to eat," she orders.

This must be what it feels like to have a grandmother.

Tabitha gives me a knowing grin and heads for the kitchen.

I watch her go then climb the stairs, not stopping until I'm safely in my room, greeted by the smell of lavender and chamomile.

Home.

Singing, I make my way to my bathroom and immediately begin to strip. *I need out of all this shit.* The fabric is making my skin crawl. I toss everything I have on directly into the trash. I'll be happier if I never see navy blue sweats again.

I turn on the shower, wait for it to warm, then hop under the spray. My mind races, trying to process everything all at once.

I'm a Bradford. *Who are the Bradfords?* What made them so important that my own mother was willing to kidnap me and try to kill her husband of almost twenty years?

Sighing, I pour shampoo into my hair and begin to scrub days of grime from it. "Dad, what the hell is going on?" I murmur to myself.

As soon as he's more stable, I'll get some answers.

I rush through the rest of my shower, remembering my siblings will be here soon. I smile at the thought of finally being home with them as I step out of the shower and towel off.

By the time I'm dressed and walking out of my closet, the three of them are in my bed. Ky and Kell are smacking each other with pillows, and Jamie is off to the side, reading a book.

Seeing that his sister isn't paying them any mind, Ky looks at Kellan. They both turn and launch their pillows in Jamie's face. She bursts out into giggles, jumping from her spot to tickle them.

"You two are going to pay for that," she shrieks, and they scramble out of her clutches.

"Gotta catch us first," Kellan exclaims, running to the other side of the room.

I lean against the wall, basking in the moment.

"Help," Ky shouts, running full speed into my stomach.

Letting out an "oof," I join in the fun and poke his side. He squeals as he makes a mad dash for the bed.

I follow after him, climbing on the mattress and patting the spots next to me. "Come on, let's watch a movie until we fall asleep."

They settle in as I flick on the television, pulling up a Spiderman movie.

The boys cheer and I ease back on my pillow, resting my eyes. Their commentary on who's the better Spiderman is the last thing I hear before sleep consumes me.

16

SEBASTIAN

She's back.

The little spitfire wasted no time showing her spark. Ariah made sure her dad was going to be taken care of. Hell, she even ensured Sam, of all people, was going to be seen. The same Sam that's tried to make her time in Edgewood miserable.

When they brought Samantha out, I began to second-guess her participation in this whole ordeal. She looked like hell ran over three times.

According to the reports, she was raped and beaten severely. It didn't stop her from trying to paw all over Wes, though. He went to give instructions on transport, and her claws snaked out, grabbing for his vest. Wes jerked out of her reach.

She asked him to ride with her, and he declined. Then, she asked him to stay with her as they did the rape kit, and he again declined. Samantha immediately threw a fit, tossing the contents of her rape kit across the room and refusing to complete the exam or cooperate further with questioning.

Her actions after were questionable, but who am I to say how someone processes their trauma? Shit. I'm probably the poster boy for how not to handle it.

Vivian has fucking ruined me.

Once I reach my room, I strip and grab a quick shower. I need to go to *Le Toucher*— it's been a fucked last few days, and I need relief.

As the water beats against my body, I lather my skin remembering a time when I thought I'd spend my life with her. She was everything I wanted and thought I needed.

Now that I'm clear-headed, I see that I never looked at her the way Wyatt and Owen look at Ariah— like whether the sun rises or sets is determined by her happiness.

I'd say it was a bit strong for something so new, but neither of them is stupid. They don't only think with their dicks, and for them to be so besotted with a girl, while uncharacteristic of their typical behavior, means she's something special.

Turning the water off, I step from the shower, grab a towel to wrap around my waist, and make my way to my closet.

Once dressed, I grab my keys and head for my car.

Driving through the town, I look up once I approach the *Welcome to Edgewood* sign and make my way to the interstate.

The tension in my spine immediately settles once I'm ten minutes outside of town. Coming home wasn't supposed to bring back all of these memories, and it certainly wasn't supposed to stir new ones.

The Selection is something I'm duty-bound to— I volunteered once things with Vivian didn't work out. Without a Bradford, there would need to be another male heir from one of the original families.

I thought we'd pick some chick, marry her, and get her pregnant. Feelings were never part of my plan. Ariah was never part of my plan.

She still isn't, but it's hard not to watch her with Owen and Wyatt and want that feeling.

"That's it. Right fucking there. Bastian never lets me take control." I hear the familiar moan of my fiancée as I walk through my house to my bedroom.

"Goddammit, if I knew you fucked like this, I would've taken you up on your offer years ago," Vivian shouts.

I grit my teeth, change gears and push down on the accelerator as the scene that haunts me plays across my mind, reminding me exactly why I can't allow feelings anywhere in this arrangement.

Women are disposable. They are for my pleasure and nothing more. However, I can't dispose of whoever we choose— I just won't love them.

I exit the highway, driving on autopilot until the club comes into view.

Le Toucher is an updated French-styled chateau. The limestone structure stands three stories high and is over twenty-thousand square feet, where you can live out your every carnal sin, no matter how depraved.

I pull up to the gate, stopping when one of the guards approaches.

"Nice to see you again, Mr. Grant. It's been quite some time. Matthieu will be happy to have you back, and so will the girls.

"Thank you, Trevor. I'm long overdue for a scene and a scotch," I reply.

He smirks, raising his hand to signal to the control room to open the gate so I can get through. Then I drive up the long winding drive-way, scan my card, and pull into the underground parking garage.

Matthieu has this place set up so that once a member scans in, their rooms are prepared for their particular tastes. By the time I make it upstairs, a girl will be in my room, ready to play.

Stepping out of the elevator, I make my way to the entrance, scanning my thumb against the sensor and waiting for the lock to disengage.

"Welcome back, Mr. Grant," a soft voice croons, oozing sex.

I turn and take in R'chelle. Her rich, umber skin glows under the lights. I bite my lip and remember those thick thighs wrapped around my neck as I brought her to orgasm for the eighth time one night.

"Good evening, Chelly. How are you?"

Heat rises to her pecan-colored eyes— she remembers that night too.

A soft whimper escapes her as she rubs the column of her neck before she finally turns, giving me a view of her heart-shaped ass.

Fuck!

I'm tempted to see if she'll be the one to join me tonight, but a hand lands on my shoulder before my lips can part to ask.

"Sebastian," Matthieu greets me. "I didn't expect to see you here. Not with everything going on back in town."

He guides me away from Chelly and down to his office in the opposite way that we usually would go to grab a cigar and a drink while we catch up.

"Aren't we going the wrong way?" I ask, and he snorts.

Matthieu doesn't speak until we're safely behind his office door.

"Have a seat. Let me get you a drink," he instructs, and I sit in the leather armchair in front of the fireplace— opting for a face-to-face without a desk separating us.

I watch as my hulking friend pours us both a glass of '79 Macallan Gran Reserva. Matthieu is six-six and easily three hundred pounds of muscle. So, it's always hilarious to watch the man who looks like he bench presses skyscrapers pick up ice cubes with small tongs.

Matthieu is always immaculately dressed, his Egyptian-blue Brioni suit highlighting his dirty-blonde quiff-styled hair and jade-green eyes. The French fucker could always make a woman's panties melt when he fixed his gaze on her.

"So, are you going to tell me why we're meeting here and not in our usual spot?" I try for the second time.

He hands me my drink and sits.

"It's simple. I like my club drama free and you being here violates the rules set in place by the Council," he says cooly.

Shit. In my haste to escape everything, I forgot about the damn no fraternization rules.

Matthieu gives me a knowing smirk, "Ahh, Bastian, my friend, you forgot," he teases, his French accent more pronounced when he uses my nickname.

"It's been a very stressful last few days," I mutter.

He grimaces, "Yes, I've heard. How is the girl? Ariah, is it?"

I dip my head confirming he's correct. "She's a fighter. A fucking spitfire. Resilient in ways that put grown men to shame. She's been thrown to the lions and became the tamer."

Matthieu's frown lifts, his olive cheeks lift into a megawatt smile that would make men and women trip at his feet. "You like her, oui?

"No. I can't allow myself to be that foolish again." I blurt before he can say more.

He laughs— fucking laughs.

"Oh, Bastian. Vous ne pouvez pas être très intelligent si vous n'avez jamais rien fait de stupide. Be a little foolish, you deserve it," he offers, reaching over to pat my knee before sitting back and sipping on his drink.

I hear him, but I wouldn't survive another heartbreak. Whenever we choose Ariah, I'll care for her— love is not an option.

17
ARIAH

"You're next. You think you're safe because of who you are? You're not. Your name won't save you from the anal pounding I'm going to give you." The shriveled dick jackass with the moldy breath proclaims as he tucks his disgusting appendage back into his soiled black pants.

He and his partner have taken turns coming in and out of this fucking room to violate Sam in so many ways. He stalks over to me, just like he has every time he's come in here.

It's always the same.

He bends, breathing his aged milk smell into my face, telling me how many ways he's going to have me and which hole he'll take first before he turns and stalks out of the room.

"Are you listening to me, you privileged bitch?" he snaps

I want desperately to deck him in the throat, but I'm chained to this damn wall. So, my fight would only piss him off and leave me at a significant disadvantage. Instead, I stay quiet, internally cursing him out as I bash his face in with his own boot.

A sudden yank of my hair pulls my head back. He grips it at the root, *reminding me of a certain someone who did this on my first day of school. My hand twitches at my side, and I have to ball it into a tight fist to prevent myself from my gut reaction to swing.*

"Do you hear me talking to you, you dumb whore? Didn't they ever tell you that when a man talks, a woman is supposed to answer unless told to shut the fuck up?"

I can't stop the sneer of disgust I feel from appearing on my face. My nose wrinkles and my eyes squeeze closed.

Does he think we're in the eighteen hundreds or some shit?

"You think you're too good to talk to me, you little cunt? Well, maybe you'll scream for me instead." *My eyes snap open, and I try to pull away, but his grip on my hair is too tight. His free hand reaches for the resistance-free sweats they put me in. For fuck's sake. I begin to struggle, flailing in his hold as I try to loosen his grip.*

"Hold still," *he grunts, changing tactics, no longer reaching for my pants. Instead, he reaches for his own.* "You won't think you're all high and mighty when I'm shoving my coc-."

"Angel, wake up."

My eyes spring open as I suck in air, my heart racing faster than my mind can register the sound of the voice.

I can't let him try to do that to me again. I swing my arm up in the direction of the sound until it connects with its target with a loud smack.

"Fuck, Angel. It's me. You're safe," I hear, and the voice finally registers. *Owen.*

My eyes come into focus on the two figures in my room.

"What, what are you guys doing here?" I ask Owen and Wyatt, looking out my window to see darkness, verifying it's still night.

"We needed to make sure you were okay. We had to make sure you were truly safe," Wyatt murmurs, taking up the spot next to Owen. *Where the hell did my siblings go?*

Noticing my gaze focused on where he's currently seated, Owen answers my silent question. "Tabitha and Jamie were bringing the twins to their rooms when we came in. You were thrashing in your sleep."

Still confused, I try to shake the remnants of my nightmare off. Thoughts of that vile man and his partner make my skin crawl.

"Hey, Love," Wyatt beckons, bending to lightly brush the hair out of my face, putting his more into view. "What's going on in that head of yours?"

I'm unsure if I'm ready to talk about everything that happened over the time I was taken. Shit, I'm not sure I'm prepared to begin to process the lies upon lies my entire life has been. *How can I?* I still don't know enough to fucking know where to start.

My annoyance at this whole fucked up lie I've been living grows. I feel the muscles in my jaw tighten with each pass of my teeth grinding against themselves.

"Riri. Ariah," Wyatt's voice snaps me from my spiraling thoughts.

"I'm sorry. What did you say?" I know it was something because I could hear him speak, but I was too lost in my thoughts to register what he said.

He lifts me from my bed, positioning me on his lap. "I said whatever you need. We're here. Tell us what's going on in your beautifully chaotic mind."

Do I tell? Can I trust them? It's the guys. Owen and Wyatt have easily bulldozed their way into my life, and before I was taken, I was definitely growing feelings for both of them. *But can I give them this piece of me?* Ever since my dad was taken by his traitorous cunt wife, that thought causes my back to stiffen. It's always been me making life continue in their absence.

"Or we can just sit here and be," Owen states, climbing over our outstretched legs and sitting beside me on my bed. His breath tickles my shoulder before he plants a chaste kiss. "You don't have to talk now or ever if you don't want to. I know a great way to exorcize your demons," he finishes, glancing up and peering his hazel gaze into mine. He gets a faraway look in his eyes like he's seeing past me, lost in his mind as I was moments ago.

Reaching up, I touch the scruff of his beard, bringing him back like he did for me. "Where did *you* go?" I ask, tipping my gaze up as his eyes clear.

"A story for another day. Right now, my- our concern is you, Angel," he endears, and I see the haunting shadows leave his stare as he refocuses his attention on me. *What happened to you?* I make a mental note to revisit this conversation.

I feel hands trace up my spine and land on my shoulders, massaging the tension away. I turn and encounter Wyatt's soft smile, fully taking him in. His once smooth skin bearded. "Did you get in a fight with your razor?" I quip, tugging at the fine, coarse, auburn hair on his chin.

He laughs, and some of the worry drains from his posture. I moan when his fingers press into a knot at the base of my neck, causing my head to lull to the side.

"Don't make those noises when we're trying to behave, Love," Wyatt grunts as he bends to kiss the same spot his hands just were. Shivers travel my spine, making goosebumps line my skin. I feel the smirk crest his lips before he lifts them from my skin.

"None of that," he taunts. *Jerk.*

Huffing, I accept that no amount of procrastination will deter them from this conversation. Not even sexual ones.

I lay back in his muscled embrace, allowing his body heat to envelope me, grounding me in the present. *I'm not still in that room.*

"While I was there, so much happened in such a short amount of time, but it felt like an eternity passed at the same time," I start, taking a fortifying breath to prepare myself for everything I'm about to divulge.

A hand grabs mine, and I know it's Owen's. Wyatt's hands are wrapped firmly around my middle. I close my eyes and nod, reassuring myself that I'm Ariah fucking Bishop or Bradford. Whoever the hell I truly am, I take whatever life throws at me and make it my bitch.

"The entire time was a mind fuck. Between some waterboarding-style tactics when I first came to, the horrifying things they did to Samantha in front of me, the asshole who tried to assault me, and finding out my mo- Elise is part of some new world order type of organization, I need more time to process it all," I verbally vomit, rambling off everything at once.

I feel Wyatt stiffen as Owen squeezes my hand almost to the point of pain.

"Did they- did they touch you, Angel?" Owen chokes out. His eyes close and his jaw clenches so tightly that his angular cheekbones are more pronounced, even through his five o'clock shadow.

I'm not ready to have this conversation. What happened to me is nowhere as severe as what I witnessed, but when that man tried to force his disgusting dick in my mouth, only my quick kick to his balls and elbow to his gut saved me long enough for some guard to rush in and drag him out of the room.

The look of retribution in his cold, dead eyes made me refuse to sleep and not for the first time, I wonder what would have happened if my dad and the guys didn't come in time.

I would've been in for the fight of my life.

"You don't have to tell me exactly what happened if you aren't ready, but I— no, *we* need to know if we have to go dig up the asshole's body and skull fuck it before we defecate on it," Owen snarls, and I know his anger isn't toward me but what happened to me.

Wyatt finally loosens his grip on me. "Please, Ariah, please," he begs.

Shaking my head, "No, I wasn't sexually assaulted in any way. There was an attempt, but it wasn't successful," I explain.

They both puff out a small sigh of relief. A little reprieve from whatever they were imagining happened to me.

"They still hurt you though, Love, and for that, every single fucking one of them will die," Wyatt commands, reaching around and turning my chin to face him so I can see the fury and seriousness in his words.

"Damn right. They won't even get to meet any of my fine ladies — they deserve nothing less than a dose of Lev," Owen adds.

A dose of Lev? What the fuck?

I'm about to ask what they're talking about when my room door bursts open, and another unannounced visitor makes their entrance. *Seriously? I'm talking to Thomas about security measures.*

"Ariah bumboclat Elaine Bishop, where the pussyclat have you been, and why di ras did no one fucking tell mi when yuh reach back?"

My attention shifts in the direction of my rider. *Shay!*

I jump from Wyatt's arms and rush my best friend. Her arms open before I reach her.

She embraces me, squeezing me tight before her hold loosens, and she smacks the shit out of my arm.

"Hey," Owen and Wyatt shout, jumping off the bed, but she aims her glare in their direction, and I fan them off, already knowing what the slap was for.

"If you ever in your life go missing again and don't find some way to let me know where the fuck you are, I'll kidnap you and lock you in a tower myself. I don't care if you have to use morse code, carrier pigeon, smoke, or bat signals. Let me know bitch," she demands, and I burst out in laughter.

Fuck. I needed that. This whole night has been too damn heavy.

"I promise," I joke, holding up the scouts' honor salute and then crossing my heart, making her glower even more.

"Tek mi fi joke and see wah happen," she states, then shifts her focus to the guys. "Time's up, she's mine. You assholes had her and didn't even tell me she was back. Wait til I see Sebastian. I told him to tell me as soon as you found her, and none of you fucks did. I'm not sure when I would've known if I didn't do my nightly sneak-in."

Wyatt chuckles. "You think we didn't know about your nightly terrible cat burglaresque activities? Then you haven't been paying attention," he says back to her as he walks toward me, Owen close behind.

Owen sneaks past Wyatt, snatching me in his muscular arms, gliding his nose up the side of my neck, causing me to tip back, allowing him to kiss a trail up my exposed skin before planting his soft mouth against mine. His lips eagerly possess mine, soft but demanding, wild but controlled— everything he is, all at once. I'm lost in the feel of his mouth on mine. His tongue gains access to mine as his hands slide up into my hair. He groans, and I melt into him, feeling the reaction his body is having to my hunger for our connection. Neither of us wants to pull away, but Shay's protests make me pull back.

"I'm not usually a cockblock, but y'all are on punishment." She motions her hand, waving it dramatically in our direction and continues. "None of this is happening. Now get the hell out!" she dictates, dragging me from Owen's hold.

Wyatt intercepts me, and before she can protest, he lifts me by my ass, making me wrap my legs around him, fearing I might fall as he nips at my bottom lip.

"I told you already no one can keep you from me, Love. Not even Shay Warren, as formidable as she may be. No one or nothing will separate me from you again," he murmurs, crashing his lips to mine. His kiss is different from Owen's, still commanding but more possessive and all-consuming as pulls me into him, squeezing my ass until my pussy is rubbing against his jeans. *This is a recipe for disaster.*

"Wy, let's give the girls their time together," Owen coaxes, and Wyatt begrudgingly releases my mouth and places me back on the ground.

"Fine, you can have her tonight, Warren, but that's only because we have to get back," Wyatt states, placing a quick peck on my forehead. He and Shay snark at each other until the guys reach the doorway, stopping to survey me one last time before winking and exiting the room.

"Seriously, now, tell me everything. I need to know who I have to kill, and I don't want to miss a single person," she implores.

I walk toward my bed, crawling back under the covers, preparing to divulge everything to her.

"Okay, have a seat. This is going to be a complete shit show."

18

LEV

I scrub my skin, trying to wash away the frustration at my lack of control. How can the Council continue to allow us to walk in absolutely blind? There are so many threats lurking— waiting for their opportunity to strike, and all of them want *her*.

The thought of Ariah makes my dick harden— the quick-witted, intelligent force of nature with a mouth that can flay you, all wrapped in the body of divine femininity— a fucking worthy adversary and an even more worthy partner.

I missed everything that was right in front of me. She's been trapped in a game bigger than all of us, and we almost lost her. *That shit can't happen again.*

Groaning, I ignore the throbbing between my legs. I don't deserve relief, not after everything I did to her. The way I disparaged her— shit, my final words to her before she was taken.

I don't get to come— not until she forgives me. The look of utter shock in her gray eyes when I spoke to her in front of the ambulance was worse than her punching my nuts. She didn't expect me to care or worry about her being taken. *How the fuck do I fix this?*

My hand grazes the scar on my shoulder, a constant reminder of what I had to do in order to get Owen help. The angry line creeps from the tip of my shoulder to my elbow.

When I dove from the car, I landed on a sharp piece of gravel that cut into my skin as I rolled across the road. I had to get over fifty stitches to close the wound. The road rash healed, but the scar welted up, leaving me with raised skin that I couldn't stand the sight of— a constant reminder of my failure to get Owen out in time before what those animals did to him.

Once I was old enough, I covered it with a chest and half-sleeve tattoo.

I can still feel the phantom grip of the man's hands on me as he dragged me to the car— like a shadow touch causing me to always be on alert, ready to jump at impending attacks. It's why I blacked out when Ariah grabbed me that day by my locker.

Water pours over my body as I stand under the shower's spray, trying to figure out how to possibly right this wrong and do it without her thinking that it's only because she went missing.

Was it the catalyst? Sure, but sometimes you have to be slapped with a stupid stick to recognize your idiocy. Her being taken, the Council's secrets, and the realization that I was fighting my attraction to her are among the many reasons I see my mistake for what it is— dumb.

Sighing, I rub my hands down my face, frustrated at myself and the almost permanent hard on I've had since I finally allowed myself to want the minx. The thought of her plush lips sassing me when I told her to leave makes my dick jump and my full sack tighten. I grunt and look down at the engorged head of my cock, the veins pulsating and angry that relief isn't coming. I moan at my level of control over myself, imagining how it would be to have Ariah under my control, tied up with her pussy spread open like a gift at Christmas time. The idea of how pretty she would look with the rope's fibers against her golden skin as her hair is fanned out above her waiting to be pulled as my tongue buries itself so deep that it could spell my name on her cervix.

The idea has precum leak from my tip, washed away by water. I want so badly to grip my shaft and jerk, imagining it's her mouth. Instead, I turn off the faucet, reach for my towel, and step out of the shower.

Wrapping the towel around my waist, I make my way over to the sink and grab my Waterpik, flossing before picking up my toothbrush and holding it up to my mouth once I've added the toothpaste. I begin my regimen, two minutes on the bottom—brushing the stress of the day away. I look up to see the dark shadows sitting like overstuffed luggage, waiting for someone to claim them from baggage claim under my eyes. My usual, closely shaven face is now thick with hair. I shut my eyes and listen to the sound of the swishing of the bristles against my teeth. *It will all be fine.* I work to make my thoughts a reality. I hear my alarm sound, and my notification system sounds.

"Sir, it appears that Wesley Edgewood and Sebastian Grant have arrived and will be parking a 2022 Bentley Mulliner Batur in the driveway in one minute and nineteen seconds. Would you like for me to open the door?" Geoffrey, my AI, informs.

Didn't we talk enough?

I move on to brushing the top row of teeth and answer, "Yes, and let them know I'll be down in five."

Moving to my closet, I grab a pair of sweats and a T-shirt, annoyed that my routine has been interrupted. As my sweats pull over my ass and the fabric glides over my raging hard-on, I bite my lip, relishing in the throbbing— it's the perfect punishment for my foolish treatment of Ariah.

Pulling on my hoodie, I head for the stairs to see what these two could possibly want to discuss further. As my bare feet hit the heated marble, I see neither Wes nor Sebastian went to wait in the spot we usually meet in. Instead, they stand in the entryway.

I run my hands through my still damp hair, fanning it out over my shoulders. I really should get a cut.

"Why are you two standing here?" I start, but once I see the look on their face, I ask, "What's going on?"

Sebastian meets my gaze, the angular set of his jaw flexing, "We've discovered more information, and we need you to look into this without the Council knowing."

I look between the two of them, trying to determine if they're serious about this. We've done many things but never once have we actively subverted the Council.

"Is there a reason this has to be kept from them, and where are Wy and O?" I probe. Something of this magnitude shouldn't be done unless we all agree.

As I finish my sentence, Geoffrey notifies me that Owen's truck is pulling into the driveways, and Wyatt is with him.

Wes smirks, reaching up to pat my shoulder, "You didn't think we would do this without all of us present, did you? I'd never unilaterally do anything that could have profound repercussions on us unless absolutely warranted." *Cocky prick.*

The cherrywood front door opens, and the looming forms of Owen and Wyatt step through, both dressed in lounge pants, sneakers, and an LWU hoodie.

I look at Wyatt, "Did you get the new chip in Ariah?"

"Of course I did. Did you forget who I am?" he jests.

He's joking now, but when that minx finds out he— no, *we* chipped her not once but twice, we're all going to get dick or throat punched— and we'd all deserve it.

"So what's so urgent that you made us leave watching Ariah?" Owen asks.

Sebastian gives him a puzzled look, narrowing his blue eyes at Owen's words. "I thought you said Shay was over and kicked you two out?"

Owen rolls his eyes like the idea that they would leave is asinine. "We weren't leaving until we made sure she was truly good."

"It's Shay, though. She's not-," Wes begins to state, but Owen interjects.

"Shay is amazing, but with what Ariah went through, we just couldn't leave until we knew. We didn't listen to anything they spoke about. That's her story to tell."

The faraway look he gets when he remembers something glints in his eyes, dilating his pupils. It's something many might miss, but I've spent years watching over my friend— a promise I made long ago to ensure the darkness never completely swallows him whole.

I nod, acknowledging I see him but not announcing it to the group. He has a far deeper understanding, one greater than any of us could ever have, of what Ariah's going through.

Clearing my throat, I change the topic of the conversation back to what we were originally here to discuss. "What have you found?"

Before anyone can answer, my mother makes her way down the stairs. Calista Washington is not a woman to trifle with. Each step commands the room— she's a force. All five feet two of her brings everyone to heel.

"Boys. What brings you all here at this hour?" she asks shrewdly. Her perfectly styled brow arches, knowing we are up to something without any of us uttering a word.

"We just needed to go over our plan for the girls for once they return to school and the dates begin, Mrs. Washington," Sebastian answers. No hitch— no hesitation. The smooth fucker could lie his way out of death, but he can't fool my mother.

She snorts, "Right. Well, just don't get caught. Your father is on his way home, Levi, and I'm quite sure if he pulls into the driveway and sees that you idiot's have parked your cars out front, then your scheming will be done before it's even begun." She finishes the last of her chastisement as her heeled slippered feet touch the landing continuing their journey until she reaches me, stopping, and I bend, knowing what she's here for.

My mother plants a kiss on the top of my head and then whispers, "Keep that girl safe," before pulling away and strolling through the foyer into the main part of the house. *What does she know?* And not for the first time, I question how many people in our lives have kept secrets from us.

"We'll have to talk more about this when it's safe. For now, what or who am I looking into?" I implore, hoping to speed this up. I'd ask Geoffrey to give me an ETA on my dad, but if my mother is warning me, I know we don't have much time.

"Our dads," Wes rushes out. "They're keeping too many secrets, and if we continue to wait for their direction, we'll always be too many steps behind."

The shared look of shock on Owen and Wyatt's faces lets me know this was a Sebastian and Wes decision.

"What exactly are we looking for?" Wyatt asks, mischief already brewing. I can almost see the wheels turning in his head at the chaos he can wreak if let off his leash.

Sebastian peers down at the yellow gold and black face of his limited edition Romain Gauthier Logical One watch, adjusting the strap. Even in his casual attire, he finds some way to elevate his look. He looks up, running his tongue over his teeth before he answers, "We need to know just how long ago they knew Elise Lockwood wasn't who she said she was."

19
ARIAH

It's been a week since I've been home, and every day since then, I've gone to sit with Dad. He's getting stronger and will be home at some point next week. I brought the kids to see him, and their elation was palpable. We still haven't broached the subject of how to tell them about *her*, but for the time being, we agreed to let them enjoy him being home and try to return to some level of normalcy.

That's why I'm currently pulling on a pair of black yoga tights and getting my ass ready for school.

Dressed, I make my way to my closet and grab my Flower Bomb perfume and my navy blue Docs to match my dad's Linkin Park hoodie. His being home is everything, but wearing his clothes always felt like a layer of armor, and I feel like I'll need it for today. Samantha's also coming back to school today, and from what Shay's been texting me, she plans to ramp up her menacing.

I roll my eyes at the fact she's even still on this campaign to try and ruin me. Didn't she get what she wanted? She's Selected, after all. Sighing, I walk downstairs, mentally telling myself to stop using logic with the illogical.

Tabitha stands at the bottom of the stairs, my coffee and steak, egg, avocado, and cheddar cheese bagel wrapped and ready to go. *God, I love this woman.*

"Thank you," I chime, grabbing my breakfast and hugging her.

She laughs, "Can't have you going into battle on an empty stomach and uncaffeinated. I don't think Edgewood could survive that."

Laughing, I shake my head, "I don't think Edgewood can survive me at all," and make my way to the car and a waiting Thomas.

I swear I hear her mumble, "That's what I'm hoping for," but I can't be sure because she's already walking to the kitchen when I turn back.

"We're going to this party, Ariah, and I'm not taking no for an answer. It's not for another month, and it's a costume party," Shay whines as we make our way down the hall. I feel eyes burrowing into my back with each step I make down the hall, whispers of what people think happened trail behind me trying to chain my legs and weigh me down with their judgment of who's at fault for their queen being taken along with me.

I'd care more if their views on the matter had any bearing on my life. *Fuck them, fuck their opinions, and double fuck their cunt-faced queen.* They can all stub their pinky toe on the corner of a dresser for all I care.

"Are you listening to me, bish?" She cuts off my vivid image of the squawkers crying out in agony at their toe jamming into furniture at the speed of sound.

"Massive party. Next month after the big Edgewood vs. Lincolnville game. Did I miss anything?" I snark.

I might have been looping the pinkytoegate in my mind, but I heard every word she said. I'm just not sure I'm ready for parties.

Turning, I begin to decline, but she cuts me off.

"Nope, I will not have it. You will not recoil into yourself and let that bitch and her organization of banshees turn you into a recluse." Determination fills her soft brown eyes. "We have a month to work up to it. If you're still not ready by the time the party comes, we'll talk, but I won't let you say no outright, especially out of fear. Your bitch of a mother doesn't get to take your autonomy from you after all she's already done."

"She's not my mother," I growl, ignoring her valuable points and zeroing in on the one thing I can handle.

We step into AP Calc, and the room is still empty. I make a beeline for my seat, just wanting this day to be over. Once seated, I turn to her. "Look, I'll think about it, and I'm not letting anyone make me do anything. I'm still me. The same wise-ass with no patience for bullshit."

My best friend surveys me, dissecting my every mannerism, searching for any signs that I'm being disingenuous. Seeing no chink in my demeanor, she smiles, lighting up her honey-bronzed face, her freckles popping with the spread of her lips, displaying almost all of her teeth, but then her lip curls. Her smile transforms into a sneer.

"Speaking of bullshit." She tips her chin in the direction of the door and I swivel my head enough to look out the corner of my eye in time to see Samantha and her pod squad enter the room.

Her nose is still in a brace. I'm almost shocked she came back with a less than pristine look. That thought makes me feel somewhat guilty. I still struggle with who she is and what happened to her. She's a total twat, but what happened to her should never happen to anyone. Then I remember her words from her hospital bed, '*it should've been you.*' That shit played on repeat most of my week off. How jaded and broken inside do you have to be to wish that on anyone? But yeah, fuck that spineless ho. May her nose jobs always be crooked.

My gaze follows her to her usual seat in the back corner opposite our side of the room. She sits, her lemmings following suit.

I turn my gaze, done with the Sam show, and begin to pull out my supplies for class.

"You'd think they would've just left her. I mean, they did come for me after all," Samantha snickers, pretending to whisper. I ignore her. We've had this conversation, and I won't engage in her shit this morning.

"I heard Wes came running for you," Meagan says, and I assume it's to Sam because we don't talk.

"Of course he did. I mean everything to him, and soon I'll be his wife."

God, her bravado is beyond delusional. Only Samantha would think being ignored positions her to be someone's wife.

I snort at the look of devastation in her eyes that night back at the hospital.

"Something funny, trash?" she shouts from her perch, and I ignore her.

I really think she has a degradation kink. I should ask Wes. My gut lurches at the idea that he would know. The feeling confuses me. Why the hell would I care where the prick sticks his dick?

An image of him pressing me against the wall, and the feelings that stirred in me at his words as he worked my body into a frenzy comes to mind. I feel my cheeks flush at the reminder of how close I was as he called me a slut. I can't like Wes. Is he attractive? Fuck yes, but he's an even bigger douche. So what if his body looks lickable, or that I wanted to follow the trail of water as it cascaded down his muscular chest to the well-defined V leading to a spectacular-looking dick. He's as big of a jerk as his junk is, super fucking huge.

"Did you not hear me addressing you, skank?" Sam tries again, jolting me from the dangerous path my thoughts were traveling.

My mouth sets in a straight line, and my eyes roll like they're doing summersaults as I begin to count, trying to remind myself it's better to be the bigger person in this instance. *Don't embarrass this ho. She's not worth it.*

"Maybe you've actually learned your pl-." Her sentence is interrupted by the husky tenor of an unexpected voice.

"Don't finish that sentence unless you want me to remind you of your place," Lev instructs.

What alternative universe have I landed in where Levi Washington, the same guy who essentially told me I was wasting my time because I wasn't good enough, is coming to my defense? Not that I needed it. She was about one more snide remark away from being read.

My gaze snaps up, our eyes locking. He looks better than when I last saw him last week. The dark circles no longer sit under his eyes, and his beard is now trimmed low. He's wearing his usual ripped jeans, a thermal shirt with a navy flannel button-up over it, and a pair of combat boots. His pectoral muscles look carved from stone with how his shirt lines his chest. I don't know if he notices me looking, but I swear he makes them flex, and I have to dip my chin to hide the blush creeping up my neck behind my hair.

"Whatever, Lev. I'm done with the bitch anyway. She bores me," Sam mumbles.

"Bores you or intimidates you?" Shay asks pointedly.

I look at her and see she's at the end of her patience, and class hasn't even started yet. I shake my head quickly, and she huffs when she notices, gritting her teeth and folding her arms across her chest but says nothing else.

I'm sure I'll get an earful about not letting her flay her later, but again Sam's an attention whore and the best way to deal with that is to suck the oxygen out of the air instead of fanning the flames of her toxic personality.

"That bitch could never intimidate me. She's not even in the same stratosphere," Sam snarls. And now I've had enough.

"She was good enough to be one the original Selected and not a replacement for dead girls," Lev challenges.

Am I wrong for bursting out into laughter at this? If I am, Shay's riding to hell with me because she does the same.

She growls but says nothing in response as the rest of the heirs walk in. Wyatt and Owen's eyes lock on me, both smiling, happy I'm finally back at school. They've been to the house daily, sometimes staying the night to keep the nightmares at bay.

I shut my mind down when images try to bombard me. Today will be a good day, even if I have to fake it until it's true.

Wes sits next to Shay, close but still at a distance, Wyatt and Owen take up their positions to my left and my right after they each kiss a cheek, causing me to flame red, and Lev sits in front of me, looking back before facing forward like he's a sentry on duty. It's weird, but I feel protected in a way I haven't since returning home.

Wes and Lev could still use a few slaps upside their domes, but for now, I enjoy the peace their protective energy brings, and because I'm a petty bitch, I turn to Sam, watching her as she takes in this display of solidarity. Malice fills her arctic eyes and she glowers.

Tipping my head to the side, I arch a brow, smirk, and wink.

Checkmate bitch.

20

SEBASTIAN

I thought I was finally done with this place and having to be in the same space as Vivian. My return to Edgewood Academy has had her visit my office twice today under the misguided assumption that my return is for her. I'm here for one thing, and Vivan Taylor is not it.

I scan over the fifth personnel file on my desk. Verifying each person's information matches Lev's files is tedious, but his meticulous attention to detail makes my job far more manageable.

This person is exceptionally dull. They've been married for forty years and spend weekends collecting bird feathers. I snort at the idea of a man skulking through the woods trying to find the feather of a bird that's eluded him for decades.

Sighing, I run my fingers through my loosely styled hair. I was so annoyed with having to be back in this building I forgot to add my styling gel. I check my watch— today's band matches my gray three-piece Tom Ford suit. There are still another four hours left in my day. *For fuck's sake.* I want to punch myself for coming up with the idea of staying in my position. I could be working on my grad school portfolio or hitting the gym. Maybe even rubbing one out since I can't have sex with my usual hate fuck.

It's been far too long since I've had a beautiful woman at my mercy. I never played with Vivian. After finding her riding my father's dick with my engagement ring on her finger, I fucked anything with legs and a pussy between them. It wasn't until I went with one of the guys from the frat house to this BDSM club that I learned how much I needed control after everything happened—how much I loved the idea of determining when and how often a woman is pleasured. The height of euphoria on a woman's face when she's riding your tongue and coming for the seventh time in a row or how distraught she looks when you take her right to the edge over and over and over again.

I wonder for a moment what the spitfire would look like riding that edge for a whole night. I can picture the frustration in her slate eyes and the anguish on her face when her orgasm eludes her time and time again. The way she'd claw my back as I make her crash over into oblivion once I finally let her taste what was just out of reach for so long.

Groaning, I reach up and rub the back of my neck. I really shouldn't be having thoughts like this at school or about a student. It doesn't matter that we're only four years apart. Until I'm done here, she's off limits in the only way I can ever allow myself to have her. The others can fall— I won't allow myself to make that mistake ever again.

There's a knock on my door, interrupting my thoughts. It's for the best, though. The last thing I need at school is a case of blue balls.

"Come in," I announce.

My door opens and the girl I was just telling myself was off limits walks through. I have to bite the inside of my cheek until it bleeds to prevent myself from pulling my lips between my teeth. Ariah Bish-Bradford is gorgeous.

"Hello, Mr. Grant," she says, walking fully into the room and thankfully leaving the door open.

I grunt at the sound of Mr. Grant on her lips and imagine her calling me 'Sir.'

Closing my eyes, I massage my fingers against my forehead. *Get your shit together, Bash.*

"Now, we've had this talk already. Please call me Sebastian," I instruct, my voice firm, and I see scarlet dust her cheeks. How prettily she turns red. I can almost imagine the shades of pink I could turn her luscious ass while she rides my fingers. *I'm fucked.*

Clearing my throat, I ask, "How can I help you?" I'm proud that I'm able to hide the hitch in my breath as her elegant throat bobs.

"I wanted to discuss a plan to complete my makeup assignments," she whispers initially, but gains her confidence by the end of her request. *Do I make the spitfire nervous?*

I'm reminded of the first day of school when she looked like a deer in headlights when she walked into the office. She had the same doe-eyed look. I had fun toying with her then, but I know nothing good will come from me toying with her now. I'm barely hanging on as it is.

Nodding, I state, "Each of your teachers was briefed about your absence and expects to hear from you. Take this form, and have each one fill it out with clear instructions on how and when your assignments should be done."

She saunters into the room. The sway of her hips enraptures me. It's not purposefully done to seduce, making it much more enticing. Her hand reaches for the paper from my outstretched one, and our fingers brush, and a jolt of something shoots through me at the quick light connection of our skin.

I snatch my hand back, but my gaze never leaves hers, stuck in a forcefield that refuses to let either one of us break our stare. I can see the dusting of freckles by her right eye and the way they darken as she takes me in.

A throat clears, and we both jump, our trance broken. I look to sneer at the uninvited intruder at such a moment, and I'm met with Vivian fucking Taylor's stern glare. Dare I say she looks almost feral, her upper lip pulled up, exposing her teeth? She's definitely a mood killer, and I can't tell if I'm glad or pissed off at her presence because it stopped whatever that was.

Returning my attention to Ariah, "If you have any trouble with any of your teachers, please let me know. They've all been made aware that they should give you enough time to catch up."

"Thank you," Ariah mumbles and darts out the door without so much as a backward glance.

"What the fuck was that, Bash?" she demands.

Standing from my seat, I grab my suit jacket, deciding I'm done here for the day. We have a meeting about the rules for our courting dates later anyway.

Once my blazer is on, I put the files away, locking them up and still ignoring the rash that is Miss Taylor.

"Did you not hear me?" she screeches, ready to cause a scene.

Now that everything is away, I grab my satchel and finally bring my attention to her.

"That was you getting the fuck out of my office and not questioning me," I command, pushing her outside and securing the lock before striding past her stunned face.

I yank the main office door open and notice Brian Porter standing on the other side "Can I help you?" I hope he's not here for anything serious, I can't stand the sniveling shit.

"I, um," he stumbles.

Sighing, I reign in my annoyance. "How can I help you Mr. Porter?" I try again.

"I wanted to see about changing some classes, but I'll come back tomorrow," he rushes out, turning and scurrying down the hallway.

"The rules are simple. You must take each girl on at least one date starting with the one you chose on Selection Night," Mr. Edgewood explains, and everyone groans except Wyatt, who looks like a twisted version of a clown with how big his smile is.

He's the only one with someone of substance. The rest of these girls are vapid leeches. The idea of spending any amount of time with them makes my head pound.

"When you say date, what exactly does that entail?" Owen inquires, and I can see him trying to take his date to the butcher shop to gut pigs.

Wes's dad steps from around the table before he replies, "I mean dinner, conversation, dancing, movies, things to get to know them. You'll have to pick one of them. Eventually. It would behoove you not to be saddled with someone you despise."

"We're choosing Riri. This is all just a formality," Wyatt states with a surety that dares someone to challenge his decree. He won't get one from me. Of all the girls, Ariah is the only one I could say I wouldn't mind having to marry. I still won't love her, but it would be great to be with someone I could respect.

Mr. Edgewood sighs, "Be that as it may, you still need to hold up your end of this arrangement. Date them, fuck them, just don't impregnate any of them. As a matter of fact, we've called in Dr. Lambert to place birth control implants in each girl's arm. Save the babies until after college."

The word baby makes Wes's face turn four shades of green and Lev stiffen while Owen and Wyatt look crestfallen. Those idiots couldn't possibly want to get a girl pregnant in high school.

"He didn't say you couldn't practice the act of making babies all you want. Fix your faces, you idiots," I snipe.

Looking at Mr. Edgewood, I nod, acknowledging his wise decision. Those two would try to fill Ariah with so much of their cum she'd be pregnant in a day. I wonder again if she knows exactly what she's signed up for.

She's got two wildly possessive and obsessed men at her beck and call, with the third and fourth closer to being team her than she might realize. Lucky for her, it will stop at four. While I may enjoy her surrender, I don't plan on surrendering in return.

"I expect the dates to begin as soon as tomorrow. You have until the end of the school year and five young women to court," Mr. Edgewood instructs, staring each of us down with his cold brown eyes. He stops before us, ensuring we understand his last point. "Boys, don't fuck this up."

21

ARIAH

After a long day at school, the last thing I want to do is to meet and discuss this Selection shit, but at least I'll be able to see Dad. I can't wait for him to be home so we can talk without watchful eyes on us.

I'm still shocked by his appearance when I open the door to my dad's room. His face is now cleanly shaved, but he still looks somewhat emaciated. Dark puffy bags sit under his gaunt gray eyes that appear paler than their usual smokey gray.

"Ry." My dad smiles wryly, his face lighting up. "What are you doing here?" he asks, pushing the button to elevate himself into a sitting position.

I step further into the room before answering, "I have some stupid meeting about what this whole Selection process entails, so I thought I'd stop by before going to the stuffy meeting." I sit at his bedside before continuing. "What madness should I expect when I get up there, Dad?"

I've wanted to push for more answers, but I didn't want to interfere with his recovery. The doctors have already made it clear that we need to keep his stress levels down, ensuring that nothing impedes his recovery.

So, I've bitten my tongue. I'm hoping this line of questioning isn't too heart rate spiking. There are too many unknowns. For every question answered, ten more arise.

Clearing his throat, he responds, "Well, I'd say it was simple, but the rules outlined for this Selection are vastly different than when I was going through it."

My eyebrows shoot to my hairline. I thought he didn't grow up here.

"Wait, I thought you never lived in Edgewood? How were you part of the process?"

Dad smirks, nodding before he replies, "Always keen on the details. No, I didn't, but I still had to participate in the tradition. I can't get into the whys or hows just yet."

My cheeks puff as I huff out in exasperation—*more answers, but always even more questions.*

Leveling him with a glare, I try a different approach. "So, you're telling me you had to do this too, and with Elise?"

"It was a bit different. We didn't have to choose one wife to share between us. We each were able to make our choice. It wasn't anything like what you're going through now."

I observe him, trying to gauge how my next question will be received.

"I know you've told me some of how you and *that* woman met." My stomach still roils whenever I think of my mom and how she was never who I thought she was. "But tell me again," I implore.

He stares as if he's replaying how they met in his head, his gaze almost wistful before he finally looks at me and answers. "She should've never been on my radar," he snorts. "You know that? Your mother—Elise," he quickly corrects when he sees my nostrils flare. "She was the help's daughter. She was never supposed to be eligible, but I fell for her so hard."

I remember this part. My supposed grandparents worked for his family, the Bishops, who until now I thought were dead. I have so many questions. I want them all answered immediately, but I know he won't because of some stupid grand plan.

"She was different. I fell hard and fast. Elise was the center of my world until she wasn't," he grits out, his teeth clenched so hard the sharp muscles of his jaw flex, and I think he'll pull something. "Elise was a plant, and I'm still trying to wrap my brain around how the woman who owned my heart could so easily drive a dagger through it."

Me too, Dad. Me too. I hurt for him. His pain is far different but similar to mine. He chose her. We had no choice in the matter. The betrayal hits differently but just as profoundly.

I see the uptick in his heart rate on the monitor. I know my quest for answers is coming to an end, so I try to see if I can push for more before time runs out. "Why didn't you tell me any of this before?"

He looks around before responding, "It was, and still is, for the best that you don't know all of what's to come. This can't seem forced, or it won't work." He squeezes my hand and continues, "But this isn't something we should discuss any further here."

I nod in agreement. He's right. Damn this town, and fuck all of these secrets.

Frustrated that I, once again, am in the dark and that it, once again, all surrounds my arrival to this town, I try to move to a different topic I think he'll answer. "What is going to happen during this Selection process?"

"Donald will explain all the finer details. Just make sure you follow all of the rules, Ariah. This part is important. You *must* follow *all of the rules*," he reiterates, emphasizing the 'all of the rules,' part.

"Donald?" My eyes narrow in confusion.

"Mr. Edgewood."

Huh, I didn't know that was his name. He looks more like a Chad or Preston to me. He does always seem to be quacking like a duck. *I guess it's fitting.*

Recognizing that he won't give me anything else, I move to a safer subject. "When are you officially out of here?"

He smiles, sensing the obvious change in subject. "Next Friday. Now go on up to the meeting. I'm sure you're just itching to find out all that comes with being the potential Edgewood heirs' wife."

Slanting my eyes, I scowl in his direction. "I think they've got you on the good stuff because you have to be high out of your mind to think that."

He chuckles and grunts, still sore from being shot. I know he's trying to make light of the situation, but I'm still pissed at the whole damn process.

I step into Mr. Edgewood's office. It's warmer than I imagined it would be. With his prickly personality, I expected sharp edges and uncomfortable furniture. Instead, there are brown leather sofas, colorful paintings, and pictures of Wes, a woman I assume is Wes's mom, and Mr. Edgewood.

I itch to take a closer look at a younger looking Wes. He's in a hunter-green Chaps cable-knit sweater, standing in front of what looks to be a log cabin of some sort at a ski resort. A bright smile plasters his face. He appears to be about six or seven because he's missing teeth in the photo. *Who knew the big grouchy ass could smile.*

Turning from the image, I make my way over to the table, taking in the group of men. Outside Mr. Edgewood, I only recognize one of them, Mr. Grant-Alex. I keep forgetting he prefers Alex.

"Ariah dear, I'm so pleased to have you back and safe." His smile reaches his eyes, warm and genuine, and I wonder for a moment how someone so even-keeled has a son like Wyatt.

Returning his smile with one of my own, I reply, "I'm thrilled to be back." I cut my answer short as Sam's scowl beats into the side of my face.

Why does she always look constipated?

I wonder if I should secretly gift her Miralax or something. And because my pettiness is still rearing its ugly head, I smirk and give her a knowing wave. The frown on her face looks like it's deepening, but between her nose brace and botox, I can't freaking tell.

The deep voice of Mr. Edgewood fills the room, pulling my attention away from Sam's bared teeth. "Ladies. Thank you for joining us this evening. Before you, you'll see a folder outlining the entire Selection process and what is expected of you. Please turn to page one where the preliminary list of rules is located. This is where we will begin."

I scan the rules, and like the meeting with the lawyers, my head begins to pound and my palms start to sweat.

1.Each Selected must go on at least two dates with each heir.

2.The Selected are required to wear their pins at all times.

3.The Selected are required to receive a birth-control implant.

4.The Selected are required to plan and attend two societal events, one of which must be the engagement ceremony, as well as three fundraisers.

5.The Selected must maintain a 3.5 GPA or higher.

6.The Selected is required to attend Lincoln-Wood University.

7.The Selected may not date anyone but the five original bloodline heirs.

That's cold blooded, having us all plan and attend an engagement party that only one of us will be the one proposed to. Yikes, talk about awkward.

He reads each rule out loud, and as they pass his lips, it feels like a collar tightening around my neck, and not the type that makes my pulse race.

If I'm being honest, some rules aren't truly an issue. It's that the choice has been snatched from me in a modern-style bridal hunt. I want to shout and ask why I have to participate since I'm supposedly an original bloodline, but I feel like I've already pieced the answer together.

I have a vagina, and of course, that will not do in this males only fucked up boys' club.

Sighing, I ponder what other female Bradfords had to do. Were they kept from their birthright because they were women, and forced to marry some other heirs to keep the line pure?

"Miss Bishop," a voice booms, and I come back into awareness. I was so lost in thought I must not have heard the first time I was called.

"I'm sorry. What did you say?"

Mr. Edgewood's eyes narrow in displeasure. *See cold and prickly.* Definitely not matching this earth-toned interior. I wonder if his wife designed this, hoping it would rub off. *Mission not accomplished.*

"I said, please turn to page fifteen of your documents to go over what happens once one of you becomes *The Chosen.*"

I nod, quickly turning the page as I internally roll my eyes. *More fucking rules.* What next, the color requirements for our underwear?

It all sounds so damn ominous, *The Selected... The Chosen,* like some cult virgin sacrifice, until I remember, not everyone around the table is a virgin. This better not be a sacrifice.

I'll be kinda pissed if I die before I can actually sample a dick or two. I snicker at my stupidity. With everything going on, I'm thinking of making sure I don't die a virgin. Obviously, while it's not my primary concern at the moment, I'd still like to scratch that fucking itch at some point.

Shaking my head from my lustful and poorly timed thoughts, I begin to read what will happen once someone is chosen.

1. The Chosen will attend Lincoln-Wood University with the heirs in a major of the Fraternitas' choosing.

2. The engagement ceremony must take place after the graduation ceremony.

3. The Chosen must maintain a 3.5 GPA.

4. The Chosen must take etiquette classes.

5.The Chosen will be legally married within one year of the engagement to the Edgewood heir and legally bound to all five bloodlines by contract and commitment ceremony.

6.The Chosen must have a baby within the first five years of marriage.

7.The Chosen must provide each heir with at least one male heir.

What the fuck? Are we broodmares? Who the hell is having five or more kids? I want kids but five? What if I don't want them until after I earn my degrees and start my career? Shouldn't this all be decided between whoever's chosen and the heir?

I can't hold my tongue any longer. "Who came up with this farce of a process?"

"Miss Bishop, you will refrain from interrupting. The rules have been set, and the primary expectations were set long before any of us were born," Mr. Edgewood states, his tone sharp.

"Of course, you'd have an issue with what's expected. You have no respect for values and tradition," Sam snarks.

I roll my eyes at her kiss-ass behavior.

"He's not who you need to impress. You can dial back your 'pick me' energy some," I snap back.

"Ladies," Wes's dad's voice cuts through our banter, silencing us both. "If you two could kindly save your bickering for outside, we can proceed."

I cross my arms over my chest and nod, confirming I'm ready. Sitting back, I wait to hear what other asinine requirements will come from his mouth.

22

ARIAH

"We have to go to etiquette classes, get married in a year, and don't get me started on the birth control shit," I shout.

Owen's and Wyatt's sprawled forms take me in from their places on my bed as I rant about the bullshit I heard in the meeting last night.

Thank fuck the kids are all out with Tabitha and their security team until later. I can picture the look on Jamie's face hearing I'm being forced to put a birth-control rod in my arm. I'm still fuming over the audacity of dead men.

This can't be real life right now. How can a group of men dictate what happens to *my* body?

"Ariah, Angel, it's precautionary." I listen to Owen try to reason with me as he and Wyatt lay on my bed.

Of course it makes sense. Who the hell wants to get pregnant at this age? But that's not the point.

"I'm not disputing the validity of what it's for. I'm trying to figure out why a group of men is dictating my uterus," I snap. *Fucking patriarchal bullshit is what this is.*

Wyatt rises to his elbows and tilts his head, processing what I've said. His brows arch, his pupils dilate when he understands my point of contention. "It's not that you don't want birth control. It's the fact that it's being demanded of you instead of you having the right to choose."

"Tell him what he's won, Alex," I snark, still annoyed at the idea that my bodily autonomy has been taken from me. "I would've gladly decided to get the implant if someone had asked. Instead, a bunch of middle-aged men, who probably have prescriptions for Viagra, have decided and that's that," I continue to gripe as I pace across my heated wooden floor. That comment was uncalled for, but so was their birth control proclamation.

Owen jumps up from the bed, reaching me in two strides, and scoops me into his arms. "I'm sorry this decision was taken from you," he breathes me in. "I'm sorry so much was taken from and forced on you. This will all be over soon. It will be June before we know it."

Sighing, I nod. He's right. As fucked as this whole situation is, there is some sort of end in sight, and again I would've wanted protection anyway. Shit, even with the implant, *no glove, no love.* Not while this whole twisted version of *The Bachelor* is happening.

His breath on my skin makes me squirm, and I feel the moment he realizes its effect because his lips brush the hollow of my neck.

"Does." *Kiss.* "This." *Nip.* "Feel good?" he murmurs as his teeth graze up my throat, sending sparks along my spine and making my body hum to life.

I moan my agreement as he walks us back toward my bed, stopping only to toss me into the waiting arms of Wyatt. *When the hell did he sit up?*

Wy's hands move from my waist up my stomach until they're under my shirt, palming and squeezing my breasts over the cups of my lilac and black lace bra. My body heats at his touch.

"I think she's wearing too many clothes, O. What do you think?" he asks, pausing his movements to pull my shirt off before unhooking my bra and sliding it down my shoulders, dropping it to the bed.

I don't fight him, eager to feel their hands on me again. My body buzzes with anticipation, my nipples hard long before the air caresses them.

Resting against his chest, Wyatt kneads his thumbs into the base of my skull, massaging his fingers into my temples, relieving some of the day's tension from my body.

I whimper, lulling my head forward to provide him greater access when I feel my right leg being hoisted into Owen's firm hold.

These tag team massages will never get old.

"I don't know who taught you both how to do this, but they deserve all the money in the world," I sigh in utter contentment.

They both huff a small snort of laughter.

"We haven't ever done this with anyone, Angel. Care isn't something we do unless you're involved," Owen professes.

I lift my eyes to his, and again I'm met with a faraway look before he blinks his gaze back into focus. I seriously need to get him alone to find out what causes that haunted stare.

However, before I can fully catalog that thought, Wyatt captures my hardened peaks and rolls them between his calloused fingers, leaning me further into his body. Pleasure spikes in my veins as he increases the pressure, pinching my nipples until my mouth falls open with a panting mewl.

My attention snaps from Wyatt's hands on my tits to the feel of air hitting my thighs and the sound of tearing fabric. Goosebumps line my legs as he cuts my pants. I gawp, too stunned to speak.

"I agree. She does indeed have on too much," Owen murmurs, slicing through the last of my leggings, leaving me in only my matching lace boyshorts.

Tossing the knife, Owen climbs on the bed until he's positioned his knees under my thighs, lifting my hips slightly off the mattress. Bending, he brings his mouth to my stomach just below my belly button, and nips his way to my pelvic bone as he peels my panties down, bringing them to his nose and inhaling once he's fully divested me of them.

"Fuck, Angel, you smell divine," he says, his voice husky and filled with desire.

I watch, my heated, half-lidded gray eyes locked on his movements, as he brings the crotch of my panties to his mouth and licks the very obvious wet spot.

Groaning, he palms himself. "You fucking taste even better."

My whole body is crimson at the debaucherous act. *Fuck, why is that so damn hot?* My eyes heat. *Shit.* I feel my muscles clench.

Wyatt must sense my excitement because he grips my hair, pulling my head to the side as he lowers his lips to my pulse point and whispers, "Discovering new things about what turns you on, Love?"

The vibration of his voice against my flesh makes me shiver. I remember the last time the three of us were like this, and I moan at the memory. The way they had me spread across the bathroom counter as they distracted me from it all.

Wyatt's teeth latch onto my neck, and I groan at the way his lips suck on my skin, contrasting the force in my hair. Heat traverses my body as every nerve ending goes on high alert.

Shit, this is better than watching porn.

"Let's discover even more," Owen commands. Wyatt leans back and I squeal as Owen flips me onto my stomach.

My face is level with Wyatt's visibly hard cock as Owen massages my ass, occasionally slipping his finger between my folds. I can feel the moisture build with every pass over my clit.

I moan as he dips another digit inside, pumping in and out before taking my juices and rubbing circles into my clit.

"Pull him out," Owen instructs, pointing to Wyatt but not stopping his assault on my pussy.

I tilt my face up and meet Wyatt's hazel stare. The hunger that greets me has me biting my lips.

Wyatt lowers his head until his mouth crashes against mine, our

tongues moving in synchronicity, neither battling for dominance, a
perfect balance of give and take. We both groan our pleasure, deepening this kiss, wanting, no needing, more before he pulls back.

"You heard him, Riri. Take me out," he dares.

Spurred on by the challenge in his eyes, I don't hesitate, unzipping his jeans and pulling him out.

I stare at the metal balls lining almost the entire length of
Wyatt's dick. My gaze snaps up to his heated whiskey eyes, which
look more whiskey when filled with yearning. "How did this not
hurt?"

He snorts, "Pain is a state of mind."

"Okay, Confucius," I quip, rolling my eyes.

The sharp sting of a palm cracks my butt. "No, rolling your eyes,
Angel," Owen commands, and because I can't help myself, I turn and
roll them slowly, exaggerating every movement of my facial
expression.

"You really are a brat sometimes, you know that?" he jokes before
his demeanor turns serious. The smile melts off his face as he grabs
the globes of my ass and squeezes, his gaze never leaving mine when
he speaks. "What should we do about that?" he asks Wyatt.

"Stuff her pretty little mouth full until the only sound she makes
is her choking on my dick," Wyatt replies as he yanks my hair tighter,
tilting my head back to meet my lips with his again.

"Eh, eh, ehhh," Owen pulls me from Wyatt's hold, and I whine in
protest. "Not yet, Angel. On all fours. Now," he commands.

My knee-jerk reaction is to lay on my back, spread my legs, and
say make me, but I'm more eager to see where they want this to go.

Pushing myself off of Wyatt, I position myself in the middle of
my bed, appreciating its size for the first time. We're all on here
comfortably. Both of their tall, muscular bodies and my curvy one
easily fit with room for more.

My skin flushes at the idea of more of them in my bed. So many
hands roaming and touching. I wonder what it would be like to hate
fuck Wes and Lev, or what it would feel like to be under the pene-

trating gaze of Sebastian. He looks like he thrives on control. How would he react to my chaos? My tongue peeks out, wetting my lips at the scene playing out in my mind.

Who knew the idea of multiple dicks could be so appealing?

I'm jerked back by my hair into Owen's tattooed hold.

"You're not allowed to disappear into your head, even when it makes your skin flush darker shades of red, Angel. The only ones allowed to do that to you right now are us," he growls in my ear, pinching my nipples hard to the point of pain as he bites down on my neck. "I told you before I don't like being ignored."

The simmering anger can be felt in the stern tone of his voice, and it only makes me clench harder, my juices leaking out, and I hear Wyatt groan.

"Fuck, Riri," he leans forward and licks the evidence of my arousal off my thighs, and I whimper when he nips my pussy lips.

Owen bites my earlobe and releases me. "Now get back on all fours," he demands, and like the wanton slut I'm discovering I am, I scramble into position and watch as a very naked Wyatt positions himself in front of me. His neck propped up on his crossed arms. Freckles dot his torso, but I'm focused on the trail that leads from his well-defined Adonis belt straight to his slightly curved cock, bobbing in my direction.

"Your dick has freckles on it," I blurt out before I can stop myself.

His mouth spreads into a smile. "Easier for you to connect the dots," he jokes, and all three of us burst into laughter.

"Sorry, I couldn't help myself."

The heat from Owen's body hovers over me right before I feel the cool steel of his knife press to the center of my spine.

"Don't apologize, Angel. We love seeing you smile," he whispers, lightly dragging the blade down my back before bending to retrace the trail with his lips. I moan at the sensation his lips cause. My nipples grow harder as blood rushes to the area.

Owen continues to work his way down my back until he reaches my tailbone, swirling his tongue as he drops the knife on the bed and spreads my ass cheeks apart just as Wyatt's hands caress my face, pulling my attention to his. Sitting up, he bends, capturing my mouth as I simultaneously feel Owen's tongue glide over my back entrance. I flinch at the foreign sensation, but my shock lasts barely a second as surprise morphs into desire. I moan as he sucks his way to my pussy. Each pass of his tongue ratchets up my whines. His movements stop and I nearly curse.

"Didn't I tell you to put that pretty mouth of yours around Wyatt's dick, Angel? Don't make me repeat myself."

I move my lips from Wyatt's and work my way down his chest, swirling my tongue over his peaked nipple and biting.

"Shit," he hisses as I continue to kiss a path over his abs to his auburn happy trail. My eyes connect with Wyatt's fat dick. He's thick all over but more at the crown than his base. Veins pop from his shaft and my mouth hungers to feel the weight of him on my tongue. I second guess myself, wondering if he'll fit. I've seen this done thousands of times in videos, but seeing and doing aren't the same thing.

Lowering my head, I open my mouth and flick the crown of his dick, tasting the pre-cum leaking from the tip. The salty tang is not off putting, and I'm eager for more.

"Yes, keep doing that," he groans as I wrap my palm around his pierced shaft, stroking as take him deeper with each bob of my head. The cool metal of the barbells glide over my tongue as it swirls around him.

I feel Owen slide under me before he wraps his arms around my middle, pulling me into him. My thighs planted on both his shoulders, giving him full access to my waiting pussy. His tongue grazes my clit before his teeth latch, sucking in the bundle of nerves and lapping relentlessly until I squeal.

"Fuck!" I shout around Wyatt's dick. My body is no longer my own. With every nip and lick, I surrender to their control.

"That's it, Love. Give us your screams," Wyatt growls, my mouth still working him. I move up and down his shaft, flattening my tongue and hollowing my cheeks to try and take him deeper before shifting my attention to his pulsating head.

With each pass of my lips, I push myself further and further until I feel my nose press against his groin, and I hum in triumph.

"Shit, Riri. Fuck, whatever this is, don't stop doing it." Wyatt throws his head back, allowing me to feel the girth of his throbbing dick in my mouth. I need it. I want to see him shatter for me the way he made me explode on his tongue in his bathroom.

I increase my pace to match Owen's as his tongue probes my entrance and his fingers pump in and out of my ass, I edge closer to the cliff. My suction on Wyatt grows more frantic.

When Owen pulls away, I curse unintelligibly as my lips stay firmly wrapped around Wyatt's cock.

Owen quickly shifts my hips back, latching his lips over my clit as three thick fingers enter my pussy. Any and all protests die with my next moan, making me take Wyatt even deeper and he groans his approval.

"Shit. O, keep doing that. Fu-ckkk." I feel his body tighten as warm ropes of his cum shoot in my mouth. I nearly choke before I adjust to catch each pump. Wyatt pulls himself from my mouth before crushing his lips to mine. "Fuck I taste good on your tongue. Now go reward O with that magical throat."

I watch as he lays back in my bed, his amber eyes trained on my movements as I turn around on Owen's face. He never stopped devouring me.

I look down at his intimidating dick before shaking off my apprehension, opening my mouth and taking him in until he triggers my gag reflex. *Fuck he's big.*

He's longer and thicker than Wy from base to tip, but I work him in, then pull him back out. Drool escapes out the side of my mouth.

"Make it nasty, Angel," Owen instructs, speaking right into my pussy. My hips buck at the vibration.

Nasty. Okay, I can do that.

I lift my mouth, gather my saliva, and spit on the head. My hand wraps around the shaft, jerking him in my firm grip as I take him in my mouth, sucking him in while my tongue circles around his slit. Doubling my pace, I suction my lips over the bulbous tip. My movements slow as I twist and fist his length before increasing my speed, pumping until I feel him jerk in my hand.

"Oh, you want to play," are his last words before the pace of his tongue against my clit doubles, and I feel something cold and metal enter my pussy.

My movements stutter and nearly stop, but a hard slap to my left ass cheek lets me know that's the wrong decision.

"No you don't, keep going," Owen commands. The handle of his knife inches a little more inside of me.

Shallow thrusts increase as he bites down on my clit, and I'm soaring. My vision blinks out. All I see is white as I scream my release, careful to not clamp my teeth on Owen's dick. My body shakes, riding out my orgasm just as he shoots down my throat.

"Shiiit-tt-tt-tt," Owen mutters, between twitches, his leg jumping slightly as he continues to work the bundle of nerves between my legs.

I suck him in until he softens in my mouth and I release him. My head angles in time to watch as he slowly pulls the handle from inside of me and sucks it into his mouth.

"Holy shit," I whimper, turned on all over again.

"One day, I'll have your virgin blood on this knife," he grunts.

My body continues to jerk until it finally settles, and I'm a pool of jelly on top of him.

He carefully lifts me, positioning my body on the bed between him and Wyatt. The three of us lie languidly in varying stages of bliss, my hands resting on their arms as Wyatt plays with my hair and Owen massages circles into the inside of my wrist.

"Now that's a way to convince me to get the implant," I joke, and they both sigh with a contented laugh.

23

WES

Owen and Wyatt sit like proud peacocks across from me, both their faces painted with a euphoric calmness. I'm tempted to ask them what has them looking like they just had the best nut of their lives, but I feel like I already know the answer. *Her*. It's always her— Ariah Bish-Bradford.

She's the reason every man in this room, myself included, has their emotions plastered on usually more stoic faces.

I can't deny I was wrong about who she was, but I wasn't wrong about the chaos her presence is causing. It's obvious she didn't know who she was. She never adhered to one rule since stepping foot in this town— constantly challenging me at every turn.

Now we know she's a goddamn original bloodline. *The original bloodline.* The Bradfords established this town, and while it may carry my last name, it was only named that because William Bradford willed it. Her existence raises more questions. How were they able to stay hidden so well? What happened to shift the power out of their control? I hope Lev was able to dig up more information on what happened to the Bradford line.

Staring in his direction, I take Lev in. He looks like he's in the battle of his life. He's focused on his computer, eyes flitting across the screen as his fingers move deftly against the keys. Whatever he sees causes his jaws to clench with enough force that it sets my teeth on edge.

"What the fuck is wrong with you?" I lean over and ask.

"Nothing," he grumbles, side-eying me. "We need to iron out the details on how we plan to dig up information on Elise and how long our fathers have known of her existence."

He's redirecting— Lev's favorite pastime. I scowl but let it go for the time being. If he doesn't want to talk yet— fine.

"Are you two love birds fighting?"

"Trouble in paradise?"

Owen and Wyatt tease at the same time, their words jumbling together.

I flip them both the middle finger and wait for Lev to start us off.

The door to the room swings open, and a frustrated Sebastian storms into the room.

"Can we send a message to whoever killed the other girls and ask them how much they'd charge to get rid of my problem?" he gripes.

I wonder what she's done now?

"Vivian still not taking the hint?" Owen asks, lifting a butterfly knife to his nose and inhaling it. His eyelids half-mast, fluttering as his lips part just enough, releasing an inaudible sigh. *This guy and his knives.* Only he would sniff metal and be turned on. "We don't need that twisted fuck... I'll gladly slice her in half for free," he volunteers.

Sebastian's scowl turns upward into a mischievous smirk, his cerulean eyes glint with the promise of being rid of Miss Taylor. "I'll definitely let you know if it really does come down to it."

"If you assholes are done, we have bigger problems than *Vivian Taylor,*" Lev snaps.

"What has his balls in a knot?" Sebastian inquires, surveying the room. "Or is it that no one has them in a knot that's got you wound so tightly?"

Glaring, Lev retorts, "Fuck off, Bash. My balls aren't your

concern. I'm just trying to get us to focus on the task that could get us all in serious shit."

Lev's words sober the atmosphere of the room. Since our impromptu trip to his house, we've all been sleuthing, but Lev's been doing the bulk of the work.

Sebastian takes his seat, and Lev instructs Geoffrey to secure the room. We're meeting at his house because we know there's no chance of The Council accessing this room. All of our electronic devices were left in a secure box at the entry point of this part of his house. The Tombs is not the place to be having this discussion.

"Tell me you found something on what happened to the Bradfords," I voice, hoping to get answers to my earlier train of thought.

Lev doesn't respond, not at first. He pulls up files to the screen at the front of the room.

I read the words and then reread them, ensuring what I'm seeing is indeed true.

"Someone was killing off the Bradfords?" Owen mumbles. I'm not sure he intended to ask his question out loud because it was barely above a whisper.

Lev clicks to another screen showing case after case of Bradfords that were killed. Some by poisoning. Others by more gruesome methods. A whole line almost wiped from existence.

"Are Ariah and her dad all that are left?" I question. So many of them died. I don't know how we kept this out of the public eye. Then I remember who we— Fraternitas is. They own everything. If they want it hidden— it never existed.

Lev brings up yet another image. "That's the thing. I'm not sure. Until we were told who Ariah and her father really were, there was no evidence of Bradfords anywhere. I had to hack into the restricted town archives to get this much," he sighs. His face still is marred with frustration, and not just from this.

"So, there can either be a town full of unknown Bradfords or only two remaining ones left?" Wyatt chimes in.

"Pretty much," Lev replies, showing another set of documents.

"Ariah's father is the rightful head of the Fraternitas, and as his daughter, Ariah is the heir to it all. Well, she would be, if she weren't born as a girl."

I look around the room, gauging the expressions on everyone's faces, seeing if theirs match my shocked one.

Sebastian massages the bridge of his nose before he speaks, "Do you-do you think our fathers had anything to do with the mysterious deaths of the Bradford line?"

That thought has crossed my mind since I discovered who Ariah truly was. Why else would they want her back in this town?

"No," Lev responds, with no hitch or hesitation. "The Fraternitas ordered Aaron hidden until college, where he reappeared as a Bishop. Our fathers let him continue to hide once Ariah was born until we came of age, and then he was expected to return."

"What the fuck? You mean Ariah could've been here with us this whole time? Why'd they do this?" Owen growls, flipping his knife open and closed as he narrows his cold gaze on the offending information.

Sebastian is the first to respond, "No, she couldn't have. Did you miss the part where Bradfords were being slaughtered? Aaron Bradford was being hidden, and once Ariah was born, not to mention her siblings, they had to stay hidden. At least until the Selection."

Piecing it all together, I shout, "She's who they expect us to pick."

It has to be that. There's no other way they'd let her come here after trying to keep them hidden for so long.

"Yup. It took you assholes long enough to figure that out. I was getting lonely being in the know," Wyatt adds.

Every head turns in his direction.

"You knew, you little shit, and you said nothing?" I snarl.

Of course he knew. It's so fucking Wyatt behavior to know and keep quiet. Sowing chaos and trying to pull strings like a puppeteer.

"Oh, chill the fuck out. I'm the smart one and knew she was ours, so I got to get the insider information until you asshats got your shit together. Only I figured it out before most of you did," he says.

There's not a hint of remorse in his tone. Instead, he casts an accusatory glare in our direction.

"Why didn't you tell us?" Lev asks, his voice strained and his hands fisted on the oak table top. He's at the end of his patience. I think if one more thing happens tonight, Lev might snap, and I haven't seen him seriously lose it in a very long time.

Wyatt turns, tilting his chin and quirking his lip, "I just said it. You all were, and some of you still are, too blind to see that a Queen walks among us, and until you do, I'm holding the cards to my chest unless I know it will cause her harm."

She's doing it again— division in our ranks. Ariah is tearing at the seams of a brotherhood— something that's never been in jeopardy before now. I expect Lev to flip shit.

"I get it," Lev says.

My jaw hits the proverbial floor.

"Just promise to give me everything so we can keep her safe, and I'll pull my head out of my ass soon enough," Lev finishes.

This response surprises me more than my dad's sudden caring attitude.

"Finally getting it, are you, Levi?" Sebastian taunts.

"At least he's not letting past bullshit continue to fuck with the present," Owen pokes, coming to Lev's aid.

That causes the smirk to fall right off Seb's golden face. *Yikes.* Nothing like a call out.

"Fuck you, O. You know it's best this way," Sebastian snaps back.

Owen lifts his tattooed-covered hands in mock surrender, "Whatever you say, Bash. Just remember to take your own advice. Or are you one of those, 'those who can't do, teach' people?"

"Burn," Wyatt heckles.

Sebastian's stubble-covered jaw flexes in annoyance. He hates being called on any shit pertaining to Vivian. I can't say I blame him. Walking in on your girl screwing your dad and then her marrying your former best friend creates a certain level of distrust in a person.

"Enough," Lev shouts. "We all have shit to figure out, but the important thing is that we do everything to keep Ariah Bradford safe. Which means no one can know she's a Bradford. Agreed?" he asks

"Agreed," we all say.

"Now, what the hell are you all planning to do for your first dates?" Wyatt broaches the other elephant in the room.

Collective groans fill the room.

"Fuck this shit," I murmur, remembering I have to actually spend time with Sam.

I stand, exiting to Wyatt's cackles following me out the now unsecured door.

24

ARIAH

The doctor's office is sterile, a mixture of steel and crisp ivory surfaces. The only pop of color comes from the impressionist paintings and plants positioned around the waiting room.

This is not how I envisioned spending my Monday afternoon.

When I told Shay about the ridiculous stipulations that came with being a Selected, her nostrils flared, and a string of curse words flew from her mouth until she calmed and tried to help me see the silver lining. How did she put it, 'endless buddy fi yuh pum pum.' The way I burst into laughter once she explained what the hell buddy and pum pum were. 'Ariah, my girl, I can't have you walking roun' here as my bestie and don't know what it means to siddown pon di buddy. Don't worry, I'll teach you how to quint it.' When she saw the look of exasperation in my crinkled brows, she bent over, roaring in delight at my utter confusion. 'It's cocky, my girl. Dick,' she finally explained, putting me out of my misery, and then it was my turn to keel over.

I chuckle as the scene replays.

A derisive snort wipes the smile off my face.

All girls selected, myself included, are seated, waiting to be called. Samantha and her clones cluster together, whispering and laughing as they openly glare in my direction.

Their constant tittering about me not deserving to be here is getting so old. I wonder how they'd feel if they knew I was actually an original bloodline? I picture Sam melting like the Wicked Witch as her flying monkeys turn on her.

I snort out a laugh, and their heads all snap in my direction. Rolling my eyes, I prepare for whatever onslaught of hate I'm about to get.

"I don't know what's so funny. Unless you're laughing at the tragedy that is your life," Meagan says, turning to see if she receives Sam's approval for her terrible attempt at bullying me. Once she notices Sam's smirk, she turns back to me and turns her nose up in my direction.

"The only tragedy here is your piss poor attempt at trying to put me in my place. It's just too bad for you that you're not even in the same zip code as me," I reply, cutting my eyes at her.

A door opens and a short woman with graying hair styled in a pixie cut and pink scrubs steps out holding a tablet.

"Okay, ladies, we're ready for you. We'll call you back one at a time. Once you receive your implant, you're free to go," her mousey voice informs us. "Summer Anderson. You're up first."

Summer pops up from her seat and walks through the open door. Once the snick of the lock is heard, Samantha takes it as her opportunity to continue where her pleb left off.

"You know you won't be chosen. It will be me in the end. I'll have them all," she decrees, with confidence only a delusional person can have. Her nose is still in the brace, but her eyes narrow in challenge, hoping I'll engage. I won't give her the satisfaction.

Pulling out my phone, I text the guys. Images of the other night in my room heating my cheeks.

Me: Why am I doing this again?

Sneaky Devil 😈: So there are no babies and you can take over

the world until you're ready to have a litter of little critters that look like the perfect blend of all of us.

The Big O: So I can shove my dick deep inside of you.

Me: So convincing... I'm out of here...

I love messing with them.

The Big O: Someone wants to be punished.

Me: I don't know what you're talking about.

Sneaky Devil😼: But I think you do.

The Big O: I think you like it when we chase you.

I shiver, chills run up my spine, and butterflies whirl in my belly. The idea of either of them, no, both of them, chasing me and what would happen once I was caught makes me squeeze my thighs together as I clench.

Me: Again....I don't know what you're referring to. I think you have me mixed up with someone else. 😉

The Big O: You'll know who we're talking about when my hand is around your throat as you choke Wy down.

Sneaky Devil😼: While O has you riding his hand.

Fuck. My eyes close as my tongue rolls in my mouth, imagining how it will feel to gag around Wyatt again. My lips lift into a grin, almost tasting him again.

"I wouldn't be smiling if I were you. It's only a matter of time before you get everything you deserve and you're kicked back to the slums where you belong," Samantha snides, interrupting my vivid daydream.

Lifting my gaze, my eyes narrow in her direction, but before I can tell the bitch where to stuff it, the door swings open, Summer steps out, and the nurse calls Sam to the back. The priss rises and heads for the back, stopping right as she's about to step inside.

"I'm so glad to get this. It will mean no more condoms between Wes and me," she smirks, winking before finally walking through the door.

My chest constricts at her words. I know she and Wes had, and maybe still have, a thing, and he's not anything to me.

So why does the idea of them being together make my blood boil? On a good day, I want to punch him in the mouth. Since I've been back, our interactions aren't as arctic, but I'd say they're still frosty.

I'm so lost in my thoughts that I don't hear when my name is called. I look up and see I'm the last one here. *How long was I thinking about Wes fucking Sam?* For fuck's sake.

"Sorry," I say to the nurse, hopping up from my seat and following her to the back.

"That's it?" I inquire.

"Yes, but remember you'll need to wear a condom since you haven't had your period until the hormones take effect. Then you're all set," Dr. Lambert instructs.

"I plan on wearing condoms even after that, Doc. Nothing's one hundred percent."

"Smart girl," she replies, but there's something in the way she's looking at me that makes me wonder if she means it. The look is gone before I can be sure it was even there.

Shaking it off, I hop down from the exam table. It's been a long ass day. I wouldn't be surprised if I saw a talking phoenix at this point.

After I thank Dr. Lambert one more time, then leave her office. I know Thomas and Erik are both waiting for me outside. Ever since my kidnapping, I've had at least two guards at all times, one of whom is always Thomas when I'm out of the house.

"Ready to go, Ariah?" T asks. I'm still working on getting him to call me Ry, but it's better than that Miss Bishop bullshit he was spewing only weeks ago.

Nodding, I lean my head back on the seat and sigh. Shutting my eyes, I let the stress of the day roll off me. Reaching up, I massage the spot the implant rests. These assholes overreached, but I'm glad to have the protection.

The vibration of my phone has my eyes snap open. I see it's a text.

Unknown: You're still behind in the race and have yet to learn your place. I'll take a girl until it's you I can finally erase.

Color leeches from my face. Another girl's been taken.

25
ARIAH

No one was taken. I sighed with such relief when Thomas told me everyone was accounted for and that security was being increased for each girl.

"Riah! Bitch. Are you with me?" Shay coaxes me from my thoughts.

I'm spending far too much time there lately.

"Yup, what did I miss?"

"Nothing, you were just five million miles away. You didn't even see when Wes dismissed Sam from their table," Shay says.

My head turns, confirming. A very pissed off Samantha stands with her hands fists at her side.

"You can't keep doing this shit and thinking it's okay, Wesley. You fucking selected me. You're supposed to treat me with respect. All of you are supposed to be," Samantha shrieks.

Shifting my focus, I close my eyes as I roll them. Doesn't she ever get tired of being the fucking drama?

"I'd laugh, but it's ridiculous at this point."

"You'd think she'd have some sense of self-respect," Shay snickers

Arching my brow, I retort, "Her and self-respect are like oil and water."

"Enough about them. Now that you have your implant, which dick will you be riding first?"

I choke on my soda, spluttering a cough as I try to clear my airway.

"Way to catch a bitch off guard," I say once my nose stops burning.

"Whatever, answer my question. When are you letting your ho fly?" she probes again.

Heat blooms, creeping up my neck to my cheeks. I'm sure my usually hidden freckles appear more prominent.

"Don't go getting bashful on me now. Which buddy are you quinting on first? My vote is for Owen. He looks like a crazy fuck in the bed. The choke you while he rearranges your insides type," she finishes. Her brown eyes darken.

My head tilts at her expression. "Are we speaking from personal experience?" I tease.

She shakes her, clearing the smoldered look from her eyes. Her gaze is now present. "Bitch, we aren't talking about me. We're talking about you. Stop trying to divert the conversation."

It's not like I haven't given this any thought. Shit, I've given it A LOT of thought, more than a few nights with my fingers between my legs. Wyatt, then Owen, and then the both of them at the same time. That image makes me bite my lip, preventing the moan rising in my chest from escaping.

Shay's mouth spreads into a beaming gapped-tooth smile, her gloss making her rose-pink lips pop. "You're thinking about it right now, aren't you? You dirty bitch," she jests. "Who? Which one has your face turning twenty shades of red?"

A hand glides up my spine. "What has you flushed, Angel?" Owen's heated breath caresses my ear before he plants a kiss on the thrumming pulse of my throat.

His hand strokes lightly against the base of my neck. I'll need to change my panties if he keeps this up.

"N-nothing," I finally stumble out, tipping my chin up to meet his stare.

The amusement lighting his eyes says he heard at least part of this conversation.

My heart rate skitters, skipping a beat as he leans down until his mouth captures mine, engulfing me in his spiced scent.

A low gasp escapes me, and he uses that opportunity to gain entry. His tongue tangles with mine. His hand moves from my neck, gripping my hair and groaning into our kiss. And for a moment, nothing else exists.

I whimper when our connection is severed.

"I'd keep going, but I don't want to give the cafeteria a show," he grumbles, pressing his lips to my forehead before he returns to his full height.

His words sober me. My head whips from side to side, taking in the shocked reactions and murmured words of the lunch room. *Fuck.* How did I forget I was at school?

"Yes, Bitch. You forgot you were at school," Shay mocks, cackling at my bewildered expression. My face is absolutely twisted in a combination of horror and embarrassment until I remember I honestly don't give a fuck who saw.

Relaxing my scrunched up face, I pull my shoulders back, arching a brow in challenge at anyone who'd have some fuck shit to say.

"There's my Riah. Fuck these people," Shay cheers, and we both stand. I grab Owen's hand as we walk out of the cafe.

"I need you to meet in your groups and prepare for your midterm presentations," Miss Taylor instructs now that she's finished with the lesson for today.

Everyone moves to their assigned groups. Wyatt, Lev, and I turn our chairs to face each other.

I feel the weight of Lev's penetrating hazel eyes boring down on me.

"What topic should we present on?" I ask, ignoring the feel of his perusal.

Ever since they rescued me, his indifference towards me has vanished, replaced by a pensive look that I swear sometimes is lustful, but that can't be.

I sneak a peek at his silhouette. He's gorgeous. Lev's stubbled chin accentuates his pronounced cheekbones and Grecian nose. Sculpted eyebrows and clear, moisturized skin depict his propensity for self-care. The muscles in his jaw flex, and I know he feels me studying him.

"Maybe we should do something on the suffrage movement," Lev suggests.

I still refuse to meet his eye, and Wyatt saves me from having to respond.

"That's an excellent idea. There is a lot of history for the fight for voting rights in this country. Shit... across the world."

A shadow appears to the side of me.

"What will your group's topic be?" Miss Taylor asks, her tone short and sharp.

I watch as Lev's demeanor shifts. His eyes turn to slits as one part of his lips curls upward.

"Do you want to walk away and try to come back when your sour-ass attitude is gone, *Vivian*?" Lev growls her name, and her posture goes rigid.

I'd say I was surprised, but they rule this town and everyone in it.

Clearing her throat Miss Taylor begins to speak, "I-I only meant."

She stutters before garbling her following words and finally saying, "I'd just like to know if your group has an idea of the topic you'd like to cover."

"We'll let you know when we've actually had time to discuss it. You only just had us break into groups. Go find your ass a seat away from us and don't bother coming back over here," Wyatt snaps.

Miss Taylor's nostrils flare in indignation as she grinds her teeth, but she turns on her black suede heels and walks to her seat at the front of the room.

I cover my mouth, pretending to rub my nose, hiding my laugh.

Lev leans over, and I stiffen at his proximity. "Does our protection of you amuse you, Dove?"

Dove? What the fuck is happening here?

Slanting my body away from him, I reply, "You're in my personal space."

His hands clench, but he nods and backs away from me. "I'm sorry," he mumbles. The hurt expression on his face threatens to gut me.

"Oh, fix your face. You didn't think you'd call her a sweet pet name and all would be forgiven, did you?" Wyatt cajoles, reminding me I still have reasons to be leery of Lev. "Make him work for it, Riri," he continues, winking at me.

I snort at his rebuff of his friend, smiling at him for always knowing what I need, and mouth 'thank you.'

"Let's go with suffrage. I like," I say, getting us back on track.

I look up at both of them in time to see resolve set in Lev's hawk-eyes gaze. He dips his head as if he's saying, 'game on,' and I can only imagine what this will mean for me.

I'm saved from my own thoughts when the signal for the end of class sounds.

Gathering my things, I ready myself to leave when a voice sounds from the front of the room, making me groan.

I should've seen this coming.

"Miss Bishop, I'd like a word with you before you leave, please,"

Miss Taylor states, her thin lips twisted and her snub nose upturned, as she turns to walk away.

I still don't know what I did to this woman for her to treat me with such disdain constantly. Her face looks like she's sucked on a lemon whenever she sees me.

Sighing, I wait for the class to empty. Wyatt stops at my side. "Do you want me to wait for you, Love?"

"No. I won't be long. She can't have much to say to me," I reply, hoping it to be true.

"In that case, I'll see you tonight," he says, pressing a quick kiss to my lips before he turns cold eyes on Miss Taylor, staring her down as he disappears out the door, distracting me from asking how he'll see me tonight. We don't have any plans for later.

Miss Taylor clears her throat, forcing my attention away from Wyatt's retreating form. Her straight platinum-blonde hair falls to the shoulders of her lilac silk blouse that I notice for the first time is unbuttoned far too low, exposing the crease between her ample chest. She can almost give me a run for my money in the breast department.

"Miss Bishop, what is the nature of your relationship with Mr. Grant?" She asks, snapping my attention from her lack of professional attire to her quirked brunette brow. *She could've at least dyed her brows too.*

I scrunch my face in confusion. "You mean Wyatt's dad?" I respond, trying to gain clarity on why she'd even ask me this dumb shit.

She huffs, crossing her arms over her chest as if my puzzlement is inconvenient.

"No," she snaps, "not Wyatt's father. Sebastian."

She can't be serious with this shit?

"At the moment, nothing, but if that changes, I'll be sure to update you," I smirk.

I internally groan at having to deal with yet another catty, jealous girl. Except, Miss Taylor isn't in high school. She's a whole grown-ass woman.

Her hand springs from their crossed position and grips my arm, digging her nails into my skin.

"You listen here, you stupid fat cow. I've waited years to have Bastian back, and I'll be damned if you or any of the other selected bitches take him from me," she seethes.

My head leans to the side, oscillating from her glowering azure eyes to where her claws begin to pierce my flesh. "You have about half a second to remove your hand before I break it," I snarl, my voice tinged with a level of violence I didn't know I possessed.

She drops her hand as if sensing the brewing storm raging below the surface.

"You'll stay away from Bash-."

I cut her off, "You'll shut the hell up, or I'll find Sebastian and fuck him for spite while you're tied to a chair and make you watch as I ride him until he screams my name."

The fucking audacity of this woman. Hell, the damn audacity of this damn town. I didn't ask for any of this shit.

Meeting her shocked stare, I smirk, then turn and storm from the room, only to be grabbed into Wyatt's waiting arms.

"Fucking brilliant, Love," he says, leaning in, crashing his mouth to mine.

Well shit. If being a smartass gets me this. I'm going to have to do it more often.

26

ARIAH

"I'm so glad to be going home," my dad says from the other side of the car.

Thomas and I went to pick him up almost two hours ago. He was finally discharged fifteen minutes ago.

"I can't wait for you to spend more time with Jamie and the twins. They're so excited for you to be coming home," I exclaim.

His smile lights his face, lines appearing as he crinkles his eyes. "I'm glad to be back. I wish it were under better circumstances," he mumbles the last part. The happiness that was glinting moments ago dims. The long look lasts a few seconds before he quirks his lip and smiles again.

My frustration with everything that's happened grows, and my anger at Elise boils. All the questions I've had about her behavior over the years resurface.

"Hey," my dad interrupts. "Don't go there, at least not today," he coaxes just as Thomas turns into the driveway.

He laughs, and I know he can see the ridiculous hand-painted welcome sign we made for him.

I look out the window and confirm that to be the case, but it's the jumping twins, dressed in their superhero costumes, that make me join him.

"Those two are ridiculous," I chuckle.

"Quite the pair, I imagine," he begins. I feel him tap my arm to get my attention, and I turn as he continues, "I want to say this again. Thank you so much for being what your mo- Elise and I couldn't be, Ry."

I shake my head, "You don't need to keep thanking me. I did what needed to be done. If you want to do anything for me, tell me what you couldn't when you were at the Edgewoods'. What don't I know?"

After everything that happened, I needed answers, and he owed them to me.

"Let me get situated, and once you brothers and sister go to bed tonight, we'll talk," he suggests.

I nod as we pull to a stop. It was fair enough.

Much like the night I returned, the car door is ripped open, and two mini-terrors dive into the car, causing dad to groan out in both shock and pain.

"Hey, you two, take it easy. Remember what we talked about," I instruct.

Kylan and Kellan pull back, their tiny identical faces scrunching up in remorse. "Sorry," they say in unison.

"I've missed that," dad chuckles. "The twinning thing you two do," he clarifies, and we all laugh.

Once we're in the house, Tabitha greets us, and her eyes begin to water, but she quickly brushes away the tear before it can fall. "You're home, Mr. Bishop," she croaks.

What is that about? I look back to see if Dad's expression will give anything away, but before I completely turn, his words shock me still.

"Mom," he gasps. "What-what are you doing here?" Dad asks.

Mom?

My gaze swings back and forth between the both of them.

"Aaron," she cries, running for him, but slowing so as not to hurt him before wrapping her arms around him.

"They need me. You needed me," Tabitha, my grandmother states. "I would never leave them here alone. Not after everything."

Jamie moves to stand beside me. "Wait, so, we've been here with our grandmother this whole time?" She turns her accusatory gaze in their direction. "What is going on?"

"That's what I'd like to know," I mutter.

Dad looks at me, imploring me to understand and wait.

"Fine," I mumble. "Jamie, let's give them a minute. I'm sure they *both* will give us answers later."

Jamie rolls her eyes and stomps away, murmuring things about stupid adults, always trying to keep kids in the dark as she coaxes the boys to follow her upstairs.

I couldn't agree more.

Turning back to my father and Tabitha, I cross my arms and demand, "I think I need some answers before they go to bed. I think it's only fair."

"Let's go to the office," Tabitha suggests.

I can't believe I've been living and spending time with my grandmother.

Once we're in the room, my dad closes the door behind him, as my grandmother and I take our seats at the same table I learned of my fate in this town.

My dad clears his throat, taking his seat before he begins. "You know I was never born in this town, but still abided by the laws set out by our founding members." He stands, pacing the room, and continues, "When I was old enough, my father, your grandfather, Tobias Bradford, explained it all to me. The assassination and kidnapping attempts. Edgewood was no longer a place they could stay. So, we hid until it was time, but our hand was forced."

"Why the hell would someone want to kill our family?" I exclaim.

My father turns, stopping in front of me, "I need you to understand, Ry, I never wanted to return here or wanted you anywhere near this. I was hoping it would never get to this point. But your conniving mother-.”

Tabitha cuts in, “What your father is trying to say is. It wasn’t safe for us. We weren’t sure who was killing off the Bradford line, but after your great-grandfather was killed when I was pregnant with your father, we knew it was time for us to leave.”

I weigh her words, processing all the information I’ve just been provided.

“Where’s my grandfather?” I ask. It probably shouldn’t be my first question after all of the revelations just shared, but I want to know if I have more family out there.

“Still back in Bronston. We couldn’t risk him being exposed. Not with your father gone,” Tabitha replies, rubbing the back of her hand.

“Colorado? Like the town over from where we used to live when we were kids?” I probe.

Dad answers this time. “Yes, but when we were living there, they were down in Texas.”

“Are there any more Bradfords out there?” Now that I know my grandmother and grandfather are alive, I’m curious to know.

“Yes.”

I wait for him to say more, but he doesn’t. I open my mouth to ask more questions, but dad raises his good arm, stopping me.

“No more questions, Ry. We can’t tell you more. We shouldn’t have told you this much. If I wasn’t so shocked to see your grand-mother, I wouldn’t have blurted out who she was.”

His face begs me to understand when he sees my jaw clench.

“Please, understand. Your safety... Kylan, Kellan, and Jamie’s safety... is most important, and I won’t risk any of you. Not for answers you’ll eventually get.”

Sighing, my shoulders slump in defeat. He’s right. I’d never risk them. While I might risk myself for the truth, I wouldn’t do anything to put them in danger.

I nod, and his posture visibly relaxes. “Why don’t you show me my room, and then we can celebrate my return with a family game night?" he suggests.

"I miss those," I say in earnest. I'm not one hundred percent over the lack of questions I've had answered, but want to enjoy his being home.

Tabitha stands. "Great! I'll get everything set up." She makes her way to the door, but I shoot from my seat and engulf her in a hug. When she squeezes me back, I bask in the feeling of being hugged by my grandmother for the first time.

I've hugged her a million times before now, but this is the first time I'm hugging her knowing who she is to me.

I feel the drop of something wet against my head and her soft whimpers. "I know, Sweet Girl. I know," she whispers in my hair.

Pulling from her embrace, I shout, "Not it for telling the kids about Elise." I want no parts in that mess.

Dad pinches the bridge of his nose, "I'd never make you have such a difficult conversation. The days of you having to be the parent are done, Ry."

Smiling, I nod. There's still much more to understand, but for now, I'll take my win. My dad and *grandmother* are both here.

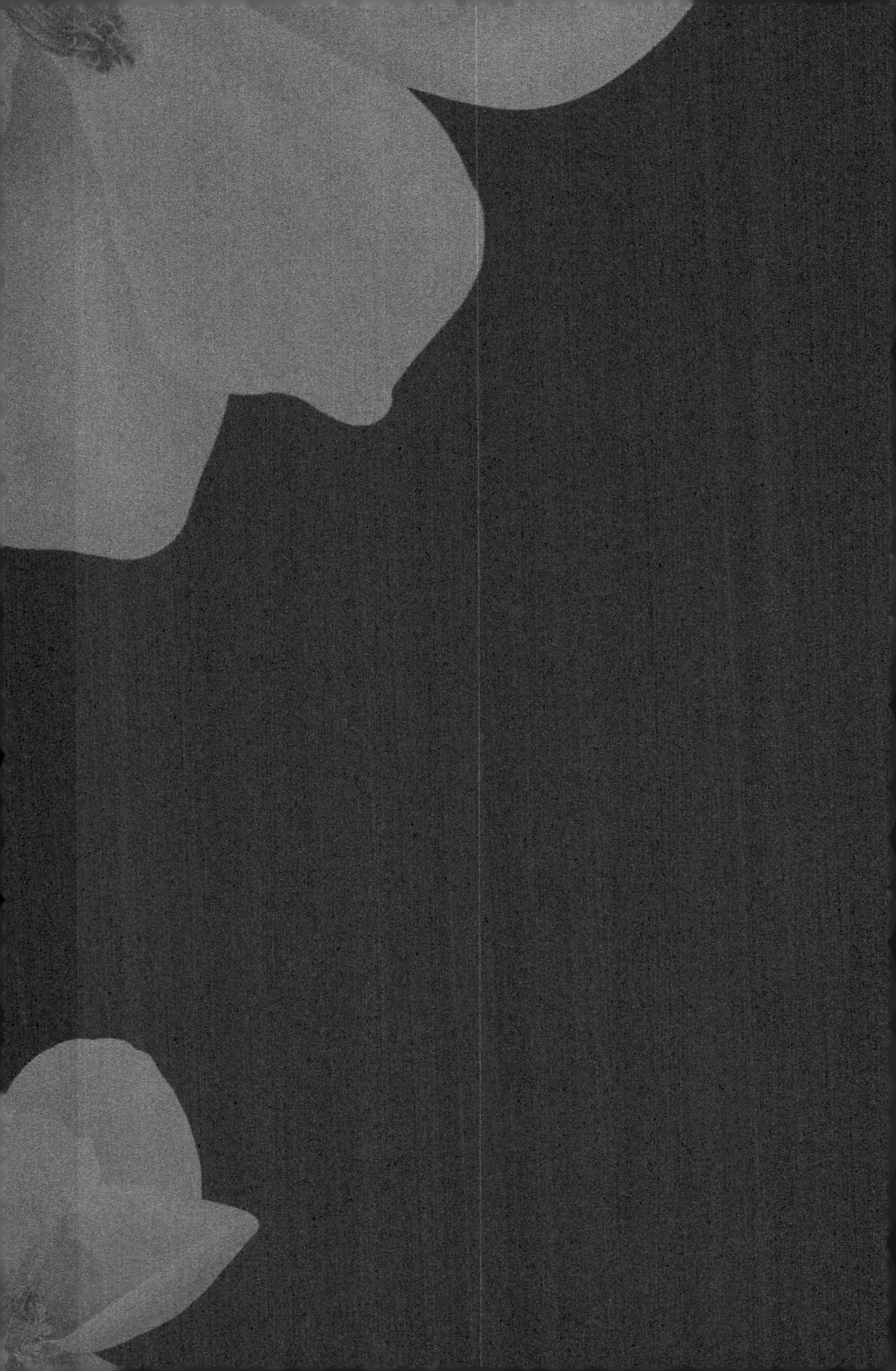

27
WYATT

The week flew by, Ariah's dad came home yesterday, and she spent some much-needed time with him and her siblings. I'm sure if we didn't have this planned, she wouldn't have left the house at all this weekend.

At the reminder of our pending date, I begin pacing the room. My nerves won't settle. I've been like this all damn day.

I'm picking Ariah up in the next hour to take her on our first of many dates.

I'm not exactly sure why I'm nervous. It's not like I haven't been out with her before. This time just feels different. I need to make sure it's special because she's everything.

From the first moment I saw her over all those months ago, and every interaction since— I've known. *She's it for me— for us.*

"You got it, Wy. Don't stress it. What you have planned is going to blow her mind. But you know, even if it were just the two of you sitting and watching a movie, she'd love it because it was with you," Sebastian encourages, distracting me.

For a guy who's so anti-love, he sure is good at laying it on thick.

Shaking out my shoulders, I quirk a brow, "Thanks, Casanova," I joke. "Seriously though, Seb. Thanks for helping me organize all of this."

He pats my back, "No thanks needed. I only helped facilitate. You came up with the ideas. Now go get your girl."

"*Our* girl," I correct.

I think Sebastian will be harder to bring around than the other two assholes. Those two are skeptics— Seb's jaded. That's a whole different ocean to cross.

He gives me a small tight smile and mumbles, "Our girl," before heading down the hall, probably to our room in The Tombs.

Pulling my phone from my black denim jeans pocket, I see I have thirty minutes to grab Ariah and make it to the airstrip. *Time to get my ass in gear.*

"I can't believe we're going on a private jet," Ariah squeaks, her excitement palpable from the passenger seat of my car.

Peering from my periphery, I take in the denim skirt, slightly riding up her fishnet-covered voluptuous thighs. My gaze flicks back to the road before taking another peek at her Pearl Jamcropped-tee. She's fucking breathtaking.

"Eyes on the road," she demands, and I focus back on the street.

"You're just so distracting," I admit.

She softly laughs, "I'm not distracting enough to warrant us veering off the road. Eyes facing front."

"I should've accepted Thomas's offer to drive us instead of having him drive behind, but I wanted you all to myself."

Her smile grows. "And where are you taking me?"

I love seeing her like this— carefree and laughing. She always looks like she has the weight of the world on her shoulders, and ever since we got her back, there's a darkness that never used to be there.

Turning to her, I smirk, "It's a surprise."

She scrunches her nose, "I'm not the biggest fan of those. I have a horrible track record with spontaneous events."

There it is. That look. It's gone almost as quickly as it appeared— just like Owen and Lev. They get these faraway looks. However, tonight isn't about the things haunting her— it's about seeing more twinkles in her eyes.

We pull up at the hangar, stopping near the runway.

"Holy shit." Ariah gawks at the sleek white Bombardier Global 7500.

I'm no aviation aficionado, but this baby moves while offering the comforts of a five-star hotel.

"Seriously, how rich are you assholes?"

"Enough," is all I say in response.

We climb the steps, and Rachel, our private attendant, greets us. She stands in a jet-black skirt suit with a matching blazer and ivory collared shirt.

"Welcome back, Mr. Grant. Will it just be you and Miss Bishop this evening, or are we waiting for others?" she inquires. Her wide, warm smile showcases pearly-white teeth.

"Just us, Rachel," I inform her.

She nods, "Very well. We'll be taking off shortly, and I'll be back to get your order."

Once she leaves, I walk Ariah to our seats.

"Are you sure you can't give me a hint about where we're going?" Ariah bats her eyelashes, trying to coax a hint out of me with her imploring gray eyes. *I worked too hard to spoil the surprise.*

Leaning over, my mouth ghosts the shell of her ear, and I whisper, "Absolutely not," before pulling back and bopping her on the tip of her nose.

Huffing, she leans back and crosses her arms, the movement garnering my attention to the delicious way her breasts rise and fall.

I imagine her riding me as she feeds me her glorious tits. I imagine them slapping me in the face as I pound deep inside her.

I feel my dick jerk, and I have to bite my lip. *Tonight isn't about sex.* I'm going to give my girl the night of her life and let her feel like a teenager for once— *carefree.* She deserves a break— no, more than a break, and it's my mission to ensure we give her that.

The pilot's voice comes through the intercom, announcing our departure and estimated time of arrival without revealing our destination.

"Tell me, Wyatt Grant. What makes you so sure this," she points between us, "is meant to be?"

"I could give you so many cliché answers. Like the first time I saw you, I just knew. But it's deeper than that. It's deeper than superficial. I feel you on a soul-deep level, Ariah. I feel you pumping through my veins— it's like I need to breathe you in to survive. You own me, and you don't even realize that you do, Love." *I guess I went cliché after all.* But it doesn't feel that way to me—it's far more profound. These are just the only words I can use to try and describe what's innate to me since finding out about her. She doesn't get it yet. She thinks the first time she saw me was our first time meeting.

I inwardly chuckle. She has no idea how long I've been watching her— no inclination of the first time I saw her coming out of school in Colorado, or the time she was bent over planting Winter Creepers along the driveway to spruce up her yard once she moved to Edgewood. Then there were the times I'd watched as her cunt of a mother would come home high off her ass, and she'd pull in from a double shift at the diner, so weary she'd sit in her car trying to catch her breath.

I know she isn't aware of how many nights I stood over her bed and watched her. Some nights, peace found her. Other nights she was haunted even in her sleep— the medication no help other than to make her unaware of my presence. She can't remember how many times I brought her to orgasm. That night in her room was the first time she shaved for me. She doesn't realize how connected we are.

I'm almost giddy at the prospect of her finding out. She's going to fight because that's who she is, and I'll enjoy it because that's who I am.

Her breath catches, and she tilts her chin like she's observing me for the first time. "You speak like we've known each other our whole lives, not just for a couple of months."

My smile grows, "You'd be surprised just how well I know you, Love," I confess, leaning over and capturing her mouth to silence her questions.

She fucking tastes like candy. Her watermelon-lemonade gloss has my hands raising to tug her into me.

I want to make us one. And not for the first time, I think how if it weren't for the bond I have with the guys, I wouldn't share her even with them— not even O... and the idea of sharing her with him makes my pants always feel tighter.

We don't usually share, but with Ariah, if the idea of me fucking Owen turned her on, I'd do it, and I know he would too.

"We will be landing in five minutes. The weather is a cool seventy-five degrees on a beautiful Saturday afternoon."

The pilot's voice clears my lust-filled movements. *Soon.* I'll have her soon. Just not right now.

"Can I take this damn blindfold off now?" Ariah whines, and I think I hear her mumble, "I swear I hate surprises. I'm still reeling from the Nirvana *In Utero* signed and framed CD."

My cheeks raise into a smile. she nearly jumped out of her skin when she saw it. It's another thing I'll need to thank Colt for later. I don't bother responding, though. She can't hear me anyway. The earplugs I had her put in ensure she has no idea what's coming and have her shouting. Every time she tries to talk, I stifle a laugh.

The level of trust she's gifted me, to not only blindfold her and take away her hearing but also lead her where she needs to go safely, is humbling.

Ariah doesn't trust easily— she's been burned too many times.

I breathe her in, enjoying the scent of jasmine and rose filling the air of the armed SUV. I don't know what perfume she's wearing, but I'm buying the company.

Resting my chin on the top of her head, I sigh, feeling the most contented I've been.

"I know you hear me! I might not be able to hear you, but you can hear me, and I can tell you're laughing, you freaking jerk," she snarks, and I tickle her sides, her sassy comments morphing into peels of laughter until she's snorting.

"I'm going to kill you for making me snort, Wyatt Grant. Mark my words, you're a dead man walking," she shouts, causing a laugh to rumble in my chest.

We pull up outside of Jacobi Arena. The sound of music can be heard from the private entrance. She's going to flip when she sees this lineup.

I'll have to thank Coop and Colt, again, for the VIP access.

Thomas pulls the door open, allowing me to ease from Ariah and step outside before I turn around to help her climb out, using the opportunity to hold her around her waist and pull her flush against me. My hands linger on the exposed flesh of her stomach as I enjoy watching color bloom up her neck— my touch having the desired effect.

A cough slows my movements. "They have the private cabana ready. For security purposes, you should take the blindfold off here," Thomas suggests.

I nod in agreement, and he turns out to look at the crowd, giving us another moment of privacy.

My hands travel up her abdomen, teasing at the exposed skin

until I reach the earplugs. Gently, I remove one and softly speak into her ear, "Here's to a night of just being young and carefree."

Leaning forward, I kiss her neck, removing the other plug and mask from her eyes.

"Oh. My. Fucking. God!" The squeal she expels almost has me covering my ears. But she turns, thrusting her arms around me.

"Is this real? Are we really here?" she asks in between peppering me with her lips.

I could stay like this forever.

"Yes," I state, feeling nothing more needs to be said.

She grabs my hand and makes a mad dash toward the stage.

"Slow down, Love. We're over here."

I tug her in the direction of our seats, still watching the sway of her hips. *She's so damn intoxicating.* Not just the sensuality of her movements but her excitement— utterly enthralling. I'm fucking rock hard, my dick pressing uncomfortably against the zipper of my jeans at her giddiness.

Once we reach the cabana, she lets go of my hand and spins to take in the stage, ignoring all the lavish amenities, choosing instead to take in the first act.

"That's fucking Good Charlotte," she screams over the music pumping through the crowd.

"I know." *I'm so verbose tonight.*

Her neck cranes, not wanting to miss a thing, but I can tell she has something to say. The words look like they want to burst from her lips, so I step into her back.

"I've always wanted to come here. Dad and I would go to concerts every time he came home," her voice cracks. "We were supposed to come here the summer he went missing."

I wrap my arms around her, bringing her into me. I don't want to lie to her and act surprised because I know. So I stay quiet. Again, enjoying being able to just be— no Selection process, no annoying Sam or fucked up secret society bullshit. *We just are.*

"Thank you," she whispers. A lone tear leaks from her glossy eyes, and I reach my thumb up and wipe it away.

That's how we stay, listening to band after band— Evanescence, Nine Inch Nails, Lauryn Hill, Tribe Called Quest, and Pierce the Veil, to name a few. Eventually, we make our way backstage, and she nearly faints countless times with each musician she meets. She has more signed band tees than I can count. I made sure to buy her two of each so she could wear the ones not signed.

"I can't believe I just saw Lizzo perform live and met her in fucking person. I can't wait to get home and tell Dad," she exclaims, popping another blackberry in her delectable mouth.

My eyes zero in on the way her pink tongue sweeps over her plush lips, wiping away the wine-colored juices.

Thank fuck we're back on the jet. I spent the majority of the day hard.

"I'm happy you had a great day," I smile.

Her gray eyes light up, "Great is not the adjective to describe the day I had. Phenomenal, extraordinary, prodigious. Those words begin to express the type of day I had with you."

My chest tightens at her confession. Not just the concert but her time with me.

Extending my hand across the table, I help her stand. I want us to have more privacy, so I make my way to the bedroom at the plane's rear.

Shutting the door with my foot, I hold Ariah's hand until I sit on the bed, and she straddles my lap. Her skirt rides up, exposing the lace of her black panties.

I groan at the sight, "Are you wet for me, Love?"

Her answering whimper invites my fingers to explore.

"Yes," her emphatic response encourages me to lift her skirt over her hips.

Sliding her damp panties to the side, my nostrils flare at the smell of her arousal as I insert two fingers into her waiting pussy.

"Mmhmm. Fuck, Wy," she moans at the stretch of her walls

around my thick middle and ring fingers, as she bites her lip, turning them blush red.

My hand pumps in, slow and deep, twisting as they pull out before slamming back in. My pace is steady until I hear the hitch of her breath on my face. Increasing the tempo, I make shallow strokes. My dick gets harder with each convulsion around my digits— her walls spasming.

"Please, Wy. I need more of you," she cries out.

"You want me to slam my cock in this pretty pussy, Love?"

She groans, nodding her plea.

"Use your words. I want to hear you beg for me to stretch you open and have your virgin pussy weeping over my fat cock," I grunt.

I don't know how much more of this I can take before I bust in my jeans. It will all be worth it, though.

My words have her shaking around my fingers, and I picture what it will be like to feel the flutters strangling my piercings.

"I want you to shatter me," she screams.

And fuck do I want that too, but I can't.

"No, Riri. I can't be your first. My piercings would hurt you," I grit out.

"What if I want to feel the pain?" She challenges.

My lip quirks. "Pain is something I'll gladly give, but not like this. Not for your first time."

I lift her chin so she can see the seriousness of my next words, "I may not be your first, but I'll be your forever." Then my lips crush to hers as she rides my fingers, and my thumb circles her clit. Her moans fill my mouth— our kisses grow violent as she gets closer to her release. Her pussy grips my fingers, and her head tips back.

"Bring that fucking mouth back to me now," I growl.

Smoldering gray eyes darken at my command— her lips returning to mine, and I recapture her mouth as I increase my pace, pumping my fingers in and out of her soaking wet walls.

She releases a quiet, stuttered moan before a loud cry explodes from her mouth as her body shakes. My other hand pulls her into me, trying to fuse us together, eating her orgasm until her body finally stills.

"Fuck," she sighs, resting her forehead to mine. "You-," she begins to speak, but a voice comes over the intercom, interrupting her and shattering the bliss we felt only seconds ago.

"Sir, we have a problem."

I pull up to the front entrance of the airstrip, parking my car next to the guys' cars, and hop out.

Everyone is standing by the iron gate at the entry point. Taking my time, I stroll toward them, wondering why no one is inside until I see what prompted us to meet here.

Summer's skewered like a scarecrow to the gate. Her head hangs limply on the shoulders of her mutilated corpse. She's covered in bruises, and dried blood can be seen from her exposed sex. A knife handle hangs from the opening. Her breasts are gone. *Why isn't this sick fuck done yet?*

"Well, that's a fucked way to end a date," Owen murmurs as I finally approach.

Shit. I forgot Wyatt was on his date with Ariah.

"Where is she now? Did she see this?" I ask, proud when my voice doesn't sound feral.

"We had Thomas and Erik take her the back way. We didn't want to freak her out after she finally had a day to be carefree," Wyatt responds. He looks wistful, as if he's replaying their date. *It must have been amazing.*

I dip my chin in understanding.

After receiving the text when she left the doctor's office, Wyatt and Owen mentioned how guilty she felt that this psycho keeps going after people because of her.

"How did you manage to get her to leave without making a fuss? Didn't you say the pilot announced it on the plane? I can't imagine her going quietly," Sebastian voices.

He's right about that. I might not be as close with her as Wyatt and Owen, but I know enough that she'd never leave without protest.

"She doesn't know what the problem is, and we should keep it that way for at least the time being," Wes suggests.

"How exactly do you plan on keeping a whole dead-ass girl hidden?" I snort.

I take his point, but she's a whole damn person and a popular one at that. Her absence will be noticed.

Sebastian interjects, "We have about a week before anyone will make a big deal about it. You know how often students go on impromptu trips with their parents. Edgewood isn't the epitome of a strict attendance policy."

He's right about that. Shit, we take off for weeks at a time doing Fraternitas shit all the time, and no one bats an eyelash.

Shifting my gaze, I glance at the metal spiked through Summer's chest. "How the hell did this happen? I thought we increased security for all of the girls?" I ask.

The sound of footsteps crunching gravel announces a new arrival.

"I think I can answer that," my father states, and I immediately stiffen. His nearness unsettles me.

Bradley Washington is an imposing form but not an evil man. The best way to explain the relationship I have with a man who I'm the carbon copy of, with the exception of me having my mother's eyes, is that he wants forgiveness for something I've not forgiven myself for. How do you let go of the pain of feeling betrayed when it's yourself you feel betrayed by the most?

"Summer was taken after she refused to let her security team follow her to her wax appointment. She was adamant that the esthetician she's been going to was the same person for the last five years," my father begins to explain, pausing only to turn his jade-green eyes on me. "When her detail noticed she hadn't exited the building fifteen minutes after the end of her scheduled session, they went inside and only found her tracker, which was left on the bed."

Lifting my hand, I massage the headache building at the bridge of my nose. "How could they let that shit happen?" I bark, angrier at the lapse in security than I am about another girl being killed. Summer was a bitch, and she didn't deserve to die for it, but her stupidity made it happen.

My father's stare returns. I feel it burning into the side of my face. "Yes, they've all been taken out of rotation. We can't have security who bend to the whims of a whiny brat. They were able to recover this, however," he says, pulling out a photo of Madeline sitting in a waiting car as a man carries the slumped form of Summer.

This prompts me to observe her mangled form again.

"Tell me we have something on her this time?" Wes asks.

I know the answer before my father even responds, "No, the license plate was untraceable."

Curses fill the air. We're all over this shit. The Filiae Bellonae has been five steps ahead of us.

My gaze connects with each of theirs, communicating silent instructions. We'll meet back at my house to discuss our next move.

A hand lands on my shoulder, and I have to bite my cheek to prevent the flinch.

"We'll get them, Levi. With you working on this, I know we'll put a stop to this."

Shrugging, I roll my shoulders out of his hold and turn to leave. Only my nod acknowledges I heard him at all.

With one last fleeting look at Summer, I make my way back to my car.

Elise is a twisted bitch for this.

I stare up at the pictures of Summer's lifeless body on the screen. Madeline didn't waste any time sending her missing parts along with pictures of her corpse to her parents, attaching a note informing them that until Ariah's handed over, Selected girls will keep going missing.

The Livingstons have been calling incessantly, wanting to know what will be done to compensate them for their daughter's death. Not an ounce of care that they lost a child— just recompense.

We're sitting around the table, working through files. We've been at this for hours and are no closer to finding Madeline.

Chair legs drag along the wooden floor as Owen stands abruptly. "We're missing something, and it's putting girls in danger— it's putting *our girl* in danger," he snarls.

He's right. Whatever it is, it's mocking our inability to see what's in front of us.

"We need to do a more thorough investigation into Madeline's connections with the law firm," Wes suggests, turning to me before he continues, "Lev, we need you to access the personnel files of every employee to see if there are any lingering ties."

My face scrunches, even more confused. I thought we already established that there must be more than one insider. This town is riddled with Filiae Bellonae. Shit, there are probably people all over this town who've infiltrated the ranks and positions, gaining access to pertinent information. How else could that bitch Madeline know when to kill Lydia and take her place.

"We knew this already," I reply.

Sebastian sighs like I'm dense and not some high-level coder with a genius IQ. "For someone so smart, you're blind to the obvious," he laments.

"What am I not seeing? We know our ranks have been compromised. I've been part of the team checking and rechecking everyone's backgrounds," I counter.

Owen returns to his seat, a bottle of soda in tow.

"Um, what are we, chopped liver?" Wyatt jokes, snatching the bottle from him.

Ignoring their antics, my attention returns to Seb. He rubs at his stubble-covered face, "You're looking for connections with Madeline digitally. Whoever is feeding her information is too smart to leave that kind of trail. I think we need to broaden our search out of the law firm and into the school."

I tip my head back, mulling over his suggestion. There are so many places we can extend our search, but the school happens to be one of the locations Ariah's been harassed and attacked.

"Okay, I see where you're going with this," I admit, shifting my attention back on him. "Expand our target area. Is there anyone in particular that we should be keeping an eye on?"

It's Wyatt who responds, "Vivian Taylor."

I look into Sebastian's angry blue eyes. They're darker than their usual azure color, to see if he's on board with this.

The fierce set of his jaw and sharp focus says it was his idea.

"Her return makes no sense. Her divorce makes no sense. And her constant push to get back together makes no fucking sense."

Hearing his argument and wanting to discuss it from all sides, I counter, "She easily could have moved back for you. She's been emphatic about wanting you back. Also, people get divorced and move back to their hometowns all the time. Not to mention, being jealous and petty doesn't make you the perfect suspect in subterfuge. If anything, it draws too much attention to you."

"True, but her timing is far too fucking coincidental, and she doesn't seem to give any of the other Selected as much trouble as Ariah. Even on her first day here, she had it out for her."

Also true. Vivian Taylor has been a thorn in Ariah's side, but I want to make sure Sebastian is doing this because he genuinely suspects her and not for some lover's scorned bullshit.

"Her records came back clear in all of the searches. Are you sure this isn't some extension of your vendetta against her?"

He slams his hands on the table. "Fuck her. I haven't thought of Vivian as anything more than a hole to shove my dick into when I'm bored since her return. She does not affect me. That ship sailed long ago."

I want to believe him. I know he considers himself over her. He might no longer love her, but she's definitely had a lasting impact on him, and that's evident by his inability to be vulnerable ever again.

A notification on my phone cuts my attention. Reaching in my pocket, I pull out the device and see it's a message from Coop. He's got the last piece of information I've been waiting for.

I guess Sebastian isn't the only one haunted by his past.

Ignoring the message, I finally respond, "Okay, I'll look into Vivian more thoroughly, and Wyatt will handle the law firm."

All in agreement, we stand, heading for the door when Wyatt stops. He turns to face Wes, and I see the mischievousness glint in his eyes, a smirk quirking his lips.

"Enjoy your date with Samantha tomorrow, asshole." Wyatt chuckles as he exits the room. We all join him, laughing over Wes's loud groans of protest.

29
WES

If there's ever a reason to fucking hate the Selection process, it's this. I can't believe I have to take Samantha on a date.

Looking at my watch, I notice I'm half an hour late. *I wish I could postpone this forever.*

I hop out of the car, huffing at what dumb shit she'll have planned for tonight.

When the Fraternitas told us we had to go on dates, they didn't say anything about having to be the ones to plan anything. So, I told Sam to pick something and let me know the time and place. She wasn't getting shit out of me.

Walking up the steps, I pull open my door and stride toward the stairs, only to be stopped by my mother.

"Wesley, I thought you were already here," her soft voice brings a smile to my face.

Changing direction, I make my way over to where she stands, donning a blue-gray terry cloth sweat suit. She must be headed for the entertainment room. It's the only time she'll wear anything remotely set for lounging.

I bend to meet her, my frame towering over hers, and kiss her cheek. "What made you think I was home? I haven't been here all day."

Standing back to my full height, I catch the look of uncertainty in her eyes. "I could've sworn I saw your Selection pick go upstairs about an hour ago," she confesses.

It's my turn to be puzzled. "Maybe it was one of the staff. I'm meeting Sam at the diner."

She looks like she's about to argue further but thinks better of it. "Perhaps you're right. My head has been hurting me."

I feel the lines in my forehead crease, worry knitting my brows. "Are the headaches back? What did the doctor say?" I rapid fire. Hoping she still has a clean bill of health. I'm going to be even more late meeting Sam, but again she can wait.

My mother brushes off my concern, "I'm fine. It's just been a long day. Go get ready. You know how miserable that brat can be if you keep her waiting."

"Sam can wait until she turns to ash. Your health is always the most important thing to me."

Reaching up, her small, delicate palm claps my face. "You've always been a good boy Wesley, I'm sorry you couldn't be born to simpler circumstances, but heavy is the head that wears the crown."

I'm about to ask her what she means by her cryptic words, but she shoos me along, refusing to entertain any of my questions.

Finally, I make my way upstairs, taking the steps two at a time. My feet carry me until I stop and notice my door is slightly ajar.

Moving my hand to the door, I push it open and see a very naked Samantha spread eagle on my bed.

For fuck's sake. Now I'm going to have to burn my bed.

"What the hell are you doing in my house?" I bark

Samantha ignores me, bringing her hand down and opening the lips of her pussy, and sliding a finger in and out.

Eager to get her the fuck out of here, I survey my room looking for her clothes, spotting them on the couch.

Storming over, I grab them from the heap they're in and stomp over to my bed, throwing them in her face.

She squeals as her fingers slip from inside in time to catch them before they smack her in the face. "What the absolute fuck Wes?" she snarls.

Tired of the day and her bullshit. "Get your skanky ass out of my fucking house before I toss you out naked," I command.

I can't believe the new level she's willing to sink to get attention.

"No," she shrieks, "You haven't touched me in over a month. I'm tired of your shit."

"And I'm just tired of you. Now get the fuck out. By the time I get out of the shower, you better not be here," I shout, turning and heading for my bathroom.

But because Sam is who she is, she doesn't know when to shut the hell up.

I hear her movements before her words.

"Fuck you, Wes! You and your merry band of dicks think you can toss me aside because some shiny new bitch moved to town. You're as fucked as she is," she screams.

Wheeling around, I yank her naked body out of my bed by her throat. "You keep testing me. You somehow have deemed yourself worthy of something you've never been positioned for." My grip around her neck tightens, my eyes boring down on her, and lust fills her eyes. I forgot how much she gets off on shit like this— how much we both do. But I'm not interested in Sam. I never have been.

I loosen my grip long enough to snap, "It's not going to be you. You're not going to be *The Chosen*. You know it. So, go through the process like everyone else, and for once in your life, have some fucking self-respect." Then I tighten my hold, squeezing until she realizes I'm not doing this for her pleasure— this is not fucking game.

Her hands fly up, trying to claw at my fingers, but I hold firm until she's seconds away from losing air. It's time she understands this isn't a joke. I no longer have to entertain her bullshit. Right before her last breaths can be drawn, I toss her on the floor at the foot of the bed, and she lands with a thud.

I hear her gasp for air and get to her feet. The sounds of her picking up her clothes satisfies me enough I finally make my way to the bathroom.

Pausing at the threshold, I bark without looking back, "Now get the fuck out of my house."

"I can't believe she was in your bed," Owen says, doubling over in laughter.

"Laugh it up, asshole. You each have to take her out at some point. At least I'm done with her for now," I counter.

That sobers the room, "Why would you put that in the atmosphere like that? You fucking dick," Lev mumbles.

The noise of the lunchroom filters around us.

"That's what you fuckheads get. All that taunting, have fun," I snark and get up from the table, leaving them to sulk.

After that bullshit with Sam last night, I was looking forward to football practice today. She's at least giving me a wide berth, but I don't trust it. She's never been one to take anything lying down.

I'm exiting the lunch room when someone walks in. I smell her before I take her in. I hear Ariah's gasp of surprise as I steady her.

"Shoot. Sor-. Oh, Wes. It's you." Her face drops.

I sigh. I deserve that reaction. It's not like I've given her any reason to think I see her differently.

"Sorry, I should've been watching where I was going," I start. "Are you okay?"

Her brows furrow further. She's trying to figure out if this is bullshit or not.

Grabbing the back of my neck and rubbing, I say, "Listen. I was a jerk when we first met."

"No, you were a dick, a grade-A level douche," she corrects, crossing her arms and bringing my attention to her chest as her plump pink lips thin. I work hard to keep my eyes connected with her serious ones.

My nostrils flare. "Right, I was all of those things. I thought you were something you aren't."

"Is this your attempt at an apology? Because you can shove it," she says and storms past me.

So much for extending an olive branch.

My jaw flexes at her brush off.

A hand pats my back. "I'll tell you, like I told Lev, your well-defined cheekbones and smile won't be enough," Wyatt states, and I twist my neck to look back in his direction before he continues. "You're going to need to let your guard down, or it will never happen. But, I have faith in all you idiots, or I wouldn't let you anywhere near her."

Then it's his turn to walk away and leave me to sulk.

Why does this shit have to be so fucking hard?

I stomp through the halls toward the bathroom, feeling my agitation with this situation mounting. Am I sorry for the way I treated Ariah when she first arrived? *Yes.* Was I a grade-A douche? *Also, yes.* But is that all I am? Why the fuck am I thinking about any of this shit? Oh, that's right— *her.*

Shoving the bathroom door open, I head straight for the sink. I need to wash my face and refocus. I'm too wound up. Thank fuck there's a game coming soon. I need an outlet for my frustration at everything.

Scooping water into my hands, I bend, letting the cold water cool my heated skin. My reflection catches my attention. Worry lines my brows. The deep set of them matching the tightness of my jaw. I scrub at the stubble as I exhale and take a deeper look in the mirror. *You did this idiot— now you need to fix it— no, you need to nurture it.* It's not going to be enough to just say I'm sorry. It's time to show her.

I run my hands through my hair as I trudge up the stairs. Between last night's game, the endless search for Madeline, and the dumbass date I had to go on earlier in the week, I'm fucking exhausted.

The memory of my date with Meagan's annoying ass makes my lip curl in disdain until I remember where I took her. My lips lift into a grin, remembering the look on her face when I had her meet me at the butcher shop. The dumb bitch thought we were just meeting there. The meltdown that ensued when she found out what we were doing was almost worth having to go out with her in the first place.

I mean, I thought what I chose was a great idea. Who doesn't like gutting pigs?

The fucking pretentious brat complained the whole damn time. It took all the fucking fun out of it. I almost turned around and sliced her down the middle.

I make my way over to my bed, throwing my phone on my nightstand as I lay down. Thoughts of her screams make my cock hard. I groan. *It's been too fucking long.* I feel my dick twitch in my basketball shorts. Sliding my palm under the elastic band, I dip my hand in my boxers and pull myself out. It's already leaking from the tip. Images of me inflicting pain morph into Ariah bent over with Wyatt's pierced cock rammed down her throat as Lola dips in and out of her drenched pussy. I wrap my hand over the tip, working my cum down my length as the scene plays out.

Why we can't just choose Ariah, marry her, and put some heirs in her belly now instead of drawing out the process with formalities, is beyond me.

The idea of Ariah stuffed with my cum to the point she gets knocked up makes my spine tingle.

"Fuck," I moan, gripping my shaft and squeezing until I feel the bite of pain. My hand moves up and down in slow strokes, pretending I'm deep inside my angel's sweet walls.

The buzzing of my phone halts my movements. Huffing, I reach for it on my nightstand, swearing at whoever is interrupting until I see my angel's name flash across the screen.

My Angel: Any chance you'll tell me where we're going later?

Me: Absolutely none

My Angel: You and Wy really suck. I hate surprises dammit.

Me: Too Bad Angel. I'll see you in a few hours.

My Angel: 🖕 🖕 🖕

Just as I'm about to place my phone on the bed and return to imagining pounding into Ariah, my phone buzzes again. This time it's a phone call. Hoping it's her giving me lip, I answer without looking.

"Eager to see me, Angel?" I tease.

A bass-filled chuckle hits my ears, making me pull the phone back to confirm who it is— Wyatt's name glows on the screen.

"I can't wait to see you, Schmuckems," he taunts, and I hear the others laughing with him in the background.

"Bite me. What do you assholes want?" I grumble.

"We might have a lead on Madeline. Get down here so we can go over some shit and move accordingly."

My gaze lands on my throbbing dick. *So much for finding relief.*

Sighing, I mumble, "A guy can't get five minutes to jerk himself off to thoughts of his girl. Fine, I'm on my way."

"How did you know?" Ariah asks. Her face filled with wonderment. "How could you possibly have known this?"

She stares down at her Oreo cookie milkshake with strawberry chunks, marshmallow and salted caramel sauce, and Bailey's Irish cream.

"A magician never reveals his secrets," I jest.

Rolling her eyes, she playfully pushes my shoulder and says, "Whatever, don't tell me then. Just know I'm on to you and Wy. Don't think I haven't figured out you all somehow know more about me than I've revealed. But I've decided to let you both be great."

I chuckle. *If only she knew the extent of it.*

We're sitting in the theater room in my house. Ariah loves books, fashion, music, comfort food, and movies.

The original plan was to take her to a red carpet movie premiere and have her meet some of her favorite stars, but after Summer's body was left to taunt her, we all agreed it would be best to keep our dates local.

So, since Plan A is no longer an option, I've settled on the next best thing— bringing the movies to her.

I've spent the last week having this room remodeled to offer the best accommodations. I swapped out the first two rows of traditional cinema recliners for a king-size obsidian tufted sofa bed covered in matching colored pillows and blankets. I had a Cretors T-

3000 popcorn maker brought in and stocked the snack bar with her favorite treats.

We've already watched *Pride & Prejudice* and *The Avengers*, but we needed a snack break.

I watch as her mouth wraps around the straw, her lips pucker as she hollows her cheeks to drink her shake. Her smoldering, pewter eyes take me in— enthralling me. I watch, frozen beside her, unable to do more than breathe as she pulls her mouth away and slowly laps the residual cream from her lips.

"See something you like?" she whispers, her voice sultry. The sound wrapping around my dick— turning my semi, hard.

"I'm trying to behave myself, Angel, but you're tempting fate," I groan.

"Fuck being good," she exclaims, reaching to put her drink on the side table before crawling across the bed. The top of her tank dips, exposing the tops of her tits.

Her intentions are made clear when she straddles my lap, grinding on my now rock hard erection.

"Fuck, Ariah. You're trying to kill me."

"Maybe a little," she confesses as she pulls her top over her head, exposing her sheer lavender bra. It's embroidered in lace around the top but leaves her rose-tipped nipples exposed.

My mouth salivates at the sight of her taking her pleasure. She rolls her hips, working herself into a frenzy.

"You look so fucking beautiful flushed and in control," I begin, then I grip the back of her neck and pull her in for a kiss. She tastes like strawberries and cream as our tongues fight for control. I let her have this moment, but tonight, control belongs to me. Flipping over, I place her on her back and then yank down her leggings. "But I'm in charge tonight," I growl.

I toss her pants and position myself over her, my hands on either side of her face, bending my elbows until my teeth nip her jaw.

"Are you going to be a good girl, Ariah?" I coax, biting my way down her neck until I reach what I want. Not waiting for her response, I suck her peaked nipple into my mouth through the fabric of her bra.

A whimpered, "Yessss," is all I hear before I brace on one forearm and reach in my back pocket for Lola.

Reluctantly, I pull my mouth away long enough to cut the center band of her bra, freeing her heavy tits.

Leaning back, I take in her sensual form. Ariah's whole body is tinted pink— her chest heaving and her lips already swollen from our earlier makeout session.

"You're wearing too many clothes, Owen," she breathily states.

Peering down, I nod in agreement before placing the knife down, pulling my hoodie over my head, and stepping off the bed to pull off my sweats.

"Better?" I smirk.

I watch her eyes rove down my naked body and then climb back in the bed, halting when her words from earlier replay in my mind.

'Until this bullshit twisted bridal hunt is over, you'll need to wear a condom.' Ariah was adamant about no glove, no love. Even after I told her no one was sleeping with any of the other girls. Her reply was about how many fucks she didn't give about our promises. 'A promise is a comfort to a fool,' were her words to end the discussion.

Reaching over, I grab the foil packets from my sweatpants pocket and drop them on the bed.

Ariah's approving smile eases something in my chest. I don't give a damn about the wants or needs of others. I'm typically single-minded in my focus until *her*. It wasn't instant. Sure, I wanted to fuck her, but the need to be anything she needed grew after seeing her at her strongest and weakest moments.

Climbing back on the bed, I position my head between her legs, spreading her open and lowering my mouth to cover her pussy.

"Shit," she shouts as my tongue darts in and out of her before gliding up to her clit. I insert thick fingers and feel her clench around them as my tongue curls around her peak and sucks.

I alternate between pumping and twisting my fingers, trying to get her ready for me, only adding another finger when I feel her hips moving in tandem. I know she's close when I hear her pants growing wilder and shorter. Renewed in my ministrations, I increase my pace and bite down on her clit just as she shatters— her juices leaking down my hand and the crack of her ass.

She's ready.

Rising off the bed, I rip a condom packet off and tear the foil with my teeth. She watches me with her heated gaze as I roll it on.

Once I'm positioned over her, I ask, "Are you sure you're ready to do this?" Everything in me hopes she doesn't say no. My dick is so hard I feel the pre-cum in the condom.

"Please," is her only response, and I position myself between her legs.

The crown of my cock pushes inside, her walls gripping me, preventing further progress.

My jaw tenses, easing back out. Even with all of our prepping, she's still not ready, but the feel of her around me is better than a scream of pain as my knife slices through flesh.

"Shit, Angel, you're so tight," I grunt.

She answers with a gasp, her mouth half open. She looks glorious. My eyes stop on her pouty lips before moving to her full hips— the site of them spread for me makes my cock jerk. Grabbing my shaft, I push back in her slowly, working my engorged head in and out of her.

Looking up from our connected bodies, I groan, "You're gonna let me in this tight cunt aren't you, Angel?"

She opens her legs wider, inviting me in.

Elated with her need matching mine, I pull out and quickly reposition myself over her. Bracing myself on my forearms, my hips slowly roll forward, feeding my dick inside— shallow thrusts allowing me to work deeper. Uncertainty stalls my pushing when she hisses. I don't want to hurt her— a feeling I'll have to process later.

She must feel my reluctance because her hand snaps up, grabbing my face to make me look into her eyes.

"Take it," she commands, and any hesitation I feel vanishes as I pull all the way out and thrust forward, driving deep inside her.

"Ooo-wennn," is all I hear her shout before I slam my cock in, pulling out to see her blood coating me.

"Fuck," I shout.

The site of her blood on my dick makes my erection pulse.

Pulling out, I slide down and cover her pussy with my mouth.

"Oh. Fuck. Shit. Holy." Her words, garbled and stuttered as I feast.

I reach for Lola and ease her in. "I told you I'd have your virgin blood on my knife," I groan, bringing the handle to my mouth, licking off the remainder of her blood before rising back over her and slamming in.

I hear the door creak, and I know my other surprise is here.

Without turning, I state, "You're just in time."

31
ARIAH

He's so fucking big. Each slam of his hips pushes him deeper.

"You look so good taking his dick, Love." The sound of Wyatt's voice pulls me from my lustful haze.

My gaze snaps right just as Owen's pace increases, his thrusts pistoning.

"W-w-yy," I moan, my voice choppy.

I watch as Wyatt climbs onto the bed, his hand cupping my breast and squeezing as Owen grips my hips and grinds into me.

"Ye-ee-ss," I scream. Owen's sudden shift causes him to brush against my clit.

Wyatt's face appears over me, lowering his lips to mine, enveloping me into a soul-wrenching kiss as he plucks my nipple as my hips lift to meet Owen's. The movement spurs Owen to slide halfway out and thrust deep, making my walls grip his cock each time my body lowers back on the bed.

"Ohhh, fuckkk! Are you trying to drain me before we've had our fill of you, Angel?" he asks. "Wy, she's wrapped around my dick so good right now. Her fucking pussy is like a vice."

Wyatt hums, nipping my lip before pulling away to climb off the bed and begin undressing. "We can't have that. Not for what we have planned," Wyatt's words make me clench in anticipation for what's coming.

The idea of living out a fantasy I've gotten myself off to has me lifting my hand to play with my nipple.

A hand yanks my arm over my head before I can touch myself.

"Your pleasure belongs to us tonight. The only ones making you come will be us. Don't touch what's not yours to take, Love," Wyatt commands.

I feel Owen slip out of me, and I whine in protest until I'm hoisted off the mattress and flipped to my stomach, his palm cracking me on my ass.

"Get your ass up here, Riah," Owen demands, and like the slut I am for them, I don't hesitate. I scramble up on all fours.

Owen's fingers trail up and down my spine before strong hands grab and squeeze the globes of my ass.

"Look how fucking amazing you look, Angel," Owen groans, pulling my cheeks apart as he slowly enters me from behind. "Fuck! I could live here forever," he mutters, sinking the rest of the way in. He feels even bigger from this angle. I can feel him everywhere. I feel the stretch as he pumps in and out at a steady pace. It's better than anything I've ever felt in my goddamn life. With the next snap of his hip, he bends over my back, grabbing a fist of hair, wrenching my head up with one hand as he pushes my chest toward the bed until I'm forced onto my forearms.

"Open that pretty mouth and get Wy ready for you," he coaxes, and my pussy flutters. This is like the other night but a million times better. This time I get to feel them both inside me. I can feel myself getting wetter at the idea.

"You like that, don't you, Love? The idea of both of us stuffing you full is making you hotter, isn't it? Is your pussy drenching Owen's dick right now? Are you picturing what it will feel like when it's more than just O and I?"

Wyatt's words make me spasm around Owen as I moan out just how fucking turned on I am at the prospect.

Lifting my eyes, I see Wyatt already positioned on his knees in front of me, his barbell-pierced cock hard and waiting. I want him. No, I fucking need him in my mouth now.

I open my mouth, lowering my head to his waiting tip when my forward progress is halted with a tug.

"Uh uh uhhh. I said open. I didn't say you'd be in control,"

I'm not sure what's about to happen, but I open my mouth, and Wyatt thrusts his hips forward, making me gag before he pumps out, giving me half a second to ready myself before his hips slam forward again. I feel the saliva dripping out of my mouth with each thrust.

Owen begins to match his pace, and I spasm around him. His grip on my hips tighten.

At this moment, I feel wholly and utterly owned.

"Look how fucking beautiful you look with your tight pussy and smart mouth filled with our dicks. I knew you'd be our good girl," Owen grunts as his thrusts increase, no longer matching Wyatt's, but never letting go of my hair.

His long deep strokes cause a squeal of pleasure to erupt from my mouth, and I moan around Wyatt's dick.

"Fucking shit! Keep that up— fuck! " Wyatt shouts, pulling out of my mouth completely. "No chance I'm coming in your mouth. I need to feel you around my dick."

I feel Owen loosen his grip on my hair and unseat himself from within me. The loss makes me feel empty, but he yanks my head back, lifting my body from my prone position until I'm flush against his hard chest as his still very erect length pokes against my ass.

"I'm going to love watching you take my friend deep into your tight snatch. I'm going to watch your pussy swallow every pierced inch of him until you feel him in your lungs."

Holy fuck. Why is that so hot?

Nodding, I whimper my excitement for what's to come. Owen turns my face so I can watch Wyatt lay back and slide on the condom. His muscled thighs flecked with freckles lay spread as his thick veiny cock bobs, waiting to feed my greedy cunt.

"Now, be a good girl and ride him," Owen instructs. My hair is still firmly in his hold, his body still pressed against mine as we both walk on our knees across the bed.

Wyatt rises slightly, resting on his elbows, groaning when my thighs spread to straddle him.

"Look at how wet she is, O. You're fucking soaked, Love," Wyatt groans, reaching forward and sliding two fingers inside, saturating them in my juices and bringing his hand back to his mouth and sucking off the evidence of my arousal on his tongue. "Mmhmm, you taste like sin."

Yup, I'm going to die right here.

I position myself over Wyatt when Owen grabs my waist with one hand, his other still fisted in my hair, and slowly lowers me, inch by inch, onto Wyatt's dick.

The stretch is different. Owen is thicker and longer, but the barbells create a different sensation, and as I'm lowered, my mouth falls open at just how different it feels.

Owen wraps a hand around me, his thumb and middle finger rolling my nipple as he lowers his mouth to my neck, sucking the skin between his teeth while Wyatt thrusts up to seat himself in me entirely, and I scream.

At first, I almost don't know what to do with myself, but Wyatt's hands grip my waist, controlling the pace until my hips begin to roll, grinding against him.

Owen releases his hold on my hair, and I feel the handle of his knife begin to rub against my clit.

My body hums at different points of stimulation, threatening to detonate, my hips bucking as Owen rubs steady circles and Wyatt deepens his strokes.

I spasm as my orgasm hits, my walls seizing.

"Oh fuck, Riri, you're going to kill me," Wyatt grits but doesn't stop. Instead, his pace increases. His thrusts pumping shallow and then deep. His hips circling before slamming back inside, and I feel myself winding up before I've even fully come down. I feel almost lightheaded.

I don't feel it when Owen removes the knife. I certainly don't remember when his body moved from behind mine. I just know I go from riding Wyatt to being slammed on the bed as Wyatt's hips buck inside me, his piercing gliding along my walls right as Owen straddles my chest, pushing his way into my mouth, and I open, welcoming him in. My tongue lapping at his crown before my lips wrap around his shaft, attempting to take some control back. I suck him in, spit escaping the corners of my mouth, running down my throat.

"God, Angel. How the fuck does your mouth feel like heaven, and your pussy feel like home," Owen grunts, his body jerking as ropes of cum shoot down my throat.

The fucker is still hard! I feel Owen's girth, thick and weighty, on my tongue, and my eyes open in shock. I thought guys were supposed to be all one nut and done, but when Owen pulls out, his dick looks like he hasn't come at all.

Noticing the expression on my, Owen smirks, reaching to grab another condom. I watch as he rolls it over his length before lowering to whisper in my ear, "We're just getting started, Angel."

My focus snaps from his when Wyatt slides his hand under my ass and pulls almost all the way out of me, then drives his hips deep, impaling me before pulling out and doing it again, making me grab the sheets on the bed for purchase. I scream when his fourth stroke hits so deep I think he's trying to write his name on my uterus. He pumps three more times before his movements become jerky. Then Wyatt pulls out, ripping off the condom.

"Open up, Love," Wyatt growls, pulling me forward until I'm back on my knees as he pushes into my waiting mouth as Owen thrusts back inside of me.

"Guys, why are neither one of you assholes answering your fucking ph-."

"Holy shit."

"Fuck!"

Three familiar and very distinct voices permeate the sex-fused air.

My eyes shift, taking in Sebastian, Wes and Lev's varying levels of shock and lust.

I should be some level of embarrassment, but I can't find it in me to care, not while Wyatt fills my mouth.

Let them watch.

My gaze somehow locks with Lev's, my eyes trailing down to see his hand wrapped firmly around his own dick. The iron grip his hand has on his shaft makes me think there's no way he can feel anything but pain, but when I peer into his green-flecked stare, I'm met with unadulterated heat and promise. Promise that if he ever gets his hands on me he'll bring me to heights I've never seen. It's that promise combined with Owen's brutal pace that has my mouth dropping open in a moan that can only be labeled as inhuman as my third orgasm rips through me and I detonate around Owen's cock with a force so immense it nearly blinds me.

Unintelligible cursing is the only thing I hear before Wyatt explodes down my throat and Owen's thrusts become jerky.

"Fuck. Fuck. Fuckkk," Owen shouts over the slapping of skin. His hold on my hips so tight, I know it'll bruise, but I'll fucking wear them like a badge of honor.

Labored breathing echoes throughout the room. Each of us panting, spent, and satisfied.

Awareness of the uninvited guests finally register, and my earlier bravado wanes. I go to pull away and cover myself but Owen holds me in place, a devilish smirk lines his satiated face. A look is exchanged between him and Wyatt, their eyes doing that silent communication thing I wish I could decipher.

Owen nods and Wyatt is the first to speak. "Our girl looks beautiful when she comes, doesn't she?"

My already flushed skin blooms eleven shades of red.

Three throats clear, but it's Sebastian who responds. "We have news. We'll wait for you upstairs." The three of them turn to leave, but not before they all peruse my body once more, their jaws clenching, and I swear I hear a mumbled, "I'm going to fucking kill Wy," before they finally make their exit.

Once we're alone again, Wyatt and Owen both pull out of me. Wyatt from my mouth, leaving a drop of his cum on my lips that I lick it off and Owen from my happily sore pussy.

Wyatt hops off the bed, and I turn, falling to my side.

Owen lands beside me and pulls me into his chest, brushing my hair off my sweaty face and kissing me on my forehead.

"You make the noise go silent," he says so quietly, I'm not sure I was supposed to hear at all. I'm about to ask what he means when I hear a door creak open and the sound of a shower turning on.

My gaze moves toward the direction of the sound in time to see Wyatt come from a room I didn't notice when I first arrived, holding a damp cloth.

"Let's get you wiped down and then you can shower while we go see what the fuss is and then we can finish this movie marathon," Owen states as Wyatt stands in front of me. He bends, spreading my legs and wiping the warm rag on my puffy lips, making me groan.

"Oh shit, I completely forgot we were watching movies. It's my turn to pick," I mumble. However, the idea of just closing my eyes and letting them rub me down has a far greater appeal. It's the last thought I have as my eyes shut.

32
SEBASTIAN

For fuck's sake! What was that? How did we— why did we? I can't even formulate the words for what I saw. She's breathtaking. The way her body looked as Wyatt and Owen worshiped her. I had to bite the inside of my cheek until it drew blood to keep myself from groaning. Shit, my dick is still hard in my pants.

"Was that?" Wes stutters, pacing the hallway upstairs.

"That was art. Living, breathing, art."

I look at Lev, his focus still focused on the door we just came through as he speaks.

"Why would Wyatt tell us to meet here if he knew— if he was going to-?" Wes still can't seem to formulate a cohesive thought.

Not that I blame him. I'd like to say I feel guilty for seeing Ariah like that, but I don't— conflicted, absolutely. I'm not supposed to want her. Yet every time I see her I feel myself being drawn closer and deeper, under some invisible spell. So, no I feel no guilt for seeing her sexy ass body being pleasured. I fucking wish it was me pleasuring her until her claw marks branded my back. But I'm not supposed to feel this way. I can't afford to.

"Because Wyatt is a schemer and in his mind, she's our end game," I state.

Stepping into my field of vision, Lev finally moves his attention from the basement. "Are you saying she isn't?" he queries, and there's a challenge in his tone.

Lev is now firmly in Team Ariah's camp. I'm not in or out of it. It's just great to see him fight his demons— I wish I could fight my own, but Lev deserves it. They all do. I would love to be a fly on the wall in the room when he gets her alone. Lev doesn't like being touched and to say his tastes are far from vanilla would be putting it lightly.

It's not like the knives or blood that Owen likes to play with or the way Wes thrives off degrading his bed buddies— it's psychological. Lev likes to play with his food before he eats it.

My dick hardens at the thought of Ariah wrapped in ropes and blindfolded after she was hunted down. It's not my usual taste, but I can understand the appeal.

I raise my hand to rub at my nose, trying to clear my mind of my lustful thoughts and answer Lev's question.

"I'm not saying that Lev. Shit if it would make this sham of a Selection end, I'd put the ring on her myself," I utter. My words are truthful, but whether it's because I want this to be over or because I genuinely love the idea of our little spitfire wearing our ring is still up for debate.

"You fucks are lucky you got to experience any of her while you're not in her good graces," Wyatt states.

We turn to see he and Owen have finally graced us with their presence.

"Why did you let us?" Wes mutters, his body rigid.

Wyatt shakes his head like Wes's question is idiotic. "It was our girl's first time, and I didn't want you assholes to miss the moment. You fucks were late though."

Lev chimes in, "How do you know she wanted us there? She loathes Wes and me."

This time it's Owen who responds, his derisive snort affirming he also thinks we're dumb. "Our girl is a bit of an exhibitionist. One that likes to be watched and gets extremely wet at the prospect of us filling all of her holes."

I was not expecting that.

"But she loathes Wes and me," Lev states, emphatically. His dark brows pinched tight in confusion. Wonderment at the idea that she could want us and equally despise us.

He should know confliction— it runs rampant in all of us. Especially Wes, Lev, and me as it pertains to a certain midnight-blue-haired siren.

"Well, she'd loathe you both less if you'd get your acts together," Wyatt grumbles. "Now, what's the news so we can get back downstairs?"

"We need a place to talk," Lev starts. "My house would've been preferred for this, but you assholes wouldn't answer."

Owen claps Lev's shoulder, "As you saw, we were busy with someone important."

"We have something, and we can't discuss it all here."

Owen nods, "Okay, let me bring Ariah upstairs to my room, and let Thomas know we're leaving."

"So much for movie night," Wyatt mutters, walking past us back toward the movie room.

"Do you think they did it on purpose?" Wes asks. His head is bent as he rubs his face with his hands.

Sighing, Lev shakes his head, "It looks that way. At least for the last two years."

"Did they know about the Lydia and Madeline switch?" Wyatt asks.

"No. From everything I've been able to find, the Filiae Bellonae snuck in Madeline right under our noses, with Lydia being adopted."

My mind is reeling from the information we've gathered. We've all known that the Fraternitas has a long history, and as we recently discovered, there's been a counter organization in existence working to take over for just as long.

The Council, however, has known longer than they let on and based on what we've discovered, they've known Aaron Bishop was married to a usurper for at least the last two years. The question here is, did they know before Aaron married her and pawned him, or did they discover it after and decide it was worth risking the last known Bradfords?

"We need to know more. I can't imagine they'd go through all of the trouble of hiding Aaron, only to sacrifice him and then his heirs," I state.

Wes stands, vacating his spot around the table to grab a bottle of water. He turns, holding it out in question to see if anyone wants one.

"Just bring over a few," Wyatt suggests.

My focus returns to the screen. Lev has more archived files up, and the number of people he's been able to link to the Filiae Bellonae is mind-blowing. We knew about Pamela and Madeline, but the police chief's wife and at least three members of our security teams were discovered.

"Does Thomas know his ranks have been compromised?" I ask.

I know he'll be pissed if he doesn't know already.

Lev brings up another image before he begins, "Considering the three were on Summer's detail, my guess is he has some idea, but he'll be updated."

Well, at least now we know it wasn't a coincidence that Summer was able to convince her detail to let her go in for a wax without them.

"We've been living in a cesspool of snakes," Owen growls, fiddling with a knife I'm not used to seeing.

Titling my chin, I say, "No Lola?"

His face immediately loses the scowl— his mouth quirks up into a shit-eating grin. "Lola will never touch the skin of anyone but my Angel's— her blood is the only one worthy of Lola."

Without any further response, he turns back to the group discussion.

Crazy fucker. It wouldn't surprise me if he already carved his name into Ariah's skin.

"The real question is do we bring this information to the Council or keep it to ourselves?" Wes voices what I'm sure we've all been internally contemplating.

I look around the room, trying to guess who will be the first to offer up an opinion, but we're interrupted by Lev's computer notification.

He clicks some keys and whatever he's reading has his eyes lighting with excitement and an uncharacteristic smile grace his face.

"What is it?" I probe, hoping that something good is happening for once.

"We have a lead on Madeline."

Fucking finally.

33
ARIAH

"God, this is long overdue," Shay moans from her table.

We're having a spa day.

"Mmhm," I sigh in agreement as hands knead my lower back.

After my night with Owen and Wyatt two days ago, this is blissful. My body hums, tightening at the remembrance of how they cared for me once they returned from wherever they went with the rest of the guys. Wyatt's hands massaged my temples as Owen's worked at my instep. It was fucking glorious. Especially when it went from touching my feet with his hands to eating me like he was a man on death row and I was his last meal.

"Please relax, Miss," the masseuse instructs, "I'll be able to work out your knots if you're relaxed."

Shay turns in my direction at the sound of the woman's voice.

"What has you tightening instead of being a pool of goo under Ana's hands? She's amazing. If I weren't trying to get you to come back with me, I would've snatched her up."

I could feel the heat rise, flushing my cheeks. I hadn't meant for my thoughts to bring this much attention to me.

"Oh, Riri's been up to something, or should I say under someone?" Shay jokes.

That makes me snort, "Maybe."

A knowing smirk lines her face, her gap-toothed smile on full
display. "Spill it. You have the face of someone who's finally been
laid."

"Shay," I admonish.

She waves me off, earning her a gentle reminder to keep still
from her masseuse. "They'll be fine. You tell me which one popped
that cherry, bitch."

My eyes bulge as I burst out into laughter, causing Ana to stop
massaging my back.

"Ladies, please give us the room. I promise we'll be on our best
behavior when you come back," Shay promises. Both women exit the
room, and she wastes no time bombarding me with questions. "Who
was it? How was it and have you done it again? It was Wyatt, wasn't
it? That man's been obsessed with you the moment your thick ass
stepped out of your car."

I sit up, wrapping the towel around me as I speak, "Girl. Slow
down and take a breath. Plus, who said anything about it only being
just one?"

The squealing gasp that she lets out makes me fold as cackles
escape me.

"You lucky bitch. Two, as in t-w-o? Fuck! I need all the details,
don't skip a single thing," she demands.

By the time I'm finished giving her some of the details, because
there's no chance I'm telling her everything they said, or the fact that
Wes, Lev, and Sebastian walked in on us, she's stunned silent. I have
to look up and see if my friend is still with me.

"Damn." She fans herself. "I think I need to call Brendan. I
wonder if he'd be opposed to me adding some more men."

I shake. "You know that man isn't going to share you. There's not
a chance."

"Ugh. You're right. He barely wants me out of his sight." She harrumphs, making me giggle. "Don't laugh at my pain, bitch. Just know I'm living through you. So when are *we* getting more D?"

I roll my eyes, "Absolutely not. You're not getting me in trouble. There will be no we in this, only an I."

"Selfishness," she mutters before laughing. "Fine. Just know I'm docking fifteen friend points from you."

I snort. "Whatever, ho, you love me. Now let's finish up so we can grab Jamie and get her nails done."

The aroma of the food in front of me makes my mouth water. Once we finished at the spa, we grabbed Jamie and went to the nail salon. Now we're grabbing lunch at the diner.

"How's the party planning going?" Shay asks.

Jamie's head pops up from the food she was drooling over. "What party? Can I come?"

"This is a fundraiser. The party for Christmas is now a dinner at Wy's house. And both are going about as well as anything can go when you have to plan it with Samantha and plebs," I mumble, reaching for my fork to begin chowing down on my chicken, shrimp, and broccoli Alfredo. Before I take a bite, I answer Jamie's question. "You'll be at the dinner but not the fundraiser. That's a black-tie, adults-only kind of event."

Jamie's eyes fill with excitement. "Finally. All the kids at school talk about the parties thrown in this town and how much fun they are, even for the kids."

"She's right. They hire a whole team of people to make sure whatever kids attend have a blast. Especially the Christmas dinner. Last year they made a winter wonderland indoor playscape that looked like walking into a snow globe," Shay explains.

Jamie squeaks, clapping her hands together.

This is how it should be. She's finally just being a kid, excited at the prospect of a party where she can play and be with her friends.

"Ky and Kell are going to flip when they find out about this," she exclaims, bouncing in her seat. All thoughts of the tenders and fries gone.

"How's school?" I ask. It's been a while since we've sat down and talked.

She plucks a fry from her plate, popping it in her mouth and chewing before she answers. "Amazing, but weird. Like ever since you got picked or whatever, everyone's tried to be my friend. But I don't pay them any mind. They weren't shooting with me in the gym."

Shay chokes on her drink and quickly picks up a napkin to wipe the excess soda from her chin. "What do you know about that?"

Jamie picks up another fry and shrugs. "I'm just saying that none of them were trying to talk to me when I first moved here. I'm only hanging with my day-one friends. Not the ones who want to be my friend because my sister got picked to play some weird game."

"How do you know what's going on?" I probe. I haven't mentioned anything outside of why we had to move. I didn't want them to know about the Selection.

"I'm not an idiot, Ry. We moved into some mansion out of nowhere. Then everyone at school kept talking about the heirs picking their choices for a wife. And poof, those same heirs are always around. Especially that red-headed one." She pauses. "I like him best, by the way. If you have to pick one, make sure it's him and not the broody one who walks around like he has a stick up his butt."

I wonder which one it could be. It sounds a lot like Lev or Wes.

Shay voices my question. "Which one is that? Long hair or short hair?"

"The one with the short black hair," Jamie replies, then returns her focus to finishing her food.

Wes. I snort. He definitely is a broody asshole. Lately, however, he's been a bit nicer. He and Lev. They both have tried talking to me, or I catch them staring, especially Lev.

The look in his eyes when Owen was inside of me is definitely what I used to get off in the shower this morning.

"Ouch!" I shout, rubbing my shin with the back of my calf. "What was that for?"

"For the look on your face. Not in front of the kid," Shay teases.

I cover my face with my hands. I know I'm beet red.

"No need to hide on my account. It's not like I haven't seen the look on her face before. She gets it whenever she's thinking about one of the heirs," Jamie confesses, and I want to slide under the table and hide.

"Eat your damn food so we can go," I mutter, and Shay cackles.

Turning to Shay, I say, "Traitor. I'm deducting fifty points from your friendship points," as I join her in laughing.

"You two are weird," Jamie states, lifting her drink to her lips.

"Better to be weird than to be boring," I rib before finally diving into my food.

We spend the remainder of the meal joking and discussing the upcoming holidays. This is exactly what I needed. Just a day with my girl to relax and forget for a moment that shit is still on the horizon.

34
LEV

"You really should just keep me on the Fraternitas payroll, you know that, right?" Colt jokes.

"Right, because the Jacobis are so hard up for cash," I retort, making him laugh.

Colter Jacobi isn't what I'd call a nice guy— fuck, he and his twin, Cooper, aren't even in the same stratosphere as the word nice, but they know their shit.

I've been working on this lead for the last few days, ever since that night.

I grit my teeth at the memory of Ariah between Owen and Wyatt. *Fuck, my dick is going to fall off at this rate.*

The lead on Madeline was a dead end, but it did get us a lead I've been working on for far longer.

Colt's question jolts me back into the conversation. "Are you going to be at the big Groveton versus Lincoln-Wood game this year? You know that shit is going to be epic, and the parties are going to be even wilder," he asks as his fingers fly across his keyboard.

I shake my head, "No, we're not making it to Texas this year, not with all the bullshit going on here. When we're at LWU next fall, we'll definitely be on the field to kick your asses."

That makes the psycho fucker cackle. "Right. Did you forget GU is literally number one in the nation? I mean, LWU is a close second, but..." he trails off.

I stick my middle finger up at the screen. I'm on track to leading Edgewood to its fourth undefeated season as quarterback. "Whatever fucker. Were you able to find anything new?"

He and Coop have been working on helping me locate the bitch ass motherfuckers that attempted to kidnap me, and successfully kidnapped Owen, five years ago.

"Yeah, hold on, I'm sending you over a file I got from King."

"Vasyl?" I question, and he nods, confirming it is indeed the crazy Bratva fuck.

My computer pings.

"Viktor and Aleksi Lenkov. Bottom feeders of the sex trafficking world. Viktor was killed two years ago, but Aleksi is hiding out in upstate New York close to the Canadian border. We still can't find this Elena chick, but we'll keep digging," Colt states, reading off the rest of the information I've been searching for, for the last two years.

I snort at the irony that the brothers' surname means defender of men. Too bad there will be no one to defend Aleksi from me—his brother escaped his fate by dying. He's lucky I don't find his grave and piss on it. Hell, after I question and kill his brother, I might do just that.

Colter interrupts my sadistic thoughts with his own favor. "Okay, is everything set for Eva Rose?"

I hit a few keys and his computer dings.

"Yup, Eva will be attending Groveton next fall," I announce.

His crystal-blue eyes darken, and the danger in their depths jumps to the surface. "Perfect. Thanks, Lev. It's always a pleasure doing business with you," he says before his screen cuts out.

The look of malice and utter glee that crossed Colt's face almost makes me feel bad for Eva— *almost.*

I pick up my phone and scroll, hitting call when I find his name.

"This better be good. I'm with our girl." His tone is lighthearted. Guilt tugs in my gut— knowing my next words will eviscerate that feeling.

"I found them," is all I say. He'll know exactly who I'm referring to. Ever since that day in the car, he's known I've been searching.

"Fuck! When?" he asks, his joking demeanor vanishing.

"King is on it. He'll be here within a day."

The line goes silent. I have to pull the phone from my ear to make sure it's still connected.

"I'll be there," Owen states and disconnects the call.

I watch on my screen as the slumped form of Lenkov is carried in a body bag through the service elevator of the Tombs.

"Is-is that really him?" Owen questions.

"Yes, that's the fucker.

I turn to my friend— my brother and see a sheen of sweat beading on his forehead.

"O," I start, "if this is too much for you, I go-."

He cuts me off. "I'm fucking fine. There's not a chance in hell I'd miss this opportunity," he snaps.

I know his anger isn't at me— it's at the sick twisted dead man walking or, in this case, being carried.

The unknown of what they did to him sets my teeth on edge. I keep replaying the events of that day over and over. Was there something I could've done differently? Why did we follow Sam outside? How come it took so long for someone to find him? Should I have fought harder? The questions play on an endless loop in my mind, and as I take in the rigid posture of Owen— I wish for the umpteenth time it was me instead of him that stayed behind that day.

The door slides open, and King steps through, two of his men trailing behind him carrying the body-sized bag containing Aleksi.

"Privet, droog moy. It's good to see you again," King says, his Russian accent heavy as he extends his hand in greeting, and I return the gesture.

We aren't friends, but we aren't enemies either. I'm just not telling this disturbed fuck that.

King is a ruthless bastard. After he was almost killed by his uncle in order to take his spot for Pakhan, he moved to America to start over. Now he's built one of the largest Bratvas stateside.

"King," I reply, nodding my head in Owen's direction. "You remember Owen."

He steps back, exposing his massive wolf throat tattoo. Its open maw spans the entirety of his neck, the upper teeth lining King's jaw, with the canines dripping in blood like the wolf just had a fresh kill. It's often the last thing his victims see before their end. King jokes that he has to feed his beast before a kill.

King turns to greet Owen, "Of course, I do. Good to see you again."

"You too," Owen responds, the earlier strain in his voice gone, but when I look at him, I can see him fighting to keep it together.

I turn to watch as King's calculating electric-blue eyes study Owen, his jaw flexing, trying to determine if he's friend or foe.

A loud thud shifts my attention to where his men have dropped Aleksi to the table.

King clears his throat, refocusing my attention on him as he adjusts the sleeve of his black shirt before running his hands through his inky-black hair. "I brought the fucking mudak. He thought he was safe behind his gates— it took me five minutes to get in and tranq the bitch," he boasts. "So much for quality security measures."

Owen snorts. "His fuck up is our party." His statement makes King laugh.

King claps his hands together once, and states, "I'll leave you both to it then. It's always a pleasure doing business with you, Levi.

Until next time." Then he and his men exit the same way they entered.

Once the door slides closed, Owen and I stand there and just look at the unmoving form still zipped in the bag. Neither one of us moves.

I'm not sure how long we've been standing here before I finally speak. "How do you want to do this?"

"Let's do to him what he and his fucked up brother did to me," Owen grits through clenched teeth.

I close my eyes. He's never told a soul what happened to him there. We know it was horrific based on the state he was in when he came back. His whole body was battered and bruised, dried blood was still caked to his skin, and the number of stitches he needed only began to tell the story of what Owen faced.

"Are you sure?" I ask, trying to gauge his temperament. I don't want him to have to relive his abuse unless he's ready.

Cold eyes meet mine— Owen isn't here anymore— his monster is firmly in place, ready to dole out justice that's long overdue.

He doesn't respond. He simply walks to the wall and pushes the button that lowers the St. Andrews cross, then heads for the closet to gather the appropriate tools.

While he's gone, I make my way to the table Aleksi lays on and begin to unzip the bag. My hands freeze when his face comes into view. His hard features are still apparent in his sedated state.

The face of the man who grabbed me makes my heart stop in my chest. I stare at the scar that's haunted my dreams. A long jagged line cuts diagonally across his otherwise normal face.

I'd like to know the person that put the scar there. I want to ask them why they didn't just stab him in the eye and kill him instead.

"We need to wake him up and question him," I state while I lean over and hoist Aleksi over my shoulder. His body being in close proximity to mine, even for this, makes me feel like a thousand fire ants are crawling on my skin.

I briefly wonder if Ariah will ever be able to touch me or if my aversion to touch will forever haunt me.

Clearing my mind of those thoughts, I quickly make my way to the chair and zip-tie him. His head still lolls to the side.

It's time for sleeping beauty to wake the fuck up and realize there's no handsome prince or a happily ever after for him.

I walk to the table and pick up my brass knuckles. The skulls between each groove should have the maximum impact necessary to wake his bitch ass up.

By the time I've returned, Owen is back with some tools of his own—the knife he used to interrogate Glen because Lola's officially retired, a bone saw, and pliers.

"I thought we'd start off easy since we need him alive for this part," he suggests, and a small smirk finally graces his face.

Returning his smile with one of my own, I slide the brass knuckles over my fingers, flexing them before I form a fist. I turn, pulling my arm back, and launch a punch straight to a still, very unaware Aleksi's solar plexus.

He gasps awake, cursing in Russian, his face swiveling side to side as he tries to make sense of where he is. But fuck his awareness. I rear back and launch another hit, this time an uppercut to his chin. Blood spurts from his mouth as he screams. A piece of flesh falls from his mouth, along with at least two teeth.

"The stupid fuck bit off the tip of his tongue," Owen snickers.

Aleksi spits the excess blood at our feet, and Owen punches him in the nose. The resounding crack of bone indicates it's broken.

"You're going to answer our questions, or things are going to get progressively worse really quickly," I inform him, and he throws his head back and laughs.

"You fucking kids want to play big bad men? Do you even have chest hair?" He taunts, and Owen launches at him, grabbing his already broken nose and squeezing, making Aleksi holler in pain.

"Not so funny now, you dumb fucking rapist dick," he screams, pulling his knife to drag across the other side of Aleksi's face. "Now your ugly can match."

Aleksi squints. Blood drips down into his eyes as the recognition of who we are finally registers. He smiles. "Oh, it's you. Were they ever able to stitch you up? By the time we were done with you, that asshole was a little loose. Your little dick was nice and hard after Elena rode you. You should be proud to have lost your virginity to someone like her. We made a man out of you."

My vision blinks out, and my heart pounds in my ears. I bite my cheek so hard to prevent the scream that wants to rip out of my chest. I never saw Elena, and Owen doesn't talk about that day— ever.

"What the fuck did you just say?" My voice sounds far off.

Aleksi's laugh taunts me, propelling me back to that day. It's the same scene on a loop.

I'm outside the school, being dragged by my arm. They're pulling me toward the black car, and they have a gun to Owen's skull.

"Stop! Stop!" I shout, but it's too late. We're both in the backseat of the car, and Owen's crying.

"Shh, we have to think. What did our dads say to do?" I whisper.

"If it's safe, try to escape, even if only one of us gets away," he sniffles.

Then I'm looking out the window, and as soon as an opportunity presented itself, I dove from the car. My hand reaches up, grabbing the phantom spot my tattoo now covers before reaching for my hair and yanking.

Why didn't I do more? I failed him, and he suffered.

A hand jolts me from the oppressive memories.

"It wasn't your fault. I never blamed you— I never will. If you didn't get out, who knows when and if they would've found us," Owen declares, gripping my shoulder and turning me until I stare into his amber eyes. "I'm not going to bullshit you and say I'm fine, but killing this fuck will do a great deal in helping me close that chapter, and I'm able to do that because of you."

A snort pulls our attention, and both of us turn to Aleksi. "Aww, couple's therapy, how nice. I want you to know I was there first, and it was nice and tight before I was through— his blood made for nice lube. Didn't it, *O?*" he mocks.

Fuck this. He dies now. I want answers on Madeline's location, but I want retribution more.

Pulling my fist back, I land three quick jabs to his temple, and his head slumps forward.

Perfect. Now we can move the sick bastard without him putting up a fight.

Owen's footsteps stop next to me. "Let's fucking do this."

35
OWEN

I stride toward the closet while Lev cuts his bindings. I need more supplies for what I plan on doing. We can ask the prick more questions after I make him feel what I felt— if he's coherent or alive enough to speak.

The hurt on Lev's face gave me the ability to squash my spiral. He's always holding in so much guilt— letting it eat at him. We were ten. There was nothing he would've been able to do if he'd stayed. Fuck, they might have killed one of us if they had the option of two heirs instead of only one.

Before I open the closet door, I push the button to lower the cross, so it's easier to tie Aleksi to it. Nothing here will be consensual — it wasn't when they had me. Consent can go fuck itself.

Opening the door, I grab three things— Wyatt's favorite whip, the one studded with nails and shards of glass, a metal pipe, and a tactical knife.

Lev's eyes pop, shocked at all the tools. His eyebrows furrow, and a crease forms on his forehead.

I see the moment his mind tries to reconcile what I've brought with whatever hellscape I endured, but I can't bring myself to answer him. I've never shared the details of all that transpired—of how I got hard when that woman put her mouth on me, or... how... I came when they took turns.

Inhaling, I shut my eyes, trying not to lose myself to the monsters — trying to ground myself in the fact that I survived and that an erection is not consent. That coming doesn't make me dirty.

I don't answer Lev's question when I open my eyes. Instead, I say, "Some of it is to return the favor tenfold."

And it's true. They beat me bloody, but not with anything like Wyatt's whip. They threatened me with knives but never used them, and they never touched me with a pipe. But I'm going to fuck Aleksi's whole existence up with this one.

I pick up the whip and ready myself, not waiting for Aleksi to wake.

"Wait!" Lev shouts. "He doesn't deserve to be asleep during any of this." He walks over to the table and picks up a syringe. Then he stabs Aleksi in his thigh and states, "Epinephrine and norepinephrine. This will keep him awake."

Lev stands back when he sees my arm rise, and I sail the whip through the air. The sound it makes when it connects with bare skin shoots straight to my cock.

Shouts of pain sing in the air, but it's the sounds of breaking flesh that make me smile.

I whir the whip, no pause between strikes. Rage engulfs my blood. Years of anguish and hidden shame fuel me. I watch as blood and chunks of skin fall to the floor.

It wasn't my fault— *crack*. I couldn't fight my body— *crack*. I didn't want it— *crack*.

Aleksi's screams aren't enough— his pain is not enough.

I sail the whip through the air again and again, but it's still not e-fucking-nough.

Growling out my frustration, I drop the whip to the ground, deciding I need to inflict more pain.

I reach over and grab the pipe. Then I hold it and swing for his ribs.

In the back of my mind, I know someone else has joined, but I'm drowning in anger. I don't know who it is until they speak.

"How long has he been here?" I hear my father ask.

"Almost two hours," Lev answers.

I should've known there was no way my kidnapper would be brought in and he not hear about it. But he's not my focus. My resentment towards him feeds my monster's need for more.

My arm rotates to swing when a hand shoots out and clasps my shoulder.

"Wait, let's see if he's willing to talk yet," Lev suggests, causing me to glare in his direction.

I fucking hate it when he's the voice of reason.

Pulling out of his grip, I mumble, "Fine."

Lev walks to the table and grabs the salt. An evil grin grows on his face as he pours a handful into his palm.

"I said question him, not a give him a break— I'm not fucking a saint," he jokes, walking over to Aleksi and slapping his hand into an open wound on his back.

I watch in satisfaction as Aleksi thrashes against his restraints.

"Where is she?" I yell, but Aleksi doesn't answer.

Lev pours another handful of salt into his hand. This time he rubs it into the chunk missing from his side.

"Where the fuck is Madeline?" Lev snaps. "I know she hired you and your brother to take us that day. So, let's cut the bullshit runaround."

Aleksi curses in Russian before responding in English, "I won't tell you little shits anything. You're nothing compared to the wrath of those fucking women."

To my shock, I watch as my dad grabs the knife from the table and shoves the blade between Aleksi's ribs. "There won't be anything left of you to be afraid. So answer the fucking question and pray to whatever higher power because it's the Fraternitas you're dealing with and not *those women*."

My father steps back. I take that as my cue and swing with such force that I hear it when the bones in his ribs snap.

"Shit! Make him stop," Aleksi begs between ragged breaths.

Lev snatches the hammer and slams it against his bound wrist. "Fuck your pleas. Answer the goddamn question," he snarls, then spits in Aleksi's face.

"Please," the bitch cries again.

"Answer the fucking question," I command.

Aleksi grunts and Lev holds up his hand, signaling me to hold.

"Okay. Okay, I'll tell you," he begins, and we wait. "Where I'm going to shove my dick once I get my hands on that stupid Bradford bitch. I've seen pictures of her. That fat ass of hers will look good stuffed with my cock. Just like yours did. How does it feel to fuck both mother and daughter?" He laughs.

Gasps sound, but I'm too fucking stunned to speak. Elena is Elise? My brain is trying to compute his last words. I never saw the woman's face. I can barely remember her voice.

I turn to stone. Hearing the recounting of everything that happened and the shock of who Elena is was enough to make me see red, but the mention of Ariah—I black out.

Lunging forward, I kneel on the ground, pull my arm back, and shove the metal pipe up his ass at full force.

Aleksi's screams make me groan, and bile fills my throat, but I don't stop. Instead, I impale Aleksi repeatedly with the pipe, driving it violently in and out of his ass.

"How does it feel now fucker? Nice and open for me, aren't you? You like feeling my big metal pipe ripping you open," I choke out. Visions of me being sodomized loop. "Y-y-you like that, d-don't you?" I mumble aloud, mimicking their words to me as I pump my arm up and down, and push the pipe in and out.

Aleksi's screams reverberate off the walls. He begs for mercy— promises to tell us all we want to know, but the time for talking is over. He foolishly hit a tripwire he didn't realize had more dire consequences than taunting me with what they did.

He mentioned *her*.

Over my words, I swear I hear Aleksi shout, "Madeline is hiding in plain sight," just as I ram the pipe so far inside him, my fist disappears, and Aleksi passes out.

"Take that, you rapist piece of shit! You'll never get anywhere near my angel now," I cry, ripping my hand from Aleksi's ass and falling to the floor. The bloodied pipe slips from my hold, rolling across the room until it's stopped by a wall.

Like a wild animal mourning the loss of its young, a sob erupts from me, filling the room. "I told them I'd get them back, and they didn't believe me," I ramble, grabbing my knees and rocking myself — reminiscent of my time in captivity.

I don't hear it when my father approaches. I only feel him wrap his arms around me. I jump at his initial touch before finally resting my face on his chest and sobbing— sobbing for the boy who's finally gotten justice.

"You got him, and I won't stop until we get her," my father whispers, kissing the top of my head.

I don't move— letting the man I've been so angry with comfort me for the first time since coming home. I've missed him. I didn't realize how much until just now.

I'm not sure how long I lay in my father's arms battling the demons before Lev says, "Go to her— go see Ariah."

That prompts me to move, and for the first time, my lungs feel like they can take a full breath.

My father eases back, his matching gaze peering into mine. No words are spoken, but so much is said. We're nowhere near where we used to be, but it's a step in the right direction. He helps me stand as Lev comes up next to us.

"I'll clean this up. Go see *our girl*," he demands, making me smile.

He's finally getting it.

I watch Lev walk toward the table, picking up another syringe before going to a still passed-out Aleksi. He deserves a far more agonizing death, but I'm sure whatever Lev has in that needle won't give him a peaceful end.

Now it's time to see the only person who can tame the monsters.

My feet move on autopilot. I'm in my car and have it started, peeling out of the driveway.

She can never find out. Ariah will be destroyed if she ever knew how truly twisted her mother is. I would never allow her to feel that pain.

I feel my stomach churn— memories flooding me.

"Such a good boy. The plans I have for you and the rest of the heirs are only just beginning," the woman's voice coos as her fingers trail up my exposed stomach.

Why won't she stop touching me?

The flashback causes me to swerve to the side of the road, slam the car into park, throw my door open, and jump out just as the bile rises. I heave the contents of my stomach outside.

It was better when I didn't know.

A scream rips from my lungs, my hands pulling at my hair.

Why did it have to happen? I want to say why me, but I'd never wish for it to be any of my friends— *brothers* either.

I feel the tears flowing down my face, the air of the night suffocating as it brushes against them. I need to get the fuck out of here. *She's waiting for me.*

Squeezing my eyes shut, I take a moment to catch my breath, then lift my body back into the car, grab a towel from the back, wipe my mouth, and shift my car back onto the road.

All the years of wondering— now I wish I still was in the dark.

By the time I look up, I'm in my driveway, with no recollection of how I got there. My mind is still buzzing— my skin still alight. I wish I could bring Aleksi back to life and use my knives this time. Shove one right into the tip of his dick.

I push my door open, staggering my way through the house and up the stairs to my room. The room is dark, illuminated only by the television. I step through the door—my eyes laser in on the perfect form on my bed, and for the first time in the last few hours, I breathe.

Ariah lies sprawled across my sheets, the blanket covering her legs, leaving the sight of her voluptuous ass on full display. My eyes travel up her body as I walk completely into the room. I have to bite my lip to hold in my groan at the sight of her in one of my tee shirts. *Fuck she's a vision.*

I make my way to the bathroom to shower. I can't climb into bed with this scum's blood on me.

Once the hot water beats against my back, the adrenaline that keyed me up dissipates, and I can feel my body getting sluggish, but I thoroughly scrub my body and wash my hair, and brush my teeth before exiting the shower and making my way over to the bed after I've dried off.

I pull the covers down and climb into bed, sliding up behind Ariah, wrapping my arm around her body, and pulling her into me.

"You're back," she mumbles, sleepily.

"I am."

"Good," she murmurs, and then her breaths even out as she falls back to sleep.

I lower my head until my mouth presses to her neck, planting a light kiss and inhaling her calming scent.

Finally, it's quiet.

Peace—is my last thought as my eyes close, and the dreams that normally haunt me are nowhere to be found.

36
ARIAH

A masculine spice hits my nose, and I immediately wake up. I'm enveloped in the warmth of two massive arms. My cheek is pressed to Owen's chest. I'm completely cocooned.

I could stay like this forever, but my bladder is a second away from reverting me into a potty-training toddler.

Pulling out of Owen's warmth, I climb out of his bed, groaning at the delicious ache between my thighs, and rush to the bathroom, making it just in time not to embarrass myself.

Once I've finished and flushed the toilet, I stand in front of his expansive mirror, staring at my disheveled state.

I turn on the faucet to wash my hands and look for toothpaste. There's no way I'm climbing back in that bed with morning breath. I don't want to be nosey, but I need at least some mouthwash, dammit.

My eyes lock on the spot Wyatt and Owen devoured me the last time I was in his bathroom. Heat rises in my cheeks as butterflies stir in my stomach. *I wonder when we can repeat that?*

I finally spot the fancy ass opening and press it open. I find mouthwash and two motorized toothbrushes. The one that's been used is obviously Owen's, and another is still in its box. A spare, maybe? Snatching it, I decide to brush my teeth. I can always replace it.

"Angel, get your fine ass out of that bathroom. I don't give a fuck about morning breath," Owen shouts from the other room, sounding like he's still in bed.

Walking to the door, I lean against it and mumble around the toothbrush, "I'm not kissing you with stale breath."

Owen smirks, lowering the covers and slowly exposing his tattooed-rippled abs two packs at a time. *Fuck!*

"You got a little something there on your chin," he teases.

I lift my hand, and sure enough, I've freaking dribbled toothpaste foam.

"That's because I should be doing this over the sink," I argue, turning and walking back into the bathroom to finish brushing.

I make it five steps inside before I'm scooped off the ground and planted on the countertop.

The way he and Wyatt are always manhandling me lets me know they don't skip leg days. At two-hundred and sixty-three pounds, I'm no lightweight.

Owen's hand grabs the toothbrush and begins to brush my teeth. My jaw drops open, not to give him better access, but in shock.

"Yuh knuh I cahn duh fis muhshelf," I garble over the motor.

His soft hazel eyes meet mine. "Let me take care of you. I like it. I've never wanted to care for anyone before—let me have this."

So, I sit and let him have this moment.

Once he's done and I've rinsed my mouth, he lifts me back off the counter and places me on the floor, smacking my ass as he reaches around to brush his own teeth.

I watch his biceps flex with each pass of the toothbrush, highlighting the reaper in his sleeve tattoo. The scythe looks almost real, like it would harvest my soul if it touched me. I'm so transfixed I don't notice when he finishes until his hands capture my face, pulling me in for a kiss.

Lust swirls in my body, firing a jolt straight to my pussy with the way his hands are gripping me. They move from my face into my hair and then down to my ass as if he's trying to touch every inch of me all at once.

I squeal, wrapping my legs around him when he hoists me up and walks us back into his room, lowering us to the bed, never once disconnecting our lips.

He nips me before finally pulling away, "We were interrupted the other night. There was so much more I wanted to give you—that I'm going to give you."

Owen's hand slides between us, slipping between my folds. His thumb finds my clit just as his middle and ring fingers enter me.

I whimper at how wet I am for him already, remembering that night and how hard I'd come at the sight of being watched, at the way Lev's blue-gray eyes burned with hunger.

"You're thinking about that night, aren't you, Angel— the way Wy and I filled you as Wes, Lev, and Seb watched?"

My only answer is to dig my nails into his muscled back, moaning as he rubs my juices over my clit, pumping his fingers inside me.

"Answer me," he commands. "Is the thought of them all lusting for you with their dicks hard in their pants turning you on right now? Is that what has your tight cunt weeping while trying to hold my hands hostage?"

My mind is a buzz of emotions as I feel my mounting orgasm with each pump of his hand. On the fourth plunge of his fingers, I scream, "Yes!"

Owen slides his fingers, soaked in my arousal, out of me, bringing them to my mouth. "Open," he directs, and my mouth falls open, sucking in his fingers just as he brings his mouth down on mine chasing my taste.

I hear a drawer open and the sound of a foil packet. Owen ends the kiss, tearing open the condom, sliding it on, and then pulling me up from the bed until he's lying down and I'm positioned on top of him.

Pressing my hands to his chest, I lift my hips and spread my legs, preparing to ease my way down his length, but Owen's hand shoots out, gripping my waist and raising his hips, thrusting up in one fast snap.

"Fuck," we both shout, pausing long enough to give me time to adjust. If I thought him filling me from behind made me feel full, me on top is in a galaxy of its own.

His hips start to roll, and I grind down on him, picking up speed once I find my rhythm.

"I love being inside of you. Your cunt wrapped on my cock is better than killing," he murmurs.

Did he say killing?

I don't have time to process his words because his thrusts intensify. Each raise of my hips is met with one of his own. My waist circles as I grind down on his dick, brushing my clit against his pubic bone.

His hands reach up, squeezing my breast.

"Put these fucking tits in my mouth." He groans when his command makes my pussy clench as I slide back down his shaft.

I lean forward, bringing my breast to his mouth, and his lips wrap around my nipple. My head falls back, my mouth falls open as I moan, "Shit. Owen!"

A click brings my face back down. He's holding the black and gold knife he used that night. I shiver, remembering the barbaric act of him licking my blood off the blade.

"Wh-what are you going to do with that?" I ask.

His mouth unlatches from my nipple, and I grumble in protest, wishing he could answer while still devouring it.

Without pulling out, he sits up, and I slowly rock my hips in our new position.

"Ah—shit. Ariah. Fuck," he grits through clenched teeth. His hand grips the knife like he's about to snap it.

Gaining a semblance of composure, he answers, "You're going to carve an 'A' into my chest."

Sexy, crazy man fucking me say what now?

"Excuse me?" I finally get my brain to tell my mouth to say.

His other hand grips my jaw, holding my face, which is unconsciously shaking my dissent, still.

"I need this, Angel. I'm going to give you a superficial cut, and then I want you to take Lola and carve the letter 'A' right here," he says, pointing to the area over his heart.

Instead of scrambling off his dick, I clench at the idea of him wanting me embedded in his skin.

"Owen, I can't do that," I begin to protest, but he brings the blade to my lips, quieting me.

"You can and you will. I've never needed something or someone as much as I need this from you, Angel."

I peer into his eyes, and I see. The darkness. The haunted look that matched mine after returning home. I'm not entirely sold on this, but I can process this shit later.

Nodding, I push my chest out, offering him what he needs. "I'll do it."

He groans, and I feel his cock pulsating inside me as the knife slides across the top of my left breast, enough that I feel my skin break. I hiss, and Owen's hand lifts as he thrusts inside me.

Owen hands me the knife, and I watch as my blood drips down the tip.

"Please, Angel," he begs, and I steel my spine, pressing the sharp edge into his flesh. "Oh fuckkkk!"

His body strains, the veins in his neck bulging as he fights to stay still. As I finish carving the line across to make the "A," he grabs the knife from my hand, tossing it somewhere on the bed, and flips me over, slamming inside of me. His hips piston, his pace relentless.

I attempt to match his pace, but he's fucking me like a man on a mission. He powers into me, thrust after thrust, no stopping in sight. My nails dig into his back as I try to hold on. His hand reaches up, touching the "A," gathering his blood before reaching between my legs and rubbing his blood-coated thumb into my clit as he slows his pace.

"You're going to come with my blood staining your pussy, and then I'll own you, and no one will be able to take you from me," he growls, snapping his hips forward, his stroke deep enough to hit that spot over and over. Then he pinches my clit, and my orgasm crests. My body shakes, my head falling back as I bow off the bed.

The last thing I hear is his curse as he jerks his release.

Owen's body slips from mine, and he lands beside me on the bed, pulling me into his bloody chest. His fingers run through my tangled hair as he says, "Thank you."

"Do you want to talk about it?" I try, hoping he'll confide in me.

He sighs but answers, "Let's get cleaned up, and we can talk." His lips press to my forehead before we both get out of bed.

Owen rolls the condom off, tying it, and tossing it in the trash can. With each step he takes, he grows distant, his armor fastening into place. Something I've never seen him do with me before. Whatever this is about, he doesn't want to talk about it.

Noting that I'm still frozen to my spot by his bed. Owen turns, a small smile on his face, "You coming, Angel?"

He's trying Ry.

Guilt tugs at me. I don't want him to have to hide just to open up.

"We-you don't have to talk about this if you don't want to," I offer. I almost pray he'll take me up on it. I'm not sure what would make the wildest and most carefree of the guys look so solemn.

Turning, Owen's in front of me in three quick strides. I nearly take a step back in surprise.

His hand encircles my throat, his grip light, coaxing me into him as he lowers his gaze to mine.

"For you, I'd slay my demons. So, no, Ariah, I don't want to put this off. I should've told you before I asked you for what I just did, and yet somehow, you glorious girl, you saw my monsters, and instead of running, you met them head on."

I tip my chin back, peering into the furthest depths of his gaze. Determination lines his features, the resignation I'd seen earlier a distant memory.

Flicking his chin toward the bathroom, he says, "Let's go shower."

Nodding, I grab his hand and squeeze, hoping he feels the sincerity in my actions. I won't give him superficial words of support. I hate that shit.

We walk into the bathroom, and he pushes some buttons. Water shoots from almost every angle, spraying like a carwash.

"Fancy fuckers," I mumble, and Owen chuckles.

"Wait until you feel it. You'll be happy we're *fancy fuckers*."

The shower is a glass enclosure lined with tile and a stone bench. On the ledge of the shower, I notice my watermelon mint body wash next to his.

Jerking my head, I ask, "Wait, why do you have this?"

Owen's hand reaches for my face again, cupping my cheek and rubbing his thumb along my cheekbone. "Because I want you to feel at home whenever you're here."

His words turn me to goo. I feel the flutter in my belly. *Shit. I'm swooning.*

"Th-thank you," I finally sputter out.

I watch as he reaches past me, grabbing the body wash, and lathers my body.

Leaning in and kissing along my neck, he whispers, "One day soon, I'm going to fuck you on that bench. You'll be on all fours, with my knife in your ass and my cock in your stomach."

Thank fuck for the heat of the shower, or he'd see the bright pink flush of my skin.

Owen smirks, the fuckhead, he knows exactly what effect he's having on me.

"But now," his demeanor goes from playful to grave. "We talk."

He continues to wash my body, his hands roaming over my rounded hips before he begins.

"When I was ten, I was kidnapped."

My eyes bulge, a shocked gasp bursts free before I can stop myself, but I don't interrupt.

"Lev and I-," Owen continues, trying to gain his composure as his hands travel up my stomach, "W-we, we were taken from school. Lured outside by Samantha—at least that's what we suspect."

The shock I felt before burns to anger, but I still wait to speak.

"As soon as she turned the corner, we lost sight of her, and a man snatched me and pointed a gun to my head to make Lev come more willingly."

I feel when he moves. His hand pauses at my belly button, his chest pressing to my back as he lowers his nose to the hollow of my neck and inhales. Then, he murmurs something that I can't make out and grips my waist as if he's trying to ensure I can't escape.

My heart ceases at his vulnerability.

"Lev was able to escape, and the guilt of that eats at him every day. It's wh-why you need to try to give him a chance— him and Wes. We *all* were different after that, especially Lev," he explains.

I stay still, allowing him to pour out his soul. It's still not the time for me to do anything other than listen.

"When— while I was there, they kept saying it w-was m-my dad's fault. All of our dads. That they didn't listen, and since they wouldn't, I would be an example for them to be taken seriously."

Each time he reveals more, my heart rate ticks up, and my stomach churns. It's like watching an oncoming accident and being powerless to stop it. You pray for a different outcome, but you know you'll drive headfirst into the brick wall at a full rate of speed. I want to turn and hold him, but he continues to wash me. So, I give him what he needs to get through this.

"I was held for over a week. A week of hell. A week where I was repeatedly raped— my innocence stolen from me by some masked woman, before I was tortured and shared by her and the men who took me. The horror of my time there plagues me. Constantly told 'I'm here' because of who *our fathers are*." He snarls the last part.

My knees buckle, a flash of a younger Owen playing in my mind, broken and helpless. Tears cascade down my face, masked by the shower, but the water can't hide the keening that rips from my chest.

Strong arms catch me before I hit the ground. Pushing back to our full height, I reach down, grab my loofa, and turn, loosening his hold. Water runs down on us, the soap washing away from our skin, neither of us caring, and I wash him. There's no soap, but I don't care. I just need to care for him.

The strength that they have— that *he* has. I turn him around and choke back my sob. Hidden under an intricate lion eating a skull tattoo are raised scars. They crisscross his back down to his butt. My hand covers my mouth, and I close my eyes.

Who the fuck would do this? Anger takes root in my gut and burns through me. I'd kill whoever did this.

Owen's earlier words play, 'your cunt wrapped around me is better than killing,' pushing me to ask, "Have-have you killed before Owen?" My voice is still choppy as I try to talk while I cry.

He spins, capturing my chin, "Would it scare you if I said we all have?"

I want to say yes, but I remember the anger I felt in that room and how I wanted to kill everyone for hurting me and for what they did to Sam. Her name sparks a recollection of part of his story.

Did Samantha play a part in this? I want to ask, but not now.

"No, I'm not scared of any of you," I confess. How can I be? I know they had to have killed people to get us out of that room. Shit, my dad was covered in blood when he burst into the room.

Reaching up on my tiptoes, I press my mouth to his before pulling back and stating, "Your monsters don't scare me."

The green pops in his usually more hazel-brown eyes, and he hoists me into his arms. I yelp when I slide before he lifts me higher, using his elbow to push open the glass door, and heads to the bedroom, leaving the shower on. He tosses me on the now made bed, and I blush at the idea of someone coming in here and cleaning up the bloody mess the sheets must have been. I don't have time to dwell on those thoughts because I hear a condom tear, and then Owen is sliding inside me.

"You have no idea what you do to me, Angel, but I'm going to spend the rest of the day showing you," he growls. His body hovering over mine as his hips slowly roll in and out of me.

I'll feed his monsters and quiet the noise.

37
WYATT

his class is dragging. The only thing making it remotely interesting is being able to stare at Riri.

I'm unsure if it's because it's the first class of the day or because I have to take the harpy on a date tonight. I argued with my dad for over an hour on all the reasons it makes no sense to subject me to any time in her presence, but he hit me with the 'if you don't, then you'll be forced to go on more than one date as a punishment.'

This might be the only time I've actually hated my dad.

When the bell finally sounds, I start to gather my things—thoughts of the nightmare date plaguing me.

"What's with the sour face?' Ariah murmurs in my ear.

I was so lost in my thoughts I didn't even feel her approach and lean in.

"I'm just being salty over the date from hell I have to go on tonight." I blurt out, averting my gaze after my stupidity. Because, of course, I'm an idiot and told the girl I want everything with about the troll I'm forced to date because of the Selection.

Ariah's silver eyes soften before glinting with mirth, "Just remember, prison doesn't allow conjugal visits unless you have a kid visiting, so try not to make her go missing," she jokes.

The frown on my face melts away, replaced by a quirk of my lip.

"Not that I'd ever be caught, but don't tempt me, Love. The idea of my baby growing in your belly because I filled you with my cum has its appeal."

My smile grows at the way her eyes pop in surprise. What was it that Sebastian said, 'we can practice.' I have every intention of practicing until she's ready for us to grow our family.

Reaching out, I grab her hand, bringing it to my mouth, "Don't worry, Riri, no babies any time soon. Not until you're ready. I don't care what the stupid rules stipulate."

She hip-checks me, "You're a smart man, Wyatt. School first, then career, and then if I like you enough, maybe babies."

"What's this about babies?" Lev asks as he, Owen, and Wes join us.

"Nothing, there's nothing about babies," she exclaims, trying to pull from my hold, but we all box her in. "Will you assholes move," she demands halfheartedly.

Lev leans in as Wes locks his arm around her middle. "Can't do that, Dove. You see, we like the idea of having you at our mercy," he growls.

I bend, capturing her lips with mine, catching her by surprise. She hesitates for a shadow of a second before moaning, allowing me access to her tantalizing mouth. I hear the hiss of breath before the sound of Wes's voice.

"You're such a lucky girl we're at school," he whispers, sparking her awareness, and she pulls back. The momentary fog of lust disappears, and she pushes out of our hold, striding over to a smirking Shay.

"Let's go. These idiots need to cool off," Ariah states, her cheeks still flushed.

"I don't know. I think you could use about five more hours of that heat," Shay teases.

Ariah throws her hands up, exasperated by all of our behavior. "You're all incorrigible," she stammers, storming out of the room.

Shay laughs and follows her out of the room.

I turn back in time to see the varying looks of adoration and lust on their faces.

"You two assholes should be happy that she was so turned on by our proximity that she didn't remember she doesn't like you," Owen jests, pointing between Lev and Wes.

They both nod. "That means there's still hope for us yet," Lev says, longing filling his tone.

Oh, he has it bad. *Welcome to the club.*

Wes is on board but still apprehensive. Seb is now the lone man on the 'I won't fall for her island.'

"Your whore won't be around for long," Samantha's annoying voice chimes as she exits the room, obliterating the moment and reminding me of my earlier frustrations.

Wes's hand comes down on my shoulder, "Good luck with that," he mocks.

I flip him off and chant to myself. *'There are no conjugal visits in prison.'*

"I know we haven't quite gotten along— not in a very long time, but don't you remember how close we used to be?"

Each time Samantha speaks, I want to rip out her vocal cords. The annoying bitch hasn't stopped yammering the entire ride. We're almost at our destination, and we can't get there soon enough.

"Are you going to just pretend like you don't hear me? This isn't in the spirit of the rules, you know, Wy," she coos, attempting to coax me to engage with her.

Ten more minutes. I can last ten more long, excruciating minutes.

"This would all be different if you'd just give me a chance. I didn't do it, you know. I swear I didn't know what would happen. I was ten, for fuck's sake," she whimpers.

I ignore the fake ho— she's a master manipulator.

Seven minutes.

"You should treat me better—you all should. If it weren't for me, your perfect Ariah would've been raped," Samantha snarls.

That gets my attention. My head turns from the road, assessing her honesty before refocusing on the road. "What the fuck are you talking about?" I demand.

"Of course, that's what would finally get you to break your silence," she mumbles, almost resignedly.

"Stop your whining and tell me what the hell you're talking about," I grit through clenched teeth. If she knew the amount of patience I'm wielding in order not to choke her, she'd just answer my question.

Five minutes.

I keep staring at the clock on the dashboard. We're so close.

Two minutes.

When she speaks again, her voice is barely audible. "They were going to rape her, but then I was taken, and they didn't want her touched, so they took me instead. They said she meant more to you all and that seeing what happened to me and what could happen to her would make you all fall in line," she's yelling by the time she finishes.

Fuck. I'm about to do the impossible— offer her comfort, but the bitch keeps speaking as I pull to a stop.

"It should've been her! That cow could've taken it— she deserves it," Samantha shrieks as I slam the car into park.

I rip open the door and storm to her side, yanking on the handle. "You're all fucking idiots!" Her fake tears are dried up, and rage consumes her cold blue eyes, "Following behind some worthless trash troll when you could have me."

Fire fills my veins as I grip her by her hair, dragging her from the car and across the dirt-covered ground. I didn't feel any remorse for my plans for the evening, but now I feel utter glee.

Her hands reach up to claw at my hands, trying to break free from my hold, but I tug her by her follicles, making her trip and land on her ass. She turns over, hoping to gain leverage—it's too late. I'm already at the fence.

I slam her body into the fence, making her wail in surprise, giving me enough time to pin her hand and lock her into the waiting handcuffs.

"You never know when to shut the fuck up," I snarl. "I was just going to kick you out of the car and make you find a ride home, but now I'm going to make you work for it."

She thrashes on the ground, attempting to yank her hand out of the cuff. "You can't fucking leave me here," Samantha shouts.

I turn, grabbing her face and squeezing. "That's where you're wrong. You haven't seemed to figure it out yet. I can do whatever the fuck I want—*we* can do whatever the fuck we want. It's you who has no control over anything," I seethe, dropping my grip and storming back to the car.

"Be happy I left one hand free and your phone so that you can dial a ride. Hopefully, they get to you before the landfill opens or an animal comes," I say without looking back.

Once I'm back in the car, I grab my phone, snap a picture, and then send it with the caption 'taking out the trash' into our group chat.

Because where else would you take garbage on a date but to the dump?

Then I put my car back in drive and head to see my heart.

38
ARIAH

As Thomas pulls up in front of Lev's house, my hand wrings my wrist. We're supposed to meet to go over our final presentation for civics.

After he and Wes grabbed me in class last week, I've been a nervous twit around them.

"Ariah, are you getting out of the car?" Thomas inquires.

When did he get out of the car?

"Ye-yeah," I mumble, stepping out of the backseat and making my way to the large ornate door.

"Welcome, Miss Bishop, Master Lev will be with you shortly," a voice says as the front door slowly opens. *What the fuck?* Rich people and their rich people shit.

I step inside and look for the person, but see no one. Then, the voice sounds again, making me jump. "Can I get you anything?"

"She's all set, Geoffrey. I'll take it from here. You scared the poor girl."

Turning in the direction of the person speaking, I'm met with the gaze of a beautiful woman. She walks with a grace only seen in high society, but her smile is welcoming, and her resemblance to Lev is apparent. I'm just not sure if she's his mother or sister.

"Sorry about that, Ariah. Levi and his dad are all about their damn high-tech toys. I'm Calista Washington, Levi's mother."

I begin to stretch out my hand when she envelops me in a hug, her petite frame towering over me.

"Uh, hi. I'm Ariah," I start, then remember she said my name. "I'm here to work on a, um, project with Lev and Wyatt."

She pulls back from the hug, "Yes, I remember him mentioning that. He's in the shower. I'll take you to where the boys always meet when they come over."

I follow behind her until we reach the end of the hall. Lev's mom opens a door on the left, and my mouth falls open.

The place looks like the lounge of a club, not some hangout spot. At least ten monitors are mounted to the wall, a blue neon sign is lit that says 'Monsters at Play,' and every gaming console known to humankind sits at designated spots around the room. PacMan and Mrs. PacMan machines sit on the far side, next to air hockey and foosball tables. My eyes keep scanning, and I land on a six-lane bowling alley. A fucking bowling alley.

Jesus.

"See what I mean about their toys," Mrs. Washington whispers in my ear, knocking me from my stupor. "You can put your bag over there on the table and help yourself to some snacks until Levi arrives. Maybe he'll even cook for you. That will be a real treat," she says before turning and leaving me in a daze.

Cook? Lev cooks? I mean, I guess I don't really know much about him other than he can be a dick when he's ready. Well, he used to be a dick. He hasn't been one lately.

I walk to the large table and place my bag down before making my way to the kitchen area with the snacks. First, I grab a bottle of hibiscus pineapple ginger iced tea and my favorite brand of choco-late-covered Oreos, trying not to overthink that either Lev and I have similar tastes or he has my favorite foods in his house. Then, I head back to the table and sit down, pulling out my work while waiting for him or Wyatt to arrive. I don't have to wait very long before I hear someone approach, causing my attention to shift toward the sound in time to see Lev walk through the door with a hesitant smile on his face.

"Oh good, you saw the snacks I got you," he says, answering my question as his hand reaches up to put his still-damp hair into a bun.

His movements draw my attention to his biceps as they work his hair off his shoulders. They flex when his arms widen, exposing a tattoo I can't make out from this distance. My gaze travels down his body, and like a perv, I stare at the bulge in his lounge pants. *Lord, he's not even hard.*

Lev clears his throat, snapping my focus back up to his face. I can feel the heat growing against my skin. Lev's once timid smile is now cocky.

"Wy's running late." He begins walking toward me. "We should get started on the outline until he arrives," he suggests, taking his seat.

Nodding in agreement, I start back in on my work, trying and failing to ignore his proximity. I squirm when his hand accidentally brushes mine as he pulls his books out.

Shaking off the feeling, I refocus on my research. That lasts about twenty minutes. I can feel Lev's eyes boring into me. Tilting my head, I peer over at him and confirm he is indeed studying me, his brows furrowed in contemplation as he bites his lush bottom lip. *Fuck.* Why do they look so inviting?

"I-I need to get something off my chest." His words pull my attention from his delectable mouth to his gold-flecked eyes.

"Go ahead. I'm listening," I encourage, halting my typing.

He coughs, clearing his throat before he speaks. "I need to apologize."

I sit back, ensuring I don't cross my arms and making sure I don't appear like I'm being defensive or dismissive because he does need to apologize. He and Wes both do, but I don't want to be a bitch about it and refuse to hear them out. Especially if I end up having to marry these fools.

"That day. Actually, both of those days. I..." He pauses, trying to collect himself, then takes a deep breath and continues. "The night of the party, I was out of line. I shouldn't have said what I did. I won't give you any excuses, but I'd like to explain the *why*. It will also explain that day in the hallway."

I clench my jaw at the memory. One minute I was grabbing his shoulder, and the next, he had me by the throat. I dick-punched him for that bullshit.

"That night. After we made our Selections, I was so suspicious of you. Everything I dug up led to nothing, but our dads wanted you as part of the process. It made no sense to me, and because of that, you were a great unknown, and I needed to be the level-headed one. Wyatt and Owen are gone for you, and Wes is pigheaded which leads him to be impulsive. I needed to protect my family," he explains.

I can understand his apprehension. New girl moves to some exclusive town and becomes part of some exclusive bullshit practice. I'd have questions too. However, it still didn't give him the right to be a fucking tool. I want to say that, instead, I wait for him to continue.

"When we were ten, Owen and I were kidnapped. Well, Owen was successfully kidnapped, but I was able to get away."

My body freezes to the spot. I don't even blink as I work to process his words.

"The same organization that took you, they took us too," Lev continues, and my gut twists.

Fucking Elise! Guilt at my mother being the reason they were taken gnaws at me. I bite the inside of my cheek, drawing blood in an attempt to stay my knee-jerk visceral reaction. I want to jump from this chair and throw something. No, I want to find the bitch who birthed me and kill her. Instead, I count and focus on Lev as he details what happened.

"I can't tell you all the details. Ever since the day I was snatched, I don't react well to people sneaking up on me or grabbing me from

behind. It triggers something, and I'm catapulted back to that day."
His usually smooth voice sounds choppy.

Lev lifts his shirt, exposing another tattoo. It looks like it
connects to the body of armor I saw on his arm, but that's not what
captures my attention. As I look closer, like Owen, he's covering scar-
ring. My hand raises to touch him, but I stop myself. He reaches out,
taking hold of my hand and gently bringing it to the raised flesh. *I
want to cry for him. I want to rage for them both.* I feel the tears before I
know I'm crying. My heart breaks even more for what they both had
to endure. The unspeakable things Owen went through and the
undeniable guilt Lev carries around for what happened to his best
friend.

"I'm sorry. I'm so, so sorry," I croak.

Lev raises his other hand to my face, brushing away the free-
flowing stream of tears leaking from my eyes. "Shh, it wasn't your
fault," he whispers, cupping my cheek, and I lean into his palm,
soaking in the heat of his comfort.

Isn't it, though? Isn't all of this my fault? I'm a Bradford. The one
my evil mother has been working to place at the helm so she can take
over.

"Stop," he grabs my chin, letting go of the hand touching his side,
and lifts my gaze to his, "I can see it on your face that you're blaming
yourself. You didn't do this. *Elise* did it."

I try to accept his comfort, but then I replay his words, *'someone
grabbed me from behind.'* My mind reels. I did that. The day in the
hallway, when he turned away. I gripped his shoulder and pulled.

"The day in the hall. You-you were having a flashback, weren't
you? And I triggered it, didn't I?" I mumble between breaths. I can
feel my body trying to lock me out as I feel the anxiety building in my
chest and my airways constricting.

My heart is ricocheting out of my body as lips press against
mine, pulling me from my mounting panic. I gasp, permitting his
tongue to find mine. My hands begin to glide up his stomach, and he
stiffens, causing me to halt my perusal. I start to pull away, but his

hand grips the back of my neck, pressing his mouth more firmly to mine.

"Please," he begs between kisses, urging me to touch him.

Encouraged by his plea, I slide my palm to his chest, holding my hand against his warm skin, feeling the skittering of his heart beating. He groans, a noise between a moan and a cry. I can feel the tears building before they fall, the saltiness mixing between our joint lips. Neither one of us is deterred. Instead, our hunger for one another becomes more ravenous. My hands move to his hair, yanking it from its bun and tugging him deeper as our tongues delve into each other's mouths, exploring, searching... yearning for more.

"Well, this isn't what I had in mind when you said 'preparing for our presentation on women's suffrage'," Wyatt's voice shocks us apart.

Both our heavy breaths are audible when I turn to see the shit-eating grin on Wyatt's face.

"Fuck off, Grant," Lev says, but his tone is light and filled with amusement before he leans in and kisses my swollen lips. "Next time, there won't be any interruptions," he whispers loud enough that only I can hear.

The promise in his voice makes my pussy clench as I remember our date is this weekend.

"Let's get to work," I blurt out, trying to cover my nervous excitement about what his words mean.

39

LEV

I look around the kitchen, ensuring all the ingredients are ready while I wait for Ariah to arrive. Thomas agreed to drive her over so I could start the prep work. I put the dough to rest and begin to work on cutting the tops off the strawberries in order to hollow them out. I don't want to make anything too elaborate tonight so that we can focus on getting to know each other more.

I grab the cheesecake filling I made earlier from the cooler and the piping bag once the strawberries have been hollowed. Then I work to fill each berry before placing them on a parchment paper-covered cookie sheet. Once they're filled, I place them back into the cooler until it's time for Ariah and me to make them.

Closing the door to the cooler, I turn to survey the kitchen—everything is ready. I walk to the pantry to grab the apron I had made for her, hoping she'll enjoy my sense of humor. After the other day, things between us have finally lost their tension—at least the tension that had her annoyed with me. The sexual type, on the other hand—. I don't finish my thought because just as I place the apron on the table, Geoffrey announces her arrival.

I take one more cursory glance around the room and make my way to the entrance to greet her.

By the time I reach the door, she's standing inside the entryway, and I come to a complete stop. My mouth falls open as I take her in. She's wearing high-waisted, distressed black denim jeans that accentuate her curves and an off-the-shoulder Nirvana hoodie. Her long bluish-black hair falls in waves down past her shoulders. *Damn.* She's fucking gorgeous.

"Hey," she smiles, alerting me to the fact that I've just been staring at her like an idiot without saying a word.

I look into her alluring eyes. I'd give anything to know what's going on in that head of hers. Is she seeing how much I really want her— want this? Does she notice how sorry I am for my dickish behavior when I first met her?

"Hi," I finally respond. Because I'm a man of many words.

We stand there momentarily just looking at each other before my brain gets the memo. It's my house. I need to be the one to get this date started.

Clearing my throat, I try to actually formulate a sentence that's not monosyllabic. "Um. Let's go to the kitchen. I thought we could make dinner together."

Way to sound confident there, my guy.

Ariah nods and begins to walk toward me. "Your mom mentioned I should get you to cook for me. I'm looking forward to seeing just how skillful you are."

Was that a double entendre?

I want to say you'll more than find out how skillful I am in and out of the kitchen, but I don't want to push my luck. The energy between us might have been hot that night, but that doesn't mean she wants to know what it feels like to have my ropes imprinting against her delectable ass.

My jaw clenches as I fight to control my ever-aching dick. It's been almost a month since she's been home, and to say that blue balls and I are intimate comrades is putting it lightly. Thank fuck for ice baths and football games.

I bite the inside of my cheek before I reply. "Cooking is a place where I can lose myself. I like to play around with ingredients." And it's true. I do like the science of creating all types of masterpieces, whether that be preparing a meal or preparing a lethal cocktail for interrogations.

Once we're back in the kitchen, I pick up the apron off the table, and then I make my way over to her. Standing before her, I pull the strap over her head before lifting her hair from under the loop. Then I move behind her and tie the strings as I pull her in, lowering my mouth to her ear and asking, "Are you ready to put my skills to the test?"

I swear I can hear her gulp before a soft gasp escapes her. "Yes," is her only reply as she steps away from me, allowing me to see her face reddening.

Smiling, I clasp her hand and pull her over to the counter.

"I thought we could make homemade pizza for dinner and then some cheesecake-filled chocolate-covered strawberries for dessert," I state once we reach everything.

Her face lights up. "Oh, I'll never say no to pizza or cheesecake anything," she snorts. Her snort morphs into a laugh. "Bitch, I'm the secret ingredient," she says once she finally takes in the words on her apron. "Do you always have snarky aprons lying around?" she asks.

"I have a few, but I got this one specifically for you," I inform her, wanting to make sure she knows that tonight was planned down to every detail.

She tilts her chin up, and a warm smile fills her face. "This is cute, thank you." Then she claps her hands. "Okay, let's get this started. I'm ready for pizza."

"Right. First, we need to make the crust," I state, grabbing the dough that's been resting. "Grab that bowl of flour over there and sprinkle it on the counter. I'm going to check on the brick oven to make sure it's set for once we've made some pies."

By the time I'm back, Ariah has the flour spread out, and she's already working the dough. Her hair is up, and her face is concentrating on the task at hand.

I can do this. I'm the one touching her. She's not touching me. I remind myself as my body presses against her back lightly. *As long as I'm controlling the touch, it's fine.*

"Let's do it together," I murmur, hoping she can't feel the pounding of my heart.

She turns slightly to the side, just enough that her profile is in view but not touching me. "Are you sure?" she asks. "I don't...you don't...we don't have to-," she sighs in frustration. "I mean, if you aren't comfortable, we can do this-."

"Shhh," I hush, interrupting her, hoping to assuage her. "I'm okay— this is okay." Then I bracket her body with mine. The tension in her shoulders eases as she places her hands gently over mine, and we stretch out the pizza dough.

We work in silence, spreading the dough into a circle. The peacefulness of this moment is not escaping me.

"Outside of cooking and gaming, what do you like to do?" she asks once I step back from her, and I already miss the feeling of her pressed against me.

I grab the bowl with the marinara sauce and the ladle before I answer. "I love computers, reading, movies, football— all sports, really," I say as I spread the sauce over the dough.

She takes the ladle and dips it back into the bowl. "I like a little more sauce on my pizza," she explains cheekily.

I smirk, letting her continue as I grab the toppings from the other side of the counter. As she tops the pizza with all of her favorite toppings, I finish telling her about my other interests, and then she tells me about hers. Many I already knew from my background checks, but some are surprising. She also likes to game— not nearly as much as I do, but enough that she knows some of the games I mentioned playing.

"What do you like to read?" Ariah questions, dipping another strawberry into the tempered white chocolate. We're on our last few. All of the milk chocolate ones are sitting on the cookie sheet.

I go to the oven, grab the wooden peel, and pull the pizza out while I answer. "Suspense, medieval times, and some dark romance," I state, placing the pizza on the cool rack.

"Seriously?" she inquires, and I turn to see the amusement on her face.

"Yeah, what's so shocking about liking suspense?' I tease, knowing full well my love of suspense and medieval times novels is not what has her looking at me with surprise.

She rolls her eyes, "You know that's not what I'm referring to. What's the last dark romance book you read? You better not say something lame either because I'll totally judge you."

Shaking my head, I cross the room and stand behind her, my fingers sliding down her forearm and covering her hand to assist in dipping the last strawberry. The tips of our fingers sink into the warm chocolate. I lift her hand from the bowl, turning her as I bring the strawberry to my mouth, my eyes locked to hers as I open and she feeds me the chocolate-covered piece of fruit. My lips wrap around her digits, and I suck as I slowly pull them from my mouth, then chew before answering. "I'll read anything that has the main male character hunting down the female main character because she decides to run."

"That's a very specific type of interest," she whispers, attempting to back away.

I grip her waist, holding her in place. "It is," I affirm. "It's letting her know that running will never work—that once you've been claimed, there's not a place or a length of time that can change that you'll always be ours," I growl the last part because I'm no longer talking about fictional men and their women.

Ariah's gray eyes pop at my words, and her chest rises and falls as her breaths quicken. "Is that so?" Her words come out as a challenge.

My hand slides up to her throat, gripping but not squeezing. "I think you already know the answer to that question," I state, then close the distance between our lips. She opens her mouth, readily accepting me, but I freeze when she places her hands on my chest.

Ariah quickly drops her hands, "Shit! I'm sorry. I got caught up in the moment," she rushes out.

"It's fine," I grit out, my frustration with myself evident. I want to bring Aleksi back to life so I can use a potato peeler to skin him alive.

"Would it help if you held my hands to my side?" she offers, not knowing what a statement like that does to me. My dick grows painfully hard. It's been too long for me to be a gentleman about this, and let's be honest— the word gentleman doesn't belong in the same state, much less in the same sentence, as me, but I try anyway.

"We should eat dinner," I suggest.

She arches her brow, "Fuck dinner. I'd much rather do more of this," she points between our mouths. "But I don't want to make you uncomfortable. So, what do you need, Lev?"

I must take too long to register what she's said because she speaks again before I can get my mouth and head to catch up. "What. Do. You. Need?" She asks again, this time her words are more sensual. Their intentions are obvious— she's no longer interested in food.

Instead of speaking, I grip her wrist and tug her in the direction of my room. It's better to show than tell.

Pushing open my room door, I walk to the wall by my closet. I punch in the code, opening the panel.

"Rich people shit," I hear Ariah mutter.

I don't acknowledge her statement. Instead, I pull her into the room and let the door slide closed behind us.

"Do you still want to skip dinner?" I probe, watching her take in the wall lined with various lengths and colors of jute and hemp ropes. While I'd love nothing more than to tie her up, I know she also has her own trauma from being kidnapped.

Ariah turns to me, determination set in her features, "I said *fuck dinner*, didn't I?"

My dick jumps at her declaration. A smile grows on my face.

"Strip," I command as I walk over to the rack of ropes, pulling off three spools.

Ariah walks toward the bed, peeling off her hoodie and bra before she bends to unlace her docs and steps out of her jeans. Once undressed, she stands back to her full height, meeting my gaze with a challenge.

I'm not sure if she thinks I doubted she'd do it, but there isn't a doubt in my mind that my little dove has bigger balls than any of us.

"Lie back on the bed. I'm going to tie your arms to the post to start. I want to make sure you're not spooked by any of this," I instruct.

I want so badly to just lay on top of her and let her hands roam— to let her explore me freely. I'm just not there yet— I don't know if I ever will be.

Before she follows my orders, she walks up to me, unabashedly naked, lust pooling in her depths. "Thank you for caring about my needs, but I'll be fine. I want you to be fine," she declares and then turns, moving for the bed.

I watch her ass bounce with each step, eager to spread her wide and bury my face between those cheeks. I grip my dick at the thought and groan when she climbs on the bed, sliding slowly to her stomach before flipping over and opening her thick thighs to give me an unobstructed view of her already glistening bare pussy.

Fuck! I nearly throw the ropes and just dive in.

My feet move of their own volition, stopping right at the foot of the bed between her spread legs. My hand finds its way between her folds, gliding the wetness leaking out her pussy to her clit and circling. I pick up speed as her breath quickens but pull away before she can reach her peak. She turns her flushed face in my direction.

"You don't play fair," she groans.

"I never said I would." I walk around the bed, leaning over to clasp the rope around her wrist, looping one end and sliding it through to make a knot. The black rope looks beautiful against her skin. I can almost picture her completely bound.

Before I tie her other wrist, I stand and disrobe. My dick throbs between my muscled thighs as I climb back on the bed, take the rope from her left wrist, reach over, and bind it to her other one. As I lean over for her other hand, I feel her breath against my shaft before I feel her mouth wrap around me.

"Shittt," I grunt, nearly buckling on top of her. She doesn't let my sudden jerk stop her. I peer down and watch as she lifts her head off the bed in order to take me deeper into her mouth.

My head falls back as I enjoy the sensation of her tongue swirling around my tip. I clench my glutes, trying to regain my focus. Then I grab Ariah's hair, pulling her from my cock. I want to cry at the loss of the feeling, but I want more, and I can't have that until she's bound.

"You're being bad, Dove. You had your chance to eat dinner. Now you have to wait to be fed," I state, releasing her hair and tying her other wrist. Finally, I bring the excess rope to the metal hook at the top of the bed. I loop it through, pulling until Ariah's arms are stretched above her head, and tie it. I double-check the knot, ensuring it will hold before I climb off the bed.

"How does that feel? Are you okay?" I ask, reaching to grab the other spool of rope.

"Ready for more," she moans. The sound causes my dick to jump.

I drop the rope. *Fuck it.* I can frog-tie her another time. Hearing her so wanton has me changing my game plan. Instead, I grab a condom and roll it on before squatting between her legs. Then I lower my nose to her pussy, and inhale. *Jesus.* She smells so fucking tantalizing. My mouth latches onto her clit while three fingers slide into her waiting walls.

"Ahh, yess," she cries out, her legs almost snapping together.

"Keep your legs open, or I'll tie them up," I growl against her pussy. Her only response is another moan of pleasure and a clench around my fingers. I twist the digits inside her, pumping in and out slowly as my teeth nip at her clit. Just as I feel her orgasm mount, I pull my fingers out, crawl on the bed and slam inside her just as she comes, squeezing my cock so hard I nearly nut.

Before she can come down from her first orgasm, I renew my pace. My hips thrust back and forth, each stroke deeper than the last. I lean over her, grabbing her hair, bringing her mouth back to mine, and biting her lip. She returns my kiss tenfold, whimpering as my hips buck.

I need more.

Pulling from the kiss, I lower her back to the bed and pull out of her long enough to flip her, the hook on the wall allowing her to not be in pain as it turns with her. I slide my hand under her stomach and help lift her to her knees. Once she's set, I spread her ass and suck from hole to hole.

"Fuck, Lev. Please, I need more," she begs.

Positioning myself behind her, I sink back in, inch by inch, enjoying the feel of her stretching around me— how deep I feel from this angle— how fucking glorious her ass looks in this position. My hand raises and lands against her cheek, the imprint of my palm showing momentarily before disappearing. The idea of my hand imprinting for longer causes me to jerk on my next thrust.

I grip the globes of her ass. "Soon, I'm going to tie you up and have my ropes all over this fucking beautiful body as I mark you as mine, and you're going to come so hard that the only dicks that will ever satisfy you will belong to my brothers and me," I growl, bucking in and out of her.

"Don't fucking stop," she cries when I pull out and slam back in.

I remove my left hand and reach around her hips until my fingers rub her clit. Her body shakes, and her walls grip me so hard I forget to roll my hips forward.

"Fuck," I snarl, finding my rhythm again. I pull my hips back and snap forward just as I pinch her clit. Ariah comes on a loud shriek, spasming around my cock. I explode into the condom so hard I get lightheaded.

Our heavy breathing fills the space, and I take a moment to let all the blood find its way back to my brain before I pull out.

Sliding off the bed, I roll off the condom as I make my way to the bathroom, tossing it in the trash. I grab a rag and wet it with warm water before heading back to clean Ariah up.

She's sprawled on the bed, her cheek resting on the bed as she pants. "That was fucking amazing," she says between gasps of air.

I'm about to wipe her down when I see her juices leaking out. *Can't let that go to waste.* I lean over and suck all her cum up until there's none left.

"Lev," she whimpers. "You're going to make me—" She doesn't finish her sentences as she cries out, squirting into my mouth.

"Fucking delicious," I grunt, slurping the last of the juices from her pussy. Then I take the rag and clean her up before I begin to untie her.

Once she's untied, I massage her shoulders, trying not to get hard each time she moans.

After I'm finished, I bend, lowering my mouth and press a kiss between her shoulder blades. She lets out a contented sigh, then her breaths even out, and I know she's asleep.

Lying next to her, I watch her as she sleeps. Her body is relaxed, and her face looks at peace. This is how I want her to always look, which means we need to deal with her mother and anyone else threatening to hurt her.

I reach over and brush the hair out of her face. A slight smirk appears as she mumbles something inaudibly. Whatever it is— she's smiling, and I want to see this always. My eyes droop, but before I lose my battle to continue watching her to the sandman, I vow never to let her go.

T he week is almost over, which means Senior Night and the big party are almost here. This also means Thanksgiving break is next week and that I need to hurry up and get all of these dates out of the way so that I can be free and clear of the bullshit.

I've only gone on dates with Brittany and Meagan at this point. I took Brittany to see a movie. She's not as annoying when she's not under Sam's skirt. Meagan, on the other hand, was so annoying I was close to ditching her. We went to the diner, and all she did was complain about how unfair the Selection process is because no one's paying her attention and that she's a real viable option.

My date with Samantha didn't count, and my father is making me relive that nonsense again. *Haven't I endured enough with the leech?*

I make my way down the hallway to AP English when I spot the hourglass silhouette of the girl who's been starring in my dreams. Ariah Bradford is a fucking sight to behold.

Quickening my step, I catch up and walk beside her.

"What do you have this period?" I ask to spark conversation. I know she's going to AP Civics.

She glances at me out of the corner of her eye. "How can I help you, Wes?"

I sigh, knowing she's lukewarm toward me on a good day because of how I treated her. I've made progress, though— before she'd ice me out completely.

"How's your dad?" I inquire, genuinely interested. Aaron Bradford seems as though he got the shit end of a deal made before he was born. His whole family is being hunted— to the point of almost extinction.

She looks at me suspiciously, her eyes narrowing to slits. "Why?"

I don't blame her for her lack of trust in me. It's not like I've been the best guy. "He went through a fuckton— you all have. I just want to make sure he's okay and settling in," I assure her.

Her posture loses its defensive stance. "He's happy to be home. Now I need to get to class, so if you'll excuse me."

"That's fine," I state, keeping pace with her. "I want to walk you to class," I say, and it's the truth. I've been waiting for my date with her for almost a month now because then I'll have the time to show her I'm more than the pompous spoiled rich jerk she met the first day of school.

She turns her head, and her right eyebrow arches. "You're walking me to class now? What's next, holding my hand and buying us matching shirts?"

I snort. "I don't know about the matching shirts, but I'd love to hold your hand." I reach my arm out to stop her. "Listen, I don't want to wait until our date to apologize. I was-."

"Wesley, what are you doing with the trash? I've been waiting for you in our spot like you asked me to. We never got to finish up earlier."

I groan at the nasally voice of Samantha.

"Right. That's my cue," Ariah says, stepping around my outstretched hand.

"Wait," I start, but she's already halfway down the hall when I recover from the bullshit Samantha just spewed.

Samantha's heels click against the linoleum floor, signaling her approach.

"Don't worry, baby. I'll never let you have to deal with that trash troll," she coos, placing her clawed hand on my bicep.

My hand snaps out, gripping the offending limb and pulling it off me. She attempts to dig her nails into my skin, but when my grip tightens to the point I can see her wince, she relents, dropping her hands to her side. I face the bitch that can't seem to stay the fuck out of my way. "What the actual fuck is your damage? We had no plans and will never have plans to meet up anywhere again," I snarl.

Hurt flashes in her eyes but is gone as quickly as it appeared— replaced by malice. "You didn't use to say that when you had me bent over and were fucking me, Wesley. The problem only began when the cheap slut arrived," Samantha snaps, preparing to slap me, but my hand squeezes her wrist, and I don't let go until she drops her arm.

Angry that her second attempt was thwarted, she shrieks. "So, the problem seems to only be her, and once she's not chosen, you can come back to me. I'll let you play with your shiny new toy, but don't fucking think I'll let you assholes replace me with some off-brand model." Then she begins to stomp away, but I snatch her by her jet-black extensions and slam her against the locker.

"Did you fucking forget the little chat we had the other day in my room when your crusty pussy was laid out on my bed? I had to burn those sheets and get a new bed, by the way," I add.

Lust fills the pain slut's eyes until I yank an extension out. She screams, no pleasure in sight.

"Stop fucking pushing me, Sam. You won't like the outcome. Each time you try to top me, I'll only crush you harder under my heel. So leave me the fuck alone," I snarl, releasing her to drop into a heap on the floor before turning and storming down the hall to class.

Stupid fucking Fraternitas and their stupid fucking need for me to dip into the wasteland pussy.

But I know it's not all their doing. Like the guys said. I didn't have to keep messing with her to get information from her. Sam's always been like putty in my hands. I just like that she always lets me debase her in the most awful ways. It was like payback for Owen and Lev— plus, I got to nut. My temper cools when I remember the last time I messed with her. Calling out Ariah's name was the best revenge.

Samantha likes all the shit I do to her. She didn't like me screaming another girl's name because I'd never once called her name. Shit. If I had known that sooner, I'd have done it before. Something tells me that it's not that another girl's name passed through my lips, but who that girl is. Ariah sets Sam on another level of batshit.

I pull open the door to English, and Mrs. Chase looks annoyed at the interruption until she sees it's me.

"Ah, you're just in time, Wesley. We're about to read Audre Lorde's *Sister Outsider*. So grab your seat and turn to page fifty-three."

I nod, taking my seat next to Owen. I love this class. Mrs. Chase is always pushing us to explore more, and Audre Lorde's essays definitely make you think about your positionality in society.

Owen leans over. "Where have you been?"

"First, I was with our girl, but then a foul creature needed to be reminded of their place," I reply.

He chuckles. "So, Sam cock-blocked you again?"

"You wouldn't be laughing if you heard the things she said. She's delusional, and it's my fucking fault." I sigh in resignation.

"The first step in recovery is admitting you have a problem, Bro," he quips.

I flip him the bird. "Whatever, asshole. I still think we should keep a close eye on her. I know our dads said we could back off some, but I think it's a bad idea. She really thinks we'll choose her in the end."

"I'd sooner cut her heart out before I'd ever agreed to be anything to that man-eater," he states, and I nod, agreeing.

Thinking back to the hallway, I lean over to Owen and whisper, "Do you think Sam knows something we don't?"

"I wouldn't put it past her. The only problem is everything that happened when she was kidnapped. It sets a level of doubt about her being involved. Which could be a smoke screen—an extreme one, but one that's plausible," he reasons.

He's right. There are so many reasons she might or might not be involved.

"Let's have Lev do more digging," I suggest, and he nods in agreement just as the discussion begins in class.

Sighing, I try to focus back on Mrs. Chase, resigned to the fact that even as we discover more answers— there are still a thousand more questions.

41
ARIAH

"We need to find you something to wear," Shay mumbles as Mr. Jameson prattles on about coefficients.

Once he turns to the board, my head cranes in her direction. "Wear to what?" I whisper.

"To Senior Night for the football team, duh. I figured you'd have the schedule memorized for someone who claims to love football like you do," she snarks.

Seeing the puzzled look on my face, she explains, "It's the last home game for the seniors on the team, the biggest game before the Turkey Game."

I cut her off. "I know what a senior night is."

Shay rolls her eyes. "So what needs to be explained, then? Ours is Friday, your men are playing, and we're going. So, you need an outfit to wear, bitch."

"Um, they aren't all my men," I mumble, hoping they don't hear me. The last thing I want is to have to deal with is growly proclamations.

I blush, remembering Lev's last week. The way he tied me up. I
want to experience more of that.

"Right," she dramatically sighs. "That's why they all look at you
like they want to infuse you into their skin. Even Wes, who was the
captain of all dicks to you, is looking at you right now like he wants
to bend you over and—"

I cut her off again. "You don't know what you're talking about.
Wes, of all people, is definitely not mine. Shit, he was just with Sam
yesterday at some private meet-up spot."

"Miss Bishop and Miss Warren, would you like to be the one to
teach this class? I'll take a seat since you both have so much to say,"
Mr. Jameson says snidely, ending our conversation.

"Or you could turn around and just teach," Wes commands from
behind me. I can't see his face, but I'm pretty sure his rich chocolate
eyes are laced with challenges, daring Mr. Jameson to test him.

Never one to care who any of the heirs are, Mr. Jameson directs
his ire to Wes. "Is that so, Mr. Edgewood? Did you mysteriously wake
up in a reality where who you are gives you authority in my class?"

That apparently was the wrong thing to say. I watch as Lev's face
tilts to the side, studying our calculus teacher and Owen's fingers
begin to drum on his desk.

"It's funny you think that, because you must be the one living in
a waking dream if you think who I am isn't the only reason I've
allowed you to hold that semblance of control, Jameson—don't let
the bit of power *we* allow make you forget that," Wes seethes.

Wyatt cracks his knuckles while giving Mr. Jameson a sinister
smile to drive home Wes's point.

Mr. Jameson recoils at the weight of Wes's words before clearing
his throat and returning to the smart board. "Like I was saying, coefficients are the values that multiply the predictor values in a linear
regression," he explains, accepting his chastisement and moving on.

"You were saying," Shay leans back in, a shit-eating grin plastered across her face.

"Shut up," I laugh, elbowing her back upright.

Maybe Wes is trying to do better, but I still wouldn't consider him mine.

The remainder of class passes, and I feel their presence as I pack my things and prepare to leave. Looking up, I see the guys standing in a semi-circle around my desk.

"Hey," I say, glancing back and forth between them. "What's going on?"

I see Shay out of the corner of my eye, and her stupid Cheshire cat grin is back in place. Turning to her, I mouth, '*Laugh it up, ho*' before returning my attention to the guys.

"As you've heard, Senior Night is tomorrow, and we'd like you to wear this." Wes holds out a jersey.

I reach to take it from him, holding it out in front of me to see the number seven printed on the back, along with Washington. It's Lev's.

"We were going to duel it out for the honor of having you wear our number, but football is Lev's thing. We just play. So, it only makes sense you wear his," Wyatt chimes in.

I'm going to wear the jersey, but I feel they should have to sweat it out for assuming I'd want to wear one and then choosing whose I'd wear.

"So, we're just out here dictating my wardrobe now?" I quip, giving each of them a pointed glare. They start to fidget, and I have to stifle my laugh.

Wes rubs the back of his neck. "We didn't mean... we just wanted... fuck. Sorry," he rushes out.

I burst into laughter. Seeing them squirm is one thing but watching Wes stumble over, trying not to be a dick, is hilarious.

"I'm just kidding. I'll gladly wear your jersey, Lev," I say, finally putting them out of their misery.

"You're cold-blooded, Love, but I'm here for it. Make us sweat it out— it keeps us on our toes," Wyatt murmurs when he leans in to press a quick kiss on my lips before he backs away, and we all start to head for the door.

Shay walks over to us once she's up and out of her seat.

"Looks like you only need to choose what you're putting on your bumpa," she begins, looping her arm through mine and hip-checking Wyatt out of the way. "It also looks like my statement earlier stands."

I flip her off again and dash out the door before she can pinch me.

It looks like I'm going to the game tomorrow night.

I'm lying in my bed when there's a knock at my door. I look up to see my dad standing at the threshold. He looks better each day. He'll still need some physical therapy, but he's coming along.

"Hey, Dad. What's up?" I ask, gesturing him in.

He walks in and takes a seat on the sofa. "Nothing much, Ry. I just wanted to come and spend some time with you. It's been a busy couple of weeks for you."

It's true. I've barely been home between dates, planning the Christmas and New Year's Eve events, and school. It's almost felt like I've been a real teenager minus the whole 'you must get married or else' bullshit. With Dad being home, I'm no longer filling the primary parental role. Of course, I still put Jamie and the twins first in almost all my decisions, but it's been great also to make a few selfish decisions. I've even had fewer instances of panic attacks.

"I'm good, Dad. We've been planning the toy drive for Christmas and working on getting baskets filled for families at the shelter in Lincolnville. One of the girls, Summer, has been away with her family for like a month. I don't know how she can leave during this whole thing since we're required not to leave, but apparently, some family emergency."

I'd be more worried, but I'm not for two reasons. One, she's a grade "A" bitch, and two, these people disappear on long vacations all the time.

Dad nods. "I'm glad you're helping with that, and I'm sure Summer will be back soon," he expresses before his face gets serious. "Look, Ry. I will be taking my seat back on the Council after the new year, but not as the leader. I don't know that I'll ever want that seat, but it's time."

Way to change the subject, Dad!

"What does that mean exactly?" I ask because I know there are always strings. Everything in this town has more strings attached than Sam's had nose jobs. *I really should stop that.* There's nothing wrong with plastic surgery, she's just a bitch, and I know it's the only other sore spot she has besides the guys. Well, besides Wes. Because, let's be honest, she only has eyes for him.

He sighs. "It means I'll have far more responsibilities for what takes place in this town. It also means that at the Christmas dinner, we'll announce the return of the Bradfords to the Fraternitas, which by default will announce your lineage."

I groan. I liked it better when people thought I was a nobody. Now I'm sure it will mean all the 'I always liked you' people will be coming out of the woodwork. "Do we have to announce it? Can't you just slide in through the back door?" I know it's not possible before I even ask, but I can dream.

Dad laughs, and I want to throw my pillow at his face. This is serious stuff. My peopling levels can't handle anyone's fakeness.

"Simply put, no. It's going to be important that the town knows for a few reasons, one of them being greater protections for Ky, Kellan, Jamie, and you," he explains. I wait for him to elaborate, but he doesn't.

"What are the other reasons?" I probe. The look on his face tells me he's about to give me the same annoying line I've gotten since coming to this town.

"I can't tell you that," we both say simultaneously.

He rubs at the bridge of his nose. "I know you're tired of hearing it. I'm tired of saying it. Nonetheless, it holds true. I won't ever put you in danger, not because I gave you information you wanted but didn't absolutely need to know."

"Okay, fine," I huff out and climb out of my bed. Once again accepting his rationale, at least for now, but I can feel my patience wearing thin on being in the dark.

He stands and walks over to me, then uses his good arm to squeeze me in a hug. "I love you, Ry. I know it frustrates you. Just be patient with me a little longer," he murmurs into my hair, pressing a kiss to the top of my head.

I hug him back, careful not to hurt him. I'm still annoyed with the situation, but I'm happy to have him home.

Before I can pull back, his arm scoops under my armpit, and I'm being flipped into the air. A loud screech flies out of my mouth as I hit the mattress with a thud.

"Dad!"

"You haven't been training. I shouldn't have been able to toss you with only one good arm," he chastises. "You're back in the gym starting tomorrow. I'll bring Mikhael here to continue your lessons until I'm well enough."

My eyes widen in surprise, "Wait, my gym teacher?"

He smiles, "You didn't think we'd have you at the school without someone to continue your training? I might still not be on board with you being part of all of this, but things were put in place to ensure you'd be prepared once you got here."

I shake my head. I should've thought it was odd that Krav Maga was being offered. Instead, I just thought it was rich people and their shit.

"Of course you did," I retort, pausing to catch my breath "I'll be ready."

"That's my girl," Dad says, then walks out of my room.

Groaning, I throw myself back onto my bed. I guess I'll be practicing before the game tomorrow night.

"Higher," Mikhael barks, easily tapping my shoulder.

We'd been at this for almost an hour now.

"Have you been training at all?" he asks, walking around me and checking my stance.

Does he think I was just home sitting on my ass? "I was kinda busy being kidnapped, asshole," I snap, dropping my hands to my side.

His leg sweeps out, clipping me behind my ankles, and I land on my back.

"Fuck," I shout.

"You're not thinking with your head," he tuts, pointing to his temple. "Never lead with emotion or anger. You know this. Get up and do it again."

Mikhael walks around my prone form, giving me only seconds to ready myself before he's on the attack again.

His foot lifts, slamming it down. "Your attacker won't wait for you to get your bearings."

I roll out from under the pending stomp of his boot into a backward shoulder roll and pivot, rearing my fist back for a kidney shot.

Mikhael grunts but aims his elbow out, preparing to hit my nose. I duck, avoiding the shot, and uppercut his chin. He sails back and kips-up as I move in on offense.

"Better," he says, wiping the blood from his chin.

My fists are up as I reposition my fighting stance. "I might have been out of commission, but I didn't suddenly forget everyth—." My words are cut off when an arm hooks around my throat and locks in.

"Always check your surroundings and never expect your opponent to fight f—," an unknown gruff voice starts to whisper in my ear, but I'm already stepping back with my left foot and tucking my chin toward my chest as I slightly twist my head and body to the right, setting my feet. Then my hands quickly snap up to my shoulders to build momentum before I bring my right hand down, swinging my open palm directly into his groin. The mystery man grunts, leaning forward with me as I bend, allowing me enough leverage to bring my right elbow up and slam it into his throat. The stranger lets out a sharp groan as his hands fall from my throat as I pivot my right foot back into my fighting stance.

"Excellent," I hear my father say, but I don't dare look. I just continue to bounce on the balls of my feet.

I watch as Mikhael gives the signal that the round is over. I don't lower my guard until I'm at the edge of the mat by my towel and water bottle. I only drop my hands to my sides when I know we're really taking a break. As I drink my water, I take in the man still holding his throat and dick on the ground.

"Damn," the unknown man exclaims between pained gasps, "that's quite the swing you got there."

I can't tell how tall he is in his bent state, but his tousled inky black hair hangs in his russet eyes as he aims his gaze at me.

Turning to my Dad, I ask, "Who's this?" My tone has an edge to it. I don't like the idea of someone I don't know sneaking up on me. However, I'm happy it didn't trip me up. After the Selection party, the idea of anyone sneaking up behind me like that makes me edgy.

Dad shakes his head, then responds, "This is Reign. Mikhael's younger brother."

I turn, looking at Reign, then at Mikhael, finally making the connection. They both have the same color eyes and facial features. As Reign gets to his feet, I see he's over six feet tall.

"Reign's a senior and will be transferring to LWU for the spring semester," Mikhael informs me. "He's going to be one of your sparring partners. After what happened at the party, we need to work on you being surprise attacked more."

I nod, understanding the importance of the sneak attack immediately. Hopefully, none of these sessions will trigger a panic attack or a flashback. "Okay, are we going again?" I inquire, knowing that I'll need to wrap this up soon if I want to have enough time to get ready for the guys' game.

My Dad's hand rests on my shoulder and squeezes before releasing it. "Let's go one more round. I know you have to get ready soon."

I grab a quick sip of my water, towel off the excess sweat, and redo my bun. "All right then. You heard the man. Prepare to get your asses kicked."

T he roar of the crowd makes me hurry up and wash my hands. *I knew I should've held it.*

Rushing from the bathroom, I hurry over to the glass of the skybox just in time to see Lev throw a pass down the field to Wes.

"Go...go...goooo," I shout, jumping up and down and motioning as if I can literally push Wes into the end zone.

He darts left and shuffles back, running around two defensive ends before breaking away and running it in for a touchdown right as the refs signal for halftime.

"Girl, take it down five octaves. You're going to make us all go deaf," Shay teases.

I turn away from the glass to face her. "Hey, you're the one who said I had to come to the game. So now you have to bear the repercussions of your actions," I snark back.

"Whatever." She grabs my wrist. "Come on, we need to get to the field before they start the ceremony."

I follow behind her as she practically drags me down the stairs toward the field. She doesn't stop or speak until we're at the entrance to the field.

"Wait, stop," I demand, pulling my hand out of her grasp. "Why are you trying to pull me out there?"

She points to Lev's jersey and then back to the field where parents and team members' partners are all making their way over to the Jumbotron.

My gaze snaps to her. "Why the hell are they all going over there? What don't I know?"

A mischievous smile crests her face. "Oh, you know, all the seniors give their jersey to a person they care about, and then that person joins the player on stage."

I try to massage away the growing headache. "I thought senior nights were just decorations, well wishes, and family and friends on the sidelines cheering you on," I huff, crossing my arms while I look for the nearest exit. *I didn't sign up for this shit.*

"You've been here long enough to know Edgewood doesn't do anything by halves. This is about to be a big spectacle, especially since the heirs are all seniors."

I groan, covering my face with my forearm. "Why didn't they tell me that before they asked me to wear Lev's jersey," I grumble. Then I remember the look on her face in the classroom. "You knew all this and didn't say anything!" I shriek.

Shay bursts into hysterical laughter, grabbing at her sides. "You should see your face right now. Freaking priceless." The traitorous ho cackles.

I hip-check her, and she nearly falls, stumbling until she rights herself. "What happened to the girl code? You know sisters before misters? Pussies before wussies?" I joke.

"I am looking out for you. It's time you stop standing on the sideline. They *all* care for you. Even the broody asshole, as Jamie calls him, and the reluctant scorned counselor."

She can't mean Sebastian? Every time we interact, he's so aloof. Not exactly cold, but definitely distant.

"*All of them,*" Shay declares emphatically, staring me down. "I see that look on your face. You don't believe me." She holds up two fingers. "Wyatt and Owen, especially Wyatt, were the least afraid to admit it. If I were a betting woman, I'd say Wyatt's been stalking you before you even knew who he was." A third and fourth finger joins the first two. She's about to list all the reasons. "Lev and Wes both looked like kicked puppies, eager for their owner's forgiveness, and by the looks of you wearing Lev's jersey, you forgave him at least. I suggest you make Wes grovel on his hands and knees for a bit longer." Shay shakes her hand once her thumb is raised. "And let's not forget the reluctant guidance counselor."

"Stop it. Don't say that. He's a teacher. There's no way he's interested in me," I interject, but she waves me off with the same annoying hand.

"Girl, shut up. Sebastian Grant is only twenty-three. If he didn't skip like two grades, he wouldn't even be a counselor here." She rolls her eyes, pausing momentarily. "He's going to be the most stubborn. That bitch Miss Taylor did a number on him when she cheated on him with his father and then married his ex-best friend, but he'll come around all the same. Shit, my money is on him falling hard and fast once he does."

Holy shit. How does she just drop that bomb on me? I knew Miss Taylor had a hard on for Sebastian, but I didn't know what she did. "Why didn't you tell me this tea before?"

"It's almost like you've been here but not paying attention to any of the gossip passing through the halls of Edgewood Academy," she quips before turning me to the field. "You can give me hell later. Get your ass out there. They're waiting on you."

I turn and see Lev standing just far enough away that he couldn't hear what we were talking about. I glance back to Shay, glaring at her one last time before sighing and pulling my shoulders back as I make my way onto the field. He takes my hand once I'm within reaching distance. "You guys could've warned me," I mutter.

"Where's the fun in that?" He smirks, leading me up the stairs to the platform. "Thank you," he murmurs, kissing my cheek and going to stand with the guys.

I try not to drool when I take them all in. Men in football uniforms? *Yes, please.* I work even harder not to stare at their jocks. It was hard enough not to drop my mouth open as I watched Lev's very toned ass walk away.

Each senior's name is called one by one, and they're given this elaborate plaque. Their loved ones cheer them on and hug them once they walk across the stage. I watch as each heir's parents wait for them. I step up next to Lev's mom and dad.

"Ariah, dear, so lovely to see you again so soon," Mrs. Washington greets.

"It's great to see you again, too," I reply with a slight wave.

A hand shoots out. "I agree with my wife. It's great to see you again," Lev's dad says. I haven't had very much interaction with him outside of Selection stuff.

I nod, shaking his hand and returning his greeting just as Lev's name is called. We all step up, cheering him on. His dad does one of those finger whistles that I've always been envious of.

"You know there are talks about him being a starting quarterback next year at LWU," Mr. Washington boasts, pride evident in every one of his features.

I knew Lev was an amazing player, but I didn't realize he was that skilled. "That's amazing," I profess right as Lev makes his way to us.

Lev hands his dad his award and scoops me into a hug, squeezing my middle and lifting me off my feet. "This is the best award," he whispers in my ear, planting a chaste kiss on my jaw.

I blush at the attention now on us but return his affections with my own, pecking him on the lips. "Congratulations," I say softly.

"Save some accolades and loving for the rest of us, Washington," Wyatt grumbles, pushing Lev out of the way for his own hug.

I laugh at their banter, hugging Owen next. When Wes steps up, he hesitates, looking unsure. I'm tempted to snub him, especially after the hallway incident, but it is his Senior Night. I reach up and hug him, catching him off guard. A shrill noise makes me step back as I watch Sam stomp from the field. "I don't think you're g—."

Wes's finger presses to my lips. "I'm going to stop you right there. She's nothing to me, and I wouldn't let her ruin this moment even if my life depended on it." Then he envelops me in his arms, squishing me into his padded body.

"Bring it in, you fools," I hear their coach shout, and Wes reluctantly lets me go. Then he steps back, staring down into my eyes before turning and running down the stairs and off the platform.

Wyatt leans in beside me. "You just made his night, Riri. Thank you!"

I follow the rest of the people down and off the field to a smug-looking Shay.

"I should've made you bet me," she teases.

"Fuck off," I quip, pushing her toward the stairs and back to the skybox, so I don't miss the guys' second half.

43
WYATT

I drop my duffel bag to the floor, lean back, and bend my knee to rest my foot against the wall. We won the game seventeen to three. Now I'm waiting for the rest of these idiots so we can leave.

The rowdiness of the locker room isn't loud enough to drown out my thoughts. It's been weeks since Ariah was rescued, and outside of Summer being killed, there's been radio silence. After Lev and Owen shared what came of their interrogation of Aleksi, I was hopeful the lead they'd gotten would lead to finding Madeline or Elise.

Elise. Even the non-verbal sound of her name makes me want to wash my brain with bleach. The rage I feel for that vile bitch can't be quantified.

After Owen finally shared what happened to him during his time in captivity, we all agreed never to tell Ariah—she doesn't deserve to carry that guilt.

"Are you going to the after party?" Coleman, one of our team-mates, asks, pulling me from my rambling mind.

"Later," is my only response, and he nods as he walks out of the locker room.

Looking up, I watch Wes, Owen, and Lev grab their shit and head my way.

"You primadonnas finally ready?" I jest.

"Shut up, asshole," Wes grumbles, pushing past me to the hallway.

Owen snorts, "One would think you'd be in a better mood since Ariah actually hugged you."

"The big baby's upset because he's still on the outs."

We're halfway down the corridor when we hear Sam's screeching voice.

"Do something about this. You promised me— you fucking promised!"

We all slow our steps, hoping to hear who she's talking to, but nothing's heard until she speaks again.

"No! I want what I was promised, and I'll accept nothing less than that, or you'll fucking pay," Sam snaps.

It's quiet again. *She's on the phone.*

The loud thud of the door makes us walk faster to the duck down a hallway.

Who the hell is she talking to, and what the hell was she promised?

"Fine. I'll be there in ten minutes. Let me just get the fuck out of this cheerleading uniform," Sam mutters.

We duck into the trainer's wing, keeping quiet and waiting a few minutes to be sure she's left.

"Who do you think she was talking to?" I ask.

Lev already has his phone out, tapping away at the screen. "Whoever it was, she wasn't talking to them through her carrier. I'd need more time to see if she's using some third-party app."

"Why don't we just follow her? She's still wearing the Selection pin with the tracker," Wes suggests.

"Okay, someone call Sebastian and tell him to meet us at Owen's Jeep. We'll stay far enough behind and only observe who she's meeting with. Then, if there's something suspicious going on, we'll make a better plan from there," Lev instructs.

Wes is already on his phone telling Seb where to meet us, and I'm texting Ariah, letting her know we'll meet her and Shay at the party later—hoping my statement is true.

By the time we all make it to Owen's car, Samantha's already gone, so Lev's brought up her chip for us to follow through GPS. "Do we all understand the plan for tonight? We're only following her until we know more," Lev states.

"You've only said it fifty times since we got in the car," I mumble.

"That's probably because you and slice and dice over there can be somewhat impulsive," Sebastian deadpans.

Owen and I look at each other and smirk, lifting our hands to our chests in mock horror. "We would never do anything rash," I state.

"I even left Lizzie at home." He pouts in the rearview mirror from the driver seat like a scolded child.

Sebastian meets his gaze, "Do I even want to know who Lizzie is?"

"Why, she's my new Spyderco Paramilitary 2 knife. She isn't Lola, but she'll gut you more efficiently," Owen answers, pulling the car to a stop. "We have to park here. Sam's tracker stopped right at the entrance to town. If we go any further, we risk her seeing our headlights."

Lev pulls out his phone and messes around with things on his screen again. Then he pulls out his laptop, and I see him bring up the controls for his drone.

"Will that make it here in time?" Wes asks.

Lev nods. "I've had it following us since we got in the car. I'm just pulling up the feed to my laptop so we can watch and listen together."

We watch as the drone feed appears on the screen. Samantha is standing outside of her silver Bentley Continental GT convertible. A man in a nondescript black car pulls up on the other side of the town line.

"Is that the same car from the night outside the diner?" Owen grits, pulling a knife from his pants pocket.

I see Sebastian shake his head out of the corner of my eye. "I thought you left it?"

"This isn't Lizzie. Now is that the car or not, Lev?"

The camera zooms in just as the audio kicks in.

"No, the make and model were different," Lev replies before he holds up his hand to silence us.

"Do you have it?" Samantha asks.

Damn, her voice is still so fucking obnoxious.

"I told you I did. Us meeting like this is fucking risky," the deep voice exclaims.

Sam's hand moves around animatedly. "I could give two fucks about risky. Give me what I asked for," she demands, and the man leans into his car and pulls out a duffel bag.

He walks right to the line and stops. "You know I don't come into the heir's territory. So, if you want this shit, you'll have to meet me here."

"Zoom in on that face," Wes commands. " I recognize that voice."

Lev angles the camera just as Sam walks over to him.

"Fucking coward. The heirs aren't anyone you should fear. I'll rain hell down on you and your family if you don't bring me the right shit," Sam snarls.

"Oh shit. That's Az," Wes shouts when the man covered in a skeleton tattoo comes into view. The intricate details of each bone contrasts with the shaded black and gray areas.

We watch as Sam steps closer, reaching out for the bag only for Az to drop it to the ground, grab Sam's arm, and yank her to the Lincolnville side of town. She screams, pushing at his chest, but his grip is firm.

"Listen here, you uptight cunt, the only reason I'm here is to drop off the fucking shoes you begged us to find for you. I'm not Trix. She's too fucking nice if you ask me. That's why she handles all the orders," he growls, and we all watch the bravado drain from Sam once she realizes she's never been the one in charge.

Not moving my eyes from the computer screen, I ask, "Who is this guy?"

"Azrael. He's one of the head members of The Lycéan," Wes replies.

The Lycéan? I thought Az was only called in when someone violated their rules. I'm about to ask for clarification when Lev's hand snaps up, quieting any further questioning.

"I'm just here to tell you to lose our information. Don't call asking us to find you anything ever again. You wasted your one and *only* request for a pair of shoes," Az barks, releasing Sam. She grabs the duffle bag and stumbles back across into Edgewood as Az storms back over to his car and peels out without a second glance.

"Stupid fucking asshole. He'll get his, just like everyone else," Sam mumbles, placing the bag on her car. Opening it, she pulls out a shoebox.

"She was really here for fucking shoes?" Sebastian seethes when Samantha takes out a pair of heels.

I rub the bridge of my nose. We were convinced she was up to something. Of course only Sam would call on the fucking Legion for a pair of shoes. Those guys can find anyone or anything, but you can only ask for their services once. They're fucking urban legends.

Owen sighs, "What now? This was obviously a bust. Is Sam off the list?"

No one immediately says anything, but we all watch as Lev brings up a website with the same shoes Sam's essentially drooling over in the middle of the road.

"Fifteen million dollars for a pair of heels?" Wes yells. "Remind me to make sure Ariah knows never to spend that much on freaking shoes."

"You don't dictate something like that. Ariah would probably tell you how many ways to go fuck yourself before you got your first words out. Not to mention, don't you have jewelry that costs more than that?" Sebastian snorts. "Those are Debbie Wingham Heels. I'd say the price point is perfectly reasonable between the eighteen-karat gold thread, the rare blue and pink diamonds, and the rose gold accent leather."

We all burst into laughter at Wes's look of confusion. The poor dummy has a lot to learn. With the way his dad dotes on his mother, he should know better. But, alas, some people must be led to the river and taught how to drink.

Lev clears his throat, "For now, we continue to keep an eye on Sam. Nothing happened this time, but until we catch Elise and Madeline and know for sure she's not involved, she's not in the clear."

I watch as Sam gently wraps her overpriced shoes back in the cloth, and places them gently back into the box before she finally gets back into her convertible. "I don't know if I should be annoyed we wasted our time when we could've been with Riri or glad that Sam was dumb enough to contact them, allowing me to catch a glimpse of the elusive Az," I concede.

"We need to get going before she sees us," Sebastian states,

"Let's go catch this party," Wes suggests.

"Drop me back off at the stadium. I'm not going to any damn party," Sebastian commands.

I don't blame him. If Ariah wasn't there, I'm not sure any of us would be going.

Owen turns the Jeep around and drives back to town. "Nobody better be touching our girl. Quinn's upset she didn't get used, so she feels quite stabby."

I would say no one would be that stupid, but past events have shown just how very dumb people can be.

"Lev, pull up the camera at the party," I demand.

The feed comes up, and my fists unclench. She's in the middle of the floor dancing with Shay. Everyone dances around them, but they all keep a safe distance back. *I guess people have a bit more sense than I give them credit for.* She has a bright smile on her face as her hand wipes her hair back from her sweaty forehead. Ariah laughs, throwing her head back, exposing the column of her neck. My eyes trail down, watching the sensual sway of her hips, and I'm mesmerized. I could watch her for hours.

My lips lift into a grin. *I have watched her for hours.*

"Earth to Wy," I hear Lev shout, causing my attention to pull away from the screen and look in his direction. "We're here."

I look around and see we have indeed arrived. "We're coming for you, Love."

44
ARIAH

Hands travel up my arms as two bodies press into me, bringing me out of my dance haze, the moment reminiscent of the time at Shay's house.

"Hello, Love."

"Hello, Angel."

Wyatt and Owen croon in my ears, causing chills to ripple down my spine.

I smile at their closeness before looking for Shay. When I finally find her, she's dancing with some girl I've seen at school but never talked to. Just as I push my ass into Wyatt, Owen presses his body into mine from the front. I ask, "Who's the girl Shay's dancing with?"

The girl is about the same height as me, maybe an inch or two taller. I can't really tell because she's in five or six-inch stilettos. Her honey-wheat hair has a wavy-curly flow to it. She's curvy, not as curvy as me, but if I had to guess, I'd say she's about a size fourteen. I can't see her eye color or distinguish her features from here. She's a smoke show.

"That's Eva," Wyatt answers.

"She's a senior like us, but she's usually quiet and doesn't come to these at all— at least not anymore," Owen states.

I arch a brow, signaling my request for more information. He knows I need more than just age, sex, and location.

Owen smirks. "She's good people. She mostly keeps to herself. I can go into more detail if you want. I'm more focused on the way you feel pressed between us again than I am on Shay dancing with Eva."

I glare at him, ready to put my hand up and stop him from moving even closer when he finally sees I mean business. I won't let my friend be left out just because I'm with my guys.

Relenting, Owen states, "She's not going to hurt Shay. They used to hang out a lot until Eva started to behave strangely. It's been a long time since she was at one of these. No one knows what exactly happened. We only know that one minute she was thick as thieves with Shay, then she was basically a hermit, going nowhere but school."

I peer over Owen's shoulder, Shay's eyes connecting with mine. When her customary smile is in place, I mouth, 'Are you okay?' Once she nods, I finally allow myself to enjoy the feel of their bodies against mine.

The music switches to Spice's *Go Down Deh,* and my hips begin to roll. My skirt rides up, exposing the top of my thigh-high fishnets. I hear matching groans and feel Wyatt's dick growing against my ass.

"Are you going to be a good girl for us and grind that body on our fingers?" Owen whispers, sliding his finger along the top of my thigh before slipping it under my skirt.

"Someone's going to see us." I protest, placing my hand on his wrist to stop his upward progress.

Two more bodies close in as Wyatt's hand trails up my other thigh before cupping my ass. "No one's going to know. Plus, we have these two helping to block us completely." He then leans over and latches onto my neck, sucking at what I'm sure is salty skin. I've been dancing for hours, so I'm covered in sweat.

Wes and Lev take a few more steps in, their hands joining the fray. So many hands. I lean my head back into Wyatt's chest, enjoying the feeling of their touch. Each one is so different. I know I must be lust drunk because I'm allowing myself to indulge in the feel of Wes's fingers dragging ever so lightly up my arms and to the opposite side of my neck before he grips my throat.

Fuck. The sensation he's causing as he squeezes, it's just enough to have a bite of pain, and I'm not repulsed, not even remotely.

I feel Wes's hot breath on my neck. "Do you like the idea of pain?" he murmurs.

"Wesley," a distinguishable whiny voice zaps all my lustful thoughts. I attempt to step out of Wes's touch, but all their holds lock me in place.

"Don't you dare, Angel. That bitch doesn't get to kill our vibe," Owen demands through gritted teeth. His hold on me matches the ire in his whiskey-colored eyes. I know his anger isn't for me but for the gnat that can't seem to know when it's her time to bow out with some grace.

Samantha approaches, but I'm not up for this bullshit tonight. I came here to have fun, not square off with the likes of her.

"Let me go. Tonight's not the night for her shit," I snap, unfurling from their hold.

Shay is already waiting. "Are we out?" she gauges, trying to decipher my plan of action.

I nod, striding toward the door. I hear the belabored temper tantrum of Samantha and the muffled curses of the guys behind me.

"She's really stale with her lack of self-awareness and ability to read a room," Shay expresses.

Sighing, I reply, "Exceedingly so. I don't know that I've actually ever met someone so clearly obtuse."

"Oh, if there's one thing Samantha Davenport isn't, it's obtuse. She knowingly pushes herself into every situation. It's her entitlement that's the issue," Shay expounds.

I nod, entirely in agreement. Samantha is more conniving than I think we give her credit for. She definitely wears the 'I want it, and I want it now,' a real Violet Beauregarde.

We step out into the crisp air, and I shiver. With December fast approaching, it's starting to feel like winter here in New England. Raising my arms, I try to warm my goose-pimpled skin, kicking myself for trying to be cute instead of practical and wearing a coat.

The warmth of a coat and strong hands envelop me as the scent of black coral and moss fill my nostrils. The undertones of lavender make me inhale a bit deeper.

"We're going to have to work on you taking care of what's ours, Dove," Lev's deep voice sing songs in my ear, renewing the chill in my body, this one not from being cold.

My lips lift into a smile as I allow myself to stand in the heat of his body. I want to touch him but don't want to push him, especially not in front of so many. "And let me guess. You're all going to ensure I do just that, right?" I tease.

Owen tugs me from Lev's hold. "That's exactly right, and you're not going to fight us on it either," he murmurs, nipping me on my nape before spinning me around. "Or— maybe you will, and then we can have even more fun." A wry grin paints his face, the left side of his mouth quirking up. "Oh please, please, please fight. I do enjoy a good game of cat and mouse."

Pecking his lips, I push against his chest, slipping from his grasp on my waist. "As long as you all know that I'll be the one doing the hunting," I smirk, looking each of them in the eyes. Wes still looks uncertain of how he should interact with me. I can almost see his brain trying to decide if he's allowed to join in on the banter or not. He can stew for a bit longer. I can only tolerate certain levels of asshole, and his still needs some work.

Turning around, I start walking to the car, enjoying their commentary on how I could never outsmart them.

"Keep sleeping on my girl, and unnuh will be left chasing your tails," Shay jokes, and we both burst into laughter as we reach her car.

We say our goodbyes. Then I turn to head toward where Thomas is parked. Owen attempts to pull me back into him, but Wyatt's hand smacks his out of the way.

"Uh-uh. She's all mine tonight. I'm not sharing." Wyatt declares.

"That's cold-blooded, but I respect it."

I'm about to argue on my behalf when Wyatt grips my hip, pulls me into his chest, and presses his lips to mine, dissolving all protests.

"You can be up in arms about your right to choose after I'm through," he mumbles against my lips, slowly disconnecting where they're joined together.

We barely make it to Wyatt's room before we're both pulling off our clothes. Items dot the floor like a trail of breadcrumbs, leading straight to our tangled limbs.

Wyatt kisses a trail up my stomach.

"Do you know how long I've waited to have you alone— all to myself, Love?" Puffs of air caress my skin as he makes his way down between my legs. His arms spread my legs open, giving him a perfect view of my wet pussy. I can feel myself dripping in anticipation. His tongue licks a slow ascent, stopping to whirl circles around my clit before sucking it between his teeth. The sensation wreaks havoc on my senses, and I moan when two thick digits slide in.

Wyatt pumps his fingers at a frantic pace. His suction on my clit is relentless as I barrel over the edge.

"Fuck!" I shout. "Please...condom...now...inside me." I babble with some semblance of coherence between gulps of air, and in less than a minute Wyatt's rolling a condom over his piercings and slowly seating himself in my pussy.

"I'm not going fast tonight, Riri. Tonight, I'm going to wring every ounce of pleasure you have to give me and then take a little more." He groans between each languorous stroke. Each drive is purposefully teasing.

If he doesn't move...

I whine a sob, a cross between frustration and satisfaction when his waist swivels creating just enough friction to graze my clit with his pelvic bone but not enough to give me what I'm seeking. I'm so tempted to take control.

As if seeing the thought play across my mind, Wyatt rocks his hips back, leaving just the pierced crown of his shaft inside me before driving back in deeply. A scream gets caught in my throat as he sets the pace.

"I'm in control." he growls, then switches his movements again, so he's now hovering over me as his hips languidly roll. His hand reaches up and palms my breast, rubbing my nipple between his fingers as he lowers his mouth, grazing the hardened peak before biting it.

"Shh-itt," I moan as he sucks and twists while sliding in and out. I feel the six sets of barbells gliding along the walls of my pussy as I match each thrust of his hips.

When he moves his mouth from my nipple, I cry out in protest until he silences me with his hand around my throat, lightly squeezing until my eyes roll back, exposing the whites of my pupils.

"Look at me, Love. Let me see those fucking gorgeous gray eyes turn metallic from how deep I'm inside you." he orders, using his grip on my throat to pull my mouth to his. His grasp tightens as our tongues dance.

I can feel my vision blurring, but the feel of his cock buried inside of me while he chokes me is mind-altering.

With a nip of his teeth on my lips, he lowers me back down to the mattress, never once loosening his grip. Instead, he squeezes tighter on his downward thrust. My walls clench, attempting to hold him hostage inside me.

"Shit, this pussy is so fucking greedy for me, isn't it?" he grunts.

I want to bellow 'yes' so loud that anyone in a five-mile radius can hear, but Wyatt's other hand reaches down between us and begins to strum at my clit while tightening his hold around my throat. It's still not enough for me to feel unsafe or like I'll pass out. Instead, my body is buzzing at the overstimulation of my senses being worked. My eyes close of their own volition.

"Eyes on me," he grits out when I squeeze around him. My walls begin to spasm. I can feel my orgasm mounting.

Wyatt's fingers rub steady circles on my clit as he pistons into me, his dick pumping deeper with each stroke as his hold on my neck tightens to the point of hesitance. The fear is creating a sensation I've never felt before. My pussy clamps down hard. My back bows off the bed as choppy squeals fight their way out. I erupt, and my pussy convulses around Wyatt's dick. I barely hear his cursed orgasm as his thrusts become jerky.

It's not until I've come down that I realize he's pulled out of me and is wiping me down with a warm cloth that I realize I must have passed out at some point.

"How long have I been out," I croak, my voice hoarse from my shrill screams.

Wyatt doesn't stop wiping the sweat from my forehead. "Twenty-three seconds," he murmurs. He looks like a lost puppy.

"Why the sad face?" I probe.

"I lost control. I didn't mean to choke you until you lost consciousness. I just wanted to heighten your experience."

I quirk my lip. "I'm more than okay, Wy. I would've stopped you if I truly thought I was in danger. I enjoyed myself. Shit, enjoyed isn't enough. I fucking loved it."

He still doesn't look convinced.

Sighing, I reach my palm up to his face. "Listen, from now on, if we ever do this again and I don't feel safe, we'll make a plan beforehand. Deal?" I suggest.

He reluctantly nods.

"Now come lay with me or fuck me again, whichever tickles your fancy," I joke, making him smile. He scoops me into his chest, resting my cheek against him so I can feel the thump of his heart until it evens out.

Just when I think he's fallen asleep, he mumbles. "I'll never hurt you on purpose, Riri. I'll cut out my own heart first."

45
SEBASTIAN

It's the day before fall break, November's rushing to an end, and I'm searching through the personnel files, combing through all the information, and cross-checking it with what Lev has provided me. It's taking longer than I expected. Some of the people who work here have interesting pasts. I've already recommended the removal of at least three predators, and by removal, I mean time with Owen or Lev. I'd take care of them myself, but I know they need this.

I stare down at Patricia Nelson's name. She's quirky, but by all accounts, everything checks out. She likes to spend her nights in the dungeons of Le Toucher. I place her file through the shredder. There's no need to expose anyone's private information unnecessarily.

The beeping of my phone signals it's time for me to wrap this up. Opening my briefcase, I place the stack of files I didn't get through inside and prepare to leave.

I'm locking up my office when I hear someone approach.

"Damn. I guess I missed office hours," Ariah mutters.

Placing my keys in my pocket, I reply, "I am done for the break, but if you walk with me, I can see if there's anything I can help you with."

She walks alongside me. "I think Miss Taylor has it in for me."

I grind my back teeth at the mention of her name. One day I'll be able to hear it and feel nothing— I'm still not there yet.

"What makes you feel that way?" I inquire, knowing it's probably the case, but I don't want to assume Vivian is stupid enough to harass Selection picks.

Ariah huffs. "She's continuously marking my grades lower than they should be, even after the situation was already addressed. And she's always making snide comments."

That sounds precisely like Vivian.

Once we reach the front office door, I hold it open, allowing Ariah to exit. She mumbles her thanks and steps through the door. The candy floral scent of her perfume fills my nose, and I have to fight the urge to flare my nostrils.

"I know she's your ex or whatever," she states, making me stumble momentarily.

"Is that so?"

"Yes. It's all over the school, and if the rumors weren't enough, her direct threat to stay away from you a couple of months ago solidified the fact," she rushes out.

I feel the headache that was a dull ache earlier double. Vivian is a fucking nuisance that I created out of my need for vengeance.

Ariah's arm swings out, stopping us before we exit the school building. "Look, I get you're not a fan of this whole process. I wasn't at first. Fuck, I'm still not completely on board, but we're in this, and I would appreciate it if you could get her to back off before I do something to make my point."

Turning, I face her, watching the flare of her nose and the flush of her cheeks. "And what exactly is it you intend to do?"

"Fuck you in front of her."

I choke on air, covering up the sound with a fake cough. "You shouldn't tempt fate."

My words cause her silver eyes to narrow. "I'm not scared of my civics teacher."

A smirk grows on my face. "She's not the fate you're tempting, Spitfire." Her eyes dilate at the shift in my voice— smooth and deep. "I'm not sure you know what you're signing up for with me," I state, stepping into her space and bending to whisper in her ear. "Your throat would be hoarse by the time we were through." I stand and step back, enjoying the flush in her skin— now from lust instead of anger. Moving around her, I say, "I'll deal with Miss Taylor. Have an amazing holiday Miss Bishop." Then, I make my way out the door, leaving her with her mouth hanging open before I tip my head in Thomas's direction as I pass him to reach my car.

I know I shouldn't have teased her like that, but the image of her counting as she's laid out on my bed shot my ability to make good decisions right out the window.

My mood sours the minute I put my car in drive. Now, I need to go and deal with a lingering problem.

The Taylor estate sits on the edge of town. Like most of Edgewood's homes, it spans acres and sits behind a gate.

I pull into the horseshoe driveway and park, jumping out and climbing the ridiculous amount of steps to the door. Before I can knock, it swings open.

"Sebastian," Vivian's mother gasps, "I have to say I never thought I'd see you at our door again. I guess Vivi was telling the truth for once when she said you two were getting back together."

Of course the lying wench would say that.

"No. We're not anything. You know the Selection has started, and even if it didn't, I'd never subject myself to your daughter's ideas of love again," I state emphatically.

Mrs. Taylor's posture visibly relaxes, stepping aside to let me in the house. "I knew you were a smart boy, Bash. I don't know where we went wrong with Vivi— she's always been so thirsty for power."

I follow her to the sitting room as she prattles on about how sorry she is and how she would've told me if she had known what her daughter was up to. I appreciate her candor. She's always been straightforward.

"Where is Vivian now? I need to discuss something important with her."

"She's in the guest house at the back of the property. She's living there until, in her words, 'I get Bash back.' I'm going to need to speak with her father now that I know she's lying again. You know where to go. It was good to see you again, Sebastian. Make sure, whatever you boys do, you don't pick that Davenport girl. She reminds me too much of Vivi," she states before leaving the room.

My stomach roils at the thought of ever being tied to another soul-sucking leech like Vivian. Samantha Davenport is a close second to the woman I thought would be mine forever.

I hear the moans before I even open the door to the guest house.

"Fuck, ride me fucking harder, Vivian or I'll flip you over and take what I want," the voice of my father nearly catapults me back to the scene in our home that day.

"Shut the fuck up. You're here to get me pregnant and nothing else. We have a limited window for Bash to believe this baby is his," Vivian's vile voice snarls.

The fucking woman doesn't seem to remember I never put my dick in her without a condom. I only ever fucked her ass since she's been home, and I haven't touched her since before the Selection two months ago.

Clapping my hands, I walk into the room. "Bravo. I guess this is your encore. I'd say, what the fuck, but nothing you two do surprises me."

Vivian springs off my father's naked prone form grabbing at the sheets, grasping for some sense of modesty— a trait she's never possessed, apparently.

"Oh no. Please continue— don't stop on my accord. I'm only here to tell you that if you threaten another Selection girl again, Vivian, it won't be me visiting you. It will be Owen, and we know how much he's been dying to slice you— I mean, spend some time with you," I gleam.

Vivian jumps off the bed, nearly tripping over the clothes sprawled across the living room floor. "Bash, please. I was doing it for us. If I were pregnant, you wouldn't have to go through with the Selection."

Is she serious?

"Stop," I shout, shocking her still. "Do you even hear yourself? Don't you think if I wanted to be out of this, I wouldn't have volunteered or, I don't know— maybe even gotten you pregnant myself?" I turn, storming back toward the entrance of the guest house, done with all this bullshit. My father is smart enough to remain silent— our relationship died that day, and the treacherous jealous bastard knows not to speak to me unless it's required.

Vivian grabs my arm, her nails trying to gain purchase, but I yank myself from her hold, rounding on her until she steps back. "I suggest you give Ariah Bishop and me a wide berth— at this point, your fucking life depends on it. Consider this my last kind act toward you, Vivian," I growl, then turn and stalk out of the guest house, choosing to walk around the main house to the car. I don't need to see the Taylors again.

As I drop to my seat, I wonder if Vivian's mother knew my father was here. I immediately dismiss that thought— Joanna Taylor would castrate my father where he stood if she knew he was here, consequences be damned. The positive of this situation is I can finally put Vivian Taylor in my rearview because fuck her and the sperm donor. I would hope he knocked her up, but no kid deserves either of them as parents.

Driving out of the estate, I head for the Tombs. We need to add my father to the list of potential turncoats. There's no reason he should be helping Vivian, not if he's with the Fraternitas.

With my mind made up, I turn on my satellite radio and let the sounds of Fallout Boy's *Light Em Up* beat through my speakers, enjoying the freedom I've just been given.

My mother and two younger brothers might be hurt by his demise, but they've all suffered far greater with him breathing—sometimes, things must die for new things to be born.

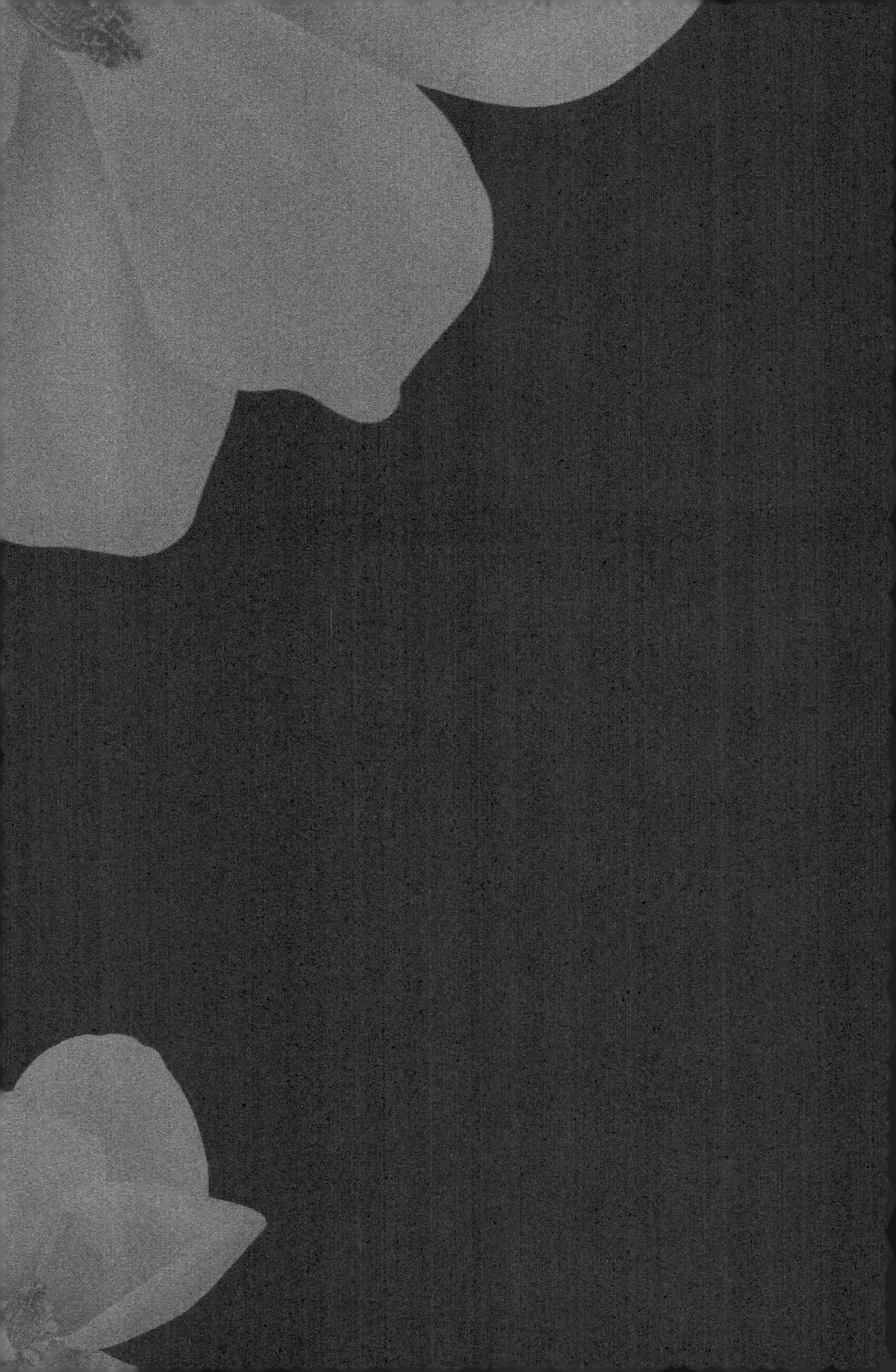

I can't believe it's already December. After the holiday break, we played in the championship game and lost. Lev was bummed, but a weekend with Ariah would make anyone feel like a champion.

Grabbing my books from the passenger seat, I exit my Jeep and head for the building. I'm late, so everyone's already inside. I was following a few leads Lev had on Madeline last night and overslept.

I grit my teeth. We haven't gotten any viable leads on her or Elise. It's been quiet— too fucking quiet. Maybe I should be happy that no more girls have gone missing and there haven't been any more anonymous packages delivered to Ariah, but it'd be foolhardy for us to believe this is done and over with.

Sighing, I scan my thumbprint and enter the building. I'm annoyed with this day, and it's only just begun. Usually, I'd say Fridays are great days. However, I have another damn date tonight. The idea of sitting across from another Samantha crony is nauseating at best.

I make it halfway down the hall when I hear hushed whispers.

"I'm not going to continue to put up with this. I'm in charge, and your attitude hasn't gone unnoticed. Get your act together, Miss Davenport. I don't want to have this conversation again."

Is that Vivian?

Sam comes storming around the corner. She's not paying attention, too busy mumbling about stupid fucking people always trying to tell her what to do, that she doesn't see me, and I have to step out of her way so she doesn't crash into me.

I don't move fast enough because she clips my shoulder.

"Hey, watch where you're fucking— oh, Owen, it's you," Samantha's snarly tone quickly smooths to coquettish. "I didn't see you there." She tries to raise her hand to touch my arm, but I fix my glare at the offending limb, and she wisely continues lifting it to brush her hair behind her ear.

I don't respond, continuing to walk past her to AP Calculus.

"Why are you so late this morning? Class is nearly over," Ariah asks, leaning in once I take my seat. The fruity scent of her lip gloss wafts in the air.

I angle my neck to take her in as she shifts back into her seat. Her hair is in a messy bun, and today's t-shirt is Bob Marley. *We really need to exchange playlists.* "I woke up late," I reply as the bell rings, ending class.

Ariah stands, Shay and the guys following suit, then we all make our way for the door. "Hopefully, it wasn't anything too bad that kept you up," she states, and I detect an undercurrent of worry.

We've talked about the day in my room, what she did for me, and some of the reasons why I needed it. She doesn't know all the details, but she knows just enough for her to understand my need for pain, mainly inflicted by a knife. I stare at her as we walk down the hall. I love how there's no judgment in her eyes, only worry.

"No, Angel. It turned out to be nothing," I respond, keeping my answers in the gray area of truth. I don't want to lie to Ariah, but we all agreed to keep her out of this as much as possible— that means skirting the truth. She's definitely going to kick our asses when she finds out.

Ariah's strong. We know all about her Krav Maga training. She's been working with her dad for years in hand-to-hand combat. I've seen videos of her shooting, and while she's no markswoman, she can hit her target from a distance. It's why we know her mom had her drugged to be taken. I'm confident she would've put up a hell of a fight if she wasn't.

An image of her throwing knives with me threatens to make my dick hard. Inspired by the vivid scene playing out in my mind, I ask, "What are you doing on Sunday?"

We're stopped at her locker. "Outside of some training with Dad, Mikhael, and Reign, nothing," she replies.

Ah, yes, Reign. A background check was run on him the minute Mikhael asked for him to be able to move into town. He'll be finishing his Bachelor's at LWU after an incident at his last school, and he was asked to leave. He wouldn't be Ariah's training anything if I didn't know the incident was related to him stalking a particular female student. Why he's stalking her doesn't matter to me— what matters is that he's so obsessed he doesn't see anyone but her.

"Owen," Ariah's hand on my arm jolts me back into the conversation. "What did you want to do this Sunday?"

A slow smile creeps on my face. "Good, keep your afternoon free. I want to take you somewhere."

I'm about to say more when Wes cuts in. "Ariah, can I talk to you for a moment," he mumbles, and I snort. The cocky fucker is nervous.

Ariah's eyes narrow. She's still running hot and cold with him on a good day. Every attempt he's made since Senior Night has been rebuffed. "What's up?"

"Uh..." Wes grabs the back of his neck and looks down both ends of the hallway before finally meeting her gaze. "I was hoping we could— I mean, I could take you out this weekend. I want to expl-."

She holds up her hand, stopping his rambling. "I'm nowhere near ready to go on a date with you, Wes, and now isn't the time to try and explain away the fucked up way you treated me when I got here," Ariah states, grabbing Shay's arm and taking off down the hall.

Wes shouts after her but she flips him off and keeps going. He turns back to us, running his hands through his inked hair. "Fucking hell. She's never going to give me the time of day. This is bullshit," Wes whines. *Fucking man-child.* He turns to Lev. "How the hell did you slide back into her good graces so easily?"

We collectively snort. Of course he thinks Lev was just magically forgiven.

"I didn't," Lev deadpans.

Wes looks even more perplexed. "But you're close, aren't you?"

Wyatt walks up next to Wes and tsks, "Guy, he didn't slide into her good graces. He's continuously putting in the work. Have you learned nothing?"

"I don't understand. What do I need to say to fix it? I just want to fix it," Wes pleads.

"You have to figure that out, but your effort should match your fuck up," I tell him before we all head to our classes before the bell rings.

And with the way Wes fucked up, he'll probably need to do something meaningful.

I knew I should've just skipped this bullshit date. These girls always get their panties in a bunch over my date ideas.

"Are we seriously at the morgue?" Brittany hisses.

I smirk. "The cadaver in front of you determines that the answer to your asinine question is yes. I told you where we were going, and you still got in the car."

Brittany stomps her heel. "That scrap of junk wasn't a car. It was a death trap."

My smirk grows, remembering the look on her face when I pulled up in my Dad's '91 Acura Legend. Like I would ever again let her or any of her other friends ride in the same car Ariah's been in. Shit, I already replaced the seats in Rubi so that Ariah would never have to sit where any of them might have once upon a time.

"Hey, that car got you here. Keep it up, and you'll have to walk back," I reprimand, grabbing the scalpel and bending over the body. My hand lowers, and I begin to press into the flesh below me, and the asshole on the slab muffles a scream behind his gag as he wiggles, messing up my incision.

Digging the blade into the wound, I growl. "You fucked up my line work, asshole."

Brittany screams at the sight of the blood, reminding me why I set this "date" here.

I look back at the idiot on the table and then back at her. "Do you know what I discovered today?" I ask her, making another slice, a better one this time, into the man's side. Brittany doesn't answer—she won't. She knows she's screwed. "I learned that a certain group of spoiled-rich, snobby girls, following the orders of a vile cunt who doesn't want to get their hands dirty, hired some idiot to pretend to stalk my girl."

Brittany begins to walk toward the exit, but it's too late for her. Wyatt walks in just as she turns to grab the door handle.

"Where do you think you're going?" he snaps, and she runs back into the room.

"You might as well sit so I can finish my storytime. I was about to get to the best part," I direct, pointing my scalpel to the chair by the slab.

She stands frozen to the spot, and I nod at Wyatt. He snatches her, causing her to yelp. He has her in the chair next to me and zip tied before she realizes she should do something.

"Please d-d-don't h-h-hurt me," she begs. She's terrified. We can't hurt her because of the stupid fucking rules, but I plan to make her sweat.

Flaring my nostrils, I inhale the scent of her fear. It doesn't have the same effect it used to— not since I found my new drug of choice.

"Imagine our surprise when we discovered what you and your little bitch squad were up to. How you wanted him to record himself chasing her and stripping her naked," I seethe, turning back to the dumbass who thought he could make a quick buck. I sink the blade deep into his Adam's apple and slice down until I reach his navel. Typically, we'd drag this out, but Lenny here sang like a canary.

Brittany's shrill cries echo off the walls, almost bursting my eardrums. I clench my jaw, fighting the urge to cut out her vocal cords. "It was all Samantha's idea. I didn't want to do it. I'm sorry, please, please, please don't kill me," she begs incessantly.

"Shut. The. Fuck. Up. Or you're next," I bark.

Wyatt laughs, and I turn to glare at him until I see his eyes aren't trained on me. I follow his line of sight. Brittany's passed out.

Chuckling, he says, "Now, this is the definition of scared straight, but in her case, she isn't yet. Let's leave her here and call someone to pick her up in two hours."

Nodding, I stop before her unconscious form and wipe my bloody palm down the front of her face. I drop the scalpel in her lap, then exit the room. If she's smart, she'll get the message.

Don't fuck with what's mine.

47
ARIAH

All the planning for this event was worth it. Everything came together nicely, and we made almost two thousand family baskets filled with everything necessary for the holiday as well as gift cards to buy presents. After distributing these, we need to go back to the Edgewood estate to finalize the details for the annual Christmas event.

"This is so dumb. Why do we have to do this at all? Isn't there a team that can drop these off, and where the fuck is Summer? That bitch has avoided every single part of putting this together," Sam complains.

I roll my eyes. Of course she'd find doing anything for someone she considers 'less than' beneath her. She and her plastics are some of the reasons why some people shout, 'Eat the Rich.'

"Imagine being so wealthy you don't see or understand how it's possible to need a helping hand. To be of the mindset that all you need to do is pull yourself up by your bootstraps and everything will work out just because opportunity, luck, and hard work lined up for you, so the reason it hasn't for someone else is that they're not trying hard enough," I state, and they look at me like I'm the stupid one.

The woefully ignorant of the systems and circumstances that don't allow access burn my soul.

Huffing out a frustrated breath, I leave the room before I let my anger get the best of me. Today isn't about me. It's about the thousands of families that will have a better Christmas. This was my situation last year. Waiting and hoping to get something to ensure the kids could have a halfway decent holiday while our loser mom was off on what I thought was a bender. Instead, she was out trying to plot how to lay siege to some shadow organization, leaving me to fend for my siblings. Until we moved to Edgewood, donations like these helped make Christmas happen, but I'm not stupid. What's happening here isn't the norm. My situation is the stuff portrayed in movies and books. How many people would have the opportunity to be some hidden powerful bloodline seated in a position of power?

"Didn't I tell you not to feed the zoo animals?" Shay jokes, knocking her shoulder into mine to get my attention. I'm so happy she's here volunteering.

Sighing, I say, "It's just." I shake my head, at a loss for how to express what I'm feeling without coming across as brash and irrational.

Shay pulls me in for a hug. "Some people won't ever get it. No matter how much evidence says otherwise, they won't. So, don't let them draw yuh out."

I squeeze her tight, thankful again to call her my bestie. Who would've thought I'd like anyone enough for that shit. "You're right."

"Duh bitch. I'm always right. You're late," she teases, stepping back. "Now, where is that ho, Summer, at? As much as I hate to agree with Sam on anything, she's right about Summer's absence. It's odd that she'd be missing from the Selection process for so long and that her friends don't know where she is."

"Do you think something happened to her? I thought it was normal for families to go traipsing off without a moment's notice," I reply, hoping that's really what happened in this instance.

Shay and I grab two baskets each, double-checking that it has everything inside before we walk them to the finished side of the room.

"I mean, yes. We all have taken impromptu trips. It's just a little weird that she wouldn't talk to any of her friends." she explains.

I try to remember the last time I've seen Summer anywhere. I know I saw her at the doctor's office when we got the freaking mandated implants, and then I saw her at school a few times after that, but that was in early November. It's mid-December. I mean, when they said she was traveling, she still could be. *Right?* But would she not speak to *any* of her friends?

Pulling out my phone, I bring up one of my social media apps. "What's her handle? Maybe she's posted some pictures?"

"Here, let me," Shay offers, taking my phone and typing the name in.

Shay hands me back my phone, and I click on the last image posted. Summer's poolside, in a barely there bikini, sipping on some fruity-looking drink. Her caption says, 'Jet setting. Leaving the Bullshit Behind.' It was dated yesterday.

"I guess she's giving a middle finger to the Selection. Good for her." I snicker as we pick up more baskets and bring them over, placing them with the others. I didn't like her, but I'm here for anyone with enough balls to do something like this.

Once we've finished with our section, we move to help the others.

"Summer's dumb for leaving. Like, who would give up such an amazing opportunity? What if they were going to pick her?" I overhear Meagan say.

"It was smart for her to leave. We all know there's no competition. I'm the one being chosen in the end, but the bitch could say something to me," Samantha snaps.

Seeing her folly, Meagan stumbles to fix it. "Of course. She was sparing herself the inevitable heartbreak."

Shay snorts, "I wonder if they ever get tired of sucking the shit out her batty hole."

"Ladies, it's time to get these baskets loaded." the event planner instructs.

Sam and her lemmings groan but finally start to help, and we're done and ready to head out to deliver baskets.

As I get in the backseat of the car, I pull my phone back out and look at Summer's picture again. *Why would you stop talking to your friends all of a sudden?* The thought niggles in the back of my mind the entire time we drop the gifts off at each center. So much that I don't realize when Thomas pulls up outside my house.

"Ariah, we're here," his voice coaxes me out of my wandering thoughts. He's standing with the door open. *Shit, I really was out of it.*

Rubbing my forehead, I step out of the car, "Sorry, T, I didn't even notice we were here."

"What's going on? You've been out of it almost the entire time," he inquires, walking me to the front door.

Stopping, I contemplate momentarily before I blurt out, "Has anyone heard from Summer or her parents?"

"The family has decided to take a break from the stress that the Selection process has caused them," he responds stoically. "Now, go inside. Tonight's a big night for you, Miss Bradford."

My thoughts begin to scatter for a different reason. "Ugh. Why did you have to remind me? I was enjoying my perfect plan of avoidance," I whine, stepping inside.

He laughs, and I know he thinks he's redirected me, but I know an evasive maneuver when I see one. I won't make a big deal out of it now, but I make a mental note to find more information on Summer's whereabouts as I climb the stairs.

I stare at my Dad and the twins, all decked out in matching tuxes.

"How long do we have to wear these stuffy penguin things again?" Kellan asks, pulling at the bowtie.

"Yeah, this thing keeps giving me a wedgie," Kylan adds, picking at said wedgie.

I have to hold my hand over my mouth to hide my laughter. Jamie, however, giggles until she's snorting. She looks beautiful in her pantsuit. She refused to wear a dress, much to the stylist's dismay. Jamie said, "I don't need to be in a stupid dress to be pretty." Dad was entirely on board with her decision.

Shaking his head, Dad says, "Just a few hours, guys." Then, we're all piling into the SUV.

As we pull up to the Edgewoods' house, Dad's expression smooths out, his laugh lines disappearing instantly. "Okay, tonight is serious. Remember what we talked about. After tonight, everyone will know you as a Bradford."

My stomach bottoms out. I'm not looking forward to this announcement.

Dad squeezes my hand. "I know, Ry. This isn't what we want, but it is what we must do," he says before turning to grab the box lying on the seat next to him.

"I know. I'll be fine." I nod, taking another deep breath before exiting the car and heading to the front door.

The door opens by the time we make our way up the stairs, and the work we've spent weeks planning is on full display. Wes's house has been transformed into Christmas in New England. A giant pine tree is off to the side by the floor-to-ceiling window. It's decorated in white, gold, and red, the color scheme for the evening.

I watch as Dad takes the box he carried in and walks to the tree before opening it and taking out our family ornament. As he hangs it, we stand by his side as a bellman announces our entrance, and I brace myself.

The burly man looks at his paper and then back to where we're standing. His gaze oscillates between what's written and the family before him. His shock is quickly masked as he puts back on his professional demeanor and bellows, "The Edgewood family would like to welcome the Bradford family to the town's annual Christmas ball."

Gasps break out around the room, the loudest shriek belonging to Samantha before a woman who looks just like her leans in and whispers in her ear. Samantha's posture straightens, and her lips thin.

I watch Donald Edgewood walk to the podium, and the whispering crowd goes silent. "As you've just heard, the Bradfords are back." My father steps away from the tree and walks toward the stage. Lev's, Owen's, and Wyatt's fathers follow suit as Mr. Edgewood continues, "The five founding bloodlines are now all back in Edgewood. Aaron Bradford will take his place among us as a leader within the community. The Selection process will go on as planned. Thank you all for coming out." Wes's father finishes, then steps from the mic, effectively cutting off any possibility for questions.

A tug on my dress has me looking down at Kylan. "Can we take off these stupid clothes yet?" His question cuts at the tension of the moment.

I smile, squatting to meet his eye. "Not yet, buddy, but if you hurry, there's a snow globe bounce house down the hall." That's all that needs to be said. His beef with the tux is forgotten as he grabs Kellan's hand and tugs him in the direction I pointed.

Standing, I turn to look for Jamie, only to see she's run off already.

"That was smooth." I look up to see Lev smirking as he and the other guys stand at the bottom of the short staircase. Sebastian holds out his hand to help me down the steps.

My feet aren't fully planted when I see a sea of people converging on me.

Wes turns around, facing the oncoming group. "Back the fuck up.

You all acted like you didn't want to know her before. Don't try to know her now," he barks, staring down the crowd of our classmates.

Shay elbows her way through the slowly dispersing crowd. "Unnuh move nuh, chuh. We nuh wan nuh fake fren roun ere. Suh, do— gwan bout yuh business," she exclaims, looping her arm through mine once she reaches me. "Fuck these people. Let's go have fun with your men."

I'm about to correct her when I'm pulled from her into a hard chest.

"We'll be back." I hear Wes state as I stare up into his mocha eyes. "We've got some shit to clear up."

48
WES

"Put me the fuck down, Wes, or I'm going feed you your balls for Christmas dinner," Ariah yells.

I ignore her and her wiggling form until we're safely in my room, and I lock the door, entering the code so she can't escape. I'm over this 'we'll talk later' shit.

Once the lock engages, I put a cursing Ariah down on her feet. She rights herself and lunges. I give her the free shot— I deserve it. I did snatch her from the party, but fuck the party— we need to talk.

When she tries to slap me again, I grab her wrist, giving her enough time to swing her balled fist into my ribs. I grunt, bearing the succession of blows before I spin her and wrap her in a bear hold from behind. Her head flies back, but I move out of the way just as she would've connected with my nose.

"Calm the fuck down. I'm going to put you back down, and then we're just going to talk— all I want to do is talk," I plead, hoping she can hear the desperation in my voice.

I hear the heaving of her breaths from our quick sparring. "Fine. Just put me the fuck down," she instructs, and I do.

Once she's finally back on her now-bare feet, her silver heels scattered on my floor, Ariah pulls down her royal blue dress. It's fucking sinful on her. There's a slit that goes up mid-thigh, just enough to show skin and still be deemed appropriate.

"Well, speak. I'm not in here so you can ogle me," she snarks, stepping toward the wall that leads to my other room.

What I wouldn't give to fill that fucking mouth of hers.

"I've been trying to tell you how sorry I am," I pause, waiting for her usual interruption. Ariah remains silent but crosses her arms, accentuating how delicious her chest looks in her dress. I fight the urge to reach out and snatch her then tease her until her nipples peak through the fabric. Instead, I grit my teeth until I know a moan won't come out, and then I continue, "There's no excuse for how I treated you when you first arrived. I was, and still am, a dick. I just don't want to be a dick to you anymore."

She rolls her eyes, and I want to fuck the brat right out of her. I can feel myself harden with each defiant look she awards me. I'm tallying up in my mind how hard I'm going to fuck her for this shit. "We've already established you're a dick, Wes. This isn't breaking news."

I close my eyes, and the blood rushes from my head straight to my dick. *Now's not the time asshole.* Refocusing I confess, "What I'm trying to say is that I'm sorry. I want to fix this— I just don't know how."

"You could start with an explanation for why the fuck you decided to target me at all. I was minding my business. You could've easily done the same," she retorts tightly.

"Look, I..." I grab the back of my neck. "I really don't have the right words."

"Spit it out, Wess-leey," she exaggerates my name, and I unconsciously step in her direction.

Clenching my fist to hold myself back, I finally blurt out. "You were a fucking unknown at a time when a lot of shit was happening. You and your family magically gained access to a town that rarely allows anyone in and were a complete and total nobody," I snap, knowing I'm holding onto my control by a razor-thin edge.

"So, let me get this straight." She walks toward me, each step punctuating a point. "You called me trash, sicced your Barbie and her-."

"She's not my-," I attempt to interject, but she silences me.

"Don't interrupt me," she yells, then continues listing my transgressions. "Cornered me in a janitor's closet and then in a hallway."

By the time she's done, we're practically nose to nose. Only a foot separates us.

"It's not like I was wrong. There was another secret society trying to converge. You were part of the game— a *major* piece on the board. Your mother has brought chaos and destruction," I seethe, stepping further into her space.

"You asshole," she snarls, cracking her palm across my face. My face whips right, and any hope of me handling this the nice way dies.

"I gave you the first slap as a courtesy for my dickish behavior. You don't get anymore," I growl, lifting her over my shoulder and swatting her on the ass as I stride to my bed and toss her on the mattress. She lands in a heap, and I'm on top of her before she can move. "You seem to like me more when I treat you this way anyway," I state, pressing her arms above her head as I latch my mouth onto her neck, sinking my teeth in just enough and sucking, knowing she'll have to wear my mark for at least a week. The idea makes me rock fucking hard.

"Get the fuck off meeee," she moans the last part when I press my dick into her, the thin fabric of the dress doing nothing to prevent me from rubbing her clit.

"That's my dirty fucking slut, moan for me," I grunt, pulling my mouth away. I grip her wrists in my left hand and yank the front of her dress down, exposing her breasts. I don't hesitate. My mouth dives for the blush-colored peaks, biting until she writhes under me.

I knew she was a pain slut. I remember the way her eyes darkened that day in the hallway. The way her pussy clenched around my fingers as my hand gripped her throat.

"Uhh, fuc-," she cries before she forces herself to stop. I need more. A taste won't be enough this time.

Climbing off her, I start to strip. She scrambles off the bed and darts for the door. I don't stop her futile attempt. She can't get out unless I let her out. So, I slowly undress, then grab a condom from my nightstand drawer and drop it on the comforter. I turn and take a seat, putting my naked ass on my bed. My cock jumps each time her ass bounces as she fights with the unmoving door.

Once she finally realizes her attempts are all in vain, she turns around— her eyes bulge at the sight of me. "Let me the hell out of here, Wes, or I'll break your dick off and fuck you with it," she yells, and said dick jumps at the thought of the fight.

"I'd welcome any attempt. Now, why don't you be a good little slut," I croon, standing and striding across the room. I watch Ariah's eyes drop to my very hard cock and continue, "And get down on your knees so I can fill that smart, little mouth of yours until you choke on my dick like I know you're gagging to." I'm standing in front of her by the time I'm finished, her mouth hanging open, whether from shock or lust. I'm not sure— nor do I care. Lifting my fingers, I wipe the little bit of saliva building at the corner of her mouth. "See, you're already drooling for it," I tease, knowing precisely what will happen next.

She growls, attempting to slap me again. I grab her by her throat and press her into the door. "You seem to like it when I treat you like my dirty little slut. Don't you?" I whisper, leaning down to bite her ear.

"Fuck you, Wes," she snaps, aiming to knee me in my junk, but I'm already moving. My grip around her neck tightens, and I press my body into hers.

Smiling, I state, "That's exactly what I plan to do."

My lips crash against hers, tasting what I've been craving for months while my other hand works its way under her dress, reaching for her panties. *Fuck!* She's already soaking wet. I slide my fingers under the seam of the lace, pulling it to the side. I feel her legs spread, granting me access.

We both groan when two digits slide in. I work my thumb over her clit as I pump in and out of her, and just as her walls squeeze around my fingers, I pull out, releasing her throat, and push her to her knees. "Open up your dirty whore mouth," I demand, and when she goes to chastise me, I thrust my hips forward into her unsuspecting mouth. The gagging noise she makes causes the muscles in my ass to flex as I try hard not to come on the spot. I'm saving all this cum for when I'm inside her.

Ariah's hands press against my thighs, and I grip the back of her neck and push just a little more. I pull out when I hear her throat catch, knowing that if I keep this up, I won't make it to the part I know we both want.

"What the hell was that shit, Wes?" Ariah demands. Her face a beautiful mess, mascara runs down her water-streaked face, and her blood-red lipstick is askew.

I smirk. "Don't tell me you didn't like it. Your fucking pussy was weeping only minutes ago. Get your ass on that bed, Bradford. Don't make me do it for you."

When I see the fire in her eyes light, my body hums in anticipation, and Ariah doesn't disappoint. She launches off the ground into my body, and I wrap my arms around her, but she bucks out of my grasp, readjusts her stance, and tackles me to the ground. I grunt when my back hits the carpeted floor.

Ariah stands and slowly slides her black panties down her thighs before she stands over my face. Then she sinks to her knees, her thighs straddling my face as she uses her knees to hold my arms in place.

Like I would fight this. I want to snort, but refrain, so I don't make her change her mind.

"Now you be a good boy and make me come," she coos, mocking

my earlier tone as she grips my hair and grinds her pussy into my mouth.

With arms pinned by her knees, I can't grip the globes of her ass. I groan in frustration at the thought as my tongue delves into her pussy. She grinds on my face, her fingers digging into my scalp when I begin to hum against her clit. The action causes her to stop holding my arms down, and I grip her ass, pulling her deeper into my mouth, sucking until I feel her juices run down my chin. "Fuck. Fuck. Fuck-kk," she shouts.

I need in her now.

Reluctantly, I stop devouring her pussy so I can get us to the bed. I toss her back on the bed, grab the condom, roll it over my shaft, and yank up her dress before I situate myself between her legs.

"This doesn't mean I forgive you, Wes. You have a fuck ton to make up for," she confesses.

"I wouldn't expect any less," I reply and then thrust forward. "Holy Shiitttt," I moan, holding my hips in place, enjoying the feel of her tight walls wrapped around me.

"Either fuck me or get off me," she commands.

I don't respond. Instead, I pull all the way out and slam back in as I grip her hair, yanking her up to me as I pound inside her. My pace is brutal. There's no kindness in this. "Is that what you want?" I ask her, pulling her head back until she's looking into my eyes. "You want me to use this fucking sopping wet, tight cunt?" My hips pound in and out with each word. "You want to be a slut Ariah, is that it? You want me fuck all your holes until you're leaking all over my bed like a dirty bitch?"

She clenches around me tighter, matching my thrusts, fighting for dominance, and I allow it this time. I feel myself getting closer.

I slip out and flip her over, "Get your ass up. On those knees like the dick-drunk slut you are."

Ariah positions herself, then turns, locking her eyes with mine. "Quit your fucking talking and put your dick to good use."

We grin at each other simultaneously, and then she bends

forward, angling her juicy ass in my face. What she does next makes me almost forget myself and come. She reaches around and holds open her ass, giving me a perfect view of both of her beautiful holes. I grab her hips and thrust back inside, watching as my dick slides in and out of her— the condom's covered in her juices, and I ache to know what my cock would look like being the one covered instead. And for the first time in my life, I want to yank off my condom and sink so deep in someone I don't know where she ends, and I begin.

Ariah's hips roll as she grinds up and squeezes the shit out of my dick. It feels so fucking good I forget to move and curse. Once I remember myself, I grip both her hips and guide her back into me, meeting me stroke for stroke. The tempo picks up every time I feel her walls try to lock me in. Her body starts to shake, and I know she's close. I drop my right hand and move my left hand to clasp her throat. Bending over her body, I then fist her hair. The leverage is just what I need. Her head tips back with a tug, her ear near my lips when I growl, "Be my good slut and come all over my dick," just as I slam deep.

Ariah screams her release as her walls spasm around me, and I come, shooting my hot cum into the condom. She falls to the mattress, and I pull out of her and roll off the bed to get something to clean her up. Again, something I've never wanted to do before.

I don't try to examine the feelings coursing through me as I warm the water and wet the rag. Instead, I punch in instructions for someone to bring Ariah new clothes for our return to the party.

When I return to my room, she's in a blissful puddle in the middle of my bed. I climb back on the mattress and begin to wipe between her legs. Her puffy pussy lips greet me, asking me to kiss them, but I refrain, not wanting to ruin the calm our fuck session has brought on. For now, I enjoy that she's in my bed and not fighting me. My determination to get her to forgive me is even greater.

49
ARIAH

"So let me get this straight. You let Wes, as in Wesley Benjamin Edgewood, rearrange your womb in the epic hate fuck of all hate fucks?" Shay questions as we get ready for the New Year's Eve party at Wyatt's house.

I massage my temples. This is the sixth day in a row she's asked this. "Why are we doing this again? This has been asked and answered a million and ten-point-five times," I exclaim.

She steps into the white sequin bodycon dress and the way the crisp white looks against her skin—my girl looks fantastic.

"Listen, I'm just trying to reconcile the Ariah of a little over a week ago talking about how she's going to make him work for it, with the one standing in front of me, not ready yet," she jabs, "who let him fuck you so sore you couldn't even sit right for two days." She snickers at the last part.

I throw my shoe at her, and she dances out of the way. I feel my cheeks flushing at the reminder of Wes's knowing smirk when we sat down for dinner that night, and I had to sit on either ass cheek. My pussy was well and thoroughly fucked. I had to soak two nights in a row after that. I've avoided his text messages every day since then.

He's tried to check on me, but I think a big part of me is slightly embarrassed by just how much I loved it when he called me his slut.

"You're thinking about it again, aren't you?" She probes, grabbing a red dress and throwing it at me. "Try this. I guarantee you'll have all your men threatening every man's balls if they look at you.

"I don't know what the hell I'm going to do with you," I snort, sliding the dress down over my hip.

"Keep me and love me forever because, like the guys, you're stuck with me, and I'll gut anyone who tries to tell you differently. Hurry up, we're late as it is," she sasses.

Grabbing my gold heels, I exit my closet and get ready for the night ahead. The adults are celebrating at the Edgewoods' which means even wilder antics will be happening.

Thomas has already made it clear that he will not wait outside, and there will be teams of security on the premises. It was the only way he'd agree to me attending. Before, I'd say he was overreacting, but ever since the night I was kidnapped, every overreach feels reassuring.

Once I'm dressed, I step into the boys' rooms. This will be the first New Year's Eve we didn't watch the ball drop together. They're both knocked out, so I make my way to Jamie's, and she's watching a movie. "Are you sure you don't want me to stay home with you tonight? I know he has to be at the Edgewoods' tonight, but I can—" I try again, and she cuts me off.

"Go have fun. You deserve it. We'll be here," she states, rolling her eyes at my fourth attempt at asking.

I arch my brow, "Ma'am, yes, Ma'am," I tease, walking toward the door. Pausing, I turn before I cross the threshold. "I know it's been a rough few years, but I feel a tide of change coming, Jamie, but once this whole thing is over, we'll get some semblance of normalcy."

"Do you promise?" She has so much hope in her emerald eyes. It's been a long time since she's let me see her this vulnerable.

I stride back across the room and scoop her into a hug, and kiss the top of her head as I mumble into her hair, "I promise to do every-thing in my power to try and make it possible." Because I won't lie like our mom did and tell her beautiful lies that only will end with tragic endings.

My heart warms when she squeezes me back and murmurs, "Thank you," as she pulls from my embrace.

T he music thumps in the room, and my body's covered in a sheen of sweat as I dance for what feels like hours. Shay and I arrived around nine, and now it's almost eleven, just a little over an hour until midnight.

Needing to cool off, I go to the bathroom with Shay. We laugh at the moping faces of the guys as I leave.

"They all got it bad," she teases as we enter the private bath-room. Wyatt only made the main-level restrooms available to every-one, but we have keycard access to the ones upstairs.

"Maybe a little," I joke, closing the door to pee while she's in the powder room. I can hear her laugh when I finally admit what she's been telling me for weeks now.

I flush the toilet and wash my hands before stepping back into the room. Shay finishes fixing her makeup and then goes to the bath-room herself.

Once she's out, we exit the bathroom when her phone rings. She looks at the screen and tells me she needs a minute, "It's Brendan. He must finally be here."

I smile, excited to finally meet the man she's been gooey over. Then I step outside to give her some privacy, walking down the hall to ensure I don't overhear anything.

"Fancy meeting you here."

My eyes snap toward the smooth tenor of Sebastian's voice.

"Are you checking up on me?" My tone is somewhat accusatory. I told the guys I'd be alright. I was only going upstairs, and security was every damn where.

Sebastian steps out of an alcove I didn't see when we first walked in. "Actually, I was here before you," he states, walking over to stand beside me. "So, I should be asking," Sebastian leans in and whispers in my ear, his breath tickling my neck, "are you following me, Ariah, because that could be dangerous for you."

An involuntary shiver tracks up my spine. Goosebumps rise at every spot his words touch along my skin.

"No, no," I stutter, "I was coming to cool off."

I nearly jump out of my skin when his chest presses against my back, and he trails his knuckle down the back of my exposed nape, my head leaning into the sensual touch.

"Such a shame. I would have loved to show you what happens when I have you under my control," he sing songs, gently pressing his lips along the back of my neck.

My breath hitches at the feel of his soft lips on my now-heated skin. "You keep talking, but that's all it is, isn't it? Conjecture? I've seen nothing that says otherwise," I retort, finding my voice.

His hand trails up my exposed thigh, resting on my hip. "Keep it up, Ariah." He groans when I push my ass into his hardening shaft before spinning me and pinning me to the wall. "And soon, I'll forget my rules and teach you just how far you can count." Sebastian nips my jaws before he presses his lips lightly against my parted ones.

I open my mouth to ask him what he means when the bathroom door opens. "Ry," Shay shouts from down the hallway,

"Until next time," he murmurs, leaning in and kissing my forehead.

The feel of Sebastian's presence disappears, taking all of his warmth with him, leaving me bereft. I turn, seeking him out, but he's already disappeared into the corner he appeared from.

"Ry." She tugs at my arm, refocusing my attention on her excited expression. The gleeful look on her face pushes the moment with Sebastian to the back of my mind. "He's here! Let's go."

I move quickly as she drags me down the stairs. The music's volume increases as we approach the main area of the party. As the room comes into view, I see a tall man standing off to the side. He's in a long sleeve black button-down collared shirt and dark wash denim jeans. His onyx-colored dreads are styled into a giant braid that hangs over his shoulder, hitting him mid-chest.

Shay drops my arm and rushes for him. I smile as I watch him catch her and wrap her in his muscled arms. *Brendan is hot.* It's the only way to describe how handsome he looks. His beard is shaped up and well-groomed. He beams down at her, lowering his lips to hers for a quick kiss.

He plants her back on the ground as I approach. "Brendan, this Ry. Ry, this is Brendan." Shay introduces him, and I give a quick wave.

"Hello. I'm Ariah, but Shay just said that," I say.

My back prickles with awareness as I feel them before they arrive.

Shay confirms their presence. "And these territorial idiots are her men."

"What's up? Nice to meet you all." Brendan chuckles, extending his hand to greet each heir. Even Sebastian found his way from upstairs to say *hello.*

I roll my eyes as Wyatt pulls me back into his arms. "You've been gone too long, Love."

"Sebastian was keeping a watchful eye on me, weren't you, Seb?" I jest.

Sebastian clears his throat when my gaze flits to his cerulean blues. My eyebrow arches in challenge.

"Is that right?" Owen asks, quirking his lip.

Sebastian smirks, nodding to confirm that the challenge has been accepted, then answers without hesitation, "That's exactly right. Our little spitfire was alone, so naturally, I had to keep a close eye on her and then do a quick inspection, ensuring no harm had come to her."

I blush at the mention of the way he *inspected me.*

"Let's give them some space," Shay announces, pulling Brendan away.

I shout, "Enjoy ringing in the new year, Bitch," and Shay flips me off before disappearing back down the hall we just came from.

Once Shay's form vanishes in the crowd, I step out of Wyatt's grasp and turn, "Let's go dance," I command, rushing to the dance floor, not waiting to see if they'll follow, knowing they will.

I'm lost in the music, my hips swaying to the beat as I dance with Owen when the DJ announces there are five minutes left until midnight. Lev grabs my hand, pulling me off the dance floor and up the stairs to the private seating area we were in earlier.

"Why'd we leave the dance floor?" I probe, grabbing a bottle of water and taking a sip before putting it back on the table.

They all close in just as the countdown begins, and the crowd starts to count.

"Ten," they yell as Wes steps in, pressing a kiss to my cheek.

"I'll do better," he whispers.

"Eight!" Sebastian's lips brush my ear, "I will do my best with you." His words sound unsure.

"Four," the room roars, and Lev steps up, bending swiftly to kiss my forehead.

"Thank you for forgiving me." Then he's pushed out of the way.

"Two!" Owen grips my hand, pressing it to the spot where I carved the "A" before bringing my hands to his lips and kissing the tips. No words need to be exchanged.

As the clock strikes midnight, I'm whirled around into Wyatt's chest, his hands gripping my throat as his lips crash against mine. The cheers of people ringing in the new year are distant background noise as Wyatt kisses me breathless.

When our lips finally separate, he leans in, whispering in my ear, "To the first of many New Year's together."

50
LEV

I can't believe it's been three weeks since the New Year's Eve party. We've all fallen into a somewhat comfortable routine.

When we're not following leads on Madeline and Elise, we spend most of our time with Ariah. The only exception is when we're being forced on the required dates for the Selection. As is the case for me now. So, while Owen, Wes, and Wyatt are all watching movies at O's house, I'm forced to suffer through a mind-numbing dinner.

The girl sitting across from me makes me want to pluck my eyes out. Meagan has to be one of the school's most superficial, stuck-up girls. Second only to Samantha.

"Can you believe he took me to a fucking butcher shop? Like, why would he think I'd want to touch pigs? Especially when I just got my nails done."

This bitch is vapid.

I'm tempted to reach across the table and push her face into the heap of grass she calls a meal.

"Lev. Lev, are you listening to me?"

I roll my eyes, "Unfortunately, I'm stuck, and I have to listen to you babble about your terrible existence from your ivory tower."

Meagan flares her nostrils, her lips pursing. "What the fuck is that supposed to mean, *Levi,*" she snaps.

My nails dig into the muscle of my thighs, trying to remind myself that I can't reach across the table and twist her neck.

I lean over the table, keeping my voice low so only she can hear, "First, don't ever call me Levi. As a matter of fact, don't call me anything— don't fucking talk to me. I've listened to your drivel far longer than anyone should have to. Just shut the fuck up and eat your rabbit food so we can end this fucked up charade."

Fury fills her eyes, her mouth curls into a scowl, and indignation is written across her pixie features. "How fucking dare you. You and those fucking idiots don't know what's coming for you. She's going to destroy you all," she screams, dissolving the semblance of decorum, slamming her hands on the table.

My fingers twitch, itching to grab her. Instead, I ease back, crossing my arms across my chest, and watch. I notice Brian Porter smiling on with glee at the scene. *Fucking tool.*

Meagan stands, forcing my attention back to her as she storms away from the table.

I watch as she makes her way for the exit, stopping at the threshold. She stops short of leaving the diner, pausing with a hand on the glass. She turns and shouts, "I hope you assholes and that stupid bitch get everything coming to you. You all fucking deserve the hell that's about to rain down on this town!" Then, she shoves open the door and stomps out.

I'd say I was embarrassed, but I'm too busy being happy that this date is over. Brittany wasn't terrible. We grabbed coffee, and that was that. Sam's date was— well, it wasn't. I refused to have that conniving skank within breathing distance. I had her meet me at the diner, then had Mary hand her a note that said, 'Not even if it would save the world from ending would I be caught dead on a date with you.'

It was worth the screaming Wes's dad gave me about the rules. What wasn't worth it was the punishment the Council gave me. I have to take her out next week or else— and I didn't want to know what the *or else* was.

Sighing, I get up from the table and drop my money to cover the meal.

Fuck this dumb ass Selection process.

A blaring ringing wakes me. I'm not sure when I fell asleep. After the date with Meagan, I came home and tried to do some more work on the lead we got on Madeline. We're so close to finding her. I can feel it.

The phone stops ringing before I can reach it, and I lift the illuminated screen to see I have twenty missed calls and ten unanswered text messages. Then, just as I'm about to unlock my phone, it lights up. Sebastian's name flashes.

"What's going on?" I ask, answering the phone.

"Meagan's dead," is his response.

The grogginess I felt a second ago dissipates.

"What?" I question, trying to ensure I heard him correctly.

"We got the call. You need to get your ass down here now. This shit doesn't make any sense," he says.

Fuck!

I was just with her.

"I'm on my way," I mutter, hopping out of my bed to find my keys and head for my car.

This is starting to feel like some B-list horror movie.

It takes me five minutes to pull up to Meagan's house. The scene mimics Summer's— cars pull up outside, our security team is running checks and no police presence.

As I step in the door, the pungent smell of cooking skin hits my nose.

"They're down this hall, sir," one of the men from security informs me, and I walk down the hallway on the left.

The vile smell increases with each step. The guys are once again clustered together when I make my approach.

"What happened?" I ask.

Wes and Owen step aside, allowing me access to the room. I pause, waiting for someone to answer, but when I see that no one is going to, I step into the room teeming with security.

Thomas isn't here. At this rate, the man might put Ariah on house arrest.

My focus locks on the half-charred torso of Meagan— still hanging partially from her tanning bed. I'd think this was an accident— that maybe she turned it up too high and fell asleep, but as I approach, I notice her face. It hangs at an awkward angle, and her eyes and mouth are sewn shut. However, that's not the wildest part of what I'm seeing.

Turning, I ask, "Have you seen this?"

They all step into the room, but it's Owen who answers, "Yes. Now, what does it mean?"

I turn back to Meagan's body, leaning to ensure I'm seeing correctly. Embroidered into her forehead is 'snitches get stitches.'

Wyatt steps up and jokes, "I guess they took the meaning literally."

I snort and then clear my throat to cover it up, trying to have a modicum of respect.

"It's okay. We all did the same thing," Owen quips, patting me on my back.

"What the hell did she do to get the rat treatment?" Wes mutters.

That's what I've been playing in my head.

"Didn't you have a date with her earlier?" Wyatt states.

I nod, "Yes, and she had a bitch fit when I told her to stop acting like a spoiled brat. Then she squawked about how we'd get ours, Ariah will, and blah, blah, blah, before she stormed off," recounting the scene from earlier.

At the time, I thought she was spewing the same whiny bullshit, but then I recall a crucial part of what she said.

"She's going to destroy you all," I mumble.

"What?" Sebastian questions, stepping in front of me.

I massage the bridge of my nose. "Before she left, she said, 'she's going to destroy you all'," I restate.

"What the fuck is that supposed to mean and who is she? Elise?" Wes snaps.

Someone had to be watching— unless this is unrelated, but that can't be possible. What did she say that made someone take this level of retribution?

"It has to be Elise. Right?" Wyatt says, running his hands through his auburn curls.

A wail cuts through the air. "No, no, no, no, noooo! Not my baby. Please tell me that's not my baby girl," Mrs. Brewster shouts as she attempts to dive between us to get to her daughter.

Sebastian's arms shoot out, wrapping around her to prevent her from reaching Meagan's body. "You can't touch her. Not yet," he explains, tone coaxing.

Mrs. Brewster pulls from his hold, wheeling around, and smacks him.

"This is all your fault. All of your faults. You and this fucked up town's rules," she continues to pound in his chest. "She's my baby, and you made them take her from me." She aims again, but this time Sebastian grabs her wrists.

"I let you get in the first shots because you're grieving. Don't take my kindness as a sign that I can be fucked with. Remember who the fuck we are," Sebastian barks, releasing her from his hold.

Mr. Brewster comes into the room and pulls his wife into his chest, "Come Ophelia. This isn't the place for you," he instructs, then looks at us, his eyes imploring for leniency. "Please, I'll take her from here. She's— Meagan was our miracle. Please try to understand."

Sebastian nods. "Just get her out of here before she does something stupid."

Mr. Brewster lifts her in his arms, bridal style, and strides toward the door. As he carries her, Mrs. Brewster's head pokes around his arm. Glaring, she mutters, "I hope you get what you deserve for taking her from me."

"Hush Ophelia, you've fucking said enough. Remember your goddamn place," Mr. Brewster snaps, storming out of the room.

I know she's grieving, but I won't make the mistake of ignoring angry confessions.

Looking back to the guys, I say, "Make sure we look into the Brewsters. Ophelia Brewster moves to high priority. She and her daughter have said things eerily similar."

I huff out a frustrated sigh, taking in Meagan's prone form. We need to get to Madeline. She's the key to finding Elise and ending this.

"If this keeps up, there won't be any girls left to choose from," Wes states.

Truer words have never been spoken.

"They won't get to Ariah ever again. I'll see to it. Meet me back at my place," I growl and make my way out of the Brewsters' house.

Determination sets in my chest as I climb back in my car.

I'm coming for you, Elise.

51
ARIAH

"And you're sure her parents are home?" I ask Shay.

We're sitting on my bed as I scroll through Summer's social media again. Another picture's been uploaded. This time she's outside of a club, and it was posted about a week ago.

When the news of Meagan's death broke two weeks ago, I started keeping tabs on Summer's accounts, but nothing suspicious has turned up.

"Yes, I saw Summer's mom in town earlier today and followed her back to her house before coming here."

This is perfect, with Thomas off training new security at the Tombs and my Dad at a meeting. Erik's here with Antonio.

I grab Shay, tugging her in the direction of the stairs. Once we hit the landing, we make our way to the security room and wait until the door is opened.

"How can I help you, Miss Bradford?" Erik says, stepping outside.

It takes me a moment to realize he's talking to me. "We need to, um, go to Summer's house," I state. His answer is the first test.

"What time do you want to leave?" Erik inquires, pulling out his phone and typing what I assume is a text to Thomas.

"I'd like to go now, please, if possible."

His phone buzzes, and he checks it and replies before he responds. "Okay, let me get a small team together, and we can leave in ten minutes." Then he turns and walks back into the room.

"Well, they aren't trying to keep you from going over there. So that's a good sign," Shay offers.

I arch my brow, "Or they're letting me go as a double-fake to make me think nothing's wrong," I surmise.

Shay shakes her head, "You need to stop watching crime shows. It's making you sound paranoid." She knocks her shoulder into mine before taking off for the coat room.

Chasing after her, we giggle as we grab our coats, and I explain my theory. "Seriously, think about it. It's not like the people in this town aren't above making Summer disappear and then posting pictures of her on social media to make it appear as if she's traveling."

Shay pauses before she continues to the car. "I'm not going to say it isn't possible. The people in this town are capable of a lot of things. Which is why we're going to talk to Summer's parents."

We arrive outside the Andersons' estate. Antonio opens the rear passenger side door while Erik waits by the steps. I know it'd be too much to ask for them to wait outside, so I don't even waste my time. Instead, I ring the bell and wait for someone to answer.

The lock disengages, "How can I help you?" A middle-aged woman with graying hair asks.

"Hi, I'm Ariah Bradford." I throw in the last name, hoping it will prompt her not to close the door in my face immediately. "I was wondering if Mr. or Mrs. Anderson was home."

Before she can answer, a deep voice sounds behind her, "Who is it, Denise?" Then a man steps into view, recognition filling his gaze. "How can we help you, Miss Bishop, or is it Bradford now?" he snarks.

I brush off his obvious annoyance with my presence."Bradford is fine. I was wondering if I could speak to Mr. or Mrs. Anderson.

We were trying to reach Summer. She's been posting on social media, but she hasn't been responding to any of our messages lately."

"I'm Summer's father, and don't you think that if you haven't heard from her, it means she doesn't want to speak to you? Isn't that how it works these days? You should take the hint, sweetheart," he leers.

So much for tact. I take a breath, preventing my snark from making an appearance. It feels like he's goading me. "We're all just worried about her. She hasn't been in touch with Sam either, and that's unlike her."

I swear I hear him mumble something about Sam being a spoiled cunt. "Summer is over this town, and she's not coming back— you and all the people here need to let her be. You've all done enough," he snaps, then slams the door in our faces.

"That went well," Shay snorts, and we turn to head back to the car.

Just as we reach the bottom step, a vehicle pulls into the circular driveway. "Oh, that's Summer's mom," Shay leans in and whispers.

Perfect. "Maybe she'll be a little more forthcoming with how Summer's doing," I retort, standing by the SUV door.

Moments later, a willowy brunette steps out from the rear door of the black Lincoln Town Car. Mrs. Anderson steps from around the door, thanking the driver before ascending the stairs. She doesn't spare us a glance.

I chase after her. "Mrs. Anderson."

She stops, her right stiletto-heeled foot landing on the step as she turns in my direction. Brown shades protect her eyes from the sun's glare. I note that they match nicely with her cream cashmere coat.

"How can I help you, Miss Bradford," she sighs.

I close my eyes to prevent her from seeing my eye roll. My annoyance with that dismissal is mounting.

Plastering on my customer service smile, I begin. "I-we," I

correct, pointing to Shay. "We wanted to check in on your daughter. No one's heard from Summer in months, and we're a bit worried."

Mrs. Anderson returns my fake smile with a saccharine one of her own, her scarlet-painted lips tip up, exposing her white teeth. "Summer has decided that Edgewood is no longer the place for her to be, and after all the death that's occurred since your arrival, I'm inclined to agree."

Is she trying to say this is my fault?

"What are you implying?" I challenge, arching a brow.

Pulling the belt of her coat tighter, and stepping up so that she's now towering above me, Mrs. Anderson replies, "Simply, that since you and *your family* wormed your way into our town, there's been nothing but chaos." The accusation is made more evident by the sneer on her face.

"Funny, I always thought it was the fucked up rules this town was founded on that caused this. Considering they're the ones that initiated it all," I seethe. Because fuck her and this bullshit town for always trying to pin all this on me.

Mrs. Anderson's lips thin, and she's about to speak when Shay interjects, saving this woman from my wrath. "Listen, we understand this whole process has been taxing. No one blames Summer for not wanting to participate. We just want to be sure that she's safe and nothing's happened to her."

"Summer is finishing her senior year at a private school abroad," Mrs. Anderson says dismissively, turning and walking up the remaining steps.

"You'd think she was hiding something," I mumble, loud enough so only Shay can hear.

She elbows me before following behind Summer's mom. "And we wish her the best. Can you confirm the last time you spoke with her, please? I promise this is the last of our questions, and then we won't bother you again," Shay says, adding the last part and tipping her head in a far more welcoming smile than my earlier one.

I swear I need more lessons from Shay. She's playing Summer's mom like Paganini's Caprices.

Mrs. Anderson waves her hands in dramatic fashion and turns, sighing as she pulls her phone from her Celine bag. Her fingers work the screen, then stalks over to us before turning her phone and showing us her call log. "Are you happy now? I spoke with her about an hour ago." She gives us enough time to see the call log and the duration of the call before yanking her hand back and shoving her phone into her coat pocket. "Now, if you two could be on your way. I have better things to do with my time than entertain either of you."

She's turned around and slamming her front door closed before Shay and I are even back to the car.

"Now, you can stop worrying," Shay murmurs, climbing in the backseat.

We both buckle up before I say anything. "It's still weird that she'd just up and leave and then stop talking to her friends."

Shay meets my eyes, "Were they really her friends, though?"

Rubbing at my temples, I acquiesce, "No. I don't suppose they were."

"I say she's better off," she replies.

Nodding, I huff, "Leaving Sam is always a great option."

We sit back, both silent on the drive to my house. Shay's texting on her phone, and I'm guessing she's talking to Brendan, by the smile on her face.

I, on the other hand, am lost in my thoughts. Even though I've seen the pictures and her parents have both confirmed she's alive and well, I still can't shake the feeling in my gut that there's more to Summer's disappearance.

"Don't you have a date to get ready for?" Shay's question distracts me from all thoughts of Summer. I can feel my face flush.

I have a date with Sebastian.

52

SEBASTIAN

"Why didn't you leave after finishing at LWU?" Ariah asks from across the dining room table.

The candlelight highlights the soft glow of her makeup. She looks radiant, and for the umpteenth time this evening, I question my acceptance to have our date here in such an intimate setting.

I know we all agreed to keep our dates with her in as controlled of an environment as possible, but nowhere in my agreement did it dictate what the date should consist of. *I* chose this setup. It's why the deep silver eyes of a girl whose very presence threatens my control stare at me from across the table.

My eyes flit across the room filled with candles and fresh bouquets before taking in the table, I had my staff set for an intimate dinner for two, and my chef prepared shrimp scampi with asparagus tips and a chocolate soufflé.

Ariah's eyebrow arches, reminding me I have yet to answer her question once my focus returns to her.

"I always knew I would be coming back home. The Selection just sped up my timeline," I finally say.

She nods, grabbing her glass of sparkling wine, and I smile. Each time she sips, I watch her cute nose scrunches from the bubbles. Then, I watch as she swirls the angel hair pasta onto her fork and places it into her fucking delectable mouth.

The sound she makes has me clear my throat and try to shift my focus. "What made you go along with the Selection process without putting up so much of a fight?" It's something I've been wondering since we found out she was Wyatt's choice. Ariah doesn't strike me as the type of person to fall in line.

She finishes chewing, grabbing another sip of her drink before she answers, "It's simple, really. My siblings. My parents weren't around, and I needed to take care of them." She stares me straight in the eyes before she says the next part— all softness and light leaving her features. "When your back is against the wall, you'll do whatever it takes to survive. Even playing in the weirdo version of pick your bride."

"We're pawns in this game of chess," I reply.

She snorts, "You only remain a pawn when you refuse to fight your way across the board and become a queen."

That answer piques my interest.

"Are you fighting, Ariah?" I hear the huskiness of my own voice.

Again she meets my eye. "Until my last breath."

I want so badly to see her fight— see her at my mercy.

Her head tilts, "Are you fighting, Bastian?"

I bite my lip at the breathy sound of my name on her lips. "More than you can imagine," I respond, no longer sure if we're talking about the Selection.

"Why?"

My jaw clenches at the challenge in her tone. How can one word hold such power? *Why?* Why what, I want to ask. Instead, I retort, "Because ceding control is not something I do— taking it, however, is. So, I will fight to keep it." Then, I grab the glass filled with amber liquid and bring it to my lips.

Ariah gently places her fork on the plate in front of her. "One could say giving over control to the right person is the most powerful show of control."

Does she even know what she's implying?

I stare at her over my glass before taking a sip of whiskey. The burn enters my bloodstream, fueling a simmering fire within me. "I don't think you understand what it means to offer yourself over to someone to control you, and you should be careful because a weaker man would take advantage," I state. I'm met with her tinkling laughter.

"I think you're full of shit Sebastian Grant. I think when met with a challenge, you hide behind your veil of perceived control when it's really just a crutch."

Placing my glass back on the table, I push out my chair as the dessert is brought out. "Is that right, Little Spitfire?" I grab the black-berry on the side of the dish and bring it to my mouth, biting off a small piece and licking the juices from the corner of my mouth, enjoying the way Ariah's eyes follow the movement of my tongue. Then I lean into her space, bringing the dark rich fruit to her lips. She opens, and I rub her lips until they're painted in the blackberry juices. "Do you think I'm afraid to control you, Ariah?" I ask, bringing the berry back to my mouth and eating it. "Do you think I am a man that denies themselves what they truly want to possess for very long?" I growl, then bring my mouth to her and suck on her black-berry-stained bottom lip. She moans, and the sound shoots straight to my dick. Reluctantly, I release her mouth and use my hand to clear everything from the table. "I think it's time you learn why I was holding back."

Her shocked gasp gives me enough time to lift her from her seat and lay her on the table. "Sebas-," she begins to object, but my finger lands on her mouth, silencing her.

"The time for talking is done— from now on, the only time I want to hear you speak is when you're asked to count and you are to address me as Sir." My dick throbs at the sight of her eyes bulging with my directives. "Do you understand, Ariah?"

She nods, and I tsk. "That's one. Let's try this again, shall we? Do you understand?"

"Yes," she mumbles, and I lift my finger from her lips. "Oh, I see we have a little brat present. That's two. Do you know two of what that is?"

She shakes her head. "That's three." I smile. "Tonight is going to be such a lovely lesson for you in what it means to relinquish control." I unbutton my sleeves and roll them to my elbow.

"The only lesson I'm getting so far is that you're all talk," she sasses.

"Four," I breathe, trying to contain my excitement. "Do you know there are many ways to elicit pleasure while teaching someone manners?" I glide my finger up her exposed thigh, thankful she's wearing a dress. I took the time earlier to admire the designer, but now, I just want the black fabric blocking her luscious curves from my sight gone.

Her breath hitches when I reach right under her breasts— the swell of them makes me eager to see how many times I can bring her right to the precipice without falling over through nipple play. As if they can hear me, the peaks fight to poke through the fabric of her bra, and I oblige their entrance, welcoming them by rubbing her left nipple between the tips of my fingers, and she whimpers. *So fucking responsive.*

I pull my hand back, and she whines. "Five. I'll keep counting until you realize everything is now under my control. I'm going to get something from my bathroom. I want you naked with your legs spread by the time I return," I instruct, turning and striding from the room. I want to rush, but anticipation is another form of foreplay.

Walking into my bedroom, I grab the box I bought months ago— the one I hoped, but wasn't sure, I'd ever use. I open it, ensuring everything's still inside before bringing it to the bathroom to clean the tools. Once everything is clean, I grab the lube and head back downstairs to see a very naked and flushed Ariah spread across my dinner table. "Fuck," I grit as I see her pussy clench and release, and I imagine what she'll feel like around cock.

"It took you fucking long enough, Sir," she mocks, and I grin.

"Seven— that's two more for that mouth. Tonight, you'll count down from seven and then back up," I announce, walking up between her legs and bending to sniff her already wet opening. No longer able to control myself, I bury my face between her legs and feast.

"Oh shit," Ariah screams, and I feel her catapult from the table, her hands gripping my hair as my tongue swirls around her clit. I feel her legs begin to shake, and I pull away. She squeals in protest.

"Count," I murmur against her pussy.

"Seven."

"Seven, what?" I demand.

"Seven, Sir," she whimpers.

I stand. "Good. Now you understand how this will work. First, you'll count down from seven each time you're denied your pleasure. Then you'll count up to seven each time you're awarded it. Do you understand?"

Ariah looks up through lidded eyes, hunger with lust and excitement. "Yes, Sir."

I drop the box and lube on the table, then return my mouth to her clit as I slide two digits into her waiting pussy. She must be still riding the near orgasm from before because her walls begin to grip my fingers when my lips increase the suction on her clit. She moans louder— her body begins to shake, and again I pull away.

"No," she shouts, and I lower my mouth and nip her clit.

"Count. That's the only words coming from you right now," I demand.

"Six, Sir," she says through clenched teeth.

"I'm not sure you can last under my control. Would you like me to stop?" I probe as I stand between her legs.

She rolls her eyes, "Didn't you just tell me not to speak?" I arch a brow. "Sir," she adds.

I can't wait to see just how much she moans 'Sir' willingly by the end of this.

Hovering over her prone form, I lower my mouth to her nipple, biting the raised peak between my teeth before swirling my tongue over the reddened tip as my hand brushes between her legs and my thumb rubs her clit. Ariah begins to squirm while she pants, signaling she's close again. I pull back again, unlatching my mouth from her nipple and removing my hands from her pussy.

I watch her nostrils flare, but no vitriol leaves her lips. Instead, she mumbles, "Five, Sir." My prompting is no longer necessary.

Smiling, I immediately begin to wind her body up again— each time inching her right to the edge before denying her— each stroke bringing her almost there, making her more eager the next time. My hunger for her grows as she counts down on moans and whines of frustration.

My mouth is between her legs as Ariah counts down for the final time. "One, Sir," she cries, and I crush my lips back over her clit, swirling my tongue until she crashes into her first orgasm, her body shaking.

I don't give her any time to recover. Instead, I slide three fingers inside her and pump in and out as my teeth nip her, and she comes again. Her juices run down my fingers, and I pull out, lifting my lips from her clit, and bring my fingers to my mouth and suck.

My hungry blue eyes peer up at her through her spread thighs.

"One and two, Sir," she sighs, almost drunk off finally being able to come, and I want so badly to bury my dick so deep in her that I can't ever leave.

I shake my head at those thoughts. *Never again.*

The moment my mouth returns to her pussy, her back bows, and her hands fist at my scalp, pushing and pulling— unsure if she wants me to stop or continue.

"Please, please. No more," she begs, and I attempt to pull away, but she pushes my face back into her soaking wet pussy. "Don't fucking stop," she snaps, and I add a number for the next time we play.

She'll learn quickly. The count never stops.

I eat her until she's rolling into orgasm five before I pull out the vibrator. Her eyes widen. "On your knees" is my only command, and she obediently flips over on the table. I make a mental note as I bring the vibrator to her clit, and Ariah's juices drip down on the wood varnish to ensure this table gets placed in my room. No one eats off this but me.

"Holy fuck," she shouts, her knees nearly buckling as I increase the suction, and I press her back, pushing her stomach down to the table, exposing her entrance enough for me to slide my three fingers in.

"That's it, beautiful. Sing for me," I coax. The sound of her orgasm makes my dick fight for freedom from my pants, but there will be no release for me tonight. As much as this is a lesson for her, this is also one for me. I'm teaching myself the cost of losing control because as much as I wanted her— her goading should never have made me give in.

"Six, Sir," she shouts, and I groan, knowing I might just nut in my pants before this night is over.

I start to thrust my fingers again.

"Ahhh. I can't...not anymore...please, Sebastian."

I pull my fingers from inside her and bring my palm down on her ass, then drive them back inside, pumping in and out as I increase the toy's suction on her clit.

"Fuck! Ohhh fuck," she moans.

"What was that?" I bark

"I can't come anymore, Sir."

Yanking my fingers out of her, I pull the toy away, flip Ariah to her back, and then stand between her legs.

"Count," is my only instruction before my fingers slide inside, pumping in and out, each thrust causing her to clench. I watch her eyes roll up in her head, and her mouth opens, but nothing comes out as I increase my pace. My free hand grabs the vibrator, pressing it to its highest speed, then places it right on her clit. She yelps right before her body begins to shake. She snaps up before falling back down. Her fingers search for something to grasp, but she's greeted with nothing but smooth cherry oak as a scream rips from her body, and her walls convulse around my fingers like they'd lock me inside forever.

I close my eyes and groan at the thought of the feel of her grip around my dick. "Jesus," I grunt, pulling the toy away and pulling my fingers out, replacing them with my tongue as I try to drink as much of her as possible— not letting a drop go to waste.

"Seven," she gasps, shutting her eyes in blissful surrender, and I smile.

"That's my good girl," I croon, bending to press a kiss to each closed eyelid before exiting to grab a warm cloth.

By the time I return, she's lightly snoring. I wipe her down, then carry her to my room to rest. Once I've placed her under my covers, I watch the rise and fall of her chest, wishing I wasn't so bitter and could give her more.

53
ARIAH

Civics is boring today. Miss Taylor is yammering on. The guys aren't at school. They haven't been in days. They're all running around with things from the Fraternitas. At least I've gotten to see them after school. Well, most of them. Wes has been texting me daily since I caved and gave him my number. The amount of Taylor Swift songs he quotes are hilarious and cute. He knows all isn't forgiven, but getting to know him has softened me some. Sebastian, on the other hand...

Sighing, I remember how he cared for me after making me a gushing mess, only to find his mask firmly back in place and him growing so distant days later. I haven't spoken more than a few words to him. All of them were him saying this is for the best in the last two weeks. I went from concerned to indifferent after the first week.

"Miss Bishop, can you answer my question, or are you too good for that now?"

My head snaps in the direction of the woman that, with each passing day, I'm tempted to punch. Masking my ire, I plaster a smile on my face. "I'm sorry. What was your question, Miss Taylor?"

Her lips curl before she restates her question. "I asked if you could tell me the importance of the Voting Rights Act."

I ramble off the answer, and she moves on to the next question, rapid firing around the room. She continues for at least fifteen more minutes before my mind wanders again.

Pulling out my phone, I scroll to check social media. It's nearly mid-February, and Summer is still posting pictures of herself from around the world. Her latest photo is of her standing in a coral pink thong bikini on the white sands of Matira Beach in Bora Bora. Her caption makes me snort, 'Sun's out, buns out.'

"Ariah," Miss Taylor shouts, and I realize I've completely zoned out again.

I murmur an apology, but that's not good enough for Vivian Taylor.

"Honestly, Miss Bishop, if you can't pay attention in my class, you can get out," she snaps, causing the room to break out in snickers.

"What's your problem? I apologized. Move on already," I shoot back, totally over her snide comments and off-the-cuff petty remarks.

Her lips thin as she works the muscles in her jaw. "My problem, *Ariah,* is you and every other entitled bitch in this town," she sneers, and I laugh, causing her fists to clench at her side.

Um, pot, meet kettle.

"I guess you're a spoiled bitch since you were born and raised in this town, and I only just arrived," I taunt.

"Holy shit, she's got you there, Taylor," someone teases. I don't recognize who it is and won't look to see either. Instead, my focus is trained on the bitch who's about to learn today.

The bell rings, but no one moves.

"Everyone out," Miss Taylor barks, but no one moves.

"Yeah right," a high-pitched voice says. This time it sounds like it was a girl, but again I can't be sure.

Vivian Taylor struts from behind the desk, her black stilettos clacking against the floor, "Either get out, or you all fail."

Grumbled curses sound before the movement of students leaving hit my ears, prompting me to slowly gather my things, never taking my eyes off the vile woman in front of me.

Sliding from my seat, I lift my bag and walk for the door. My back is finally turned to her, but my senses are on alert. I'm steps away from the entrance when I feel her. I twist left just before she screams, announcing her attack. She misses me by a mile and falls into the students exiting the classroom before hitting the floor with a thud.

"You ruined everything," she wails, scrambling off the ground, her shirt askew as she charges for me, and I deflect her wild, uncoordinated movements.

"Aww, is Vivian hurt because Sebastian doesn't want her anymore?"

"Shut up, you stupid trashy cunt. He does want me. It's you and this stupid fucking process," she screams, aiming her nails at my face.

I bat her hands to the side, refusing to engage in combat. It would be cruel to beat someone like her. She can't fight for shit.

Vivian's movements become more erratic each time her strikes don't land. I hold my free hand to my mouth and mock yawn. The wild set of her eyes signal her next movement. Vivian screeches as she lunges to my left, and my arm bends, extending my elbow right into her temple. I watch as she falls to the ground before quickly springing back to her feet and backing away to reassess.

"You're nothing. You and your worthless bloodline should be eradicated," she seethes, and I wonder for a moment what she knows.

"The fact that I'm a Selected and you're not says I'm not the one who's nothing here."

Vivian launches herself at me again. "They're using you. Once this is over, Bastian will be mine again," she cries, and I know she undoubtedly believes this. *She's like another fucking Sam.* I'm starting to wonder if delusional is in the water in Edgewood.

I sigh, sticking my right foot out and tripping her to the floor. Her remaining heel flies off as she turns to sit back up, ready to strike out another time.

She has some fight, but I'm bored with her shit.

"Sebastian loves me. It's always been me," Vivian exclaims, standing back to her feet. I could clock her one time and end this, but I want her to talk more about my family. How the hell did she know the Bradfords were being hunted?

My next words are uncalled for, but who the fuck cares. I need her to talk. "Is that why his face was buried so deep in my pussy that I can still feel the lingering effects of his tongue?"

"You're lying," she shrieks. "He wouldn't touch you!"

"Oh, but he did. Over and over and over again." I grin.

Miss Taylor grabs the chair next to her and charges for me, "I don't give a fuck who your mother and father are. I'm going to kill you— you stupid bitch,"

My ears perk at the mention of my mother, but I have no time to process before Vivian hurls the chair at my face. I duck, avoiding it, but not her, as she tackles me to the ground.

We both hit the ground with a thud, then she's up, attempting to wrap her hands around my throat. I push my wrists between her forearms and press out, forcing her to release her grip. Then I quickly scoop my arms around her and twist us around until I'm on top of her.

Grabbing her hair to hold her steady, I land three successive blows to her face. Her arms finally fall to the ground, but I don't stop, striking her twice more, my punches not hard enough to knock her out, just enough to subdue her.

"You should've never come here. This is all her fault," she grits through pained sobs. The devastation in her tear-stained eyes should move me, but they don't.

I smile and say, "I told you not to fuck with me." Then, I drop her head back to the ground and stand.

Vivian curls into herself and cries. She's murmuring something over and over, but it's unintelligible.

Looking up, I see five sets of hungry eyes boring into me. Owen is visibly hard as he twiddles his knife. Lev's calculating gaze is taking me in. His eyes survey every inch of me for what I'm not sure. Wyatt looks ready to skin Vivian alive, his teeth bared as his jaw flexes, and Sebastian and Wes stand like sentries by the door, collecting everyone's phones and instructing anyone caught with footage of what happened will not like the consequences.

Where the fuck did they come from?

I'm walking toward them when the hair on my neck stands. A keening sound rips through the air like a battle cry as I hear the guys shout their warnings. I turn in time to see Vivian launch herself in the air, giving me just enough space to ready myself. My arm pulls back, my hand balled into a fist, and I punch her. The crunch of bone against my knuckles alerting me to something breaking. I prepare to aim again when I'm pulled back and hoisted into someone's arms.

I begin to fight, resisting whoever has me. "It's me. Relax. She's out." Wes's sharp tone finally registers. Turning, I see an unconscious Miss Taylor sprawled on the classroom floor. "You calm now, Rocky?" he teases.

"Shut up before I knock you out too," I retort, hiding my smirk. The banter between us is new, but I like it.

Wes laughs before he leans in and whispers, "You know how much I enjoy your fight," then nips my ear before placing me back on my feet.

I roll my eyes, then take in the room. *Shit.* I'm about to be in so much trouble for this.

"**W**hat were you thinking?" Mr. Edgewood shouts from his desk.

I'm standing in his office, being chewed out for yesterday's fight. Even though the guys took everyone's cameras, word got back, and I was summoned.

"I was defending myself," I said dryly for the tenth time.

Wes's dad has been lecturing me for the last thirty minutes about how a *lady* handles herself and the expectations of a *Selected*. I want to shout 'fuck that', but my dad is giving me the eyes.

"Rules are rules, Miss Bradford, and one of those rules clearly states that you're to behave like a Selected," he barks.

"Easy on the growl, Donald," my Dad snaps. "She gets it. I think there should be some exception because of how Miss Taylor handled herself," my father continues.

Take that, asshole. I internally cheer my Dad on.

"Miss Taylor has officially been dismissed from her duties and will be escorted out of town within the week. Her stay in Edgewood has been rescinded," Mr. Edgewood explains. "Now, what did she say to you?" he probes.

I dig my nails into my palms, preventing the smartass remark on the tip of my tongue. "She said the Bradford line should be eliminated and that she didn't care who my mother and father were. She was going to kill me."

My Dad's jaw clenches, and Mr. Edgewoods brown eyes darken.

"Thank you, Ariah. You'll have three etiquette training sessions to help you learn how to handle yourself in situations like this— you're dismissed," Wes's dad instructs.

I bite the inside of my cheek until I draw blood before I look at my father, and he gives a quick shake of his head, signaling me to go.

Turning, I storm out of the room but carefully shut the door before pressing my ear to it, hoping to overhear something.

"Miss Bradford, there's a camera on you," I hear Wes's father sigh.

Shit.

Accepting defeat, I skulk down the hall and try to make sense of their reactions.

54
WYATT

Vivian being fired and forced to leave town is the perfect cover-up for what she has coming to her.

"I think we should go grab Ariah," Sebastian suggests from the passenger seat.

My gaze whips from watching Vivian pack her car with suitcases to the only idiot left among us. "I thought you were 'keeping your distance.' Why would you want Ariah to come to the farm?"

I wanted to throat chop his Adam's apple a few weeks ago after their date. Ariah was sullen for almost a week over his fuckboy behavior. We've all given him hell for it since then. He's supposed to be the most mature of the five of us— Sebastian is acting like an emotionally stunted goofball.

A wry grin lines Sebastian's stubbled jaw. "Something she mentioned in my office before Christmas break."

"Were any of them in reference to your extreme case of douchery?" Owen asks, making me snicker.

Seb sighs, "Seriously, how long are you all going to keep this shit up?"

"As long as it takes for you to realize your fuck up. Now, what did she say?" Lev inquires.

I turn back to the window. Vivian's loading the last of her things in the passenger side of her car. She closes the door before turning back to speak with her parents. "Is the audio on?" I ask when I see her hands moving animatedly.

"Give me a second," Lev says, and I hear his fingers fly across the keyboard.

"You two didn't even fight for me to stay," Vivian yells.

"This is for the best, Vivi. You'll be better off away from all of this," Mr. Taylor reasons.

"If you didn't let all your delusions blind you, you wouldn't be here now. This falls on you, Vivian. *You* slept with Sebastian's father, *you* married his best friend, and *you* threatened a Selected— one of your own students, no less. What's there to fight for? Salvage your dignity and move on with your life," Mrs. Taylor scolds.

That woman never bites her tongue.

"I always liked Mrs. Taylor," Wes chimes.

"He is coming— Sebastian is going to be mine. I was fucking promised," Vivian screams. Her next words are mumbled, but the drone's audio is magnified. "She fucking promised me."

"Did you catch that? Rewind it," I demand.

Lev replays her words.

"She knows something. I fucking knew it," Seb growls, slamming his fist on the armrest.

That comment makes me turn from Lev's computer screen. "Care to fill the rest of us in?"

Sebastian sighs, "It wasn't anything concrete— just a gut feeling. The timing of her move— her willingness to take whatever bullshit I slung at her— fuck, the ways she always would claim I'd be hers."

"I wouldn't beat yourself up over any of this. We just had her in the crazy ex category as well," Lev adds. "All of her background checks cleared— even the more extensive one I had Colt run on her."

Sebastian doesn't look at all appeased.

Owen turns from the window, "Doesn't matter either way— now we get to kill her for more than just fucking with our girl."

I look back to the computer and watch as Vivian gets into her car and pulls off, exiting her driveway. We watch the drone follow her, driving through town and crossing the town line.

"She gets seventy-two hours— that's it, not a millisecond longer. We need her to be seen, so they don't suspect foul play once she goes missing," Lev begins. "Seb, tomorrow you'll call her and tell her to meet you up at the farm to talk things out. Once she arrives, we'll question her and decide the rest from there."

Sebastian nods before he says, "We need to bring Ariah, but I don't think she needs to be there for the zesty interrogation portion of the evening— just for what comes later."

My auburn brow arches, "Why exactly does she need to be there?" I question. We've all agreed to keep her as far away from this shit as possible.

Sebastian turns, the smirk back on his face. "She told Vivian the next time she messed with her, she'd fuck me in front of her, and I, for one, think that's an excellent send-off for Vivi— don't you?"

The cackle that escapes me can only be classified as hysterical. That bitch karma always gets her due.

"I t's time to wake up, Vivi," I taunt, pouring the water over her face.

She splutters, fighting for air as awareness settles in.

"What the fuck? Where the hell am I?" she demands, tugging at her restraints.

"Uh, uh, uh," Wes chides. "You don't ask questions— only answer them."

Vivian's head swivels, taking in each of us before landing on

Sebastian. Her face crumples in a momentary defeat. "Bash," she pleads, but he doesn't respond. Her nostrils flare. "Why would you let them do this to us?"

Owen laughs, stepping into her field of vision and blocking her view of Sebastian. "There is no you and him— there hasn't been in a very long time, Vivian. You saw to that, or don't you remember?"

"I had to," she screams. "I had. If I didn't..." she stops, not finishing her sentences.

"If you didn't, what?" Sebastian snaps, stepping around Owen. "You keep saying that and never explain why— tell us why!"

Vivian's shoulders slump. " I can't tell you," she sighs.

"Can't or won't?" I challenge seeing the play long before her eyes lift.

She glares at me. "Wouldn't you like to know," she seethes before smirking. "You and this town are full of men who think they run everything. You know nothing."

"And you do?" Lev goads. "You, who was so easily swayed that you gave up the supposed love of your life and, like a coward, did whatever you were told. You think you're in charge?"

Vivian screams and tries to launch herself at Lev, but she's securely strapped to the chair. "I did whatever the fuck I had to in order to survive. I fucked whoever I was required to in order to win, and I killed whoever the fuck I had to, to get you back," she shrieks, facing Sebastian.

I look at the guys and know we're all thinking it. *Bethany, Trisha, Summer, and Meagan.* All four girls— dead because of some twisted obsession.

"You had me, Vivian. *You* fucked that up with all your lies and scheming," he reminds her.

She shakes her head. "No! No— I did this all for you— for us. We can be together soon, Bash. I just need to do one more thing, and you're mine. All mine. She promised me." Vivian mutters the last sentence repeatedly, more to herself than anyone in the room.

"Who's she, Vivi?" Sebastian coaxes. "Tell me who she is, and we can work this out."

Hope lights her eyes, but I see the moment she remembers herself. "No. I can't tell you. If I tell you, then I can't have you."

I try a different tactic. "Who is the last person you have to get to? Tell us, and we'll help you so you and Bash can be together."

"The Bradford cunts. All of them, starting with the twin boys. They're going to be next. They have to be next," she mumbles to herself again.

She's losing it.

"This bitch is wrapped tight, and that's saying a lot coming from me," Owen states, and I nod in agreement.

"What the fuck?"

All our heads snap in the direction of the voice at the door.

55
ARIAH

S hocked gazes meet mine.

"Fuck, you're early, Angel," Owen says.

I ignore him, walking to the bitch that said she would kill my siblings. Starting with my brothers.

"Repeat what you just said," I snarl, grabbing a fist of her hair. She's still mottled with bruises. She needs more, in my opinion.

Manic eyes bore into mine. "You heard me, you trash whore. I'm going to start with their eye-."

I punch Vivian in the mouth. Then I strike her in the eye, and she screams. *Fuck her cries.*

Arms attempt to grab me, but I throw my elbow back. I hear a grunt of protest but ignore it.

"Twisted fucking bitch," I shout, stepping back and kicking her in the chest.

Hands wrap around my waist, and I fight to break free, but I'm squeezed tighter. "She deserves this and more, Dove, but we need answers," Lev's voice soothes.

I know he's right, but it doesn't stop the rage roiling in my stomach. Inhaling, I take in my surroundings. When Owen called and told me Thomas would bring me to meet them, this wasn't what I expected to find.

We're in a barn. There's a table to the left filled with all types of tools. I remember seeing weapons like these in the storage room at the building my Dad used to train me. My eyes land on a baton. It's one I recognize. It doubles as a taser.

"Okay," I raise my hands in surrender.

"If I put you down, will you behave?" Lev probes.

I side-eye him. "I promise to try."

The second my feet hit the floor, I take a step in the direction of the table. Wyatt sees me and smirks, shaking his head, but doesn't signal for me to stop. Instead, he winks and dips his chin, encouraging me to take another step. "How would getting rid of the Bradfords help?" Wyatt inquires, bringing everyone's focus back to a very bloody Vivian at the center of the room.

She sneers, her once-white teeth stained red. "I don't know, and I don't care. Those were my orders if I wanted to have *my* Sebastian. This cunt and her family were just a means to an end."

I snatch the baton off the table and click the charge, standing away from the table when Wes's gaze lands on me. His eyes narrow, and I shrug, careful not to touch the wand to my leg.

"At least they were until you touched Bastian," Vivian snarls. "Now, I'm going to enjoy making this bitch suffer."

I take another step forward. "How do you plan on doing that? Your dumbass is tied to a chair," I taunt.

"You think I can't get out of this?" Vivian quips.

I burst into laughter. "I'd love to see you try. It would make my day if you got free, believe me."

Sebastian clears his throat, and Vivian's attention refocuses on him. "Who wants the Bradfords gone?"

"Not the Bradfords— just..." Vivian purses her lips, refusing to say anything else.

Wes storms up to her. "You just said they wanted all of them gone. Quit fucking playing around. Which is it?"

Vivian tilts her head back and spits in his face. Wes rears his hand back but drops it at the last minute. Cursing, he stalks off, giving me the opening that I needed.

"He won't hit you, but I will," I growl, pulling the baton from behind my back and swinging it three times across her face. Her body jolts, foam forming at the corners of her mouth, and her head slumps. "Dumb bitch," I mumble, turning off the wand and dropping it to the ground.

"I thought you were going to behave?" Lev asks, and I turn to see him scratching at his beard in an effort to mask his amusement.

"She's not dead, is she?" I state, pointing to the rise and fall of Vivian's chest.

Lev snorts, "No."

"Then, I behaved. You didn't say how I needed to behave," I retort.

Owen and Wyatt's laughter fills the room.

"She's got you there," Wes says, striding back into the room, his face now free of blood.

Turning, I finally ask the question I've been wondering since I walked in here. "Why did you call me out here?"

"Payback," Sebastian explains, and a smile creeps onto my face.

Payback.

The heat from the hood of Sebastian's car warms my barely-covered ass. I might have said forget it if spite and fury weren't warming my blood. It's freaking cold out here.

"You can't do this to me! Bastian! Make them stop," Vivian shrieks, trying to squirm from Owen and Wyatt's hold, but zip ties bind her as they drag her to the metal-enclosed pigsty.

Once they tie her to the gate. Wes and Lev secure barbed wire around her arms.

That's going to fucking hurt.

"Bastian, please. I can make us work. I'm sorry, please. Don't do this," Vivian pleads.

Sebastian ignores her cries, instead moving to stand between my legs and spreading them.

"Don't think you and I aren't going to talk, asshole," I snap.

He sighs. "I fucked up. I'm sor-."

"Not now. Now, we send your bitch of an ex off with a lovely parting gift," I instruct. Shock registers in his features. "What? You think I don't know she's about to die? I'd have killed her if you let her go. She threatened my family. She's fucking dead." I mean every word I'm saying. Anyone who's a threat to my family dies. I'm over this bullshit.

Sebastian opens his mouth to speak, but I lean forward and yank his tie. "Shut up and fuck me."

Lust illuminates his darkened blue eyes. "Two," is all he says, and my skin chills for a different reason. I feel my nipples pressing at the fabric of my thermal shirt. He steps back and runs three fingers down the length of my exposed pussy, smearing my already-leaking juices against them before his gaze locks on mine as he brings the digits to his mouth and groans, "Fuck. You taste even better than the last time I tasted you on my tongue."

I whimper and lean back, bracing on my elbows. "I'm ready to count, Sir," I breathe, and his pupils dilate.

"Sebastian, please. Stop. Don't you fucking touch her again," Vivian screams.

He ignores her, moving slightly to the side, so she has a better view of what will happen.

Fury. She's pissed. Vivian attempts to launch herself at us, but a pained cry bursts from her, and blood begins to trickle from the barbed wire around her wrists.

Owen and Wyatt laugh. "Not a fan of this show?" Owen teases.

"It's becoming one of my favorites," Lev adds, causing me to look at the hunger in all of their eyes.

I lean around him and stare into her rage-filled eyes, reaching for his fingers and dragging them to my entrance. "Touch," I gasp as he works his ring and middle finger in and out of me.

"Eyes on me," Sebastian growls. "She might be here, but your attention," he pounds deeper, "belongs only to me." Each syllable is punctuated with each drive of his fingers.

My body begins to hum to life when I feel a third finger slide in with the next thrust. I clench at the intrusion, his wrist twisting, angling his movements to hit a new spot, a deeper one, while giving his thumb access to my clit.

"Ahhh," I squeak when the pressure of this thumb on my clit doubles as his pace picks up. "I'm...I'm...I'm," I can't get the words out.

Sebastian's other hand presses down on my abdomen just as his fingers pump in and out of me at a rapid pace, and a scream rips through the wintry night air. Our heavy breathing is evident through the wisps of air huffing from our mouths.

"Count," he orders over a wailing Vivian.

"I'm going to kill her. I'm going to kill her and make you watch," she shrieks.

I'm still too high on the euphoria of my orgasm. Ignoring her, I mumble, "One."

"That's my good girl," Sebastian groans.

Sitting up, I unfasten his belt and unzip his pants, eager to finally see his dick. I bite my lip to hold back the moan at the sight of him. I run my fingers down his length, just barely able to wrap my hands around him.

Sebastian grips my hair, yanking my face up to look at him, "Put those pretty fucking lips around my cock, Ariah." Then he lowers my head until my mouth is wrapped around his shaft.

"Fuck."

"Shit."

"Yes, Angel."

"I'm so fucking hard right now."

I hear the guys groan, but I'm too focused on tasting more of Seb. My hands shoot out, landing on his ass and pulling him in. The action has him hitting my throat, and I gag. I can feel the spit trickling out the corners of my mouth, but I don't stop. Instead, I bring my hand to his shaft, wrapping my fingers around it, working him up and down while my tongue swirls over the tip and my mouth applies pressure to the head.

"Holy— fuck," Sebastian grunts, pulling my hair until I remove my mouth.

I look up in confusion. "If you didn't stop, I'd nut in your mouth, and tonight the only place I plan to come is inside you."

Sebastian pushes me back against the car's hood as he tears open a condom Wes hands him. "This isn't how I wanted our first time to be," he mutters, rolling the condom on and positioning himself between my legs.

My eyes travel the length of him as he lowers himself on top of me. His hand lifts my right leg over his shoulder before slowly working his shaft in my pussy. "You feel..." He bites his lip as he peers down at me. "Jesus," he groans once he's fully seated inside me, his hips rolling steadily.

I cry out when he snaps forward, driving himself even deeper before pulling out and snapping forward again. His pace doesn't increase, but each thrust of his hips buries him until I feel full. Sebastian rolls his hips, his dick hitting a spot that makes me see stars. I have to dig my nails into his back to prevent blowing his eardrum.

"Don't hide from me," he pants, increasing in pace, repeatedly hitting that same spot.

I want to shout, 'you hide from me,' but his hand slips between our bodies, finding the spot between my lips and pinching until I look up. "Scream," he commands. His hips piston, his fingers rub circles around my clit, and I do as I'm told. I cry out so loud Vivian's choked sobs are a distant memory. I shout so loud my body jerks, and my pussy clamps down, forcing Sebastian still.

"Fucking shit," he snarls, and I feel him tense. His cerulean irises roll back, leaving only the whites of his eyes visible before warmth coats my insides.

Sebastian rests his forehead on mine, working to catch his breath as his hand trails up and down my arm.

"I'm going to fucking kill you. I will bathe in your family's blood and make you watch. You stupid fucking cunt." Vivian's rants finally permeate the small semblance of our lust cocoon.

I start to pull away, but Sebastian holds me still. "I never said I was through with you."

My eyebrows nearly hit my hairline when I'm flipped over, and I finally feel how hard Sebastian still is. I see the foil wrapper fall just as his hand cracks against my ass. "You didn't count. Now you're back up to two," he states before grinding into me.

I can't form words because his hand is pushing my back down until my stomach is pressed on the hood of the car. Then he grabs my thighs in his arms and immediately pounds into my soaking wet pussy. He's relentless. I have no time to catch my breath as his grip on my legs pulls me into each thrust. The familiar tug in my lower belly builds when I feel another hand between my legs. My eyes snap up to see Wes's arm before I feel more hands. Owen and Wyatt both play with my nipples. Wyatt squeezes while Owen ducks his head to bring my other breast into his mouth. Sparks shoot over every area of my skin as my hair is fisted, the length wrapped around Lev's hand, and he lowers his mouth to mine. I moan into the taste of him, whimpering when our lips part.

Lev nips my lip. "You're ours now, Dove."

His proclamation made clear, Sebastian slams his hips forward, our skin slapping, and I come at the same time I feel him shoot into me again.

"Two," is all I get out before I feel myself being wrapped into a blanket, and then my eyes close.

56

LEV

The sight of Ariah on the top of Seb's car is something I'll use to jerk off to for the rest of my life. The way her legs were spread so fucking nicely as he pounded into her over Vivian's anguished screams was breathtaking. My dick is growing hard again just thinking about it.

Owen is the one that gets off to screams, but the combination of Ariah's moans of pleasure mixed in with the broken sobs of the bitch who's been killing off the Selected girls and helping Elise went straight to my cock.

Once Seb left to take Ariah home, where he hopefully pleaded to her for forgiveness, we sliced Vivian's Achilles tendons and cut her down from the gate. She was a sobbing, delusional mess— even when we tossed her in the pen, she kept mumbling she would fix this and Sebastian would be hers. We stayed until the pigs silenced her screams. Then we all left to handle shit.

Wes, Owen, and Wyatt went to the Tombs— our fathers had a possible lead on Elise, and they needed to follow it up. I came back to my house. I was waiting to see if Colt found anything in the information I sent him.

When I went through Vivian's phone, I was able to find encrypted text message conversations between her and someone, but their identity is still unknown. So now, Colt and I are running a trace. My gut is telling me it's Madeline, but I need confirmation. I'd love to get that bitch on my table.

My phone rings, pulling my attention from the computer. Once I see Coop's name, I answer.

"Hey. I thought Colt was the one handling this?" I state.

"He's been occupied with a few things," Cooper replies.

"A few things or one person? Isn't Eva in town, touring the campus?"

"Fuck off, Lev. Do you want what I have or not," he snaps. His voice is almost identical to his brother's. Most people wouldn't be able to tell them apart, but where Cooper's tone is curt, Colter's is beguiling, making for different inflections on certain words.

Huffing a laugh, I reply, "What did Eva do anyway that has you two so out of sorts and investing this much energy into her?"

"*She* didn't— her brother did, and she's going to pay his penance. Now stop asking fucking questions about shit that doesn't concern you," he orders.

I'd argue with him, but I understand what it's like to want people to stay out of your business.

Clearing my throat, I ask what he's found, and he sends over a doc that confirms my earlier reaction— Madeline. We've found her.

I mumble my thanks, disconnect the call, and text the group chat.

Me: HW's been found.

We call Madeline the Huntswoman, HW, since she's like a hunter for the evil queen in *Snow White*. It's a nice play on words in case someone's dumb enough to try to hack our shit.

It doesn't take long for the chat to indicate responses are imminent.

Wy: Good shit. This lead was a bust.

Wes: Finally. What's the plan?

O: 🔪 💧 🐷

I snort at Owen's response— he's going home to get all his girls.

M e: 😂 😂 😂 O, seriously?
O: Sharpening Lizzie and the girls as we speak.
Seb: Ariah's asleep. Should I leave now?
Wes: Did you have to get on your hands and knees?
Seb: Fuck off.

Wyatt: I hope she made you lick the ground or some shit. You deserve it, dick.

Seb: 😶 No assholes. But I did try to explain....I'll tell you later.

Me: Focus...we have HW!
Wes: Are we grabbing her now?
Me: I called in King.

T hat has my phone ringing— a video call.
"You called in the crazy Russian fuck?" Wes gapes.
I shrug, "King needs information on his uncle. I found it. So, he'll grab Madeline in exchange. She won't expect him."

"Hopefully, she doesn't say something to make him kill her before he delivers," Wyatt states.

When Madeline was Lydia, she had a mouth on her. We should've noticed the change. Lydia was quiet, but we chalked the change in behavior to the Selection. She wasn't a big fan of what was happening and was vocal about it before she was murdered, and Madeline took her place.

"How long before he grabs her?" Owen inquires.
"King is on it already. I'll have an update soon."
Sebastian clears his throat, and I see Ariah's sleeping form sprawled out on his chest. Her lips slightly parted, soft snores escaping her. She's fucking stunning. "Should we go to the Tombs

now?" he asks, pressing a kiss to her forehead and brushing the few strands of hair from her face. I don't think the idiot recognizes he's gone for her already— just like the rest of us.

"Nah. King won't get her here for at least eight hours. I'll see you fuckheads in the morning," I say before ending the call.

Dropping my phone on my desk, I get to work drawing up the files on the sex trafficking warehouse King's uncle's been running stateside.

"No friend this time?" King observes once he's placed Madeline on the table.

"They're on their way," I reply, unzipping the bag Madeline's in.

King watches me for a moment, then nods, "Where are the files on my uncle?"

Once I have Madeline strapped in, I walk to the table and grab the flash drive. "It's all on here. Your uncle's into some seriously sick shit."

"What did you find?" he probes, taking the drive and putting it in his pants' pocket.

Rubbing the bridge of my nose, I explain. "He traffics women, men, kids— fucking whole families. The warehouse you're looking for isn't even a speck of sand in the desert with the number of holdings he has."

King sighs. "I know, but this is my foot in the door."

I open my mouth to speak but pause for a moment, thinking through my words carefully, knowing what it will mean for us if he ever decides to do it. Then I say, "If there ever comes a day you need help taking this piece of shit down, let us know."

King reaches his hand out, signaling a gentleman's agreement. "I have your word?"

"Have your word for what?" Wes asks, his eyes narrowing suspiciously to where King's reaching for my hand.

"To help when the time comes," I reply, holding my hand out.

Owen, Wyatt, and Sebastian walk in and take positions around the room. Owen stands over Madeline— one of his knives in hand, ready to play.

Wyatt quirks a brow, looking away from the table of tools. "What's going on?"

King and I drop our hands, accepting I need to explain the situation before an agreement can be made.

"King's going to take back his birthright from a sick, twisted fuck, and we're going to help whenever the time comes," I state, then peer around the room into each of their eyes for confirmation. Once I have, I turn back to King. His arm is already outstretched. I return the gesture, our hands clasp, shaking on it. "You do."

King steps back and says, "I'll leave you all to it then. Until next time, be well, Levi," before exiting the room.

"How fucked are we because you made the deal?" Wes sighs.

I rub the back of my neck. "As long as we can get rid of the Filiae Bellonae and take over the Fraternitas, we'll be more than ready for Serge Volkov.

Owen drags his blade down Madeline's arm. "Can we wake the bitch yet?"

Stalking to the table, I grab the syringe, then approach Madeline and plunge it into her neck.

Seconds later, she gasps awake and immediately attempts to pull from her restraints. Once she realizes she can't get free, she takes stock of her surroundings. "What the hell am I doing here?"

"You're here to answer questions." Wes begins, grabbing a corkscrew before slowly approaching her.

Madeline laughs. "You stupid little shits are in over your heads, and none of you fucks even realize it." Her laughs promptly turn to cries when Wes buries the corkscrew into her thigh and turns it.

"Now, where's Elise?" Sebastian growls.

"You think one stab to my leg will get me to tell you fools anything?" she seethes.

A loud smack turns into a crunch before morphing into a shrill cry. I look to see Wyatt hammering away at the bones in Madeline's leg. He pounds the hammer until her left femur is nearly nonexistent. His chin dips, and he smiles. "You have so many more bones to crush. Are you sure we're in over our heads and that you have nothing to say?"

An idea comes to me, and I walk to the closet, grabbing the container.

"I'm going to give you one more opportunity to tell us where Elise is," I explain, standing over her, my hand on the top of the dropper.

Madeline's nostrils flare as she meets my eyes. "Fuck you and your opportunities. I'm not saying sh-."

Before she can finish, I pour the bottle of hydrochloric acid down her leg, forgoing the dropper. Then I pour the lye on the newly exposed skin.

"Marinate for a while. I'm sure by the time we return, you'll be singing a new tune," I taunt, before signaling the guys to meet me by my computer.

"Did you really just tell her to marinate, like you just basted her with a marinade or some shit?" Owen snorts, wiping the blood off his blade.

I shrug, "I mean, with the lye, she's pretty much cooking."

He and Wyatt burst into laughter while I plug Madeline's phone into my laptop.

"Do you think we'll find anything on it?" Sebastian asks.

"Only one way to find out," I reply without looking, my focus on the text messages pulling up on the screen.

Wes's finger lands on the screen, honing in on a set of messages.

"Does that say what I think it does?"

I nod, confirming what he said but keep sifting. We can digest all the information later. But, for now, I need to know if there's anything in here I can use to get Madeline to cooperate.

After what feels like hours, I store the information we've found on my drive and send the files to Colt for a more in-depth analysis.

"We need her to tell us what she knows about Elise. Unfortunately, there wasn't enough on her phone to discover her location," I inform them.

Madeline screams from her spot on my table, and I'm tempted to shove a metal pipe down her throat to shut her the fuck up.

The last fucker on this table didn't talk enough. Now, this bitch won't stop squealing. If I were truly fucked in the head, I'd shove a knife inside her like she did to Summer— not that I cared for her. It was just a shitty way to die.

Looking at my watch, I notice it's only been an hour since I doused her skin.

"Fuck, that looks fucking mangled." Sebastian grunts when we finally reach the table.

Madeline's skin is peeled away, exposing ligaments, bones, and tendons.

Grabbing a chisel, I round the edge of the table. "Let's try this again. Where," I lightly tap the bone. "Is." I increase the force. She tries to move but can't. "Elise?"

"I don't know what you're talking about," she squeals.

She's lying. Her eyes flit in every direction but mine, and her heart rate is galloping. That might have something to do with the needles being shoved under her nails by Sebastian, but I feel it in my gut— she knows more.

"Stop fucking lying to us," Wes snaps, taking the chisel from my hand and stabbing it through whatever is left of her right leg.

"I'm not lying," she screams. "The only person I was ever focused on was Ariah. It was my job to make sure she was in place, but never marry any of y-" Madeline stops the second she recognizes her slip up.

Not marry any of us? That's not what Ariah said. Her distinct words were that her mother wants her to.

Before we can question her, foam starts to leak from her mouth, her head falls to the table, and sightless eyes stare up at me. Once her face droops to the side, a tooth falls from her mouth onto the metal slab.

"Fuck. Shit. Fucking dammit," I yell.

"Cyanide," Owen growls.

I yank my hair from its bun, trying to cool some of my anger.

"What if Ariah isn't the endgame?" Wes voices my concern.

Wyatt shoves his shoulder, "Don't you fucking start that shit again."

"I don't mean our endgame— that's a given. There's no chance we'd ever choose anyone else," he corrects. "What I'm saying is, what if Elise never planned for Ariah to actually take power? What if, once Ariah got it, Elise plans to kill her and take control for herself?"

Fuck. Have we been missing a vital piece?

"No, it's something else. She was about to say make sure she never marries any of you," Owen explains, pacing the room while he twirls his knife. "Maybe it was Vivian. Maybe Madeline and Vivian were working together behind Elise's back."

That theory held weight.

"In which case, they're both dead. So, no more shadow within a shadow government," Wyatt adds, chuckling a little to himself at his joke.

As the guys make their way to the door, I take one last look at Madeline's dead body and hope her and Vivian's death is really the end of people trying to kill Ariah, but my gut tells me I'm far from right.

Y I snort, perusing the hallway, and once again, my classmates don't know what to make of me. They've looked on in
a combination of fear, awe, and contempt over the last few days
since word spread about Miss Taylor not only being fired but having
to leave Edgewood. Sam and what's left of her clones are the only
ones daring enough to taunt me. I wonder if they'd continue to do
that if they knew I was also the reason Vivian was killed.

"Earth to Riri," Shay says, tapping my shoulder.

"Huh?" I reply, knowing I missed everything she's just said.

She sighs, her brows furrowing. "Lawd gal, you're always in your
head. I said are you ready for your date with Wes tonight?"

Ready is subjective. I have possible outfits selected, but am I
ready? I'm not sure.

"I don't know," I answer honestly.

We stop at her locker. "What is it? Do you still hate him?"

I think over the last few months, our text conversations, the
many times he's stopped by just to watch TV or play with the twins.
He's done nothing but try. "No," I say confidently. "I don't honestly

believe I ever hated him, but even my annoyance and anger toward him has simmered."

Shay nods, not voicing an opinion, just encouraging me to continue.

"Wes has spent the last few months apologizing without pushing. And after the New Year's Eve party, he's worked even harder to show that he made a mistake, but he's more than his past behaviors," I explain.

Shay closes her locker before she finally speaks. "So, what has you feeling hesitant? I can see apprehension all over your face."

Of course she'd see that, but can I tell her what has me the most in knots? I look at my best friend. She's never judged me. Clearing my throat, I shake off my nerves and blurt, "I want him to treat me like a slut. I fucking loved when he did it that night, and I spend a shit ton of time thinking about it."

The smile that grows on Shay's face has me turning fifty shades of red. "Bitch, so let him do it. Be his dirty slut. Liking to be degraded in the bedroom isn't a bad thing. Shit, when Brendan." She pauses. "Nope, never mind, this isn't about me. Just let him do all the things. Fucking embrace the dirty, nasty freak in you. None of it is wrong. You're both consenting."

Inhaling, I joke, "So I won't lose my progressive woman card?"

She rolls her eyes, "Progressive women respect a woman's right to choose. That means if you *choose* to be dominated in and out of the bedroom, that's your motherfucking right."

"Agreed," I state, grabbing her hand and dragging her to class. "Oh, don't think I didn't notice how you glazed over you and Brendan. We'll discuss later."

"Whatever bitch. Just remember we're going shopping this weekend to find something for the party at LWU."

I mutter my protests, and Shay laughs as we take our seats.

"What is it with you guys and freaking blindfolds?" I quip, holding Wes's hand as we travel down the hallway of his house.

When he asked if I wanted to eat first or get my surprise, I obviously went with surprise. Hence the walking sightless down a wing of his massive mansion.

"Hmmm, a group of extremely dominant men, and the girl they're enthralled with at their mercy? I can't imagine what the appeal could be," he whispers, his breath tickling my nape.

I'd elbow him, but I won't chance it in these heels. "Oh, shut it. How much longer?"

His arm grasps my waist, halting my steps. "We're here," he says, pulling the blindfold from my eyes.

It takes me a second to register where we are and what's happening.

"Miss Bradford, it's a pleasure to meet you."

I look to Wes and back to the world-renowned fashion instructor standing only feet away. "Is...is she really here? Pinch me so I know I'm not dreaming," I plea.

"Ouch," I hiss when Wes's teeth nip my neck. He quickly soothes the sting with smattering kisses. I lean into his touch but then remember we aren't alone.

Straightening, I cover my obvious embarrassment with a cough. "I guess I'm not dreaming," I joke, trying not to freak out that Chloé René is in the same room as me.

"I'm definitely here. Why don't you come in? Wes had this studio set up with everything we'll need for today," she instructs.

Looking around the room, I see a designer's dream: fabrics, mannequins, accessories, and sewing and embroidery machines.

Everything's here. My feet carry me to the Brother Entrepreneur Pro X 10-Needle embroidery machine, and I get a lady boner.

"It's a beauty, isn't it?" Chloé hums. "The things you can do with all the designs in your portfolio," she muses, and my attention snaps in her direction.

"How'd you know about-," my question dying on my tongue when I see my sketch pad on the table.

I turn an accusing glare on Wes. His hands are up in surrender. "I got a little help from Jams," he admits.

Jams. Right, I forgot they're two peas in a pod now. They game together at least once a week with Lev. She's still a traitor.

"Uh-huh, you can explain how you got my sister to betray me later," I tease before returning my attention to my instructor.

For the next three hours, I get an introductory course in design from the top instructor at Parson's School of Design while Wes plays assistant, getting me anything I need. It's the hottest thing ever, especially when he volunteers to be my model, and he has to strip down to his navy-blue boxer briefs.

We finally end our lesson, and Chloé informs me that she will be giving me private lessons for the remainder of the school year.

I nearly bulldoze Wes after she leaves. "Thank you so much," I squeak when he catches me, his bare chest pressing against mine.

"Anything for you, Ariah," he mumbles, staring down into my eyes. Wes lowers his head until our lips connect, our mouths drawn together like magnets.

My hands fist his hair, and I feel the minute our need grows when his dick presses into me through the material of his briefs.

He pulls his mouth back, and I whimper. "I should feed you," he groans, almost as if he regrets having to say the words.

"Unless you're feeding me your dick, no thank you."

He growls, "Don't tempt me."

I reach between our bodies and slide my hand inside his boxers, jerking his shaft. "Tempted enough yet?" I coax.

"You're being a brat, Ariah."

"What are you going to do about it, Wes?" I taunt, twisting my palm around the crown of cock, using the pre-cum for lubrication.

He grunts, fisting my hair. "On your knees."

Chills shoot up my spine. The anticipation of a repeat of our last encounter provokes me to disobey. Twisting out of his grip, I move across the room, pressing my back against the wall closest to all the fabric, and meet his eyes in challenge. "No."

A predatory smile creeps along his closely shaven jaw. "Come here," Wes commands, and I shake my head, refusing him again.

"Make me."

My pulse skips when he stalks toward me. I dart left and run through the door. I'm not sure where the hell I am in this damn house, but I take a chance, turn left, and take off running.

"I love the chase," Wes shouts.

I can't tell how close behind me he is, and I refuse to look back to check. Instead, my eyes quickly survey my surroundings. *Fuck.* Left was the wrong choice. This is a dead end.

Slowing, I catch my breath and notice a door. I sigh in relief when I try the knob, and it opens. Slipping inside, I secure my hiding spot with a quiet snick of the lock. Shrouded in darkness, I give my eyes a moment to adjust before seeking a light switch.

I begin to turn when a hand clamps over my mouth, shocking me still. "But catching you is so much sweeter," Wes sing songs in my ear as the lights in the room flick on. I'm yanked into his chest by my hair. "Disobedient sluts with smartass mouths belong on their knees," he growls, gripping my throat and turning me to face him before pushing me to the ground.

My mouth is filled with his dick before I can utter a rebuttal. I moan at the fullness and the weight of him on my tongue, bobbing to meet each thrust of his hips into my mouth. I reach my hands around the back of his muscular thighs, pulling him deeper.

"Fucking shit. That's my dirty girl," Wes grunts, using my hair to control the pace. It's not long before his hips jerk, and I feel his cock pulsating as he mutters a string of curses. On his next thrust, I hollow my cheeks and relax my jaw until I feel him hit the back of my throat. Wes rips himself from my mouth and comes all over my face and my chest. Then he bends and licks his cum from my lips before he uses his fingers to open my mouth. Understanding his motives, I stick my tongue out and nearly come on the spot when he spits his cum into my mouth. "Such a good fucking slut," he grits, then grasps my throat and pulls me to my feet.

I'm barely standing when his lips close the distance, and he's chasing the taste of himself. My hands grip his dick and rub the tip against the lace of my exposed panties. "Please," I beg between kisses.

Wes releases my throat, slow-walking us until my knees hit something soft. I recognize it's a bed as he lowers me to the mattress. Our mouths separate long enough for him to pull my dress off and toss it. That's when I notice for the first time I'm back in his room. He reaches into his nightstand drawer, takes out a condom, and rolls it on by the time I've divested myself of my boyshorts.

I spread my legs in invitation only to find my thighs wrapped around his neck. "Oh fuck," I groan at the first swipe of his tongue. Wes sucks the already dripping evidence of my arousal, his tongue scooping all traces of my excitement from my pussy. He hums in delight before turning his attention to my clit. His lips latch onto the raised peak as he flicks it with the tip of his tongue.

As the fire pooling in my stomach builds, I try to squirm out of his hold, only for him to stop, raise his palm, and smack my pussy. "Don't move, or I'll strap you to the bed," he instructs before returning to devour me as he lowers my ass to the bed. He slides two fingers inside me as his tongue swirls my clit. My pussy squeezes his fingers, and my back arches off the mattress when my orgasm barrels through.

Wes lifts his head, grabbing my thighs and slamming inside me, giving me no time to come down from my first orgasm. "Is this what you wanted?" he asks, but I'm so lust drunk I can't formulate words. He leans over, capturing my nipples between his teeth and biting so hard I shriek, but it turns into a moan when he sucks the bruised peak. His mouth unlatches from my breast. "Answer me, slut," he demands. "Or I'll make sure you can't crawl, much less walk, from this room by the time I'm finished."

If he thinks that's a punishment. I make the mistake of snorting at that thought. His eyes darken before he pulls out of me and flips me over to my stomach. Five quick swats to my ass, each one progressively harder. I clench with each strike, and I feel my pussy leaking down my thighs. When Wes's hand dips between my legs and feels how turned on I am, he growls. "You depraved whore. I knew you'd be my good little slut. You're fucking weeping for it."

Wes spreads my cheeks and thrusts back in, gripping my hips for purchase. Mid-stroke, I lower my stomach to the bed and clamp my walls around his dick. The motion causes him to go feral. He yanks my hair, pulling my back to his chest as he grips my throat, squeezing until I'm gasping for air. Wes pounds into me, and the combination of the pressure on my neck with the brutal pace in my pussy sends me over the edge, my walls spasming until my vision blinks out. I barely hear Wes shout as he comes.

I fall to the bed in a heap of blissful contentment. Only for me to be turned on my back seconds later. Wes powers back inside me, rolling his hips at a steady pace before leaning forward to whisper in my ear, "Did you think I was done? I said you wouldn't be able to crawl."

The freaking school year is flying by. I can't believe it's seriously April already. The last month has been quiet. With the death of two Selection girls, all the dates are finished. We all still take Ariah out, but we're not forced to spend time with Samantha or Brittany.

Samantha made the biggest stink about it at one of the planning meetings, and she was shut down and reminded that as long as we met the required dates, we didn't have to go on anymore. It was one of the few times I was thankful about the damn rules.

If it weren't for the constant updates about potential leads on Elise, I'd think all was quiet, and we'd coast to the final Selection, but as I walk into the Tombs, I know bullshit is on the horizon. Especially after what we saw on Madeline's phone. Lev has only been able to start decrypting the list of known traitors in our midst. The code has been running ever since that night, and he and Colt have been trying to speed up the process, but we've only been able to unlock the first batch of names. All of which have led to dead ends. The families either moved or we've dealt with them.

I step into the chamber and see everyone's already here.

"Good, we can begin," Mr. Edgewood directs as I take my seat.

All of our fathers are seated around the room, which is normal. What isn't is Sebastian's father. He's never in these meetings— not since his loyalty's been in question.

"Thank you for joining us, Theo. I know it was last minute, but we've gotten news," Wyatt's dad says.

I look at the guys, but they give off no indication of knowing what this meeting's about.

"Of course, it's no problem, Alex. I'm always available when the Fraternitas calls," Sebastian's father says to his brother, placing his hands on the table.

Apparently, that was a wrong move because the moment his wrists touch the wood, the table opens up, and metal straps lock him into place.

I watch as Sebastian arches an amused blond brow.

"What is the meaning of this?" Theo barks, his face reddening in anger.

The room door opens, and Thomas strides in with five more men following behind him. One of them carts in a table full of some of my favorite toys.

My father makes a derisive snort, then launches himself at Sebastian's father and punches him until Thomas pulls him back. He holds his hands up. "I'm fine," my dad huffs, straightening his tie and cleaning invisible lint from his suit. "The meaning is, you traitorous scum, that we found the link to your part in the kidnapping of *my fucking son*," he snarls, and Thomas has to hold him back before he attacks Theo again.

It takes seconds for his words to finally penetrate the haze. My pulse gallops so loud the noise around me feels a million miles away. I know things are being shouted, but I can't register anything— not until I hear Lev coaxing me from the fog. That's when I realize the shouts were for me to stop. I hear the choked cries of someone, and I look down to see my hands covered in blood. Lifting my gaze, I take in Sebastian's father. My knife protrudes from his hand, and he's covered in lacerations— none of them lethal, but all enough to draw blood and cause immense pain.

I watch as my dad approaches me cautiously. There's no fear in his eyes— just reassurance that he means no harm. "I know you want him dead, Son— I do too, but we need to question him first."

Lev's hand squeezes my shoulder. I nod, taking my seat and trying to reign in my anger. My hand instinctively goes to the spot near my heart where the only person who calms me marked me. I absently trace the "A" while I await answers.

"I didn't do it. I wouldn't— couldn't. Owen is like a son," Sebastian's father stammers.

Sebastian stands, nearly knocking over his chair. "Bullshit. You sleep with your flesh and blood's fiancée, and then again once she's my ex to help impregnate her— if that's what you call fatherly love to me, I'd hate to see what it would look like to O," he snaps.

Theo turns his face up in disdain at his son's words. "I was doing what was best to get you in the best position of power," he snarls, dropping the facade of innocence. "I was passed over because my asshole brother was the favorite. That seat on the Council was supposed to be mine. Your position as an original was stolen!"

"Nothing was stolen from you. You lost it in your blind quest for power. When you betrayed your oath and sought to take a seat that didn't belong to you— mine," Mr. Edgewood shouts, and shocked gasps fill the air. This is news to us— the heirs. We always knew something happened that caused Sebastian's dad to be skipped and Wyatt's to hold the seat.

"I did what was necessary, and I'd do it again," Theo retorts.

Ariah's father slams his palms on the table. "Including aiding in the kidnapping of two innocent boys?"

"What can I say? Your wife has a pretty convincing cunt. Are you sure those kids are even yours? I fucked Elise so much I wouldn't be surprised if your bitch of an oldest daughter was mine," Theo taunts.

He doesn't get to say anything more before Aaron Bradford whips out a dagger and throws it with such precision it embeds itself between Theo's shoulder and collarbone.

Sebastian is across the room, pushing the blade deeper and turning it before anyone can stop him. "You were always a selfish shit. Tell me where the fuck Elise is, and I'll end it quickly even though you deserve to dissolve alive in a vat of acid." Theo screams, pleading for his son to stop, but Seb pushes deeper. "Tell me," Sebastian shouts again.

"I don't know," Theo wails. "I've only been dealing with Vivian in the last year. I haven't seen or spoken to Elise in nearly two years, and when I did talk to her, I was only given instructions on what to do next."

He's useless. Outside of finding out the vile asshole is part of the reason Lev and I were kidnapped, he knows nothing more than what we know. Over the bullshit, I pull Lizzie from my ankle holster and sink the blade into his neck.

"Enjoy hell with that bitch, Vivan," Sebastian snarls, as I grab Theo's pocket square and wipe the remnants of his blood off Lizzie before dropping it at his dying feet.

Closing my eyes, I bask in the gurgle of his last breath escaping.

"I'd ask why you did that, but we all know Theo wasn't even on the last rung of the ladder. First, Elise used him and tossed him aside, then Vivian took advantage of his thirst for power," Ariah's father explains, and I dip my chin in agreement.

"What now?" Wes asks. "We still keep hitting roadblocks."

Mr. Edgewood clears his throat, signaling for clean up, before he states, "Elise will make herself known soon enough. If we can't get to her— she'll make another attempt to get to her daughter. With only two months left until the Choosing Ceremony, we only need to be patient while we continue our search."

Wes's dad updates us on a few more items and then dismisses us.

We don't speak until we're outside. "I don't like the way he made it seem like Ariah was going to be bait," Wyatt says, and I grunt, having felt the same feeling when he said to be patient and Elise would come for her daughter.

"We're not waiting for shit," Lev exclaims. "Colt, Coop, and I are going to double our efforts— triple them if we have to, and decode that fucking list."

"Until then, we don't leave Ariah alone," Sebastian directs, and we all nod.

Breaking away from them, I head to my car, "Dibs on first watch," I shout, jumping into my Jeep and peeling out of the driveway. My phone buzzes, but I ignore them.

Snooze, you lose, assholes.

59
ARIAH

I stand outside and bask in the May sunshine. We're six weeks from graduation and the final part of this Selection process. It's Friday. The school day passed without any real issues outside of Sam's usual snide comments. She's been extra cocky lately. Her attitude has become almost unbearable with each day closer to the choosing ceremony.

"Stop soaking up the sun and get your ass in the car. We have to get ready for the party tonight," Shay says, poking me in my side.

Laughing, we hop in the back of the car, and Thomas drives us to my house. "You're lucky I love you, or I wouldn't be going to this thing at all," I state as we enter my driveway.

Shay ignores me over my whining. "Do you finally know what you're wearing? Since you didn't want to get anything when we went shopping last time," she grumbles.

Now who's whining?

"My closet is full of clothes. So I didn't need to buy anything new," I retort.

Her eyebrow arches. "You have so much to learn." she sighs as Thomas parks the car.

As we step inside, my grandmother informs me Dad wants to see me in his office. I tell Shay I'll meet her upstairs then walk down the hall.

The door is open. "Ry, come in," my Dad signals.

"What's up?"

"Thomas won't be able to come with you tonight. Instead, he'll accompany me on a lead we got on your moth— Elise. So, Antonio and Erik will guard you. It's of the utmost importance that you don't go anywhere without either of them and don't take off your pin for any reason," he explains.

I nod in agreement. I wouldn't go anywhere without them, not after the freaking Selection ceremony last year. "How solid of a lead do you have?"

"Visual confirmation in the last twenty-four hours. I think this is it," he says, rubbing his fingers against his jaw. I can't imagine how he's feeling. She was our mom, but she was the love of his life, and she betrayed him the entire time.

My gut twists in anger and sadness at the trail of destruction Elise has left in her wake. "What will the Fraternitas do once she's captured?" I secretly hope she's killed instead of brought in because the alternative isn't something I want for my father. I know him, and his subsequent response proves that point.

"I'll kill her. She was my fuck up," he states in a voice void of any affection for the woman he's spent his adult life with.

"Dad," I start, but he holds up his hand, silencing me.

"No, Ry. Whatever consequences she faces must be at my hand." He gets up from his seat, steps around the desk, and hugs me. "I have to do this," he whispers into my hair.

I hug him back, still grateful he's home.

Releasing me, he says, "I love you, Ry. Now, go on. Go get ready for your party."

"Love you, too, Dad."

As I cross the door, he shouts, "Please be safe."

"I will. I promise." Then I turn and head to my room.

"**I** can't believe you're out at another party," Shay says to Eva. "The end of the world must be upon us," she jokes.

Eva laughs. "Hey, I wasn't that much of a recluse."

"Yes you were, bitch," she quips. "If I didn't see you around school on occasion, I would've thought your parents shipped you off to boarding school or some shit."

"Riri, bring that ass over here," Wyatt demands.

I try to muster a scowl, but the sight of them all standing on the dance floor makes that an impossible feat.

"You better get out there," Eva teases.

After hanging with her all night, I've decided she's okay people. I wouldn't call us fast friends, but she has potential.

I smirk, "Always make them work for—" My remark is cut off when I'm dragged into Wes's waiting arms.

"Do I need to find a better use for that mouth, Ariah?" Wes whispers in my ear as his hand possessively grips my pussy through my leggings. He rubs his palm back and forth, creating enough friction that my body comes to life.

I curse when he pulls his hand away.

"Not yet, Angel," Owen says, yanking me into his chest.

"I'm not a yo-yo, you know," I tease.

He spins me to grind against my ass. "No, you're our everything."

We're all dancing and having a good time when Lev pulls out his phone. Whoever's texting him must say something he doesn't like because he grimaces. "It's Colt," he says, and I see Eva tense before she excuses herself. "We need to call him back," Lev explains.

Owen presses a kiss to my neck, "Behave and don't go anywhere unattended. We'll be back," he instructs.

I roll my eyes and point to where Erik and Antonio are standing, "Like I could go anywhere with my shadows on duty."

"You and that smart mouth," Wes states, pecking my cheek before following behind the guys.

Once they disappear, I turn to Shay. "Who's Colt, and why did Eva look like the devil was on her tail at the mention of his name?"

She tugs me off the dance floor and over to the bar, grabbing two bottles of water before finding a quiet enough corner. Erik and Antonio take up spots far enough away not to hear but close enough to be in reach.

"Colter is one of the Jacobi twins," she begins, sighing when the name doesn't register. "Seriously? You should know all of the power-house families by now," she chastises but continues. "They aren't an original bloodline, but their family is amongst the major powers in the world."

"Okay, powerful family, got it. That still doesn't answer my question," I retort.

Shay's eyes narrow, her lips draw into a thin line. "I didn't get to the part. I was answering the first part of your question. Miss Impatient," she snarks.

"My bad. Please continue," I tease.

"Let's just say Colter and Cooper are assholes of epic proportions. As to why Eva took off, I'm not sure. We haven't spoken much until recently, and whenever I ask her what happened, she clams up."

We talk for at least another hour before I realize the guys still aren't back. Shay begins to yawn, and I look at my cell and see it's almost three in the morning. "It's late, and I don't know how long it will be before the guys return," I announce before texting the group chat saying we're leaving. The guys make a stink until I remind them about security. I smile down at my phone when they say they'll be over to tuck me in soon.

We're almost to the car when the headlights of a car flash on. Erik positions himself in front of me, and Antonio is at my back.

The door to the car opens, and out steps my fucking mother.

"You've played long enough. Get your ass in the car, you spoiled bitch," Elise seethes.

Before I can tell her to take a long walk off a short cliff, a shot sounds, Erik crumples to the pavement, and Shay screams as Antonio holds a gun to her head.

"Why?" I snarl at Antonio, but Elise cuts off his answer.

"We don't have time for your shit. Drop your phone and the pin, or your friend will join your bodyguard," she instructs.

I grit my teeth, quickly stealing a glance at Erik on the ground, his chest is barely rising and falling, and a dark pool is trickling out from under him. I'm still unsure where he was shot or his chances of surviving.

"Hurry the fuck up," Elise barks.

"Ariah, don't do it," Shay begs.

I turn in time to see Antonio strike her in the face. "Shut up, or I'll put a bullet between your eyes," he growls.

Shay shows no fear. Her nostrils flare in annoyance. She looks at me, and I shake my head for her to keep quiet. Her lips scrunch in protest, but she remains silent.

"Do you promise to leave her alone if I get in the car?" I ask, facing my mother. I begin to pull the pin off my jacket and await her response.

"Leave the jacket, and I'll leave her here," Elise states, a smarmy smile pulling at her lips.

Dropping my jacket with my phone and the Selection pin to the ground, I approach the car. Elise moves and gestures for me to climb in. I look back at Shay one last time, seeing Antonio holding her still, her eyes pleading with me to stay, but I can't. I can't let her be hurt, not for me.

I climb into the backseat, Elise following promptly behind me. She closes the door and signals for the driver to take off. Just before we leave, she winds down her window.

"Kill her," she instructs, and I scream, launching myself at her as

I hear the distinct ricochet of a gunshot, and I watch my best friend fall to the ground as we speed out of the parking lot.

"You fucking promised," I snap as my fist connects with her face. I'm dragged back into the chest of someone before the familiar prick pinches my neck.

Elise tsks, "You need to learn how to ask for things, darling daughter. I left her as I said I would. I never promised she'd be alive. Now sit back. We have a long drive ahead of us."

My body won't cooperate, my arms feel heavy, and my eyes droop. However, before I give in to the sedative working its way through my system, I mumble, "I'm going to fucking kill you before this is over."

60

WYATT

"Seriously, I thought there'd be more than this," I mumble. We've been at this for hours, and we've only decrypted ten names— all people we've known about.

"You can't rush the process. The scraper we've created will decode each change in the encryption," Coop says through the screen.

A notification sounds and I watch three more names populate.

Sighing, I turn back to my laptop and continue combing through the records I pulled for my dad's law firm.

"They're all already dead." My gaze lifts at the sound of Sebastian's disgruntled voice. He flips his computer, displaying all the names that were just revealed. "They were discovered in the last round-up the Council oversaw."

I bring up the log from last week's mission. Thirteen families betrayed us in their thirst for power. Elise promised them all something she never would give. We didn't kill them all. Most are sitting in the cells under the Tombs until a decision can be made on what will happen next.

"Was the whole fucking town in on this?" Owen growls, throwing his blade at the wall.

It's a fair question, given the situation. "Enough of them were," I reply.

"The Fraternitas needs an overhaul. We can't keep leading like this— Elise was only able to get where she is because of the arcane rules the Council refuses to see the need to change," Wes explains.

A ping sounds— another batch of names appear just as all our phones go off.

"Fuck," Wes shouts.

"I'm going to rip his balls off and feed them to him," Owen snarls.

I watch as Antonio's name pops on the screen, and I grab my phone to see my worst fears confirmed. I'm hitting call before I even register the action.

"Ariah's been taken. Shay and Erik have been rushed to the hospital, and we don't know if either of them will make it," my father explains.

"Where?" is my only question, but he understands what I want.

"The Tombs— we leave as soon as you all arrive and gear up," he replies.

I disconnect the call. "We have to go. Colt, Coop, keep us posted. We have a cunt to murder."

The fact that we're outside another building to get our girl back isn't lost on us— it just fuels us.

We don't have time to process the guilt we all feel for leaving her— we're focused on getting her back. We'll beg for her forgiveness later. But bringing her home is priority number one.

"You all have your instructions. We know from surveillance and heat signatures there are twenty-four people inside— twenty-three are targets— one's my daughter," I watch the moment of anguish in Aaron Bradford's eyes before it dissolves into determination. "All targets are shoot-to-kill unless you know they can be captured." Aaron walks down the line of his team as we stand back by the truck, ready to go. Our fathers— also suited up, are like a looming presence behind the *true* leader of the Fraternitas. "I want to make this clear— we *do not* leave this building without *my daughter,* and *Elise Lockwood* is *mine!*"

I want to say we all agree on this— all of us understanding why he wants this kill. But we *all* have reasons for wanting the walking human carcass eviscerated. I turn to Owen— his jaw is clenched. I'm not sure which girl he has strapped to his back. I just know it's a Katana, and Thelma and Louise are in his hands.

"Let's go," Aaron's voice booms.

We pull our skull balaclavas down. Then we breach— two men work in tandem to pick the locks and open the front doors. The first wave moves in.

"Where in the building is she?" I ask Lev, knowing he's already got her chip location on the screen.

"Third floor, last room on the left," he responds.

Our dads make their way to us, and Lev puts his phone away. "We're going to go in before you boys. Get Ariah and detain Elise. We need her alive— she has all the answers," Wes's father instructs.

We nod and watch Mr. Bradford and Thomas lead our dads into the building.

"Antonio is mine," Wes seethes. We grunt our agreement and head inside.

Ignoring the fighting around us, we creep toward the stairwell.

"Gas masks on," Sebastian directs, then kicks the door open, tossing in the smoke bomb.

With our masks in place, we pick off the choking men. Owen chops a gagging man in the head clear to the bone and leans over, dragging his blade across his jugular. Lev and Wes shoot three men between the eyes with quick successive pops.

I ascend the first three steps, my rifle aimed and ready, clearing the path. "First floor cleared."

We make it to the third floor with no hiccups or resistance.

"I'll breach first," Sebastian states, moving to the lead position.

We can't use the gas on this floor because we know Ariah's here and won't risk hurting her.

Before Sebastian's gloved hand grabs the knob, gunfire rings out — bullets pepper the door.

"Shit," I growl when a bullet zips past my face.

"How the fuck are we supposed to get inside?" Lev snaps.

Owen slides past us, heading for the stairs, "On it," he says, running up the stairs.

"Crazy fuck," Wes groans, chasing after him.

Sebastian signals for us to move back down to the second-floor landing.

"What do you think they're up to?" I ask after twenty minutes pass.

I don't have to wait long for the answer when I hear screams and shots before the third-floor door opens. "Clear," Owen shouts, and when we climb the stairs, Owen's standing there covered in blood.

"Is that— is that a piece of skin?" Lev asks, pointing to something hanging off Owen's shoulder.

Owen shrugs. "Maybe, I didn't really take the time to look," he says, before wiping his Katana on the dead man missing a chunk of his face, and sheathing it.

Wes steps through the door. "Let's go," he commands, reloading his side piece.

Sebastian takes point, and we move down the hall.

We're coming for you, Riri. Just hold on.

61

ARIAH

An annoying sense of déjà vu sets in at the cotton feel of my mouth. The only difference is, this time, I remember every fucking thing that's transpired.

"Oh good, you're awake. I made sure the dosage wasn't as strong this time. We have a lot to discuss and not a lot of time to do it," Elise begins.

I'm seated in a leather chair across from her. I flex my fingers, realizing I'm not tied down.

Big mistake.

Elise slides bottled water toward me. "Drink up, and no, it's not laced with anything. I need you coherent for this conversation."

I eye the bottle in suspicion. She can't honestly believe I'd take her word for it, not after Shay. My eyes close, and I force the image of my tenacious best friend falling to the ground, hoping to whatever higher power that she's alive.

"Honestly," she says, opening the cap, pouring some into a glass, and drinking it. "Do you think I have time to poison you?"

Snorting, I retort, "Says the woman that's had me injected with sedative twice now."

She slams the cup down on the table. "Drink the damn water or don't. I was just trying to help."

I bite back the *'shove the help up your ass'* rebuff sitting on the tip of my tongue and aim for answers. "What do you want to discuss?"

Her eyes light with excitement, and my hands slide down the arm of the chair, looking for anything I can use before I remember the blade strapped to my ankle in the boot of my Docs.

I'm going to kiss Owen for giving this to me when he took me knife-throwing.

"Let's start with a little history lesson," she begins, reclining in her seat. "Imagine the birth of a new nation. A country, in its infancy, where rules were being established, but the only ones able to make those rules that will govern the masses were men, even though women played an instrumental role in winning the country's sovereignty."

I sigh, leaning forward to rest my hands on my knees. "Yes, I know, the American Revolution."

Elise's eyes narrow. "No, you don't. It was long before then. It started from the time our families' ships touched this land. Our voices were silenced," she seethes.

"You mean like the indigenous nations here before us?" I snap.

Her lip curls. "That's not what we're here to discuss."

Typical.

"When the Fraternitas was formed, women were and still are not allowed. Power was to only pass through the male lineage," she continues.

I roll my eyes. "And let me guess. Your solution is to shift the power from patriarchal to matriarchal?" I scoff.

Annoyed with my question, she challenges, "Look what men have done across the globe. The wars they've started, the famine, global warming, and the division amongst nations. Why would anyone want that to continue?"

"Right, because killing girls part of the Selection and aiding in the near annihilation of an entire family line screams the pillar of morality," I snap.

Elise places her hand on her chest, appearing affronted by my claims. "Name a person with any real power that doesn't have blood on their hands?" she counters.

"I'm not the one pointing fingers here. You are. I'm simply informing you that the moral high horse is bullshit. It's the problem with absolutes and extremes," I explain.

She throws her head back and laughs. "You think the middle ground holds power? Extremes always win. You just need to be on the right side of the pendulum. It doesn't matter that the majority of the country is even-keeled. They're never the loudest voice in the room. Now, shut up and let me finish."

I watch as Elise stands from her chair and walks around the table. I halt any attempts to grab the knife.

"Our family has been working on a way to take over the Fraternitas for generations— a place we belonged from the start, and I've succeeded where many before me have failed. Do you want to know why, Daughter?" she probes, sitting on the table and crossing her legs.

Refusing to give her the satisfaction of a response, I sit back in my seat.

She tips her chin up and smirks. "Always so fucking stubborn," she mumbles before continuing. "It's because I am willing to do everything and sacrifice anyone to do it," Elise boasts.

I watch, still shocked that this woman is my mother. The same sweet woman who baked cookies and planned playdates when I was younger.

"So why wait for me? Why not just take it all yourself?" I ask.

Her eyes flare as her lips twist into a sneer. "Because it wasn't fucking allowed. It has to be you. You're the oldest and will unite the powers once you have one of their babies."

What the fuck is it with these people and babies?

"If you don't want me to kill Jamie, Kellan, or Kylan, you're going to do exactly what you're told," she demands, and my chest gets tight at the mention of their names.

I take a deep breath, trying to combat the building panic. Before, I would call bullshit, but after Antonio, I know the guards might not all be loyal to the Fraternitas.

"Don't you start your shit, Ariah," she shouts.

"How could you ever threaten your own kids?" Disgust oozes from my words. This woman is beyond vile.

Elise looks amused by my confusion. "They were spares and nothing else. If you weren't necessary, you'd be dead."

Rage engulfs me, and I spring from my seat, tackling her to the table. I land on top of her, wrapping my hands around her throat. "I'm going to end your miserable life, you heartless bitch," I grit through clenched teeth.

Her nails claw at my hands, but I refuse to be deterred. I'm going to end her.

I'm so focused on strangling the miserable life out of Elise that I don't hear the door open or the footsteps approaching until it's too late. I'm hauled off just as I watch a blood vessel pop in her left eye.

"You fucking brat," she rasps, sucking in air.

I see my handprints around her neck and smile in satisfaction. It's unfortunate I was pulled off her. I'm sure I could've killed her if I had a few more minutes.

"Sit her ass down and leave us. I'll take it from here, Antonio," Elise instructs, and I'm carted back to my seat.

"You fucking traitor," I shout.

"We all have roles to play," Antonio mutters before turning and exiting the room.

Elise stalks back to the other side of the table, ensuring something separates us. I'd say it was a smart decision, but it won't keep her safe. I've already decided she dies tonight.

"You're trying the last of my patience, Ariah. You'll do what you're told, or you'll be responsible for the death of your siblings. I'm done playing games with you," she hisses.

Over her bullshit, I bend, pretending to tie my shoe, and reach for the blade but come up empty. The holster is there. There's just no knife.

I'm yanked up by my hair. "Did you think I wouldn't search you?" Elise taunts. "You're just starting. I've been at this for decades."

Pitching forward, I clench my teeth, using her hold on my hair as leverage to flip her over my back. She lands with a thud, and I punch her in the throat, forcing her to release my hair. Her hands clasp her neck before her legs swing up, and her booted foot connects with my face.

I tumble back before rolling to my feet.

"You're going to fucking pay for that. I'm going to make sure the same thing happens to those little brats that I made happen to Owen," Elise snarls.

What she had done to Owen? I don't have enough time to process her words before she charges me. I'm ready for her attack, and once she's in range, I jump, scissor-kicking her, and she stumbles backward but doesn't go down.

She shrieks in frustration, grabbing the glass and breaking it on the side of the table. "Fuck this. You're not worth the trouble. I'll figure out another way. Jamie will be eighteen soon enough. What're a few more years?"

"You'll be dead long before Jamie hits her teens," I snap.

We dance around each other. I parry her attempts until I see her tiring. Then, I slap her lazy thrust away, knocking the shard of glass from her bloody hand, and side-kick her.

I'm on top of her before she fully hits the ground.

Grabbing the shard, I yank her up by her roots and aim the broken glass at her exposed throat.

"I hope you enjoy hell," I scream, pressing the serrated edge to her throat. The door bursts open just as I feel the glass cut her skin.

"Stop."

62

SEBASTIAN

"We need her alive," I finish, hoping my words get through to Ariah.

My fucking spitfire looks breathtaking. I'll question my claim of ownership later.

Wyatt and Owen bring up the rear as I step into the room. Wes and Lev secure Antonio— he'll be dealt with later.

"Why? This bitch deserves death," Ariah yells, pressing the blooded piece of glass into Elise's neck.

Holster my gun, I hold my hands up, trying to get her to see reason. "She's going to die. We need answers first," I explain.

"Let's get her in the seat over there, Love," Wyatt coaxes, pointing to a leather office chair.

Ariah mutters to herself but eventually drops the shard from Elise's neck. "Fine," she grumbles, then slams Elise's face into the ground three times before dropping her.

Elise makes one muffled cry but nothing else. It's not until her body slumps to the ground I realize Ariah knocked her out.

Ariah points to Elise's crumpled form. "She shouldn't be hard to tie up."

Wyatt snorts, causing my attention to shift in his direction. That's when I see the frozen gaze of Owen transfixed on Elise. Wyatt, noticing where my eyes are trained, leans and whispers something in Owen's ear. Owen nods, expelling a deep breath and shaking his head clear.

When my focus shifts back to Ariah, her brows furrow, observing our exchange. She doesn't say anything. Wyatt and I pick up Elise while Owen stalks toward Ariah.

Once Elise is tied to the chair, I radio everyone, telling them where we are.

"Who did this?" Owen asks, making Wyatt and my focus whip to where he and Ariah are standing. Owen has her chin tipped up as he examines the bruise forming on her face and a cut to her cheek.

Ariah allows him to fuss but mumbles she's fine and it's nothing.

Wyatt and I snicker at their banter when the Council walks into the room, followed by Lev and Wes.

Mr. Bradford beelines straight for Ariah, enveloping her in a hug. "Ry." He breathes into her hair. "I'm sorry. I'm so sorry," he chokes out.

Ariah wraps her arms around him. "I'm okay, Dad. I let her take me. I had to. Sh-," she tries to say her name, but the words get caught in her throat.

Aaron pulls slightly from her hold and wipes the stream of tears from her eyes. The guys all step forward, but I signal them to stop—this is their moment.

Ariah closes her eyes, welcoming the comfort from her father. "Please tell me she's okay," she finally stutters.

"We're not sure. She was taken to the hospital, Angel," Owen answers—his tone gentle.

"Well, isn't this fucking touching," Elise croaks, and all our heads swivel in her direction. "The only thing missing from this pitiful family reunion are the other three pissants I had to ruin my body for."

My hands clench at my side. Elise is like my father, but worse. Self-serving and power-hungry—lacking any moral compass.

"Good, you're awake. Let's question the hag and kill her," Lev snarls.

"I second that idea," Wes adds.

Aaron whispers something in his daughter's ear. Then kisses the top of her head before striding across the room. "This has been a long time coming, you traitorous bitch," he sneers.

Elise smiles, her blood-stained teeth on full display. "Aww, is widdle Aaron upset that I played with his widdle feelings," she coos like she's talking to a baby. "Too fucking bad. Build a bridge and get over it," she taunts.

Aaron whips a knife from its sheath and drives it into her right thigh.

Elise shrieks, jerking behind her restraints as she reflexively tries to move her arms.

"Funny you think I give a fuck about you playing. All I want are answers, and you'll give them to me before you die," Aaron demands.

Ariah steps in closer— no one attempting to stop her. She stands to the left of her father, still giving him room to interrogate Elise.

"Who else is in on this?" Mr. Bradford asks.

Elise doesn't answer, still whimpering at the sight of the blade lodged in her leg.

Aaron turns the blade, and Elise screeches. She pushes back against the chair, attempting to escape the pain.

"Who else?" he barks again.

I look around the room. Everyone is frozen to their spots— no one dares to interfere. Ariah's father looks as if he's grown two times as large as he looms over his wife.

Elise's green eyes look crazed when she lifts her gaze to meet Aaron's stare head-on. One of her pupils is tinged with red, making her appear almost animalistic. She must have popped a blood vessel at some point. "You might as well kill me because I'm not telling you shit," she grits.

A shrill cry rips from her throat as another knife impales her other thigh. "I have plenty of knives and endless time, Elise. You know better than most— I *always* get the answers. I'm relentless in that regard," Aaron states emphatically.

"F-fuck you," she spits.

"Never again," Aaron responds, reaching down and turning both knives, driving them deeper.

Lev steps up and pulls a vial from his vest. "Try this," he offers, and Aaron takes the proffered bottle.

"What's in that?" I whisper once he steps alongside me.

"Acid," he murmurs as Elise screams until she's hoarse.

I arch my brow. "You just walk around with acid?"

"Never leave home without a few different methods to aid in compelling people to answer questions," Lev quips, and I'm not sure if I should be worried or impressed.

Shaking my head, I turn back to see Aaron dripping another drop of the acid into Elise's wound. "Who the fuck else, Elise?" he demands.

Snot runs down her tear-streaked face. Elise hangs her head in defeat. "No one you don't already know about."

The Council steps forward at that answer. "That can't be true," Wes's dad snaps. "What about Senator Baker?"

"A convenient distraction you idiots believed," Elise mutters. "You fools were so focused on a *man* coming for your seats you missed all the signs in front of you."

"It's not possible," Donald grumbles. "There have to be more people in on this."

Elise thrusts her neck back, resting it on the back of her chair. It looks like it took all her strength to muster the move. "And that's how I was able to do everything. You're too fucking arrogant." She angles her neck to stare at Owen. "It's how I was able to take your sons," then she turns to Ariah. "It's how I was able to fuck your son. The little shit got hard for me, too," she cackles.

A distorted cry fills the air, and we all watch in what feels like expedited slow motion as Ariah pulls a dagger from Owen's belt, pushes her dad out of the way, and plunges the blade into her mother's throat before pulling it out and stabbing her repeatedly. "You fucking monster," she shouts. Her arm raises and lowers, over and over again, until Owen grips her wrist before her next downward strike.

Owen leans into her, saying something inaudible to our ears, and she drops the knife to the ground as she falls into his arms.

He scoops her up and carries her from the room without a backward glance.

Sudden movement causes me to turn in time to see Aaron open the top of the vial and pour the contents all over Elise's lifeless face. Then he turns and exits the room after his daughter.

I stare at Elise's mutilated corpse— *monster* isn't great enough of a word to describe who she was, but now it's over.

"Do we think she was telling the truth about Senator Baker?" Wes inquires.

"We're still working on uncovering names, but so far, everyone that's been discovered, we've known about," Lev answers.

A throat clears. "Keep digging. For now, we'll call this finished. Elise was the primary focus — she was the leader of the Filiae Bellonae, and with her and the key players taken out, we can work to find the remainder of the scum in hiding," Donald Edgewood instructs. "Meet us back at the Tombs once you've ensured Miss Brad- Ariah's okay, and you've dealt with Antonio."

I growl at the mention of his name. Wes might've called dibs, but I'm sure we'll all get our turns before he's disposed of.

We nod our agreement before leaving to find Owen and Ariah.

63

ARIAH

I lie on Owen's lap, refusing to be parted from him. After Elise dropped her bomb, I lost it. My vision blacked out, and then I was being stopped and carried from the room by Owen. He walked us to one of the armored trucks, and we haven't moved since then.

Dad came to check on me, refusing to leave until I convinced him I'd talk with him later. Finally, he relented and left to break the news to Jamie, Ky, and Kell, about Elise. I can only hope it won't devastate them too severely. I'm old enough to see the repugnant person she was. Jamie might also be able to see, but the twins were close to her. So, this will hurt them. Just another way Elise's selfishness has impacted someone.

A loop of the night plays, and I see Erik fall. Antonio shoots him and then takes Shay hostage, forcing me into the car with Elise. I watch in horror as Shay falls before I'm knocked out again. Then I'm listening to the repulsive words spewed from Elise's mouth.

I grip Owen tighter as he continues to console me. *Me.* He's comforting me after what that bitch did to him.

"Angel," his voice is like a balm to the turbulent storm raging inside me. "I'm okay," he soothes.

His surety renews my tears as I remember the night I carved my initial into his chest. The way he trusted me enough to confide in, to ease his anguish and quiet the noise. A single drop can ripple through time, causing everlasting repercussions.

I don't know how to broach this subject. My fucking mother molested and raped him when he was just a boy.

Sighing, I say, "I want to talk, but only when you're ready to."

His hand runs through my hair. "I will, Ry. Just not tonight. I don't like that you know. I would do anything to have plunged the dagger into Elise's throat so you'd never find out."

Even now, he's putting me before his pain.

"I'm glad it was me. I didn't want it to be my dad or you," I say quietly, still in shock that I'd killed someone.

"Do you want to talk about it?" he asks.

I play with his fingers while I stall. I'm not sure how I should answer this. *Am I ready? Do I want to talk about it?* "I don't feel anything. She was dead to me the moment I found out all she was doing and what she did to our family. But after what she did to you," I trail off. "Every possible tie I had to her was severed."

Owen hums his understanding. "If you ever feel otherwise, I'm always— we're always here," he quickly corrects.

I kiss the tips of his fingers, remembering how I said something along those lines. I jump up at the memory. "Where's the knife I used on you that night?"

"Lola?"

Right. I almost forgot he names them. "Yes, where's Lola?"

He unzips his vest and reaches inside, pulling the blade from some pocket.

I tug at the collar of my shirt, revealing my collarbone. "I want you to mark me," I state confidently.

Owen's eyes nearly pop out of his skull before he shakes his head. "No, Angel. You don't need to-."

I cut him off. "Yes, yes, I do. Please, O," I plead.

His eyes close before he looks around for something in the truck. I see when he spots it, and he stands, grabbing the first aid kit.

I watch as he cleans the blade and then my skin.

"Are you sure?" he probes, peering into my eyes.

"Yes," I reply, grabbing his hand and bringing the tip of the knife to my chest, pressing it in until it breaks skin. I hiss at the initial feel but lose myself in my thoughts as he carves an "O" in the spot that matches his, right near my heart. "Now you're mine," I whisper, "and you'll never have to fight the noise alone again."

My hand subconsciously reaches for the bandage on my chest, anchoring me as I walk into the hospital where Shay's condition is still unknown.

Owen holds my hand as we approach Mr. and Mrs. Warren, and the rest of their family. I recognize her brother from school and a few others from the cookout. One noticeably absent presence is Brendan.

Where the fuck is he?

"Ariah, sweet girl," Mrs. Warren says, calling me to her. Her eyes are bloodshot from crying.

This is all my fucking fault.

"I'm so sorry," I begin, and she swats at my arm, pulling me into her arms.

"Don't chu dare apologize for the wicked ways of man. Elise was a sick woman, and she deserves everyting coming her way. I'm just glad yuh ere now," Shay's mom says.

I squeeze her. "Elise is dead. She won't be hurting anyone ever again," I inform her. Then I pull from her embrace. "Any word?"

Her face crumples, and she hangs her head. "She's flatlined twice. Di fucka shot her in the spleen. But it's the blood loss. It took so long for someone to find her." Shay's mom's voice breaks, and her husband comes up behind her, taking her into his arms to comfort her.

"We're waiting to hear from the doctors. They should be out soon," Shay's father finishes for his wife and then walks her to take a seat.

I take a seat next to Owen, and he grabs my hand. "Where are the guys?" I've been so out of it that I haven't thought to ask until now.

"Once they saw you were with me and needed time, they went to the Tombs to deal with Antonio," he replies.

"I hope they dissect him," I growl.

Owen snorts, "You're turning into a blood-thirsty avenging angel."

I think over his words. I really have. "It's deserved. People keep trying to hurt those I care about, and I can't fucking have that."

"Just don't put yourself in harm's way to get justice. I know you'd do what you did for Shay again, and I don't blame you. I'd do it for you or any of the guys without hesitation. I'm just asking you to make sure it's your last possible resort," Owen begs, and I squeeze his hand.

"I promise to try as long as you do the same."

Before he can respond, someone calls Shay's parents' names, and my gaze snaps up. I grip Owen's hand watching the doctors speak to the Warrens, looking for a sign of what's happening. When Shay's mom falls, my heart stops.

"No. No fucking way." I jump from my seat and run across the hospital lobby.

"She's out of surgery and in stable condition." I hear the female physician say, and relief floods me so fast I also fall, only for Owen to catch me before I hit the ground.

"Shay's okay?" I ask for clarity.

Mr. Warren helps his wife off the ground before he answers, "Yes."

Then the doctor continues, "Miss Warren isn't out of the woods yet. We need to see how well she does once she wakes, and then she'll need time to heal."

I don't hear anything except that my best friend is alive. That news zaps the leftover adrenaline that's kept me going, and everything that's happened finally comes crashing in. "I think it's time for me to go home," I mumble to Owen.

"Then let's get you home, Angel," he bends to whisper in my ear before saying our goodbyes to the Warrens, letting them know I'll be back once I've rested, before he guides me to his Jeep.

64
ARIAH

Things have settled. Now that we no longer have to worry about Elise, and Shay's home from the hospital, I finally feel a sense of peace. I only wish my nerves got the memo and would settle the fuck down.

Between headaches, loss of appetite, and random panic attacks, I'm exhausted. I'm hoping a night with my guys will be just what the doctor ordered.

I settle between Owen's legs, waiting for the movie to start. Lev and Sebastian are on either side of us. Wyatt grabs my foot as he sits near the bottom of the bed, and begins to massage the sole, making me groan.

"Don't make those noises if you ever want to see this movie," Wes mumbles from his spot on the giant bed in Owen's theater room.

I close my eyes, enjoying the feel of Wyatt kneading my instep. "I make no promises. Wy is a god amongst men."

Sebastian snorts. "Foot rubs get you god status. What title do orgasms get?" he quips before I feel the tip of his finger brush my already puckered nipple, causing my pussy to clench.

"I was wondering the same thing," Lev adds while sliding his hand under the band of my shorts.

My breath hitches when he pinches my clit. "None of you are playing fair," I moan.

"We're not in the business of fair," Owen growls before his hand palms my other breast as he sucks on my proffered neck.

I feel the tug at my shorts, and I lift, allowing them to be pulled off. I'm guessing by Wyatt since he's no longer rubbing my foot.

My eyes pop open at the feel of a mouth between my legs, the scruff of a beard tickling my thighs.

"You always taste so fucking good," Wes groans.

Lev's fingers leave my clit, and I grumble in protest until I feel a tongue swipe across it. "Mmmm. I absolutely fucking agree," Wyatt says before sucking my clit between his lips.

My back arches when Lev's mouth replaces Owen's hand on my nipple. "Shit," I shout when Sebastian's teeth nip at my other breast.

Someone's hand pushes me back to the bed as Owen pulls my head back to capture my mouth.

"You look so fucking good with all our hands on you," Lev murmurs. His voice barely audible above the buzzing in my ears.

I feel around until I find his dick and squeeze him through his sweats. He groans before assisting me and pulling himself out. My hand jerks his length, using his pre-cum for lubricant since I can't put him in my mouth.

Wes and Wyatt both stop eating my pussy, and I whine into Owen's mouth.

"Our girl's greedy," Sebastian states. "Why don't we fix that?"

Seconds later, I'm being filled, and fingers are rubbing my clit.

"Is that what you needed?" Wyatt asks, snapping his hips and driving deeper inside me.

I'm not even sure if he's wearing a condom, but I'm too focused on wondering if I'll survive this. All of them touching me has my mind in a different stratosphere. An image of me being filled in every available hole as I'm pleasuring them and they please me flits through my mind. The thought causing my walls to spasm.

Sebastian and Lev's mouths suck my nipples with such fervor as Wes's fingers pick up the pace.

Owen lifts his mouth from mine. I look to see him and Wyatt speaking with their eyes before Wes taps Lev and Owen taps Sebastian, seeing the silent conversation between them.

"Straddle him, Angel," Owen instructs, pointing to where Wyatt now lays on the bed.

I crawl over to him, happy to see he is actually wearing a condom, and position myself before sinking down his length. My hips grind against him each time I bounce up and down his cock.

"She takes him so well," Wes groans and positions himself behind me.

I tense until I realize he's rubbing some of my juices against my puckered hole. I don't think I'm ready for anal yet, but every time one of them fucks me in the ass with their fingers, I'm tempted to beg.

Wes's palm cracks against my skin, before he slides one finger inside and begins pumping.

"Bring that fucking mouth over here," Owen commands, and I turn my face, opening for him to thrust his dick into my mouth.

Sebastian's fingers find my clit, and Lev's tongue swirls against my nipple.

I scream when all of them pick up their paces at the same time.

Wyatt's thrusts outpace mine. Wes works in a second finger, making me feel so full as his pumping matches Wyatt's. Sebastian pinches my clit seconds before Lev bites my nipple, and I crash over the cliff. My body is no longer able to fight off the orgasm, and Wyatt fucks me right through it, pounding into me so hard I barrel into a second orgasm before fully coming down from my first. I feel my juices leaking out of me just as Owen roars and comes in my mouth.

I'm pulled into Wyatt's arms. He brushes the hair out of my sweaty face and kisses my forehead. "Sleep," he whispers, and I don't fight his command.

I don't know how long I've been asleep, but the shuffling of clothes and muttered curses wakes me.

Turning, I see Owen fumbling to put on his pants in the dark. "Where are you going?"

He jumps. "Shit. I thought you were sleeping."

"Surprise," I joke.

He shakes his head and continues to pull on his clothes.

I climb over sleeping bodies before asking again, "Where are you going?"

He zips up his pants and then answers. "I have a hunch I need to check on."

I open my mouth to ask what's the hunch when his finger presses to my lips. "I'll tell you once I know for sure if I'm right or not. I won't be gone long. Get back in bed," he suggests before placing a quick peck on my lips.

"Shouldn't you bring someone with you?" I start and search for clothes of my own to join him. I don't want him going by himself.

"Nope. This isn't that kind of situation. I'll be fine, I promise."

Owen pulls on his shirt and walks toward the door.

"Hey," I whisper-shout, and he looks back. "Don't do anything stupid."

He turns back and scoops me in a hug. "I'll be back before you know it, Angel," he murmurs, kissing me, this time coaxing my mouth open.

I grumble when he pulls back. *I love you* is on the tip of my tongue, but I swallow it. Instead, I say, "I'll be here waiting."

65
OWEN

Following up on a hunch, I pull up outside Senator Baker's house and wait.

Based on the information Lev's been able to dig up, I have a theory on who could be meeting with the Senator.

Madeline kept saying shit like we'd never see it coming, but we saw Elise coming. At least we did once we had all of the information.

The number of families in Edgewood who were stripped of their titles and either forced to move or be killed is almost surprising. The Bellonae Filiae planned this for a long time, and they almost succeeded— because we got cocky. I refuse to be caught sleeping again. Not with Ariah's life at stake.

Elise is gone, but that doesn't mean the threat is. *I refuse to believe it's all that simple.*

Senator Baker is tied to this— I fucking know he is. Antonio, I snicker, remembering his cries, said as much, and so does all the evidence.

Madeline wouldn't say shit about it. The stupid cunt died protecting him, and Elise laughed and said she'd never partner with the dumb fuck. But I know something's there— which is why, just like the last few nights, I sit here and watch.

I have a few hours before I need to head to the Tombs for our vote.

Like there's anything to vote about.

Ariah is our Chosen, and I'll fucking cut out the heart of any idiot who is dumb enough to say otherwise.

Everyone is on board, though. So I won't need to slice anyone. Seb is still a ways off from falling for her, but that hasn't stopped him from seeing how many times he can make her come before she taps out.

I snort, remembering the scene on the hood of the car when we tied that bitch Vivian to the gate and made her watch Sebastian fuck Ariah. Vivian's threats and wails in protest paled in comparison to the sound of Ariah coming. I wasn't sure if it was the sight of Ariah on the car as we all made her come or her doing what she told *Miss Taylor* she'd do if she didn't stop fucking playing around that had me hard all the way home.

My dick was so hard that night. Fuck. It's hard now just thinking about it.

Sliding my hand down, I grip my shaft, squeezing and contemplating whether I should rub one out while I wait when a black car pulls up, turning into the driveway. Finally, the garage opens, and the car drives in, prohibiting me from seeing who's driving. *Fuck.*

I climb out of my car and make my way around the back of the house. I know it's not Baker. That prick's car is sitting in the driveway. This leads me to ask myself why he would park there, while the vehicle visiting pulls into the garage.

It's a good thing I already had the scoop of this place and know he likes to leave his back door cracked.

I creep along the hedges beside the door and poke my head around. No one's there, but I hear voices.

"Matthew, I told you I'd handle it, didn't I? I have them all eating out the palm of my hand. I made them all think Elise was in control," a distorted voice says.

I fucking knew this wasn't over.

I can't make out who it is, but I need to capture this.

Pulling out my phone, I duck when I hear the voices get closer and hit record.

"I never doubted you, not for one minute," the other person states, whom I can make out as the Senator.

"It won't be long now," the gleeful voice responds.

Who the fuck is this person? They sound like they're using some voice distortion device.

"Good, then you'll be mine, and so will the presidency," Senator Bakers exclaims.

Gotcha fucker. He won't live long enough to make it to the first primary, much less become president.

Taking a chance, I peek again, hoping to glimpse something, and I fucking do.

"Holy fucking shit," I mumble.

I can't snap a picture without being caught, but my word will be enough for Lev to start digging. That plus this recording. I need to get the fuck out of here before I'm caught.

Turning, I squat, creeping back to my car. Only periodically looking to ensure no one's seen me.

Once I'm inside. I start my jeep and drive back to Edgewood—my trip to Lincolnville a success.

Check-fucking-mate.

66

WES

Thoughts of last night with Ariah— the way she was with all of us makes my dick lengthen in my pants.

Fuck. I need to get myself in control, or I'm going to bust right in my acid-washed jeans.

"Having a flashback of our girl?" Wyatt asks. A knowing grin stretches across his face, making his freckles more pronounced.

Sighing, I nod, "She's everything I stupidly took too long to appreciate."

"I should make you eat crow for all the shit you put her through trying to sort out your bullshit. You're lucky she likes your pretty face, or I'd deck you in it for taking so damn long," he jokes, punching my arm.

We're sitting in the Tombs shooting the shit, waiting for Owen to get here so we can make our final choice. Though, there isn't much discussion that needs to happen. Ariah is our girl. She's exactly who we've always needed— she completes, strengthens, and owns us. A fucking queen.

"What the fuck is taking Owen so long?" Lev shouts, groaning from his space by the bar. He's much more carefree partly because the Filiae Bellonae is no longer a threat and primarily because of her — Ariah. She's done so much to bring out the friend I remember growing up with.

After the death of Elise and Madeline, it's been quiet. Graduation is next week, and the party where we announce our Chosen happens that weekend.

"Yeah, where the fuck is that shithead? I figured he'd be beating down the door to make sure we all choose Ariah," Sebastian states. He's still fighting his feelings for Ariah, but it's all over his face— he's a fucking goner, just like the rest of us.

Laughing, I reply, "So you're prepared for the beat down he's going to give you for still fighting your obvious feelings for *his* angel?"

A blond brow arches in my direction as his lips twist. *Oh, a direct hit.*

"What, you don't like being called on your bullshit? You're always dishing it— take it for once," I quip.

The asshole is constantly giving directives about what we should be doing or how we should be honest with ourselves, and here he is.

Continuing to poke fun, I jest, "Don't you think you should take your own advice, Yoda?"

The guys break out in laughter, and even he chuckles before replying. "Ariah is amazing, and I'll treat her like the queen she is, but what you all have with her," Sebastian pauses, leaning his head back to stare up at the ceiling. His wheat hair, uncharacteristically not styled, falls away from his eyes before he speaks, "But love isn't in the cards for me ever again."

I go to rebuff his asinine statement when there's a buzz in my pocket, indicating I have a notification. Pulling the device from my pocket, I see it's a text message.

Opening it, I see a video file attachment with a message. Reading the message, my jaw clenches, and I squeeze my phone, nearly cracking it before I hit play. When I see what's playing, I immediately hit stop before any noise can be heard.

Schooling my features, I announce, "Emergency meeting. We have to make our choice now."

"What do you mean, we're making our selection now? I thought we were waiting on Owen?" Wyatt's puzzled gaze probes mine.

"His choice is Ariah. So are ours. Let's go make it happen so we can be done with this bullshit Selection process," I state, rising from my seat and heading for the door, ignoring their questions as I send word to our fathers to alert the girls we've made our decision.

S he's here— Ariah. *Damn, she's so fucking beautiful.* Her blue-black hair hangs in waves loosely down her back. Blush pink lips pull up in a smile as she takes us in.

"What's going on? Why are we meeting here?" she inquires.

Before I can answer her, my dad interjects, "The boys have made their decision."

Varying looks line the faces of each girl— the three that remain. Four girls have been murdered since the start of the Selection. If our fathers hadn't been able to end Elise and Madeline, I'm sure more would've met the same fate.

I take in the room.

Brittany's face is lined with a mixture of apprehension and resignation because she knows she's not even in the running. She's ready to be done with this farce. Samantha has her usual overly confident smug grin plastered on like she knows the outcome before it happens, while Ariah is confused.

"Why are we doing this now instead of next weekend?" Ariah asks.

They've all put so much work into the culminating event, the engagement announcement party, the societal event of the year.

"We know who we want, and it doesn't make sense to prolong

the process another week. The event will just be a formality. We want to stop having to go out and string girls along who'll never be Fraternitas wife material," I reply. Then, looking directly in Sam's direction, I continue, "Why should we pretend when the person we want has been right here all along? The rest of you are worthless, and only one of you was ever worthy of becoming our Chosen."

My glare makes her confident posture stiffen for a fraction of a second, her polished demeanor cracking before her plastic air of confidence cements itself into her filler-injected face.

I'm surprised it was able to move at all.

"Oh, okay. That makes sense," she hesitates, then takes her place in line with the rest of the girls.

"To fulfill the last rite into the Fraternitas, the original male heir must select a bride when they come of age. But five original blood-line male heirs must come together every five generations to choose one wife, ensuring the continuation of a strong original bloodline," my father begins.

He wasn't originally on board with doing this now. However, I relayed our grievances over continuing in a long courtship process when we haven't gone on a single date since our first ones with any of the girls, except Ariah.

Pulling the black cube-shaped box from his pinstriped suit pocket, he hands it to me and continues, "Wesley as the original head male heir, you are charged with proposing. Who have you all selected to be your bride?"

I step forward, taking the box from his hand and turning to face the girls. Then, clearing my throat, I announce, "We, the heirs of Edgewood, in our last act before becoming full members of the Fraternitas select," I open the box to the sparkling princess-cut four-carat diamond centered on a platinum band lined with four two-carat stones. "Samantha—."

I don't finish my words before chaos erupts. A fist flies at my face just before I see Ariah run from the room, a hand covering her mouth and tears streaming down her face.

"Ariah, I'm so-," but it's too late. She's gone.

I was hoping to explain to make it all make sense. I'm only trying to do what's best. I know I could make it all right if I had time, but I didn't have any time.

"Don't be mad because he made the best choice," Sam's godforsaken voice chimes.

Lev launches himself at her, hoisting her up by her neck. "You better shut the fuck up before another ends up dead," he shouts.

Another fist flies, cracking me in my ribs, and I don't fight.

Wyatt points at me and snarls, "You better pray I catch her before she leaves!" Then he tears out of the room in the same direction she went.

I slump to the floor, my face in my palms.

What does one do when you're forced to choose?

Either decision would have fucked us. I just went with the one that leaves the girl I think I'm in love with shattered.

Fuck!

67
ARIAH

I'm going to be sick. I head straight for the bushes and throw up. Once the contents of my stomach are emptied into the green bushes, I run straight for Thomas and the waiting car.

"Miss Bradford?" He stares in confusion but opens the door.

I don't think I'll ever get used to this stupid fucking last name. This name brought me to this fucked up town where my heart was yanked from my chest.

Tears stream freely down my face. I try to compose myself as I hear the car door slam.

"Ariah," Thomas tries again.

"Please just get me out of here," I plead.

He takes off as I see Wyatt run out of the building, but their treachery needs no explanation.

They didn't choose me. I thought their feelings were genuine, but as Wes said, they selected the person who would be Fraternitas's wife material, and I'm not that.

My stomach churns as we pull up to the house. I don't wait for Thomas to let me out. Once the car's in park, I throw the car door open and rush for the bathroom, praying I make it before I heave again.

I make it up the stairs in time to put my face into the toilet bowl. The events of the last thirty minutes and the stress of the last few weeks have finally caught up to me.

How fucking stupid of you, Ry. I let them in, and they played me.

My grandmother appears, and I hear the sound of the faucet turning on between retches.

She kneels next, her hand rubbing my back. "Get it all out."

Once my stomach finally settles, she flushes the toilet as I fall to my ass on the bathroom floor.

She takes the cool cloth and wipes at my feverish skin. Tears still stream down my face as I try to speak, but nothing comes out.

"Shh, child. Just let it out," she whispers, sitting on the floor next to me and pulling me into her arms. "We can worry about the who's and what's later." And I do just that.

After what feels like twenty minutes, my tears finally cease. I need a plan.

Sitting up, I brace my hand on the floor when the room feels like it's spinning.

Fucking Hell. I'm over these damn dizzy spells.

"Are you okay?" she asks.

Finally getting to my feet, I huff a sigh and reply, "I'll be fine. I've just been having dizzy spells lately."

"Let me get you some tea," she offers.

"No, I'll be okay. I just need a moment."

I feel my grandmother's eyes on me, but she says nothing.

Turning, I face her and give her a slight nod, and she finally relents, leaving the bathroom.

I make my way to the sink, peering at my face in the mirror. My eyes are bloodshot and puffy from crying, and my skin looks pale.

Footsteps sound, and I turn in time to see my grandmother approach and then place the things in her hands on the counter.

Touching my shoulder, she leans over and kisses my cheek, "No matter what the outcome, you don't have to face anything alone." Then, she walks from the bathroom, closing the door behind her, granting me privacy.

Looking at what she left, my heart begins to race.

Get your shit together and pussy up.

Sweat starts to line my forehead, and my lungs tighten.

This can't be happening. The re-emergence of tears streak down my face, pooling under my chin.

"This can't be happening," I repeat out loud. *How could you be so fucking stupid?*

"Don't worry, Ry. We'll figure it out," my dad ensures.

My head snaps at the sound of his voice. I was so distracted I didn't hear the door open or anyone approach. But he's right.

Using my sleeve, I wipe the ever-flowing stream trailing my cheeks. Inhaling until my sobs are under control. Renewed in my purpose, I clear my throat, affirming his sentiments.

"You're fucking right we are."

re you sure about this?" I ask, looking at both of them.

"Yes," they answer in unison.

"It's not safe here anymore. I've reached out to my contact, and he'll be waiting for you all to arrive. Dominic has already lined up a place for you all to stay and has a connection that will keep you off the grid."

I hesitate, looking back at the place that was starting to feel like home, tempted to stay until I remember what's at stake.

"Let's get you out of here, Ry. Nothing is holding us in Edgewood anymore," my dad says.

He's right.

Nothing and no one is left for me here.

Nodding, I let the car door close and wind down the window. "Will I ever see you again?"

Thomas nods, "Of course, but for now, Edgewood isn't where you should be."

Sighing, I agree and say my last goodbye.

It's time to leave this fucked up town in my rearview.

68

WYATT

By the time I make my way back into the building, I'm seeing red.

How fucking dare he— Wes. I'm going to kill him.

Storming back into the room, I shout, "What the fuck is wrong with you?" I dive for him, but Sebastian grabs me around the middle, and I fight in his hold.

"Get off me, you fucker. Just because you can't love her doesn't mean you get to defend this bullshit," I snarl.

I feel Sebastian stiffen, but his hold doesn't relax. His next words freeze me— draining all of my fight.

"Owen's been kidnapped."

Lev walks in the door as Sebastian continues speaking, "Wes got a text message he needs to share."

Looking, I see Wes still sitting on the floor, his hands running through his inky hair and pulling on the ends. Blood drips down the side of his mouth where I punched him— a bruise already forming.

Serves the fucker right. He should've come to us.

"Well, where the fuck is it?" I snap.

Sebastian hands Lev the phone, and Lev pushes some buttons, pulling the video up on the screen in Mr. Edgewood's office.

My heart stops.

Owen's slumped form is tied to a chair. He's been badly beaten. Parts of his face are mottled with dirt and blood, he's been stripped down to his hunter-green boxer briefs, and the "A" Ariah carved into his chest looks like someone's tried to slash through it.

My fists clench at my side, trying to keep my composure and not throw a chair at the screen while I wait to hear something.

As my patience begins to wane, the audio plays.

A distorted voice speaks, "You've played too long, and now times up. If you pick Ariah Bradford, Owen Jefferson is fucked."

"Fuck," Sebastian shouts before I hear a fist connect with plaster.

Who the hell is doing this? I thought we handled this with the death of Elise and Madeline. This was supposed to be finished. We were supposed to choose Ariah and be done.

I grit my teeth, trying to reign in the snarl that's building in my chest.

The voice continues, "I've killed them all to get you. Only Samantha Davenport will do."

"No! No fucking way," Lev barks.

Those are my sentiments exactly. *Fuck that rusty dusty cunt.*

"To choose otherwise will ensure Owen Jefferson's demise," the voice cuts out and loops back to the beginning.

Lev cuts the video, then turns to meet our gazes.

Anguish— his eyes fall to the floor, and his shoulder slump.

"We-we have to get him back— h-h-he can't go through this again. Not again. Not again," Lev rambles. There's so much pain in his tone that I close my eyes, trying to temper my own feelings.

I survey the room for the first time since storming back in and notice Brittany and the devil in question are missing.

"Where the fuck is the soulless skank on plastic legs?" I shout. "There's no way this person mysteriously chose Samantha Davenport— that bitch is in on it."

Sebastian answers, "She took off in the height of the fray. When we went to clear the room after the outburst, she was gone, and when we questioned Brittany, she said Sam ran out right after you did. We just didn't see it."

Of course she did— she's in on this. She'd need to make a quick exit.

Piecing the events of the day together— everything becomes very clear.

I turn to my friend, still bent with his head in his hands.

"That's why you called the emergency meeting. You needed to move fast," I stammer and then face a distraught Donald Edgewood. "Do we have a location?"

Mr. Edgewood's jaw clenches, "We're working on it. Right now, they're scrambling the signal. Thomas has a friend he believes can hack into the network and lock in on Owen's location."

Wes's father looks up, squeezing his eyes shut to compose himself. His mask is firmly back in place when his stare meets us again.

"I need you boys to go get Ariah. If this person went this far to ensure Sam was chosen, it means she isn't safe. When you bring her back, we can devise a plan. Once Owen is back, we can call off the sham engagement and make an official choice. The Chosen won't be selected under duress, and the Fraternitas won't fall at the hands of some usurper," he commands.

"I want to wait to hear about Owen," I say.

As much as it pains me. I know Ariah would be more pissed if we went to her and she found out Owen's missing, and we chose to rush to her aid instead of his.

"We won't have any updates for now, and she's not safe," Mr. Edgewood's tone allows no room for arguments.

Wes stands from the ground, wiping the remainder of the blood from his face with the back of his hand. "My dad's right. Let's go get our girl."

I open Ariah's front door and immediately know something's wrong.

The house is too quiet.

Kell and Ky aren't running around wreaking havoc. I can't hear Jamie anywhere. There's no noise.

I take off for the stairs— my feet carrying me to her room on autopilot.

Ariah's bedroom door is ajar, and I push it the rest of the way open.

Clothes and boxes are everywhere.

I rush into the room, hoping I'm wrong and she's just thrown a fit, but I know. I know it before I see it.

She's gone.

Storming out of her room, I run to her siblings' rooms, checking their closets and drawers— empty.

Racing back to her room, I don't hear the guys approach.

"Where is she?" Sebastian asks, looking around at the state of Ariah's room.

"She's gone," I mutter.

"What do you mean she's gone?" Lev balks.

Wes storms into the room, searching through whatever remains of her things.

"How-how could she be gone?" he mumbles, barely loud enough for us to hear as falls to his knees, pulling at the roots of his disheveled ink-black hair.

I want to punch him again, but I know this isn't his fault.

He should've said something and let us all decide together. Instead, he was high-handed—now Ariah's left, and we're stuck in some fucked up arrangement to marry quicksand pussy.

"I'm sorry," he professes, but I'm not sure if it's an apology for us or to her. He falls forward and when comes back up his eyes are wet. "I was just trying to do what I thought was best" He breathes. The torment in his voice softens me.

I understand what Wes did— it doesn't make the consequences of his actions any more palatable.

Sighing, I make my way over to the bed and drop to the mattress, landing on a pile of clothes. Leaning to the side to pull them from under me, my hand brushes over something hard.

I stand and toss the clothes to the side to see what's there.

My eyes glaze over before refocusing, and I shout, "Fuck!"

EPILOGUE

They underestimated me for far too long. I've been patiently waiting for them to see me, but they were going to choose her. I saw the writing on the wall, and I'd be damned if I let all my years of work, and sacrificing my body go to waste.

"Did it work?"

I take in Senator Baker, "Of course it fucking did, Matthew, I told you it would."

My half-brother grins at the news. Years of planning finally coming together. His onyx-wavy black hair is cut short, framing his conventionally handsome face. Matthew was a mistake made ten years before I was born. One my mother never let our father forget.

She made sure Matthew could never find out who his birth father was. Only being able to dig deep enough to know he was a member of the Fraternitas.

It made the recruitment for getting back at the organization that our father is part of an easier sell. He doesn't know it's *our* father. The idiot thinks he's an Edgewood— the long lost brother of Donald Edgewood.

When my mother came to me and told me I'd rule this town, all I needed to do was follow her lead. I hesitated at first, stalling for months until she told me the plan was for some bitch named Ariah to marry the boys unless I got my shit together.

I went along with her plan until I found out she was fucking using me too. I was never meant to rule shit. They created some bull-shit rigged game for her to win. I was never meant to be in fucking charge. Those fuckers thought I was dumb, but I overheard my mother and Elise talking about how everything was falling into place and Ariah would finally give them what they wanted.

So, I made my own fucking plan, one that would take out every bitch in the Selection. I only missed a few.

Everything fell into place when Matthew announced he was running for Senate, I saw an opportunity, and I took it. Men always think with their dicks, and he was no different.

I smirk, thinking back to the night I seduced my older half-brother and slowly manipulated him into thinking it was all his idea. *Fucking idiot.*

Lips press to my neck, snapping me from the memory. His hand reaches up for my bra, lowering the cups to reveal my breasts, and flicks my nipple, making me groan. I throw my head back when his mouth wraps around my nipple. His mouth was always my favorite part of him.

I really need to stop sleeping with him, but I have to do this. It's the only way to keep control.

Matthew has the connection to the company that implanted the chip. If I don't keep him happy, then I can lose everything, and all he wants is my pussy and the presidency. I'm sure that wouldn't be the case if he knew he was my brother. *What he doesn't know won't hurt him.* Plus, I won't need him much longer. With the chip in Owen's body, I can use it to make them all do what I want, or he'll die.

With that bitch gone and the heirs under my control, I can finally get what I've always wanted— *power*. Until I have it, everyone is expendable. So, if they don't do what I want, I'll kill each one and never lose a wink of sleep.

I smile, remembering the look on Ariah's face when Wes broke her gullible-ass heart. She had such hope in those stupid fucking gray eyes. She was so cocky, thinking they'd choose her. I orchestrated that perfectly. *You fucking genius.*

"Who's laughing now?"

"What?" Matthew asks, removing his mouth from my nipple.

I thought I'd said that in my head.

"Nothing. Fuck me already," I command.

His mouth lifts into a smarmy smile.

"Gladly," he croons, pulling out his decent-sized dick and aiming for my entrance.

Seeing that he's lost his mind, I shout, "Condom!"

He scowls, "You promised me a baby, and I'm going to get that now."

The fucking things you do to get what you want.

He'll be dead long before he cashes in on that promise. I smooth out my features, rising up and pressing my lips to his mouth before pulling back, "Soon, Matthew. Remember, I can't get pregnant until I've finished this. Only a bit longer, Baby, I promise."

My answer seems to appease him because he nods his head in understanding and reaches for the foil packet, tearing it open, sliding it on, and thrusts in my unready pussy, as he begins haphazardly pounding into me.

God, sex with him is always lame. You'd think a man his age would've learned how to fuck a bitch.

That's why I need Wes. The way he controls me. I feel myself tighten at the thought of Wes's hand around my throat and lift my finger to my clit. I need to hurry up. Matthew can never last.

Less than five minutes later and orgasmless, I'm dressed.

Fucking waste of pussy miles.

Grabbing my bag, I prepare to exit his office.

Everything is falling into place. Elise almost messed everything up by shooting Shay and taking Ariah, but I was able to salvage a plan.

She was another fucking idiot blinded by power. She didn't see me coming— none of them did.

Stopping by the mirror near the door, I make sure nothing's out of place. Just as I place my hand on the doorknob, I feel Matthew grip my arm. I look back at the offending limb and then up into calculating, cold eyes that are a lot like mine.

"Remember the plan. Don't try and cross me. You won't like what happens if you do," he instructs.

I shake him off. "Don't threaten me, Matthew," I snap.

His nostrils flare until I soften my next words. "It's you and me in the end. We just need access to the Fraternitas, and that's coming. Once we have it, we'll kill them," I coo, planting a kiss on his lips.

My reassurance that nothing's changed relaxes his posture, and he kisses me back. *Yes.* His tongue swirls in my mouth, reigniting my pussy.

Reaching for his hand, I push his fingers between my legs.

"Give me what I want," I demand. He pushes two digits inside of me, and I ride until I finally get the orgasm I needed.

Fuck knows when I'll get good dick again. A girl's gotta do what a girl's gotta do.

Pulling out of his embrace, I take one last look at myself and then exit his office.

I step out of the building, putting on my Chopard shades when the sun glares in my eyes, and walk toward my car.

My driver opens the back door before taking his seat behind the wheel. He lowers the partition. "Where to?"

Lowering my shades, I meet his eyes. A smile fills my face, and state, "To Edgewood. It's high time I lay down some ground rules."

I hope the heirs are ready for the hell I'm about to rain down on them for fucking with my plans.

ACKNOWLEDGMENTS

Are you still with me? I promise I love you all!
First, thank you to all of my readers. This baby author journey has been the best ride! It's seriously been amazing, and I'm grateful to have all of you along with me.
To my sister Shay! Thank you for always being there and reminding me to fuck all the haters! To my daughter, Meg (insider), thank you for warming up coffee I forgot to drink and being the chillest kid I know. To my mom, for telling me to never lose hope.
To my PA Jess. Again there still aren't enough words to express all of the things!! Your constant belief in me when I doubted myself, the reminder to fix my crown if I let it tip too far one way or the other, and the ways you support me are unmatched. You and your team at Boss Bitch3s PA Services are a force!
My Alpha Team (Jess, Val, Teri, Jenna, Chayde & Lo)!! Muhahaha, we created more chaos in the streets of Edgewood, and you have to promise to hide me until it's safe. Seriously, every single one of you made this book what it is, and I couldn't be more See you in The Tombs.
To my teams (TikTok, Street & Promo), y'all are the best, and I'm grateful for the continued support!!!
To my sister-wife, Celeste, thank you for taking me under your wing and always condoning the fuckery—here's to more late-night random searches for Mark.
And to Raven, plank poses forever heaux!!
See you in book three!

ABOUT THE AUTHOR

P.H. Nix is an up-and-coming romance author. She's a lover of morally gray heroes and kick-ass heroines. When she isn't dreaming up another story for you to sink your teeth into or lost in the world of her favorite authors, she's raising her own kick-ass heroine!

For news and updates about Nix's writing, visit https://link-tr.ee/authorphnix and join her reader group on Facebook, The Tombs.

Made in the USA
Middletown, DE
17 April 2023

28754498R00303